LOVE AND OTHER
OTHER
Champagne Problems

SARAH SUTTON

For information, contact:

http://www.sarah-sutton.com

Illustration and Design by Melody Jeffries

ALSO BY SARAH SUTTON

Love in Fenton County

What Are Friends For?

Out of My League

If the Broom Fits

Can't Catch My Breath

Two Kinds of Us

Christmas As We Know It

Most Likely To

Teaching the Teacher's Pet

Dreaming About the Boy Next Door

Rebelling With the Bad Boy

Fake Dating the Football Player

Aunt Sherry,
Thank you for cheering me on from day one. You always
believed in my dream, and always believed in me.
You will be forever missed.

Chapter 1

*I*t'd been a long time since I'd had to attend a fundraiser at the Alderton-Du Ponte Country Club, and I'd forgotten how hellish they were.

The corner I stood in was a comfortable distance from the hors d'oeuvres table while not being too close to the rest of the partygoers. The strict black-tie dress code ensured that everyone surrounding me dressed to impress, showcasing their expensive jewelry for the evening. Diamonds glittered on necks and wrists as each country club attendee attempted to make another jealous with their various karat sizes.

My, what a beautiful bracelet!

That necklace is to die for!

Let me get a closer look at those earrings!

Perhaps I should've made a drinking game of it all—with each empty, false compliment, I'd take a sip of my champagne. Not that I'd stopped sipping it anyway.

While I attended college in New York, it'd been easy to forget the suffocation that was the Alderton-Du Ponte Country Club. It had been easy to let the posh high society of Addison disappear like morning dew in the

1

back of my mind. Now, I felt sticky with it, covered in the inescapable condensation of condescension.

I'd forgotten how small these walls made me feel, like they could swallow me whole without flinching. And they would.

The corner I stood in was a vacant one. Tucked near the windows that overlooked the now dark golf course, it held nothing but shadows and a young woman dressed in a navy blue, custom-made Gilfman suit. No one wandered close, aside from the revolving waiter that kept me well-stocked with champagne flutes, but even he was faceless. Everyone was. They all flitted about like little butterflies, tittering on about meaningless drivel. I wanted nothing more than to clip their wings.

I tipped my head back and gazed at the chandelier, dozens of bulbs and crystals throwing light around the room in a haphazardly beautiful manner. It was a lovely thing, yet hardly anyone looked up. Its grandness seemed small from where I stood, but I knew it must truly be massive up close, blinding—I found myself wondering how much it weighed.

I pictured it breaking free from the ceiling and plummeting to the ground.

I pictured it crushing me.

Better yet, crushing every other damned soul in the ballroom. That also would've been acceptable.

I drained the last bit of the champagne, and my empty flute was swiftly taken by a shadow that stepped in front of me. The worst butterfly of them all: my mother.

"Margot Massey," she hissed in a voice that had not even a drop of patience, though you'd never guess from how perfect her expression was. Charlotte Massey was a refined woman, not looking a day over forty-five, though she was pushing sixty. She'd nearly mastered the art of hiding her frustrations with me. "How many of these have you had?"

I tried to remember how many times the waiter had walked over. "Four? Five? It started blurring after three."

"Are you out of your mind?"

"I'd like to think I'm the only sane one within a five-hundred-foot radius," I returned evenly, straightening my cuff where it fell against my wrist. I hadn't worn this suit in months, if not years; I'd left it here while I was away at college. It felt snugger than I remembered, almost hard to breathe. I debated on unfastening the single button closure on the jacket, but refused to fidget before the eyes of the masses.

My mother's watery blue eyes flashed as she shook the empty champagne flute. "I know you haven't been to one of these in a while, but let me provide the refresher—you aren't to have more than one glass here."

"Who made that rule? A twenty-two-year-old can't have a bit of champagne?"

"Which waiter did you get your drinks from?"

I cast a glance about the room, searching the faces that all blended together in a shade of gray. Amid the glitz and glamor and gold, everything felt gray. "Why does it matter?"

The champagne had done practically nothing to dull my surroundings. I suspected it was non-alcoholic. Either that or my tolerance had built at an alarming rate.

"You two hiding in the corner?" A woman in a lowcut

3

black dress sauntered up to us, her auburn hair in loose ringlets around her face. Ms. Allyson Jennings—mid-fifties, never married, but had a ball "mingling" with the men of the club who were. Her mauve shade of lipstick smeared onto the skin above her mouth. She brought two women at her heel, but I didn't look closely enough at them to place their faces. "I know Margot's an antisocial fly on the wall, but it isn't like you to be hiding, Charlotte. Did her tendencies rub off on you in New York?"

When I'd left for college, instead of letting me go on my own to spread my wings, my mother had followed me. Granted, the trip was only an hour flight from Addison, so it was easy on her to keep her leash on me tight. If it'd been any further, surely she would've hired someone to follow me around like a shadow. But in her absence, the country clubgoers had seemingly allowed people to forget her level on the propriety tier. She'd been at the top before New York, but ever since we returned a week ago, it was like she struggled to find her footing.

It was a little satisfying, watching someone other than me struggle.

"I was only catching my breath," my mother replied. She laughed a little, a tittering sound that was far too similar to the rest of the room. It was as if everyone had one laugh soundtrack, and they each took turns playing it. "Just as you were doing when you stepped out into the hall, Allyson."

Ms. Jennings flashed my mother a shark-like smile.

"This event is so lovely, as usual," one of the women gushed to my mother. She had a champagne flute of her own in her hand, gesturing a little too carelessly with it. "It's such a good cause, fundraising for missing children."

The third woman batted her arm. "This one's for saving the bees."

"Oh, yes, yes! Even better!"

My gaze flicked back up to the chandelier, as if my will alone could cause it to fall.

"I was *just* telling Henry about the bees. He's been killing them, but I say, 'what about the honey, honey?'"

Everyone gave a giggling laugh. Except me.

"Oh, Margot." Ms. Jennings made a *tsking* sound as she looked me up and down—more specifically, looked my designer suit up and down—the disdain in her eyes clear. "Let me take you shopping, dear. We'll find you a dress you feel pretty in."

"Doubtful."

"Wouldn't you like to feel feminine?"

I fought the urge to tug on my sleeve again. Though it might've been my favorite jacquard fabric, the navy material light as it draped over my figure, it would not do to fidget like a grade schooler in it. I made a mental note to throw the jacket out the second I got back to my room. "I feel feminine."

Ms. Jennings scrunched her nose. "How? You're wearing *men's clothing.*"

No man would be caught dead in any of the suits I wore, with the waist narrowly tailored and the pantlegs tapered to accentuate the curve of my thighs. The way my lace dress shirt stretched to emphasize my chest had been fit for my figure, something a suit tailored for men would never have. But Ms. Jennings didn't see any of that. No one ever did. She simply saw lapels and cufflinks and thought *man*.

"I don't need to put skin on display to feel feminine," I told her flatly. "But judging by the fact that you had your dress tailored with a hemline four inches shorter than its stock design is, and had the neckline deepened two extra inches to reveal most of your sagging cleavage, I'd argue you *do*."

The white skin Ms. Jennings had exposed now flushed a splotchy red, nearly matching her smudged lipstick. The surrounding women murmured amongst each other. "I—I didn't have it tailored—"

"It's a Malstoni from their spring collection two years ago," I interjected, bored. "Though you practically massacred it, it's still recognizable."

My mother grabbed my arm, fingers crinkling my jacket. "Margot Massey, not another word—"

"And if you're going to continue making out with men in the coat closet, check your lipstick when you're finished, at the very least." I tapped my lips with a finger.

I wondered if her partner had thought to wipe their own mouth off. A game of *guess which married man Ms. Jennings kissed this time* might've been just what I needed to lighten my mood.

"At least I can find a man to kiss," Ms. Jennings snapped as she scrubbed the back of her hand against her mouth, stooping to the level of a sixteen-year-old girl once backed into a corner. "I bet you haven't even kissed a man yet."

I tilted my head. "Who said I'm into men?"

"*Margot!*" Mother's scandalized voice screeched loud

enough to cut through the piano being played in the center of the room.

This time, I did allow myself to smile a little, if only because of the sound of her distress coupled with the horrified expression on Ms. Jennings's face.

My gaze caught on the waiter standing a few feet from our little bubble. He looked possibly my age or a little older, maybe twenty-five, and he stood out even further from the careless way he held his drink tray. It tilted haphazardly, not supported correctly with his fingers. It was obvious from the way the two champagne flutes tilted in one direction.

The servers at the Alderton-Du Ponte Country Club were trained to maintain masks of indifference for events, and here this man was, staring straight at me as if I'd called out his name.

The waiter must've been new, but the club typically put new servers through extensive training before assigning them to serve at events. High-profile guests deserved the best waitstaff. This one slipped through the cracks.

He was also the one, I realized, who'd been stopping by me time and time again to drop off a champagne glass. The one who'd been strangely attentive.

"Oh, Charlotte!" a new voice chimed, joining the already dreadful circle surrounding me like a swarm of relentless insects. I didn't even try to cover my sigh.

Yvette Conan, another former cheerleader type who'd never grown out of that phase, smiled up at my mother. She was on the board of directors for the country club.

"There you are!" she exclaimed. "I've been bouncing

around from group to group looking for you—and got pulled in to talk to everyone, of course!"

Yvette clearly didn't pick up on the tense atmosphere, but then again, judging by the way she stumbled in her kitten heels, it seemed she'd gotten the good champagne. Dr. Conan, her husband, came up alongside her, his hand curving around her waist lightly enough to not be reprehensible for the event.

The touch was most likely a gesture for show, anyway, given that he had mauve lipstick smudged on the corner of his thin mouth.

"Mary and I were just talking about Annalise's wedding next month," Yvette said, pressing her hand to her collarbones. The way she laid her wrist caused her diamond bracelet to catch in the light, just as I knew she'd intended. "You've RSVP'd, right? And you heard about the change in destination, right? Because Ms. Nancy's been... well, on the decline." She gave a *poor little bird* expression.

I drew in a slow breath that no one noticed.

"What a nightmare!" one woman in our bubble said. "And to give up Hawaii? Oh, I'm not sure I could!"

Yvette nodded with the woman's sympathy. "Yes, well, it's very important to Annalise for Ms. Nancy to be able to come comfortably."

More like it was important for Annalise to get Nancy's wedding gift. I stared at the drink tray of the waiter, fingers itching for another flute. Once more, he glanced over, and our eyes locked for a beat before he rushed to look away.

"Of course, I've RSVP'd," my mother answered good-naturedly, mellow to the animated eccentricity. "She booked at *our* club, after all. How embarrassing would it be if I'd forgotten to respond to the invitation?"

Our club. She made it sound as if she owned the place. She didn't. While my parents might've been on the board of directors, and they might've owned the hotel next door, the Alderton-Du Ponte Country Club was not hers.

If my mother could've heard my thoughts, she'd no doubt have tacked "*yet*" on the end of that sentence.

Yvette's eyes slid to me, the excitement dimming. "And you, Margot?"

It wasn't lost on me that her voice had completely changed when directed in my direction. My mother was a welcome presence. She wasn't a celebrity, but among the high society of Alderton-Du Ponte Country Club's best— and richest—my mother was quite close. Perhaps everyone clustered around her now because of her prolonged absence while we'd been away to New York, and they never wanted to go back to that. Perhaps it was because when my parents achieved their lofty goals of broadening their hotel chain to the west coast, everyone wanted to be in their good graces to catch any scraps.

Even though I was the daughter of such an influential woman, they treated me as a pariah, a title I'd learned to welcome with open arms. "I've already sent my regrets," I told Yvette.

"Of course, Margot is coming," my mother immediately replied for me. "The Astors will be in town then for the wedding, of course—you knew the groom was a family friend of theirs, didn't you?—and it'll be Margot's first event she attends with Aaron."

In response to the expensive name, everyone gasped. I hadn't thought it possible, but my sour mood reached an all-time low. *Aaron Astor.* The name alone was similar enough to fingernails on a chalkboard. I didn't think some-one's name could elicit so much disdain in me, brewing hotly in my chest, but his did so.

"Oh, goodness!" Yvette's tipsy smile grew wider, though more plastic-like, and she pressed a hand to her mouth to smother a tittering laugh. "I didn't realize you were still trying to win Aaron's affections for her, Char-lotte. And that's going...well?"

She sounded surprised. She most likely was surprised. None of them could fathom a man as influential and well-off as Aaron Astor to like someone such as me.

"*Very* well," my mother assured. She lifted her chin, looking down her nose at the drunken Yvette. "He's expressed his interest many, many times. He's been patient while she's been away at college, but has made it clear he's eager to meet her. So much dedication. Kind of you to be so interested, though, Yvette."

She turned an ugly shade of pink.

Aaron Astor. I didn't even know what he looked like. Someday soon, I'd have a face to the name, but for now, I could make him look however I wanted in my head.

Giant forehead. Bucked teeth. Upturned nose. Balding.

Apathy sunk its teeth into me, just as it always did, dousing the derision. *You shouldn't think of ways to insult him,* the placating voice in my head mused. *Not when you're more than likely going to marry him.*

I never understood how Aaron could be so smitten with me, given that we'd never officially met. My mother had brought me along to a holiday event for travel empires in New York City, though I'd stayed out on the rooftop the entire night, freezing. My black suit had easily disguised me in the cold and shadow, and I thought I'd gotten through without catching anyone's attention.

Aaron had been present that night, apparently, and despite not having the guts to come up and talk to me—and not even hearing me speak once—he had fallen in love. Perhaps he was more so smitten over the amount of assets I had as an extension of my parents. The only daughter of two millionaire parents who owned an east coast hotel empire was attractive, indeed. Who cared about looks when someone had deep pockets?

The Astors themselves, of course, had money. The rich flocked to the rich.

"We're anticipating something big when he comes into town," my mother murmured in a hushed sort of excitement. She pressed her fingers to her lips. "Something with a few *carats.*"

The two women Ms. Jennings brought over all but giggled while Ms. Jennings smirked a little. "How exciting. A wedding *and* a proposal."

"Surely he wouldn't propose at someone else's wedding." Yvette's pink shade turned red as she imagined the possibility. "Surely. You think...you think a proposal is *that* imminent, Charlotte?"

My mother winked. "You should see the emails he sends Margot. I think it's coming sooner than later."

I'd never received any emails. I wondered if it was a lie, or if she and my father had decided not to show me the drivel lover boy wrote up.

While Yvette tried to weasel my mother for more information, Ms. Jennings mimed ever so discreetly to Dr. Conan's lips. He wiped everywhere *but* at the mauve smudge. When Ms. Jennings peered around our group to check if anyone noticed, I didn't bother averting my eyes.

"M-Margot," Ms. Jennings said quickly, nervously, though everyone else would've mistaken it for tension over interacting with me in general. "How do you feel about the engagement?"

Everyone looked to me for my answer.

Marrying Aaron Astor had never been a choice given to me. My mother hadn't even told me she met him at Christmas until February. She'd gushed over the fact that the elegant Vivienne Astor, Aaron's mother, had reached out in the new year asking if Charlotte Massey's *dearest daughter* was single.

"*He's the perfect match,*" my mother had said while we were on a video call with my father. "*He's everything we've been waiting for.*"

I lifted my chin now. "I think any rich 25-year-old desperate to marry someone he's never met must be a poor sight to see."

The conversation stalled in awkward silence. The butterflies all looked at each other as if debating to flutter away to a new flower, one that would actually give them the titillating conversation they were hoping for. My mother just looked like a furious wasp.

"Then again, I should be honored—a man, as rich as Aaron Astor, is interested in *me*." I left no room for emotion in my voice as I stared Ms. Jennings down, a challenge.

She broke away first, of course. They always did.

I turned my attention back to the ballroom, watching as the space, thankfully, held signs of winding down as the hour stretched closer to eleven. The catering staff had begun clearing the buffet tables and gathering the dirty dishes. A few still milled about with trays of drinks, but all the small hors d'oeuvres had stopped being served. *So close*, I thought to myself, glancing at the massive clock on the far end of the room. *So close to turning into a pumpkin.*

"Margot's never been interested in dating before," I heard my mother explain to our little gaggle of big mouths. "And of course, when she starts, she goes for the big one."

"And here I thought she wasn't interested in romance in general," Ms. Jennings replied. "Not even the slightest little crush?"

"Must've been boring," someone muttered.

My mother's voice was firm. "She's been very focused on her studies. Theo and I have a dedicated daughter."

The words made my stomach feel sour. I stood there amidst the nonsense, wondering why they had to bat it back and forth around me. I was no flower.

I looked back to where the waiter stood with his tilting tray, still shifting uneasily from foot to foot. He hadn't moved since I last glanced over, hadn't found someone else to serve the remaining drinks to. His shoulders were stiff, and despite his black pants and white shirt, he seemed out of place. His eyes bounced all over the ballroom, ending up on a revolving pivot back in my direction.

He tried to be smooth about it, but it was obvious— he'd still been watching.

It piqued my interest to the point that I could no longer ignore it. Without a word of polite excuse, I stepped away from the group, making my way to the cater waiter.

His eyes widened as I closed in on him, and he took a step backward. It was choppy enough that the champagne glasses swung again, his tray too far from his torso to give it the proper balance. Though he tried, he didn't have a chance to run before I was upon him, stopping within an inch from his teetering tray.

"Intriguing, am I?" I asked as I swiped up a champagne flute. I kept my back to my mother, but highly doubted she'd march over and pull it from my hands again. Not with her underlings to distract her.

The waiter's shoulders seemed even stiffer now, and he held the tray with the singular champagne flute between us almost as if a barricade. "I was just looking to see if you needed another drink."

"You mean my sixth?" I lifted my eyebrows. "It was you who kept me stocked, wasn't it? Trying to get me drunk?"

He blinked rapidly, dark lashes fluttering. They were

quite pretty. "No, I just—wanted to make sure you had what you needed."

"Not anyone else in this room. Me, specifically." I didn't smile, but the expression I offered was close. "Are you trying to get on my good side? That could be tough— I'm not known to have one."

He looked around helplessly, as if trying to find an escape path, but couldn't get his feet to move. "You looked lonely. Over there, by yourself. That's why...I came around a few times."

Lonely. The word looped around in my head, almost foreign in the context. Lonely, in a room filled with so many people that the air was thick with heat and Chanel No.5? Lonely, when I resented the thought of anyone walking up to me? Lonely, when I refused to even make eye contact with someone? *Lonely*. For a moment, it didn't make sense.

Finally, something in me sighed in a sort of revelation. *Somebody noticed*.

"I prefer my own company over this lot's," I returned, taking a sip of the champagne. I wasn't sure if it was just my tastebuds, but it almost tasted *sugary*. Almost as if it were sparkling juice.

I looked the waiter over a bit closer. The uniform of the country club for the serving attire was a black turtle-neck paired with a white shirt and a black apron tied around their waist. His didn't quite fit him right, as if he wore shirts two sizes too big. Not name brand; not the standard uniform the country club doled out.

The watch latched to his wrist looked clunky and old, like something a child would dig out from a cereal box—a violation of dress code, since no jewelry or watches were allowed when serving. He almost looked like he was pretending to be on the staff, as if he'd found a tray somewhere and just swiped it up.

That thought only increased my curiosity.

A woman walked past us then with a flute in her hand, and I eyed it. The bubbles in hers were far more of a light golden color, whereas mine seemed almost a burnt amber. Indeed, different. I nearly laughed. He *was* serving me sparkling juice. Which meant there was only one culprit behind this imposter and his poorly done-up hoax—my mother.

Perhaps I should've been more annoyed with the situation, but it more so amused me than anything. It definitely livened up the night as it began to calm down. "It's very unusual," I mused, "that you were put on a serving rotation, but don't seem to know the proper etiquette. Is the country club slacking, or are you somewhere you aren't supposed to be?"

"I'm supposed to be here," he said, but his voice lacked conviction as I inched closer to his con. "They— they asked me to join the waitstaff tonight."

"Who asked?" I pulled out a name who wouldn't have anything to do with it. "Ms. Jennings?"

The dimwit took the bait. "Yes, I—I think that was her name."

Again, I nearly smiled. If Ms. Jennings would've asked this man to do anything, it would've been to accompany her to the coat closet. She hadn't seen him yet; she surely wouldn't be making kissing faces with Dr. Conan if that'd been the case. No, the waiter was just her type—young, tall, handsome.

At least I can find a man to kiss, she'd said. *I bet you haven't even kissed a man yet.* A small thrill skated through me, and with my free hand, I reached out and smoothed my fingers down the fabric of the waiter's shirt collar. The cotton was, in fact, well-worn, too soft to the touch, but I allowed my fingertips to linger. "Do you think you could do me a favor?" I asked in a slow, measured voice. "Because I could use your help with something. If you are, in fact, wanting to get on my good side."

Wariness filled his gaze. "What kind of favor?"

"I just need you to stand there and look pretty." For him, it shouldn't be too hard. It wasn't often I was met with attractive men my age, but this waiter, objectively, was. Not in a way that stirred my pulse—nothing could stir a block of ice, after all—but in a way that made this moment even more perfect. I moved my fingertips from his collar to the top of his shoulder, feeling the muscle beneath the fabric. "I'll give you whatever you ask for in return."

"What are you going to do?"

"I'm going to kiss you."

It was clear that hadn't been the response he expected. His eyes flashed wide, and he sucked in a sharp breath. "You—you can't kiss me."

"Why?" His stuttering was a little endearing. Once more, I looked around the ballroom, noting the number of people remaining. They were tipsy, mostly unreliable. "Do you have a girlfriend?"

"No, but—"

"A boyfriend?"

He became even more panicked. "*No*." Then a resolute expression crossed his features. "I—I am an employee of the Alderton-Du Ponte Country Club, and it would be wrong...for me to kiss you."

"You wouldn't be kissing me. I would be kissing *you*."

The waiter swallowed hard. "Miss Margot."

There it was. A confession, in a way. He knew me, at least by name. It confirmed my suspicions—my mother *must've* hired him. For what, I wasn't sure, but discovering her spy was a small victory.

It was then that a tiny smile slipped, my lips curving upward, and the waiter's eyes fell to my mouth. A spark tingled in my stomach, watching him watching my lips, for a reason I couldn't explain. It wasn't just a quick glance either, but a lingering one, one that prickled my skin.

The waiter seemed to relax by a fraction. He must've thought that the longer our conversation went on, the safer he was.

Unfortunately for him, he'd been wrong. He'd learn it the hard way—Margot Massey was not one to talk to, lest she decide to use you for her enjoyment. "This isn't personal," I assured him. After taking one last sip of what mostly likely was juice—and swallowing the strange feeling that'd surfaced—I placed my flute back on his teetering tray. I eyed it for a moment, gauging where the weakest spot was.

"But thank you for taking one for the team."

He almost seemed afraid to ask. "Whose team?"

"Mine."

I lifted my arm sharply, as if shaking out my jacket sleeve, and the movement would've seemed casual to anyone glancing over, not calculated the way it was. The back of my hand smacked the bottom of the waiter's tray, and, due to the improper positioning of the way he'd held it, it toppled. The champagne flutes practically flew up before crashing to the ground with a scream, throwing liquid and shattered glass across the marble tiles.

Every head in the room turned toward the two of us, startled by the sound. Even the pianist cut off with a sharp error of the keys. *Just Margot*, I could practically hear them say, shaking their heads with scorn. *She* would *be at the center of it.*

I didn't look to see if my mother was watching, because I knew she was.

Yes, I thought to them, smiling ever so slightly. Once more, it was a genuine smile, and in the briefest moment of stillness, I saw the waiter's eyes drop to my lips, noting it. *I would be.*

I reached out and grabbed ahold of the now pale waiter's face, drawing him in and pressing my lips to his.

Chapter 2

Disorder wasn't allowed in the world I grew up in, where everything was scheduled and orchestrated down to every minute of every day. Chaos, in its pure form, was too wildly unpredictable and created too much conflict. A temper tantrum rarely gave a child what it wanted in the end, unless the time and place were correct.

However, if done correctly, a child throwing a fit to get what it wanted could yield results. Exasperated results, but results, nonetheless.

Calculated chaos—that was my specialty.

"I'm so very sorry about my daughter's behavior," my father, the head of staff management at both the hotel and country club, repeated the same phrase over and over, each time growing higher in pitch. "I apologize profusely for her actions—it never should've happened."

He wasn't speaking to me, of course. After I pulled back from the kiss, my parents hustled the waiter and me from Alderton-Du Ponte Country Club to Massey Hotel & Suites quickly and as quietly. The club and the hotel were bridged by a long-windowed corridor that stretched between the two buildings. We all sat in my mother's office now, a room that had floor to ceiling windows covering the far wall. During the day, it overlooked the beautiful rolling hills of the golf course, the weeping willows drooping low into the pond.

At night, it almost looked like a scene from a horror movie, the light illuminating the course just enough to cast all sorts of wicked shadows. I liked it better this way.

"I mentioned to you before that my daughter can lean toward the...stranger side," my father went on. He paced my mother's office while the other three of us sat at the table. My mother had her arms folded on the surface professionally. The waiter sat stiffly. I lounged in my seat, using my feet to oscillate back and forth. "Margot does have some...well...some unique tendencies."

The waiter slowly turned his attention from my mother to me, almost as if he didn't want to look. His hair was so light a brown that it almost looked golden, loose and ungelled over his forehead in a way that wasn't typical for the staff.

He was handsome, though. So much so that if someone put him in a Malstoni suit, he would've blended into high society without anyone thinking twice.

"Our daughter likes to cross the line," my mother cut in levelly. Her business tone held every drop of authority in the room, as professional as my father wasn't. She wasn't flustered, not even a bit. "She takes pleasure in shocking people. Please know that it was nothing more than a child's attempt to get her parents' attention. I deeply apologize for her immature, inappropriate actions."

The cater waiter held onto his reply. I watched him while turning to and fro, but there was nothing in his expression that belied a hint of what he was feeling. His poker face was top-notch, better than some people at the club. If it hadn't been for his nervous shifting earlier, I could've convinced myself that perhaps he, too, truly was unfazed.

My mother turned to me. "Margot."

"I deeply apologize for my immature and inappropriate actions," I repeated, echoing the line she'd set up for me. I looked at her lazily. "You were there when Ms. Jennings said I'd probably never been kissed by a man. I figured you'd want me clearing the air."

A muscle ticked in my mother's jaw. "By kissing our staff?"

"I'd be a hard sell for Aaron if word got around that I wasn't interested in men, don't you think?"

"And you *wouldn't* be a hard sell for kissing other men?"

I didn't want to admit it. "I didn't think that far."

My mother drew in a breath as if she were going to launch into a lecture, but swallowed the air instead in a grapple for patience. The waiter's eyes darted between us, and I could practically read his mind. *What is wrong with these people?* I looked at his mouth, the same mouth that I'd pressed my own against earlier, and smirked.

Standing just behind her chair, my father stood nervously, glancing between the waiter and my mother. It was almost comical how contrasting their behaviors were, my parents. I resented how much I was like my mother, who could remain cool, calm, and collected even in the face of another instance of mine. She wasn't bothered in the slightest.

"Margot," she said without looking at me. It was my mother beginning the conversation, speaking to me as if I was a business associate and we were discussing a contract. "Mr. Pennington, here, is not a simple cater waiter."

Mr. Pennington. I rolled the surname around in my head, marinating on it. A cater waiter with an expensive-sounding last name. I liked it. "He is an undercover spy, is he?" I'd guessed correctly.

"He *was*. Only for tonight. A worker called in sick, and I figured him giving a helping hand would let him get a lay of the land. To try not to have attention drawn to him, but... well." She fought to keep the annoyance from her tone. "We've hired on Mr. Pennington to be your personal secretary."

Personal secretary. The words didn't quite connect at first. My parents had secretaries, of course, but it made no sense for *me* to have one. Not when I barely left my parents' sight as it was. If she was going to hire me a personal secretary, she should've hired one *before* I left for college, and she wouldn't have had to move with me. I didn't need one now, back on their home turf.

And then, as if guessing my thoughts, she said, "With the Conan's daughter's wedding coming up next month, and the country club transitioning into its summer activities list, your father and I can't possibly monitor you twenty-four-seven. We've hired Mr. Pennington to be with you whenever you leave your room."

She paused there, allowing me to connect the dots myself. "You hired him as my babysitter?"

"Your secretary," my father insisted, as if I hadn't heard the word the first time. "As you know, Margot, we don't quite trust you to be on your own. Your impulsivity could ruin these chances of Aaron's approval for you, which we know you don't want. Think of this as us trying to save you from yourself."

Ruin these chances *for them*, they meant. One slip up, and my marriage with Aaron could fall through—which meant their dream of joining hands with Astro Agencies, one of the biggest travel agencies on the west coast, would sink along with it.

"Surely you can't keep Mr. Pennington on now," I said with a tinge of tension in my voice. "Not when everyone saw him kiss me." While I'd guessed my mother hired him, if I'd known he was meant to *stay* around me, I would've caused more of a scene. Kissed him longer than two seconds. Because it *had* been chaste—brief enough that I barely registered the softness of his lips before I pulled back. "Can you imagine the rumors? Them getting back to the Astors?"

My mother didn't even flinch. "We already have it covered with Aaron Astor."

"How could you possibly already have it covered?"

"He has been made aware of an *incident* tonight."

Which meant she downplayed it with my potential suitor as much as possible. Of course. "Why do you trust *me* not to do anything else?"

"Because your shock factor has been used up." My mother gave me a challenging look. "There's nothing else to prove. It isn't as if you kissed him because you're *trying* to sabotage your chances with Aaron. You were trying to prove a point to Ms. Jennings. You just don't think things through."

To this, I said nothing.

"Besides, Mr. Pennington has seen your *eccentricities* firsthand and took them in stride," my father said, his nerves melting into a pleased excitement. "He has proved to be unflappable."

"So far," I murmured, staring him down. We'd only had one interaction, to be fair. Sure, it had flare, but it was only the tip of the iceberg. I was sure I could make him flap if I tried hard enough.

Mr. Pennington shifted uncomfortably in his seat, as if he could see the thought in my eyes.

"Whenever you leave the hotel, you are to take Mr. Pennington with you," my mother said, now diving into the rules. "That means going to Nancy's, any trips to town, he's to go with you. We'll speak with his shift manager so that Mr. Pennington has a free pass if you request him. And please—listen to us, Margot."

It was ironic to me how they treated me as a rebellious teenager now, when I was well past those years. I wondered if they ever regretted how things had unfolded, if only because they realized they'd wasted my prime manipulation years. If they'd paid more attention to me when I was younger, perhaps I would've been more desperate to please them now, and they wouldn't have to go to such lengths as to hire me a babysitter. Perhaps they would've effectively brainwashed me into marrying Aaron Astor willingly and not had to extort me into it.

Instead, they'd set me to boarding school during those younger years.

But even though they hadn't sunk their teeth into me fully, they'd bitten in enough. I might not have been the happy robot they wanted me to be, but in the end, I still did what they wanted.

"Not to Nancy's." I leaned my elbow on to the table's surface. There was another fuzz on this sleeve, and when my eye caught it, something like panic fluttered behind my ribs. I laid my arm flat to obscure it. "It isn't as if I'd do anything impulsive there. And no one would even be around to see. Not..." I hated the way slight desperation leaked into my voice. "Not to Nancy's."

I could tell my mother wanted to refuse. Of course she did. But as my one and only condition, how could she? "Not to Nancy's," she allowed. "But you're to go straight there and back. We'll be checking your car's GPS, if need be."

I let out a small breath at the victory, pulling myself back together. "I'll drag around a babysitter to keep me in check. I would hate to do anything to unintentionally ruin my chances with *the* Aaron Astor."

My parents exchanged a brief look. The derision in my tone was not missed.

"Mr. Pennington, if you ever need a break, or a sick day, please let us know."

Again, he nodded to my mother. His wordlessness was beginning to irk me, but it was clear they'd met before this. They'd probably already talked about the requirements, the concerns, the expectations. Everyone in this room knew of the predicament except for me. It made me resent the situation so much more.

"I suppose we'll start now," my mother said, and gestured her palms at us. "Margot, don't antagonize him or run him ragged. Do I make myself clear?"

I raised my eyebrows once. "Very." With the politest tone I could muster, I said to my parents, "Thank you for hiring a friend for me. It's very touching. I'll try my absolute hardest to not disappoint you."

My father's reaction came by way of a furrowed brow, and my mother was not appeased by my words. "You may head back to your room for the night." She sounded like a mother, putting a child in time out. I suppose that was the case, though. The only difference was that once she sent me to my room, she never came back to let me out. I always saw to that myself.

Without another word, I departed from their office, not surprised to find Mr. Pennington already on my heels. So, it began now.

The hallway, strangely enough, felt stuffier the moment we stepped into it, as if the office air had been lighter and clearer. Perhaps it was because the hallway was more closed off, with no windows to let light in. All we had was the ugly florescent glow to shine down on us, illuminating our new relationship—baby and babysitter.

Mr. Pennington pulled the door shut behind us, his teeth grazing along his bottom lip as he did so. "I thought I liked you," I said to him.

"And you don't anymore?"

"If my parents like you, it means I most likely will not." I looked him over slowly, from his eyes to the toes of his shoes. I was once more confronted with the disappointing revelation that the shiny new toy that piqued my interest turned out to be nothing more than another cog in my parents' machine. It figured—the one person who'd caught the slightest bit of my intrigue had been ensnared by my parents first. "How did you win them over so fast? No, better question—how much are they paying you to babysit their problem child?"

"They may be paying me," he began. Weirdly enough, he looked almost *happy* as he regarded me, like an eager student on their first day of school. The light-heartedness about him practically seeped from those blue eyes, exuding an energy that felt near impossible to remain frustrated with. "But I hope that doesn't change your mind about me too much. I hope we can still get to know each other...pleasantly."

Pleasantly. It was an interesting word choice; a word rarely ever used to describe me.

And before I could reply, the happiness had indeed leached from his gaze to the rest of his face, and Mr. Pennington smiled. With over a decade of watching facial expressions under my belt, I'd quickly learned how to detect a genuine smile from a fake one. Mr. Pennington's smile, in all its glory, was real. The first real smile I'd received in a long, long time.

I wasn't sure I liked it.

I started down the corridor from my parents' office, back toward the common space of the hotel lobby. Mr. Pennington's footsteps in his generic loafers continued after me faithfully, all the way through the lobby and into the elevators.

"Why did you do it?" he asked once the doors closed. The mirrored panels reflected our images back to us, and I watched him in the glass just as he watched me. "Why did you...kiss me?"

It was cute that he hesitated before saying it, as if he were a little boy saying a curse word. I considered not answering him. He was, after all, a stranger who needed no excuse from me. He'd learn in time, from the gossip of other workers, that Margot Massey did things for no reason. "Were you not listening?"

"You really kissed me to prove a point to someone? Just because you could?"

I let out a slow breath, watching as my shoulders fell with it in the mirror. "Maybe."

"You go around kissing strangers," Mr. Pennington began. "But aren't you engaged?"

"My," I exclaimed theatrically. "You enjoy gossip, do you? You'll fit in quite well around here."

It amused me more than irritated me how he spoke as if he knew my situation. His rapid blinking like a scolded child also was entertaining. What did irritate me, though, was him bringing up Aaron Astor in the first place.

I'd always known it, but it was another thing to be confronted with the truth that my name did not come up unless tied to another man's.

The elevator door dinged as it opened up to the eighth floor, the warm glow of lighting illuminating the golden hallway. I started down the thin carpet toward my room. "Think about what you want in return for the kiss," I said without looking back at him. "Despite you being a spy for my parents, I keep my word. Whatever you want."

Mr. Pennington didn't immediately respond, and for a moment, I thought he stayed on the elevator. "I'll think about it."

"Thank you for your service." I stopped at my hotel room door and faced him before unlocking it. "Thank you for taking one for my team."

Even from here, I could see the tips of his cheeks pinken. "Next time...you should work on your technique."

My eyes dropped to his lips on their own accord. Even though it happened no more than an hour ago, kissing him was hazy in my mind. I'd focused too much on the gasps that immediately rang out. Despite the strangeness of it, I found myself wishing I'd been paying more attention, if only to recall what they felt like. "That sounds an awful lot like flirting, Mr. Pennington."

"I meant—I meant asking for favors, not—"

"I got it."

Now his skin definitely flushed, and in the golden light of the hotel hallway, it almost made him seem angelic. "And it's Sumner," he said softly. "Sumner Pennington."

"Sumner Pennington," I echoed, and even if I couldn't remember what his lips felt like, I focused on the way mine curve around his name now. *Sumner*. It was a unique name; one I'd never heard before. It suited him.

I slid my keycard along my hotel room door. It unlocked with a click, and I twisted the handle. Before disappearing inside, I turned back to him. "Tomorrow, in the morning, I'll be going to visit Nancy. You're not coming with me." I lifted my chin as I looked at him, letting out a contented breath. "But I'll be wanting brunch afterward, so I'll come back to the hotel for you."

"I'll be waiting for you," Sumner said, holding my gaze as he did. There was something boyish about his expression, too—the face of someone wholly untouched by this world. It was a useless wish, but I hoped it would remain that way.

This world swallowed people like him whole. It was only a matter of time.

With the dull thought, I inclined my head and retreated into my hotel room, allowing the door to close loudly between us.

Chapter 3

$\mathcal{I}$ woke up to the sound of an alarm the next morning, but it wasn't mine. Ever since I moved into the penthouse suite last week, the entire floor had been quiet. I knew the suites on this level were more expensive, more rarely rented out, but I hadn't realized how vacant it'd be. How alone I'd be.

At least, I had been alone until the blaring nuclear meltdown of someone's alarm woke me the next morning.

I removed my silk eye mask. The alarm continued to ring from the room beside mine. How was it that the person could sleep through the alarm when it was right by their ear, and yet it woke me up through the wall? Were our beds butted up against the same wall? Were they deaf?

I gave it four more seconds. On the fifth, I banged my fist into the built-in headboard, once, hard. The impact jarred my hand, but a moment later, the alarm stopped.

It was six in the morning, and I gave up on falling back to sleep. In my closet, I took my time picking my outfit, ultimately deciding on a sand colored Gilfman. The suit's fabric was made of rayon and linen, which made it the perfect lightweight suit for the increasing temperatures. I picked out a loose silk shirt to go underneath, opting out of a vest for today. More of a casual look, but still elegant. My dark hair would look best down, where it would fall just to my collarbones, a beautiful contrast with the beige material. I moved into the bathroom, already picturing how I'd style it.

It was funny, my parents accusing me of growing too isolated when they were the reason I was alone. Instead of allowing me to remain in their house, they moved me to the penthouse suite on the eighth floor of Massey Suites with no hesitation. They didn't invite me for family dinners. They never stopped by my room unless it was for something they needed, and were almost always vaguely threatening.

It was easy to become a recluse when everyone forced you into the role.

Once I finished getting ready—and double checking my suit for any wrinkles or loose threads—I opened the door to the hallway, wincing at the stark contrast from my dark room to the bright corridor. A second later, the door to the hotel room beside mine jerked inward, the mechanism jamming as whoever ripped it open.

I stilled as the person spilled into the hallway, not quite believing what I was seeing.

Sumner Pennington, stumbling from the suite beside mine. Gone was the white shirt and dress pants from the night before, replaced with a black sweatshirt and a pair of loose sweatpants. His face scrunched up as he, too, grimaced against the bright light of the hallway, looking as if he'd just rolled from his bed to the corridor.

Last night felt a bit like a fever dream, especially looking at him now.

Sumner stretched his long arms before opening his eyes wide enough to realize I stood before him. He cleared his throat, attempting to stand straight and appear professional despite stumbling out of his hotel room in his pajamas. His smile was awkward. "Morning."

"What are you doing?"

"Um...standing? Standing. I'm definitely standing."

I blamed his dimwitted response on his clear sleep deprivation. "No, what are you doing on this floor? In that room?"

"Your parents put me in the room beside yours...so I can hear when you come and go."

Sumner's voice was friendly as he explained the lengths my parents would go to, keeping me controlled. As if it were the most common thing in the world. As if asking him to listen to my comings and goings *wasn't* creepy.

They truly must've been paying him well if they were putting him up in one of their expensive suites. "Don't you have a house? An apartment?"

"I'm, uh—well, I'm in between places at the moment. I actually just moved here—"

That was why he took on the job, then. Who would've refused when they got a suite and given a salary most dreamed of? "You were the one with that alarm, then?"

"You could hear it?"

"I thought my fist banging on the wall made that clear."

"Is *that* what that sound was?" Sumner scratched the back of his head. "I thought it was the air conditioning kicking on."

Without a word, I turned on my heel and headed toward the elevator.

Of course, Sumner trailed behind me.

"I told you that you weren't coming with me this morning," I said, running a hand down the front flap of my suit jacket to make sure it was straight.

"I know," Sumner said as he followed. "I'm going down for the free breakfast. It's on the ground floor, right?"

I stopped in front of the elevator and paused, and it didn't take him more than a handful of seconds to realize I waited for him to press the button. He hit it, and it took its sweet time to draw all the way up to us. "Eat at the country club," I told him, disinterested. "The ambiance is better."

Sumner rocked on his heels. "That's okay. I don't really care about *ambiance*."

The way he said it had me frowning. "You *do* know what that word means, right?"

Sumner hesitated a second too long. "Of course."

"What are your qualifications to be a secretary?" I asked as the elevator arrived, and for the second time in twenty-four hours, we stepped on together. "Where did my parents find you?"

"We can go over my resume at brunch if you want." Sumner scrubbed a fist into his eye, looking very much like a toddler that just woken from a nap. "And maybe we can get to know each other more."

"We don't need to get to know each other." The elevator began its rapid descent, and I kept my chin set. "You're my secretary. Not my friend."

I watched Sumner tilt his head in the mirror a second before the elevator doors opened at the lobby, taking away his image. We both stepped out, and to the left was the direction of the entrance, and to the right was the way to the breakfast bar. I paused at the crossroads, as if wanting to linger in the conversation a moment longer.

Sumner, however, had his sights set on food. "Have a good morning," he told me with a lopsided smile. He took a step backward, toward the right, still holding my gaze. "Your parents gave me your number yesterday, so I'll text you, so you have mine. Shoot me a message when you get back to the hotel, and I'll meet you out front for brunch."

"Wear something business casual," I told him, to which he ducked his head in acknowledgement.

"I'll see you when you get back." And with that, Sumner turned around fully and set off in the direction of the breakfast bar.

I stared after him, trying to decipher what about that interaction left me feeling so unsettled. No, perhaps that wasn't the right word. Off-kilter. Maybe it was because I was so unused to interacting with people in general. Even in New York, my connections to the outside world were minimal. I knew people in college, but never grew close to them. With my mother always hovering, it was hard to interact with anyone outside of whom she deemed acceptable.

Normally, I hated anyone she gave the green light on. Sumner got her gold stamp of approval, and yet here I was, almost anticipating coming back to the hotel for brunch.

It was unacceptable.

There was only one person left in Addison high society that I could stand, and that was Nancy Priscilla Du Pont.

Nancy, or Ms. Nancy to those trying to schmooze her in hopes of getting a slice of her will, was one of a kind when it came to the elite. While she had ample money, Nancy chose a simple one-story ranch style home out in the country. When she could drive, she'd continued on in her simple sedan she'd been driving for over twenty years. It sat parked in the driveway now, allowing the elements to rain down on it, the rust to eat at it, without care.

Even though she and her husband founded the Alderton-Du Ponte Country Club and didn't hold back to erect it with glitz and grandeur, she preferred a simpler life. No maids, no staff, nothing. From the outside looking in, one would guess she had money, but no one would've guessed how much.

Her husband died decades ago, and with no children, it left her all alone. She often told me she was happier alone.

We were two peas in the same pod, Nancy and me, and it'd been far too long since I'd spoken with her last.

"Hello?" I called into the house when I opened the front door. The scent of medicated ointment hung in the air, and it burned my nose. After so long away, the house felt...*wrong*. What should've been familiar and lulling only seemed out of place.

I found a woman sitting at Nancy's small dining room table with a magazine open, and recognized her immediately. Then I fought the urge to groan.

"You're here?" Yvette asked, not bothering to hide the disdain from her voice. Her blouse had a blooming neckline, one that only fell low enough to display the diamond necklace that hung around her neck.

"It appears so." I looked around the kitchen, but Yvette was alone. "You're here?"

"It appears so," Yvette replied in a snotty voice, returning her attention to her magazine.

"Why? Where's Nancy?"

"The ladies at the country club rotate who stays with her during the day. She's too sick to be left alone for too long."

Despite the warm air of the house—Nancy apparently didn't believe in air conditioning anymore—a chill snaked its way up my spine. "Where is she?"

"Out back."

I stared at her for a beat as I digested her words. "I thought you said she shouldn't be left alone."

Yvette decided I was no longer worthy of a response, because she simply flipped another magazine page.

It was almost amusing how different people behaved when my mother wasn't around. I gritted my teeth together now, and ultimately deciding against picking a fight with my least favorite person, and moving through the house. It'd be unfortunate if I shed demon blood on Nancy's hardwood floors.

I found Nancy on a hill about a hundred feet from her back porch that overlooked her wide, expansive acreage. The land had once been beautiful with lush green grass and a small manmade pond set into the land with the golden sunlight shining down on it. Now, the grass had thinned and overgrown, the pond more of an algae pit than anything to sink even a toe into. Nancy had parked her wheelchair underneath the shade of an oak tree, its buds doing little to keep the sunlight off her frail skin. Her back was to me, her shoulders hunched over as if she were cold in the early summer sun.

Even from the brief glimpse, it was clear that, in the four months since I'd last seen her, she had declined further. She hadn't been in the best state when I'd been home for New Year's, but her frame seemed thinner, frailer. Even from here, I could see a blanket draped over her lap, but still watched as her shoulders shook as if cold.

Drawing in a breath, I started toward her. "What'd you do to piss Yvette off?"

Nancy jumped at my voice, and if I'd been hoping for a loud and excited reunion, I'd have been horribly mistaken. Nancy took my sudden reappearance in stride, hardly batting an eye twice in my direction. "What makes you think I did anything?" she snapped back at me, her voice ornery comforting. It contrasted the scent of medication in her house.

"She let you wheel yourself out here unsupervised."

"*Unsupervised*," she scoffed. I came around to her side, joining her in gazing at her pond. "I'm not a toddler."

"You've got the temper of one." I withdrew the small bag of Dutch dark chocolate from the pocket in my suit jacket, offering halfway to her. "Brought you something. Only if you behave."

Nancy snatched the candy out of my grip. "Would've much more preferred a pack of Marlboros. You got any on you?"

"Your lungs are already functioning at thirty percent capacity. Do you want to wheel an oxygen tank around?" I slipped my hand into my pant pocket. "Besides, I quit. Years ago. I told you."

For a moment, the only sound between us was the rustling of plastic as Nancy fought to unwrap the candy. "Good. Nasty habit. And everyone knew you were just doing it for teenage rebellion—tacky, that."

"I'm sure you did worse."

"I did *do* worse. It's much more fun to flirt with men than with lung cancer." She grumbled. "Today, it's Yvette. Friday, it was Alice. The day before that, it was Brenda. When's your mother coming to pay her fairy godmother a visit?"

"Don't hold your breath."

"Tell her if she wants to harass me into selling her the land that hotel of hers sits on, she's running out of time." Nancy began to wheeze with effort.

With heavy sarcasm, I said, "How sweet that they're worried about you."

She then attempted to tear the chocolate open with her teeth. "Worried about *something*. Funny that my 'declining health' and 'making sure my affairs are in order' comes up in every conversation with them. Piranhas, the lot of them."

"I haven't asked yet. Are your affairs in order?"

"I wish I could see the looks on their faces when they find out I left everything all to charity. Even the land your parents' hotel is on. Waiting over my will only—stupid wrapper—only to see that they're not getting a cent."

I smiled a little already thinking about it. "I'll enjoy the view for you."

Nancy tried tearing the chocolate one last time before she let out an exasperated sound. "Are you just going to sit here and watch a poor old lady struggle?" Her tone was a snarl.

I took the candy from her and tore open the wrapper, ignoring how easy it'd been. I passed it back to her without looking, focusing on the pond. The water had grown murky over the years, with algae skimming the top. It looked more swampy than manmade. Beautiful in its prime, but aging poorly.

"You've been back for a week, and you're only just coming to visit me," Nancy grumbled as she chewed, not caring in the slightest about the politeness of it. "Too busy for me, huh?"

"I've been busy attending fundraisers. Ones that *you* skipped."

"I heard about that. I also heard about your little tryst last night." Nancy gave an almost witch-like laugh. "Macking on the waitstaff. Can't say I haven't done it myself a time or two, but never right out in the open. That sort of thing never did it for me."

Of course it had gotten back to her. I wondered who spilled the beans about it, and when they would've had the time. Ms. Jennings, most likely. I couldn't imagine Yvette in there recounting the tale with Nancy; she'd have to have known that Nancy would've been on my side. Gossiping wasn't fun unless people could swap judgment back and forth.

"Was he handsome, at least?"

I pictured Sumner Pennington's lopsided smile when we parted ways this morning. "Passably."

"*Passably*, ha. Send him to me if you're going to be so picky."

Now *that* was a mental image I smiled at, though I tried to tuck the corners of my mouth down as quickly as possible.

"Tell me about him," she said, turning to squint up at me. Her eyes were rimmed with deep wrinkles, but her face lacked the fullness it once had. A perpetual tiredness clung to her features now, weighing down the brightness in her gaze. "Does he have a good tush?"

"I didn't get a chance to look," I said.

Nancy's lips curled with disappointment. "You kissed a man and you didn't grab the goods? Was he not your type?"

"You know I've never had a type." Sumner, though, could've fallen into it if I'd had one, perhaps. He was pretty enough, in a way that didn't brim with an arrogant elegance. He actually made eye contact. Actually looked at me as if I were more than a shadow.

"That Aaron fellow—he still interested in you after that spectacle?"

"As of right now, according to my parents, yes."

Nancy nodded slowly, sagely, munching along on her chocolate. "Hubert and I had a marriage like that, you know. Arranged. My mama and his mama really did most of the deciding. Worked out well enough."

I peered at her from the corner of my eye. "He died early."

"As I said, worked out well enough. He was at least handsome enough to look at while he was alive." She balled the wrapper up in her fist and laid it on the blanket covering her lap. Her skin was so pale, the backs of her hands looking as if they were bruised. "He probably hoped I'd die first, that snake. But look at me now. Just turned ninety and still kicking."

It was the sort of future that awaited me, my husband and I both hoping the other would pass first. "I'm not bothered by the idea of marrying Aaron." I shifted my weight onto another foot, finding it hard to stand still. "At least I won't be alone."

I hated how pathetic the words were, but since it was just Nancy, I wasn't too embarrassed. She always seemed to know what I was thinking before I spoke anyway, but in a more refreshing way than my mother. I felt clear minded even when we were like this, not facing each other, staring out at the pond that stretched before us. We only focused on our voices and the way the sun's rays reflected off the faint ripple in the water.

Nancy coughed, but it quickly turned into a hacking sound that had her doubling over. I stood rigid beside her, drawing in a breath and holding it while. The wrapper in her lap fluttered to the ground. Just as I decided the fit was going on too long, just when I was about to run back inside to get her something to drink, it cleared. "By God," she exclaimed breathlessly.

My heart pounded, and I forced my chin to the side, trying to calm the brimming panic. "Those pack-a-day cigs are catching up to you."

She cleared her throat a few more times, her wheezing breaths slowly returning to normal. "Being alone is a choice," she said finally, not looking at me. Her gaze, too, fixed back on the pond, as if all answers rested beneath the surface. "It isn't forced upon you like you think it is, Margot. You can choose to be alone, or you can choose to have people in your life."

I thought of my mother, her grip on my chin earlier this morning. "People don't want me in their lives." Except for Aaron Astor.

"Then find someone who does. That's your choice." Nancy reached down and laid her hands on the handles of her wheelchair, her grip looking frail as she tried to maneuver it around. She was decidedly finished with viewing the water. "You've already got one person to try with."

I reached for the back handles of her wheelchair. "Who?"

She swatted at my arm hard enough to sting. Not *that* frail, apparently. "Get your hands off," she snapped in her usual grouchy tone, but continued on. "The waiter boy. The one you already kissed."

"You mean Sumner."

"Sumner, eh? Interesting name." She huffed as she wheeled toward the house. I followed just behind her, resting my hand on one of the handles, urging her along as unnoticeably as possible. "Yes, I mean him. Go make friends with him, and I might consider putting you in my will."

"I'm sure if you gave Ms. Jennings that opportunity, she'd jump on it."

"She'd jump more things than that," Nancy muttered with a shake of her head, but I saw her lips raise a little at her joke. She made her way to the back door ramp, and we went up it. When we got to the door, though, she wheeled herself inside but stopped just over the threshold, refusing to let me enter. "Go. Make a friend. And check out his tush this time for me, would you? If it's a nice one, send me a picture."

With that, Nancy snapped the sliding glass door shut, flipping over the lock with no remorse.

Chapter 4

The vast estate of the Alderton-Du Ponte Country Club with Massey Suites looming off to its side was stunning during the day. Willow trees lined the smooth roadway leading up to the grand building, their branches swaying in the wind as I drove underneath. They cleared to display the beautiful eighteen-hundreds-style architecture that expanded with an impressive square-footage.

The structure had gone through many renovations and additions over the years, but still held the charm Mr. Hubert Alderton had fought so hard to maintain. The estate itself was over fifty acres, accommodated with private pools and spas, with their grand golf course spreading out over the greenery. Even the air itself smelled expensive.

Such a beautiful place, but it was as if I could feel my soul shrivel each time I got close.

"Good afternoon, Miss Margot," one of the valets greeted me as he opened my door. He was in his mid-thirties, tall, but would never look me in my eye.

Please leave, his expression read. When the other

valets saw me looking, they pretended to be busy with other things at their station, but it was clear they all shared one uniform thought: *Please be on your way, Margot Massey.*

No one liked to interact with Ice Queen Margot any longer than they needed to, lest she freeze their hearts. I wasn't sure when it'd become that way, that even the staff began avoiding me, but I'd grown to expect it.

I passed the man my car key. "Keep it out," I told him flatly. "I'll be just a moment." Without another glance, continuing on toward the pearly gates of hell. I could've sworn I heard a sigh of relief behind me.

The Massey Hotel & Suites lobby was just as magnificent as Alderton-Du Ponte, with floor to ceiling windows in the entryway that let in an enormous amount of natural light. The heels of my loafers clacked on the marble floor as I walked through the entrance. I didn't expect to find Sumner waiting for me—after all, I hadn't given him a time I'd be back by—but when I did a quick scan, I found him sitting in one of the lounge chairs, bathed in sunlight.

His attention was on his phone, thumbs moving fast as he typed something out. His golden hair was once more ungelled and loose across his forehead, long enough to curve around his ears. *I'll be waiting for you*, he'd said hours before, and here he was.

As I approached, the first thing my gaze locked on were his shoes. They were *sneakers*. Old, dirt ridden. The untied laces on his left shoe were nearly black with grime. He wore dark wash jeans with a tear in the knees and a loose-fitting white T-shirt tucked into the band. He hadn't been the definition of elegance last night, but at least he'd been wearing *khakis.*

"Your shoes," I said without preamble, causing Sumner to jump in his seat. His hands fumbled on his phone, causing it to fall from his grip and bounce into his lap. "Your clothes. Go change them."

Sumner rose to his feet and looked down at himself once more, his golden hair falling into his eyes. "What's wrong with them?"

"You cannot be following me around looking like you're homeless."

Finally, some of his neutral expression cracked, drawing a line between his eyebrows. It made him look less like a mannequin and more like a person. "*Homeless?*" His tone was a little more than mildly offended. "I don't have anything like *that.*"

He was directing his attention to the suit I had on, and I narrowed my eyes at the Gilfman slander. I felt perfectly put together, and my confidence grew from that solid feeling. How he could feel confident sitting in a luxury hotel lobby looking like he'd just taken the walk of shame was beyond me. "Business casual will do."

"Jeans aren't casual?"

I could've gasped. "You can't possibly think *jeans* are *business casual.* They have *tears.*"

Sumner stared at me until he could no longer hold back the tiny smile that quirked at his lips. "I know what business casual is. I was just joking. It was a little funny, wasn't it?"

I just blinked at him.

"I don't have anything on your level, though. All I

have is my work uniform, and the khakis from last night are in the wash, so—" Sumner gave a *what can you do* shrug.

He was testing me. He had to be. He was acting so... casual. Teasing and acting flippant. There was no professionalism anywhere to be seen for a man hired to be my secretary.

There was no condescension that I was used to from other clubgoers, either. No fear that was common amongst the staff.

The place I'd made our breakfast reservation, Pierre's, would've barred Sumner at entry, dressed like that. It was a rooftop restaurant on one of the tallest buildings in Bayview, with the best views and avocado toast in the county. I'd been looking forward to it ever since moving back from New York, and I debated pushing the issue, forcing him to go scrounge up *something* more presentable.

Ultimately, I scrunched my nose. "Tie your shoe before you trip."

In a sort of startled realization, Sumner fell to his knee and tied up the shoe. It hit me then it wasn't necessarily lunatic behavior he exhibited—he more was like a puppy with its energy unbridled.

He followed me out into the mid-May air, and when I started toward the valet section between the hotel and the country club, Sumner picked up pace until he walked at my side.

I glanced at him from the corner of my eye. "Why are you walking so close?"

"I—am I not supposed to?"

It was quite the conundrum, Sumner's hiring. Sure, my parents thought him unflappable, but how could they hire a man so genuinely unknowledgeable in all things decorum? "A secretary is a shadow," I told him. "A shadow doesn't walk *beside* its focus."

"Actually, it would depend on the position of the sun—"

I stopped mid-stride. "Do you have a response for everything?"

"I don't know about *everything*—"

"A secretary isn't supposed to ramble on. They're supposed to be seen, not heard."

Sumner, true to my parents' word, remained unruffled. "I don't remember a 'vow of silence' clause in my contract."

The longer I stared at him, the more clearly I could see the mirth swirling in the blue depths of his eyes like they were a new color of their own. He *was* teasing me. Not mocking, as I was used to, but *teasing*.

Without another word, I started back toward the valet, shaking my head. Sumner's clomping footfalls followed faithfully.

The valet barely looked either of us in the eye as he passed me my keys back, rounding the car to open my door for me. I debated on having Sumner drive, to milk his secretary services for all they were worth, but slid into the driver's seat and revved the engine. Once Sumner sealed himself inside, I stepped on the gas before he slid his seatbelt on.

In the four years I'd been in New York City, I hadn't driven once. Even on the rare occasions I'd come back to

Addison with my mother for events, I'd rarely had a chance to take my car out for a spin. The route to Nancy's yesterday had far too many hills and blind spots to drive as freely as I did now.

This route to Bayview had no traffic, no hills, no crosswalks—nothing but a clean stretch of asphalt that I could barrel down, and bask in the adrenaline as I did so. If the windows had been open, my hair would be flying everywhere.

Sumner, though, was not as entertained.

"Can you—" He clutched the handle above his head. I almost thought it'd rip from the ceiling. "Can you slow down?"

Now it was my turn to bask in the mirth of the moment. I revved the engine in response to his desperation, adrenaline pouring into my veins at the glorious sound. I was already in the top gear, but let my hand rest on the shifter. The tires sang in response, creating a beautiful symphony of noise. I teased the speedometer, daring it as high as I could before allowing the speed to creep back down, only to make it spike again.

"You may not care about dying, but I do," he bit out, his other hand coming down and grabbing where mine rested on the gear shift. Grabbing it *tight*—the bones in my hand shifted, and I jumped at the sudden touch. "Slow down."

I tried not to think about how his hand swallowed mine, but allowed myself one glance to see the tendons accentuated through his skin. *A nice hand.* "Say please."

Sumner didn't, but he also didn't let go. His eyes were squeezed shut.

"Don't tell me you lost your parents in a car accident or something."

"I don't have to have a tragic backstory to hate you driving a hundred miles an hour."

"Oh, *please*, we only hit one hundred *once*. We've been sitting at a calm ninety-five—"

"Just slow down," Sumner repeated for the millionth time, but only then did he tack on, quietly, "*please*."

I lifted my foot off the gas pedal and shifted the gearstick, the car slowing with the speedometer following suit. Sumner loosened in his seat, as if melting into it. A part of me loved that I could draw out a reaction, while another part—an irritating part—felt a little guilty. "Because you and your sorry excuse for *business casual*, we'll most likely have to eat somewhere else. The place I made reservations for would rather close its doors than let a sneaker as dirty as yours touch their floors."

Sumner still didn't open his eyes despite the decline in speed. "You should've told me we'd be eating at a Michelin Star restaurant for breakfast."

"It's *brunch*." The correction came out exasperated. "And you should've told me that you didn't have more than one pair of dress pants."

"What, you would've lent me some of yours?"

"I'm not sure if I'm flattered or offended if you think my pants will fit you." From the corner of my eye, I looked down at the gearshift—at his curved fingers. "How long are you going to hold my hand for?"

Sumner's eyes popped open, focusing down on our hands in shock, as if he thought he'd been gripping the gearshift itself the entire time. He snatched his fingers back as if I burned him. "Your parents hired me to be your shadow," he said, bringing back what I'd said at the country club. "They hired me because you have crap people skills, which—yeah, I found that out within five minutes of knowing you. Having to follow around a rich girl because she can't keep herself from causing trouble isn't really ideal, I'll be honest. We could fight this, and be bickering for the two weeks until your fiancé comes to town, or we can actually try to be...pleasant with each other."

Again, that word. *Pleasant.* I listened to his self-proclaimed honesty with a straight face, my sunglasses shielding my gaze. Though his voice was firm as he spoke, his hands fidgeted in his lap, fingers tracing his knuckles. Something about the way he looked at me now, the way he spoke while attempting to hide his nerves, reminded me of last night after my parents left us alone. Like these were his true colors.

It wasn't as if the casual, teasing nature of his *wasn't* his true self, but this was Sumner Pennington when his buttons were pushed.

"I've thought about what I want," Sumner went on, staring straight through the windshield. "In exchange for letting you kiss me."

I curved my fingers over the leather of the steering wheel. "Go on."

He hesitated. "You said it could be anything I wanted."

"I also said *go on.*"

"Instead of me being your secretary," he began slowly, "I want us to be friends."

I'd been anticipating some sort of outlandish request, due to his hesitation, but the direct way he spoke once more caught me off guard. *Friends*. A nonchalant, easy word that slipped off his tongue, one that was near alien to me. The word felt as if it only could apply to Destelle, who was however many miles away from me. *Friends*. I narrowed my eyes at him. "Did Nancy talk to you?"

Sumner blinked. "Who?"

I knew the old lady had a strangeness to her, but it was uncanny that Nancy pushed me toward Sumner and here he was, meeting me halfway. He was a stranger to me—granted, a stranger I'd kissed.

I fought a smile. "Interesting."

"W-What is?"

"You are."

"I thought you said I was disappointing."

"I suppose the jury's still out." I glanced over at him. "Trying to find out which side you're on is what's interesting."

"I'm not on anyone's side," he said, but it sounded like a lie.

And even if it was a lie, I didn't mind it. I didn't know what was so different, a secretary or a friend, and why he requested the latter, but it worked in my favor. My parents might've had the influence of money over Sumner, but they weren't the ones spending time with him, after all. I was. I slowed even further as we entered Bayview city limits, allowing myself a small smirk. "Good. That means I can still sway you over onto mine."

Chapter 5

*I*t didn't take too long to find a parking space, since most weren't exploring this side of Bayview on a weekday morning. I parallel parked on the street and Sumner practically stumbled out onto the sidewalk, leaning a hand against the roof of my car. I slid from the driver's seat and dusted a hand down my dress shirt, smoothing out the wrinkles from the drive over.

"I guess we know who's going to be driving from now on," Sumner said as I rounded the car. "And it isn't going to be you."

"Poor little thing," I said without affection, chuffing him on the shoulder. With my key fob, I locked the car with a beep. "Come on. Let's see if I can bribe the staff of Pierre's to let you in." It was a doubtful longshot, but my craving for their avocado toast was enough to make me desperate. At the very least, I might've even been willing to risk my parents' wrath and ditch Sumner at the entrance for it.

With my gesture, Sumner began walking down the sidewalk first. Just a half step behind him, I let my eyes travel down to the back of his pants, at the slight curve that stretched the denim material. I wasn't about to pull my phone out and take a photo, but I could report back to Nancy: he did have a nice *tush*.

At that exact moment, Sumner looked over his shoulder and found me staring. "Are—are you checking out my butt?"

"Would you be offended if I said yes?"

He immediately fell back the half-step to match my pace, refusing to be a step ahead anymore. He put his hands behind his back. "I'm not sure this is going to work if you're going to look at my butt."

"You can look at mine if you'd like."

Sumner choked a little on the breath he drew in, the tips of his ears growing red. He seemed to blush quite easily.

"If you must know, I'm not looking for me." I blinked at him, trying to convey my lack of interest—trying to *feign* my lack of interest. "Someone even asked me to send a picture. Be grateful I'm just looking."

"*Someone.*" He didn't ask who it was, but just kept his hands behind his back. We walked side by side on the cracked sidewalk. His shoulder brushed the edge of my jacket with each movement. "So, you *do* have friends?"

"She's more of a frenemy." Nancy would've concurred with the term.

The tall building Pierre's sat atop of came into view, and my heart warmed at the sight.

Sumner halted in the middle of the sidewalk. "Can we eat here?" He looked through a window set into a brick building at our left.

I didn't even look at the restaurant's sign. "No."

"Let's go to your fancy place when I'm dressed right for it," he pressed, eyes light as he looked at me. Now that I thought it once, I couldn't get it out of my head—the only term that came to mind was that it was very much so *puppy-like*. "Come on, doesn't diner food sound really good right about now?"

It absolutely did not. Did diner food ever sound *good*? Now I did look up at the signage, and *O'Hare's* greeted me in lettering that was barely legible. Sumner didn't know how much of a downgrade it was, ditching Pierre's in favor of a dingy hole-in-the-wall diner where everything probably tasted of grease.

Being alone is a choice, Nancy had said.

Clearly, because if I'd been alone, I would've gone to the rooftop restaurant and enjoyed my avocado toast.

Apparently, though, being alone *wasn't* a choice, because before I could refuse a second time, Sumner snagged my wrist and tugged my unwilling feet toward the diner's door.

"It'll be good," Sumner tried to assure as he wrenched the fingerprinted glass door open.

And I wasn't buying it. "It'll taste like heartburn."

While people would've stared at Sumner as he entered at Pierre's wondering if he was the help, this crowd of people gawked at *me* as we walked in. Some patrons even stopped mid-bite to gape at the overdressed woman who sauntered into the space.

"Sit wherever," came a disembodied voice from somewhere in the diner, but I was too distracted with the actual prospect. Sit...where? Some tables weren't even bussed free of dishes, while others had crumbs from left-over customers dotting the surface.

"Let's take the booth," Sumner said as he walked toward the table near the window, leaving me to stare with mild horror after him.

My two decades of pushing through to do something when I didn't want to kicked in, forcing my steps toward him. I stared at the cracked red booth seat for a long moment, ultimately pulling the handkerchief out of my pocket to drape on its surface before sitting. Sumner watched in a way that appeared as if he were fighting a smile.

"Note to self," I said, staring at a splatter of what looked like gravy dried to the table's surface. "Do not let Sumner Pennington pick eating establishments."

"I'll admit, the atmosphere's probably different from what you're used to." Sumner laughed as he reached for the menus tucked at the end of the table, and he pried them apart with a sticking sound. "But it's cool to try new places sometimes."

"Cool? I wouldn't be surprised to find a cockroach underneath the table."

A woman in jeans came over to take our drink order. Sumner laid his menu on the table and looked it over while I looked at him. I'd long since grown used to my own company, enjoying meals in solitude. Sumner must've felt my eyes on him and looked up, doing a double take at my stare. "What are you thinking?"

"I'm thinking that if I end up with food poisoning, it's your fault."

"Well, *I'm* thinking about eggs. And bacon—lots of bacon."

"And *I'm* thinking about my avocado toast with smoked salmon." I gave him a flat stare. "If I can't have what I want, neither can you."

He took my stubbornness in stride. "Fine, pick the worst item on the menu, and I'll have that for breakfast."

"*Brunch.*"

"Right. Brunch."

I doubted this was a place that recognized brunch as a meal, though. Pierre's had a special menu for brunch, served specifically between eleven and noon. My avocado toast was only available on that menu.

I closed my eyes to will myself to stop thinking about it. Yes, I'd pick the worst meal for him possible from this place—or just let him go hungry.

"Why did you take this job?" I asked him while the waitress took her sweet time coming over, attempting to nonchalantly sit back into the booth. It gave a wheezing creak as I did so. "What was the selling factor that made you put your life on hold for a rich girl who can't keep herself out of trouble? Was it the fact that they're letting you live in the hotel?"

"I worked as a secretary at a different company back home," he said, jumping into my interrogation. "I figured it was a good use of my skills."

"And my kiss didn't run you off?"

I didn't think Sumner would take the question as seriously as he did. The fingers holding onto his menu tensed a little, but I noticed it. Years of training to pick up every minor detail had my mind focusing in on it all. "At the event Saturday. You were standing alone in the corner of the room, looking up at the chandelier, and in a room filled with people, it was like you were the only one in the world."

A small smirk tugged at my lips. "You fell in love with me at first sight, didn't you? One kiss and it was over for you?"

Sumner didn't look amused, and this time, he did not blush at my teasing. "No. I felt *sorry* for you."

I felt the traces of my smile disappear from my face.

He redirected his attention to his menu. "I told you that I couldn't help but think how lonely you looked. That's why I'm being nice."

It was strange to hear, because while, in that moment, I'd *felt* alone, I hadn't realized it'd been so obvious to anyone who bothered to look. To a complete stranger. Which meant that either no one ever looked closely, or no one cared enough to do anything about it.

Underneath the table, my hand twitched into a loose fist. "So, you're being nice out of pity?"

"You're trying to spin it into a negative."

"No positive is without its negative."

"That's a sad thought process, isn't it?"

It didn't feel sad. It was right, justified given what environment I'd grown up around in. Even Nancy, with how refreshing she was, wasn't without her negativity. No positive without a negative. No give without a take.

Being alone is a choice, Nancy had said. *It isn't forced upon you like you think it is.*

"It's easier," I said, answering his sentence and Nancy's aloud. "To always assume there's a negative."

Sumner didn't argue the fact. He looked as if he genuinely thought about it. That was another thing about him that was so different from anyone else around here— he listened when I spoke, digested it. He didn't give a fake laugh and empty assurances. Even just from seeing him twice, that was one thing about his character I was sure about.

"It doesn't have to be that way with me," he said at last. "As your friend, you don't have to worry about any negatives with my positives."

"We aren't friends."

Sumner held my gaze evenly, unwaveringly, not intimidated in the slightest. "We could be."

The waitress dropped off our waters, giving us a few more minutes to look over the menu. I hadn't glanced at the array of foods they offered yet; I hadn't even picked up the menu. It even looked sticky, as if it hadn't been wiped down in days. Maybe I could get Sumner to recite some dishes for me so I wouldn't have to touch it.

"Why..." I began, but trailed to a pause, unable to decipher his answer on my own. "Why do you want to be my friend? Why do you want to be more than just my secretary?"

"It's like I said." Sumner reached for his water. "When I first saw you, I couldn't help but think how lonely you looked. You deserve to have someone around you who isn't a shadow. Because... because I know what it's like to feel alone in a room full of people. And no one should feel that way."

Time, for a moment, seemed to slow as his words wound around in my head. I stared at him from across the

61

booth, my pulse thudding loudly in my ears. If it were anyone else, I would've thought he was mocking me in some way, but Sumner seemed so... earnest. And I didn't know how to feel. I needed to say something, to scoff at his words, but he'd rendered me speechless.

Sumner's phone gave a little chime, which prompted him to pull it out and check the screen. I watched him while he did so, and took that moment to appraise him in this different—albeit grubbier—light. Although his clothes hinted at a former frat boy, he, admittedly, looked good in the loose shirt that'd been tucked into the band of his jeans. I couldn't remember the last time I'd been around someone who'd worn jeans, at least a pair that wasn't designer. It gave him a very causal, *normal* air.

We probably looked funny sitting across from each other like this. I found myself enjoying the juxtaposition. Not that I'd ever admit it aloud.

Sumner pocketed his phone without texting. "If we're going to be around each other, we might as well know a bit about each other, yeah?" Sumner folded his hands over his menu. "So...tell me something about yourself."

It was a clear, horrible attempt at a segue, but I allowed him the pass for now, raising an eyebrow. "What do you know about me?" Meaning: *what have my parents told you about me?*

"You just graduated college a week ago," he said. "Business administration major. You're a bit of a social outcast. You have an affinity for suits. You're engaged—or, well, is that right? I don't see a ring on your finger."

I glanced down at my hand as if one would magically appear. "I'm sure I'll be given some ugly rock, eventually."

"But you *are* engaged?"

"Not *technically*." Underneath the table, I began bouncing my foot, and it took me a second to realize I was unconsciously tapping it to the country song's beat. "That's why my parents enlisted your babysitting services, because they don't want me scaring off the world's best match."

"What's he like?" Sumer picked up his water and tucked the straw between his teeth. "Your fiancé?"

I wouldn't know, I almost said. It wasn't wholly true, though. I knew bits and pieces about him, things here and there that'd trickled down the gossip mine. "The mysterious sort."

"Mysterious?"

"I don't know what he looks like."

I expected Sumner to have more of a response to this —more surprise, confusion, at the very least, asking more questions—but he just tilted his head to the side. "So, you've never met him."

"A point to Sumner Pennington for his deductive reasoning." Now it was my turn to pick up my water, though the thought of the most likely unfiltered tap deterred my thirst. I tried not to look too closely at it. "I didn't know it was possible to be completely digital footprint free in this day and age, but Aaron Astor seems to be the exception."

"I could say the same about you. You don't have social media."

A corner of my mouth tipped up. "You tried to dig up information about me?"

His eyes dropped back to his menu. With how

quickly they bounced the surface, I doubted he truly absorbed what he was reading. With a nonchalant voice, he murmured, "Out of curiosity."

It was true, like Aaron, I kept as much as my life possible off the internet. I wasn't the extreme as Aaron, though. If one typed my name, or at least my parents' names, my picture would eventually come up in search. For Aaron, though, it was like he was a ghost. His brother's pictures came up, along with articles about their investments in the company, but Aaron was never in the lineup with them. He was mentioned by name, but always followed with "*not pictured*."

I debated drawing out teasing Sumner, my foot continuing to bounce. Where was the waitress? "Did my mother give you a bonus for hazard pay yesterday? Play your cards right, and you could walk away from this little job a millionaire yourself."

"Does that happen often? Your mom paying people off?"

"So, she did pay you."

"She tried to." Sumner met my eyes again. "Does she do that a lot?"

"I don't often go around kissing people, if that's what you're asking."

"Just me?"

"Just you."

Sumner returned to gaze down at his menu, caressing the corner of it with his thumb. I watched his lips press together, but I couldn't tell with what emotion. Sumner was hard to figure out. There were times that it seemed as if he were laying all of his cards down on the table, and others where it seemed like he held them close. When he seemed transparent, it almost felt as if he were leading me into a false sense of security surety. *Or maybe that's your paranoia talking.*

"You have a staring habit, you know," he said.

"I'm aware."

Sumner stretched his legs out underneath the table, and my foot, which was mid-bounce, brushed against his pantleg. He yanked his leg away, jerking back into his seat, as if the slight touch had been scandalous. My eyes followed his movement as amusement bubbled within me, and I half-debated on stretching my leg out to find his again, if only to torture him further with the game of footsie.

I finally turned my attention to the sticky menus, scanning. There were no pictures to provide me any insight, though that was most likely a good thing—it could've ruined my appetite altogether. The list of items was mostly normal, run-of-the-mill diner food, save for—

"Beans on toast."

"*What?*"

"Beans on toast," I repeated. "It's a popular British dish, and exactly how it sounds. Baked beans in tomato sauce on toasted bread."

The visual in my mind brought about instant revulsion, and it must've been the same for Sumner. A line formed between his brows as he frowned—the first time I'd ever seen him do so. "Margot," he all but whispered. "Not that."

I couldn't pinpoint what was strange about him saying my name until I realized he dropped the *miss*. It solidified

65

my decision more, and I fought off a smile. "If you want to be friends, that's what you have to order."

Whether he intentionally gave his puppy dog pleading gaze, I wasn't sure, but I didn't budge underneath it. Instead, it just made me smile, though it was small. Sumner's eyes, much like they had Saturday night, dropped to my mouth. And, much like Saturday night, something in my stomach tightened in response. "Fine."

I let him order it with a side of bacon strips and hash-browns—I wasn't *that* torturous. I ended up ordering a Belgian waffle, though I'm sure it would taste nothing like the waffles from the country of origin. Anything had to be better than what he got, though.

"I have another question," I said when the waitress went to relay our order, once more leaving us alone. "When I kissed you, why did you just stand there? Why didn't you push me away?"

Sumner pressed his lips together again, in a way that looked like he tucked them into his mouth as he did so. "We should..." He cleared his throat. "We should probably forget that happened, okay?"

"And why is that?"

"For plenty of reasons. I'm technically your employee now, for one. We can't really be friends if we've kissed, for two. And for three..." Sumner couldn't quite look me in the eye; instead, it looked as if he focused on my forehead. "It's never going to happen again."

"Ooh." I leaned back further in my seat, and this time, I did stretch my legs out further. I couldn't find his underneath the table. "That sounds like a challenge, doesn't it?"

He didn't appear amused. "I don't want to upset Aaron."

Any of my own amusement vanished. It was funny how a simple name could do that, as if pulling a drain on a sink and letting all the water out.

"I'd hate for it to create a problem for things," Sumner went on. "Especially when you only did it to prove a point about something."

I looked out the window at the street, where a car would pass by here and there. If I leaned closer to the glass, I would've been able to see Pierre's from here, or at least the top of the building it resided in. I wished I had gone there instead. Sumner could eat his beans and toast himself. "Why did you do it?" I repeated as if he hadn't spoken, my voice flatter than before. "Why didn't you push me away?"

I half expected him to ignore the question a second time, but, reluctantly, he said, "You act like I had time to. It was like you'd been a little kid stealing a kiss behind a slide or something—I barely had any time to react before you were pulling away. Besides... it wasn't that much of a hardship. A pretty girl kissing me—"

"You think I'm pretty?"

I'd let far too much surprise seep into my tone than I intended. Sumner's word choice just didn't make sense to me, and I didn't think it'd been a joke either. *Pretty*. It wasn't a word anyone had used to describe me, ever. I didn't wear enough makeup to be pretty, didn't wear the right clothes to be pretty. I didn't style my hair or smile enough. I wore men's clothes and had a poor personality. I wasn't *pretty*.

At first, Sumner almost seemed embarrassed, as if he hadn't meant for the words to slip through, but that morphed into something different the longer we stared at each other. His gaze bounced over my expression, as if gauging the sincerity of my bewilderment. I wondered if he was taking me in—my suit, my hair, my stature—and was changing his mind. *Mmm, she's right*, he probably thought. *Pretty isn't the right word.*

"God," Sumner murmured, something in his eyes shifting. "They ate you right up, didn't they?"

I frowned, because the words were so quiet that it was almost as if he hadn't meant for them to come out.

Before I had a chance to say anything, though, the waitress returned and laid down our plates, and all thought of our conversation sprinted away in fear. Sumner's features matched what my face felt like. "No *way*."

The plate she'd laid in front of him had to be something they scraped up from the floor. Surely it wasn't something edible. Surely it wasn't something people *paid* to eat. There was a piece of bread buried by reddish-tan colored beans, swimming in some sort of red base. It oozed off the sides of the toasted bread, pooling on the plate. She laid the hashbrowns and bacon down beside it, but I couldn't look away from his main plate.

A part of me wondered if I'd gone too far, but the other part of me was too entertained.

"How's everything looking for you?" the waitress asked good-naturedly, ignoring Sumner's outburst.

"Fantastic," I answered before Sumner could, picking up my silverware. "Thank you so much."

"It's *supposed* to look like that?" he demanded. The

stench of it hit him then, and he jerked back in his seat, squeezing his nose between his finger and thumb. "You've got to be kidding."

I drew my attention away long enough to look at my waffle, which didn't look as bad as whatever monstrosity donned his plate. At least mine appeared edible. I'd been to England on multiple occasions, though had never experienced the trauma that was beans on toast.

"The price of our friendship isn't very appetizing, is it?" I murmured as I applied the butter to my waffle, waiting for the mild nausea from the sight of his plate to pass. "You might be better off remaining my secretary."

Sumner regarded the plate as if it were stewed garbage, no doubt agreeing with me.

I found myself waiting for him to move before taking a bite myself. He'd picked up his own silverware, but didn't make any move toward the oozing beans. Disappointment trickled in at his hesitation, but I forced it down. "Order something else," I said, my tone flattening. "And next time, we'll go to the place I want—"

In one sharp movement, Sumner stabbed into the beans on toast, scooped it up onto his fork, and shoved the bite into his mouth. I gasped on instinct, bracing myself for him to choke or gag on the taste that no doubt had to mimic its scent. Sumner chewed fearfully, but slowly the grimace on his face blended into a neutral expression.

With a shocked sort of reluctance, he admitted, "It's actually not bad."

"Liar."

"No, truly. It's weird—the texture is...interesting—but

it's not bad." Sumner cut into another forkful, this time offering the bread and beans to me. "Try it."

I leaned as far back into my seat as I could. The booth wheezed pitifully. "I'd rather die."

He popped the forkful into his mouth, lips quirking. "My friend," he said after he swallowed, covering his mouth with his hand. "His mom would make him beans on toast all the time. I never believed him when he said they were good."

I felt a little miffed; I didn't realize he'd heard of it before. "Why do you want to be my friend so badly if you already have one?"

"People can have more than one friend," he replied patiently. "Besides, he's on the other side of the country right now. He's not exactly competing for my time."

"The other side of the country?"

"I lived in California before coming here." He scooped up another bite of toast, and before he ate it, he added, "He's there now."

"California," I echoed. It made sense that I knew nothing about Sumner, given we'd only met last night, but the easy way he'd just jumped into being friendly with me had made me forget it hadn't even been twenty-four hours yet. "How'd you end up on the east coast, then?"

"Short, condensed version? I went to college, double majored in business communications and business finance, worked in that field for a few years, then wanted to try something new."

"I thought you said you were someone's secretary before this."

I hadn't said it with tact, conditioned to never using it,

but Sumner nodded good-naturedly. "I was. I graduated college about...two years ago? Three? I worked as a secretary for a company until I moved here. But it's funny. Choosing a path just because everyone tells you—it's never as fulfilling as one you choose for yourself, is it?" He gave his head a little shake, taking another bite. "Not funny ha-ha."

"Someone chose your path as a secretary for you?"

"In a way."

I studied him, silent. Unsettled. Attending college, following that path because people had told him to, disliking it in the end. Was he just regurgitating my own life back to me, trying to get on my good side to show that we were so similar? Was he telling the truth? "Being a secretary in California wasn't fulfilling, so you decided to be a secretary here?"

"It wasn't the job itself that I didn't like, I just..." He shrugged. "I just wanted something different."

"Why here? Why Addison?"

"My friend—the one whose mom makes beans on toast—suggested it," he answered without missing a beat. "When I talked about wanting a change of pace, he said he knew some people in this area, and directed me here."

Even as I listened, I couldn't find a trace of a lie in his words. It didn't cause me to lower my guard, though. "And that's how you ended up in Addison."

Sumner nodded, chewing through his bite. "Working here isn't a bad gig to help get my feet under me. Gives me time to...find myself, I guess."

Sumner's backstory had more meat to it than I'd given him credit for. Going to college, double majoring, getting a job only to abandon it because he wanted something *new*. Some might've said it was reckless, idiotic—my mother would've. But I understood him almost as plain as day. If I could've abandoned my major, I would've. In a heartbeat. Knowing Sumner did...it made me look at him differently.

Sumner spoke of his similar experience with all the self-assurance I'd wanted. I wanted to tell him I was envious that he was trying to find his dream, since I'd let mine be taken from me.

"My fiancé," I began slowly. "You don't want to upset him by talking about our kiss, but you think he'd be fine with us being friends?"

"I'm sure he'd be okay with it."

"How are you so sure?"

"No one would want their fiancé to feel like they're the last person on earth." His blue gaze was serious as he watched me, dark lashes sweeping down against his cheekbones in a slow blink. "I wouldn't want you to feel that way, if I were him."

Again, it was as if he knew exactly what to say to drain all the thoughts from my mind. He didn't speak as if he were flirting, but warmth skated over my skin, as if I'd stepped outside into the summer air. To hear him say that he didn't want me to be alone—to hear *someone* say that— left me off-kilter. I almost questioned if they were the words he'd truly spoken, or the words I just longed for someone to say. And here he was, not even hesitating before speaking them to me.

No one in the world lowered my guard, not even Nancy. And yet the person across the table from me, with his beans and toast and boyish grin, had me wondering if maybe there was one person in the world I could relax around. One person I could let my guard down for.

Interesting, I decided then. My initial gut feeling had been right. Sumner Pennington *was* interesting.

Sumner picked up a slice of bacon, but before he brought it to his lips, he paused. "You're staring again."

Because I can't decide if you're a breath of fresh air or something terrifying.

"You have toast crumbs on the corner of your mouth," I said to him, returning my attention to my soggy waffle. When I began cutting into it while Sumner wiped at his nonexistent crumbs.

Chapter 6

"I've always known you were impulsive, but I guess I never realized *how* impulsive."

My phone's speaker volume threw my best friend's voice off my hotel room's walls. If I closed my eyes, I might've been able to convince myself she'd been present with me. I didn't, though. I laid on my bed and stared at the ceiling, the patterns in the plaster that I once found pretty, but now hated the sight of. I'd spent far too many hours of my life staring up at this ceiling.

"You kissed a waiter," Destelle went on, half amused but fully shocked. "Who then turned out to be your newly hired secretary. I wish I'd been there to see it. I bet Ms. Nancy had a field day with that one."

"She wasn't there, unfortunately," I replied. "But you're right, the old bat would've shoved me out of the way to get a turn herself."

Destelle laughed, the familiar sound taking away some of the tension in my chest. But only some. "Why did you kiss him, again?"

"To prove to Ms. Jennings I could."

She laughed. "Now I really wish I'd been there, just to see the look on her face."

In a way, Destelle and I were one and the same. Both of us were forced into the life of diamonds and glitz at a young age, destined to follow in the sparkling heeled foot-steps of our parents. The parties and galas were bearable in high school because I at least had someone at my side who hated it all, too. Not as much, though. Whereas I was cast out, Destelle still fit in.

Sometimes, though, I wondered what life would've been like if our situations had been reversed. What it would've been like if I fit in.

Another major difference between us, of course, was that she got away from it all.

"How's life in California?" I asked, tapping my foot on the mattress. "Sunny, warm, and surrounded with matcha lattes?"

Destelle had gone out on a country-wide road trip with her boyfriend and his band out of high school and never came back. Not for good, anyway. The band discovered they could reach a far wider audience in Los Angeles than they could in little ol' Fenton County, which was fair. Destelle came back for the holidays, but the divide between us seemed larger, the gap never quite returning to the size it'd been before.

"*Finally* warming up," Destelle replied, then groaned. "I sound like a local now, complaining about sixty-degree winters."

"Figures. I was over here freezing my butt off in ten-degree winters, but you go and whine about that Cali air."

"I'll try to bring some of it back with me when I come

for Annalise's wedding—which, my mother has made it clear I need to attend, unfortunately."

"Of course you do," I replied. "Even if your mother hadn't made it clear, I'm making it clear—you are not allowed to leave me to the wolves at the event of the century."

She chuckled again. "I hear the condescension in your voice loud and clear. Don't stress, I'll be there."

My foot began tapping more firmly. I tried to force myself to stop, but the lack of movement only made my restlessness feel worse. "You'll get to meet Aaron then. And you'll get to hear all the '*so, what do you want for your wedding*' talk."

Destelle was quiet on the other end of the phone, and I listened to the white noise. I instantly regretted bringing it up. I could focus on nothing but the white noise that stretched between us. We'd been close enough in high school that there was a time I would've known exactly what she'd say. Known exactly what she'd been thinking.

Now, I found more comfort in her silence than I did in her words. "You're still going through with it?" Destelle asked. "The engagement?"

"I suppose, technically, we aren't engaged yet. My mother says he'll propose when he arrives, though. She says the Astors look upon me *favorably*." Like I was a fat cow, prime for slaughter.

"Margot." Destelle sighed. "You don't have to go through with it. Marrying a complete stranger. Letting your parents decide that for you. You can say no."

Once upon a time, I was the one pushing Destelle toward freedom and independence. She'd resented the fact that her parents controlled her life, dictated how she acted, and I'd been the one to encourage her to break free from those restraints. That was before my parents closed ranks around me, before my own freedom went up in smoke.

It was an embarrassment when I thought about it now. Hypocritical. The memory of the previous version of me, with hopes and dreams and grit, made me sick. "You're worrying about something you shouldn't be," I told her, forcing my tone level. "I don't mind being pushed toward Aaron."

"You *don't mind*. Shouldn't you *want* to be pushed toward him? Shouldn't you *want* to marry someone?"

While I envied Destelle for living the life she wanted, I did resent it when she brought the possibility up for myself. Throwing away everything you'd ever known was easy when your parents were ones you could fall back on. Destelle could've gone rogue, dropped out of school, got knocked up—*anything*, and her parents still have accepted her when she came back. They'd have grumbled and complained and probably made her feel like crap, but they would've had their arms open.

My parents would disown me, no question. No hesitation. They'd cut their hand off before the infection could run any deeper. They'd already threatened it once.

A brisk knock on my hotel room door pulled me out of my thoughts. "I have to go. It was nice catching up." I said it, but I wasn't completely sure if I meant it.

"Text me later."

"I will." Yet another one of those thoughts—I said it, but I wasn't sure if I meant it.

I padded across the suite in my slippers to the front door, exiting my bedroom and coming out into the sitting area and attached kitchenette. I rarely used it; it was far easier to order room service. It felt a bit like a small apartment, under the security of the valet holding my car hostage and Sumner's listening ear next door. Sometimes I was surprised my parents gave up their penthouse suite to me, but I always wondered if they thought their nicest room would make up for the fact that they wanted me around as little as possible.

I didn't bother checking through the peephole. There were only two people who would come without announcing themselves.

"Good morning," I greeted my mother's shadowy figure as she stood in the hallway. She wore a pair of linen pants and a loose-fitting sweater. The outfit itself made her look much younger than her fifty-nine years old. That, and the work she'd had done. "I wondered when you were going to show up."

"Your father convinced me to calm down before I came to visit you," she returned, showing herself in and shutting the door behind her. I'd already crossed my room to the settee, lounging against it. My outfit was much like hers—linen pants with a cashmere sweater. It made me want to take it off and throw it into the trash. "And I was far too exhausted to deal with you yesterday. Believe it or not, Margot, you're not always the most important person in the world."

The quip was snotty, but easy to deflect. I used to spend nights waiting for her to come find me. Even if I had just been waiting for her to yell, I'd look forward to whenever she sought me out, like a pathetic child waiting for Santa Claus. She never came. I stopped waiting. "Glad you could enjoy your Sunday without me, then," I told her.

"I heard you and Mr. Pennington went out for brunch yesterday."

Eyes and ears everywhere all the time. "Mm."

"What did you talk about?"

"I have to report every single conversation to you, too?" I rubbed a finger into my temple. "Ask Mr. Pennington. With how much you're paying him, I'm sure he'll sing like a canary."

I wasn't sure what my mother was afraid we'd discussed, but in truth, our conversation had been simple. Normal. Talking about Sumner's collegiate, his move east. Anyone else would've found the conversation boring, but the mundane details...intrigued me. It was interesting to hear about someone's life without them attempting to glamorize it. Sumner hadn't been trying to impress me; he'd been being honest.

His easy honesty still left me a little unsettled.

"How is Ms. Nancy?" my mother asked.

If I hadn't wanted to recap my conversation with Sumner, I surely did not want to talk about my visit with Nancy. "Fine."

"Yvette said she's declining. Her doctor doesn't think it'll be much longer, with the remaining function of her heart. Quite the perfect time for you to come back to town. Try to stop in there more often, Margot." My mother's voice was thoughtful, though I didn't turn to look at her expression. "Allyson Jennings has been going over there more often lately. We need to remind Ms. Nancy how you're her favorite."

"So I can beat Ms. Jennings out from top spot in Nancy's will, you mean." My lips curved, but it wasn't a smile. "Yes, good thing you brought me back to Addison when you did. Would've been a shame if Nancy died before you could secure her fortune. Could you imagine if she left the land Massey Suites sits on to Ms. Jennings? How unfortunate would that be."

My mother entered my peripheral. "Everything is such a joke to you, isn't it? I don't know when you're going to stop acting so childish." And with that, she launched into it all. "Kissing the staff at the fundraiser? You're twenty-two, Margot, not twelve. I know you're intentionally trying to create problems for your father and me, but to be so impulsive just isn't acceptable."

I know I had signed up for it, and even yesterday, I'd been ready to pass the bickering back and forth, but now, I found myself wishing I could be anywhere in front of her. I was suddenly and abruptly too tired to pick an argument.

"I can't even begin to try to get into your head, either. What did you think kissing a worker would accomplish? Were you *trying* to get him to call the police?"

I hadn't done it for a police report, but now I almost wished he had—would Aaron Astor have wanted to marry me so desperately then? Probably. If the man was willing to fall in love at first sight and propose through his parents without having ever met me in person, he didn't seem like the type easily swayed by a rap sheet.

"Knowing you," my mother went on, still standing in

the middle of the room. It was as if she planned on running blocker if I tried to escape. "You probably just wanted to get everyone else to grasp their pearls."

"People don't say that phrase unironically."

"Margot."

My mere exasperated name felt like a small victory in that moment. A tiny, little smile tugged at my mouth, but it dropped back into place. "You said so yourself, I'm impulsive. Ms. Jennings said I hadn't kissed a man, and there was one ripe for the kissing."

"Or maybe you were hoping I'd change my mind about Aaron Astor."

My finger, which had still been rubbing circles into my temple, stilled. "I didn't kiss Sumner because I was hoping you'd change your mind," I said to my mother now, finally looking up at her. "I know how important the business deal with the Astors is to you."

"No, you were just hoping *Aaron* would change his mind."

At the moment I'd kissed Sumner, Aaron hadn't been on my mind. Right? Had the subconscious thought of him spurred me to action? I resented how she could wheedle my thoughts out of me. She'd barely tried, too. She'd been in the room not even for five minutes, and already could see right through me.

"It *is* an arcane thing to do," I said before I could think better of it. "Marrying your child off for the sake of your business flourishing."

"*Arcane.*" She gave a little scoff, pacing her way closer. "Who got that idea in your head? Destelle? Marriage itself is a contract. Do you know statistically how many marriages based on love fail, Margot? Many. Most. Any life-altering decision based on emotion isn't going to end well. That's just common sense."

She made it sound as if I had a lover that I intended to run off with. I didn't. And it wasn't as if I *wanted* to marry for love. At twenty-two, I just didn't know if I wanted to get married to begin with. Not right now, especially not to a stranger, not even if he was the son of a goldmine.

"Mr. and Mrs. Holland's marriage was based on mutual beneficiation, not love."

"Yes, and they both cheat on each other every chance they get."

"It's not cheating. It's their agreement." She gave a sigh, one that indicated her decaying patience. "You know my relationship with your father is the same, in a sense. Not founded on love, but because we were a good match. Could keep up with each other. You've always known that. We've never raised you on fairytales and love stories, so I don't know why you're acting so childish like this."

Yes, I'd always grown-up thinking love to be ridiculous. I'd never had crushes on people, never found myself googly-eyed over a celebrity. I couldn't even picture myself with a partner, lying next to them at night. Even when I tried, the visual was empty, nonexistent. So now, I didn't have a concrete answer for my mother. It was just as if something unknown grabbed my shoulders and held me in place.

You cannot do this, it said. *This is something you cannot do.*

"You live a beautiful life, Margot Massey. You'd really give it up?" My mother's hand suddenly reached out and snatched my chin, jerking my head to the side. I hadn't even realized she'd gotten close enough to touch me, and her grip was a painful pinch, forcing my stare to hold hers. "Your entire wardrobe, gone," she threatened, those blue eyes snapping fire. It was almost a comforting sight, despite her grip on my face. It was one I was used to. "Your penthouse suite, gone. Your sportscar, gone. Your inheritance, your fortune. We have given you a luxurious life, and I will not hesitate to take it back if you won't appreciate it."

My parents' relationship held no love, and neither did their relationship with me. I wasn't sure if it was because I'd been sent away so young, but we never bonded in the way a family should bond. My parents never saw me as their loved daughter; they saw me as their business asset.

It was times like this, with her threatening everything I'd ever known, that I felt small. Young. Sixteen instead of twenty-two, a child instead of an adult.

"Appreciate it by getting married to whomever you wish." It was hard to speak with my jaw held captive. "That's what you mean."

"You understand me, then." My mother dropped my chin just as quickly as she'd grabbed it. "You're in a wonderful position, Margot. You truly are. One of the Astor sons is interested in you—I don't see why you're fighting it so much."

"And *I* don't see how you don't find his obsession with me creepy." I returned my gaze out the window, fighting the urge to rub my chin. "I've never met the man, and yet he's wanting to marry me?"

"I've met him," she reminded me. "He came up to me

at the Christmas party. *I* know his intentions. And it's perfect. The hard part of catching his attention has already been done for you. You don't have to worry about wooing him." She stared at me, but I refused to look over. "You can do this for your father and me. And you will."

Her unyielding tone reminded me of the day my dreams shattered. My senior year, my parents had allowed me to apply to any fashion institutes and colleges I wanted, as long as I also applied to a few universities on their list. Looking back, that should've been a sign. I'd gotten accepted into most of the fashion schools I applied for, with the portfolio I'd built over the four years of high school, but when it was time to pay tuition, that was the first time my parents took the choice out of my hands.

Instead of fashion school, they paid for my tuition at their alma mater for a business program.

It had been like someone had shaken me awake, the peaceful life I'd been living vanishing into the icy grip of reality. I could do nothing without my parents' money—couldn't live on my own, couldn't attend the school I chose, couldn't chase the dreams I wanted—and never again would they let me forget it.

My mother began toward the door. A sudden tightness seized my chest at the fact that she walked away from me, a buzzing, ridiculous desperation to make her stay. "I want to speak to him first," I called after her. "Before I meet Aaron for the first time at Annalise's wedding, I want to speak to him first. If you want me to be coopera-tive, you could arrange that at the very least."

It was a suffocating thought, meeting Aaron for the first time surrounded by the eyes of the elite. Our every move measured, scrutinized. *He can do so much better*, they'd think; they'd say. It was bad enough to go through it, but worse to add them to it.

"You'll have to arrange it with your father," my mother said, and if I hadn't been looking, I wouldn't have noticed the way her shoulders fell in relief. *Finally*, I could see her thinking. *My robot is functioning as she should*. With the details finalized, she left my bedroom.

I was sure my skin was red from her grip, and I sat while the stinging pain receded. The settee wasn't even comfortable; I didn't know why I still sat in it. They couldn't have invested in higher quality furniture for a penthouse? Much of my life seemed consistent with that train of thought. *I don't like it; why am I doing it?*

The answer, as always, was a simple one: It wasn't as if I had anything else to do anymore. I had no possessions that didn't belong to my parents. I no longer had hopes and dreams that weren't created by my parents. My life had always been a calculated one, fully planned and no room for deviation, but they'd allowed me the first few years to taste freedom. It was a mercy of theirs. Now, they had a use for me.

I pushed to my feet and made my way back to my bedroom, continuing into my closet. It was the size of a small bathroom, rows of suits on hangers, beautiful at first sight. I'd bought my first suit at thirteen, and since then, I'd spent years collecting them. Gilfman, Malstoni, Beaumont Couture, Hefman & Italia—brands I'd never have been able to consider without my parents' credit card. Without them, I'd never have been able to express myself the way I did. I traced my fingertips over the fabrics, the satin and the cotton, letting it bolster me.

My mother, so confused as to why I acted out, wasn't alone in that bewilderment. I didn't understand it either. I didn't know why I instinctively tried to move puzzle pieces into spots they didn't fit in.

I knew one thing for certain, though, over the past three years—fighting it got me nowhere. I might as well just give in.

Chapter 7

I didn't have a great relationship with my
father. He'd always been the absent type,
catering more to his clients and business partners than his
family. That was what a wife was for, after all. And, in my
mother's opinion, that was what boarding school and
nannies were for. My relationship dynamics with my
parents had been doomed from the moment of
conception.

Or, really, doomed the moment they found out I'd be
a girl.

But whereas my mother and I both battled it out, my
father had a consistent, exhausted approach when it came
to me, like even just breathing the same air was taxing on
his time.

Tuesday afternoon, I rapped my knuckles on the
closed door with my free hand, waiting for the call. "You
may enter," my father said in a clear voice, not bothering
asking who it was.

I pushed open the door to his office at the hotel,
immediately greeted with the differences between his
office and my mother's. Where hers had been light and

airy, my father's office had dark mahogany wood and lots of it. His desk was dark, his bookshelves were dark, though they held nothing notable on them. My father never cared much to flaunt books he never read. *A clean space is a productive space*, he'd always say. *People who collect books they never touch are trying to help themselves feel more important than they are.*

He had a lot of sayings that never made much sense to me.

"I thought you might be in need of a mid-day drink," I said as I entered, holding a short-stemmed glass of brandy, no ice.

My father didn't hesitate before stretching out his hand. "Where's Mr. Pennington?"

"Mother asked for his help at the country club today. Don't worry, I don't plan on leaving the grounds and causing a scene."

He made a displeased face as he took in his first measly sip. After letting his tastebuds adjust, he took a longer drink.

Sometimes I allowed myself to think dark thoughts with a small glimmer of amusement. Picturing the chandelier falling at Saturday's event was one example. Thinking about what it'd be like to shatter every floor to ceiling window in the Massey Suites hotel was another. Sometimes I acted on those impulsive thoughts, like kissing Sumner. Most of the time I didn't, though. I was calculated with my temper tantrums, as I'd said.

But as my father took his first sip of brandy, I always wondered what would happen if I spiked it with something.

I studied him closer. My father was a prim and proper man, no facial hair marring his face, never let a hair on his gray head stray out of place. It was a little tousled now, as if he'd been running his fingers through it. "Bad day?" I asked with only a glimmer of true curiosity.

My father mumbled under his breath and drained the rest of the brandy. Three drinks; that was practically a record for him. "I'm not pleased with you after your latest scandal."

"Which one?"

"Your little display Saturday. With your behaviors, the Astors may call everything off. I doubt they'd want a *party girl* ruining their reputation."

"I can't imagine one measly little kiss would get them to reconsider letting me marry their son, not when there's a multi-million-dollar business deal on the line."

"I know it's not ideal for your generation," my father went on as if I hadn't spoken. His eyes already looked a little glassy. "This generation is all about loving who you want and not working unless it's your dream. Bah. That's the biggest piece of baloney this world is trying to sell right now."

I let him rant away, uninterested, but letting him get it out now would turn in my favor later.

"It's work. It's not supposed to be fun. Marriage— back in the old days, a woman couldn't marry a man without a dowry. Marriages have always been contracts. People have forgotten that."

Well, he was in a particular mood today, wasn't he? They'd said that Aaron Astor had been made aware of the incident, but I wondered if the Astors were more displeased than my parents let on. I forced my lips flat, knowing that a smile would be suicide. "Is Aaron still wanting to marry me?"

"His parents, as of now, are still wanting to carry through with it. They, fortunately, see the benefits of our families merging."

"But what about Aaron?"

"How should I know what he's thinking? I just know about his parents."

Interesting. Was there a possibility that he was a pawn in this game as well? I'd never considered it in all the times I'd thought about him. Bad teeth, thinning hair, but never like me, forced against his will.

"From here on out, you need to be on your best behavior, Margot." He rubbed his brow. "You'll appreciate everything down the road, a few years into marriage, when you've got kids to enjoy—"

"You can force me to marry a man," I snapped. "But you can't force me to have his children."

My father buried his head in his hands. "What do you want from us, Margot?" he asked with a suffering sigh. "What will make you be a good girl about this?"

For a moment, I relished in his defeated posture and the fact that I'd been the one to curve those broad shoulders. All the years of ignoring me were biting them in the tush, and it was more than a little satisfying to see. Though as much as I resented them, there was always that small voice in the back of my mind that wanted to make them proud. The relationship wasn't a healthy one, but it never had been.

However, it segued beautifully into the reason why I'd brought him brandy in the first place.

"I want to talk to him," I said finally. "I want to talk to Aaron before we meet."

"Your mother and I don't trust you on the phone with him. Knowing you, you'll say something ridiculous, and he'll call it off."

"I don't know what he looks like; I don't even know what his voice sounds like." I stood firmer, my hands curling into loose fists. "You expect me to give you my full cooperation, and yet you're keeping me in the dark. Tell me, is that a business strategy *you* would go along with?"

It was an angle I should've brought up before, because I could see the realization sink in for him. No. Of course he wouldn't. One didn't need a bachelor's in business to know it was a horrible way to manage a contract.

"A video call." When he opened his mouth to object, I added, "You can be present for it. That doesn't matter. I just...I want to see the face of who I'm marrying."

My negotiation skills had come from him, our giving and taking like tugging on a rope. With my mother, she only knew how to pull. My father knew how to take a step forward, to give me an inch in order to gather his footing, because he knew it'd mean success later on when he was ready for the final, sharp tug. As I suspected, he acquiesced. "Fine, I will see about a video call. Just... *please* don't make me regret it, Margot."

The win was a small one, but a win, nonetheless. Even though I knew my father would tug the rope down the line and throw my world into a remorseless tailspin, I allowed myself to bask in the victory of this small pull in my direction. "I won't."

～

There weren't many clothing brands I put on my body.

Fashion was the one thing I let myself behave that way about. It was the one way I expressed myself, the emotions that I kept bottled up spilling out onto the fabric. Malstoni was an Italian designer brand that created absolutely darling event suits, the sleek cuts and fabric types perfect to match the showiness that the elitist crowd surrounding me put off. If I were to get married, I'd be in a Malstoni.

Gilfman, however—a French brand that only had three stores in the United States total—owned my heart and soul.

A soft knock on the dressing room came, followed by a pleasant male voice. "How is everything fitting, Miss Margot?"

"Almost finished," I said to the salesman as I fastened the buttons of my shirtsleeves below my wristwatch.

"Brilliant." A moment later, he asked, "Are you sure I can't get you something to drink? We have champagne, wine—white and red."

The salesman wasn't asking me, though, because my champagne flute was already sitting on a table in my dressing room, its bubbles licking up the glass. "Oh, uh, no, thank you," Sumner answered hesitantly in the waiting room.

"Something stronger, perhaps? We have a lovely maple whisky."

"No, I'm—I'm fine, thank you."

As I shrugged on my outer suit jacket, I smiled at the discomfort in Sumner's voice. It was clear he wasn't used to the attention, such service, and I enjoyed introducing him to it. "Forgive him," I said as I exited the dressing room, smoothing my hand down the arm of the jacket. "This is a new experience for him."

There were no mirrors inside the dressing room, so stepping out into the open seating area that was ceiling to floor reflective glass, I took in my outfit for the first time. The pastel blue suit fit me like a glove, not that I was surprised. It wasn't often that Gilfman got my sizing wrong, not anymore. The double-breasted vest tapered in tightly at my waist, more so than a man's would. It illuminated my silhouette elegantly. The pants narrowed down my thigh to accentuate the shape of my legs, but not so much that they looked like a pair of skinny jeans.

Anyone who thought my suits looked like something men wore wouldn't think that if they ever saw a man try to put one on.

"It's exactly like the sketch I gave," I said as I appraised my reflection, turning to see how the suit jacket fell against my back. "It's quite lovely. What do you think?" In the mirror, I looked at Sumner.

He sat on one of the plush couches in the sitting area. Sumner held his phone in his hand, presumedly had been looking at it before I walked out, but his attention was on me now. I watched as his eyes roamed down my body, taking the fitted suit. It was vastly different from the looks

I normally received, but I couldn't pick apart what emotion shone in his expression. Finally, he came to rest on my face. "Very nice."

A lackluster response.

"It is quite perfect, isn't it?" the salesman, Jordan, murmured, coming up to me. He checked that the stitches fell exactly where they were supposed to. "Are there any specific things you notice you'd like changed?"

The jacket seemed satisfactory, so I shrugged it off and examined the look without it. The suit itself was more of a casual one. Though double-breasted, the material was on the slimmer side, and the shoulders had no padding, which gave it a more relaxed look. I pinched the material of the vest, debating on whether I liked how much of a gap there was.

Jordan seemed to agree, his fingers replacing mine near my hip where I'd pinched the fabric. "About half an inch, hmm?" he murmured, analyzing the silhouette. "This wouldn't be a hard fix at all. I could take it into the back and alter it right quick, if you've got the time."

One of the best things about this Gilfman store was that each of the salesmen were tailors, which made for easy and quick fixes. "We've got the time," I said, passing Sumner my wine glass. He took it wordlessly, and I began to undo my vest's buttons. "As long as I can get another wine."

"Of course, of course." Jordan draped the material over his arm. "Feel free to look about the store as well. It shouldn't take too long." And with that, he was gone.

The waiting area grew quiet, save for an orchestra playing faintly over the speakers. I walked over to Sumner and stopped above him, forcing him to tip his head back to peer at me. "You design your own suits?" he asked, passing back my wine glass.

"I give suggestions. The beautiful clothiers bring it to life. My Malstoni suits, though, are all his designs. One does not mess with perfection."

"Why suits?"

"Why not?"

Sumner blinked a little before donning a sheepish expression. "Fashion design, though. Not that I know the slightest thing about fashion, but that's cool. Have you ever thought of doing something more with it?"

Though he'd been vulnerable with me yesterday at brunch, I wouldn't do the same now. He'd chosen to share those snippets of himself; I did not. I didn't want to tell him about the hopes and dreams of seventeen-year-old Margot Massey, and didn't want to resurrect the pain that came from thinking about it. "No." The word was flat. "Speaking of fashion, we should have you fitted for a few pairs of pants while we're here."

Sumner at least showed up in the lobby this morning with khakis on, but the horror of his torn jeans still lingered in my mind. "I'm okay," he said, casting an almost nervous glance toward where Jordan went off to. "I bought a few pairs already."

"When?"

"Last night."

I blinked. "You bought dress pants *online*?"

"I got free two-day shipping, too."

I wondered when Sumner would stop surprising me with the clueless things he did. He bought dress pants *online.* I couldn't even begin to imagine the quality—what were they made of, polyester? I very nearly brought him to his feet anyway, to force him to try on a few pairs of pants while we were here—like some mother corralling her rebelling son—but I held myself back.

"I bet you're bored out of your mind, hmm? Watching that rich girl you have to babysit play dress up."

Sumner winced a little. "I'm not bored."

"I used to have to drag my friend along with me." I brought my champagne to my lips and gave a small smirk to him over the rim. "But in New York City, I went to my tailorings alone. It isn't fun playing dress up when there's no one to show off for."

As if on their own accord, Sumner's eyes fell to my body once again, but this time, there was no suit to inspect. I had on just the dress shirt now, two buttons undone near the top to expose my throat. It stretched across my chest, just how I preferred, and I watched as he forced his attention back to my face. "I thought you said you didn't have friends."

"Actually, *you* said I didn't have any friends. Which, looking back, is quite rude to assume."

The sheepish smile returned, accompanied by a blush on the top of his cheek bones. It complimented his already warm skin nicely.

"I haven't seen her in ages," I told him, slipping a hand into my pants pocket. "College kept me busy; her courses kept her busy. She's touring with her boyfriend now. He's in a band. She doesn't come home all that often."

He tilted his head as he listened to me speak. "Are you're upset with her? For leaving?"

I wasn't sure what gave him that impression, since I'd been quite careful about my tone. I thought about it, sipping my champagne. It was almost drained now. Apparently, Jordan thought I meant to bring the refill after he'd tailored the vest. "Slightly."

"It'd be hard to drift apart from the one person you were close with. Even though you went off to college too, you must've felt abandoned a little, huh?"

"Are you my therapist now?"

He rested his hands on his knees, giving a small shrug. "Just a friend who's assuming you've never talked about it before. And you *should* talk about the things that bother you. If you leave them bottled up, it can make you bitter."

I arched an eyebrow at him. "Bitterness is one of my better qualities."

"Happiness is better."

"I'm not a happy person."

The words sounded like more of a confession, the momentary banter dissolving into something more serious. He was able to lull my thoughts out of me, ones that seemed harmless in my mind but pathetic when spoken aloud. I didn't like it. I blamed the wine.

I moved to turn away, to go and wander the store as Jordan said I could—and go to investigate where my refill of wine had disappeared off to—when Sumner snatched my hand. His fingers wrapped around my wrist, brushing against my pulse point. "You can be," he said with far too much seriousness in his voice. "You can be a happy person."

The sudden contact had me freezing on instinct, focusing all my attention at the touch. *When was the last time someone touched me?* It was a ridiculous thought, but it surfaced anyway. My mother, gripping my chin. Before that... who'd reached out with a gentle touch instead of a demanding one?

I sniffed. "I hope you didn't take this job in an attempt to fix me. That would be quite disappointing."

"There's nothing wrong with you."

"A million and one people would disagree with you about that." I still focused on where he still held me in place, the tension of his fingers not loosening. His skin was soft; I couldn't feel any callouses. "One would argue, too, that you don't know me well enough to make such a judgement."

"Then tell me." Sumner released my wrist and sat back more comfortably on the sofa, his arm lining the back of the beige material. The tension of the moment relaxed with his posture, though even with his touch gone, I could still feel the ghost of the pressure. "What do you think turned you into an unhappy person?"

"I need a tragic backstory to justify my bitterness?" I asked, bringing his own words back.

"Most people do, yeah."

It was such an amusing question that I didn't let it sink in for a long moment, didn't let myself think of it beyond its entertainment. What turned me into an unhappy person? We might've had enough time to get my vest tailored, but we didn't have *that* much time. Besides, what he'd told me about himself the other day might've been vulnerable, but I hadn't been asking for his deepest secrets and insecurities. In fact, he'd said it all so off-the-cuff that I wasn't sure they *were* insecurities of his to begin with. Sumner couldn't ask me about mine and expect an answer.

I leaned down and brought my face near level to his, closer. He blinked at the proximity, his beautiful blue eyes widening a fraction of an inch, but he didn't pull back. "You'll soon discover, Mr. Pennington, but I'm not like *most people*."

"I'm finding that out, yeah."

I studied him from that close distance for a moment longer. The blue in his eyes was very deep; up close like this, I could almost convince myself they were gray. A speckling of freckles dotted underneath his right eye, like a little constellation.

Sumner held still through my studying, and it took me a moment to notice he was holding his breath. I made him nervous. Perhaps because he thought I'd try to kiss him again. The realization caused a tingle to glance across my skin.

Satisfied, I dropped down on the sofa beside him, realizing belatedly that two couldn't quite fit comfortably on it, at least not without touching. Where Sumner had his arm stretched, the back of my neck brushed it. Our thighs were another thing that pressed together on accident, drawn together by the gravity of the sinking cushion.

Sumner moved first, just like always, shifting to create an inch between us. "So, last night, I couldn't sleep, and I did some internet scrolling," he began. "Did I tell you I'm pretty good at digging up information? I think I might've found out a few things about your fiancé."

I narrowed my eyes. "Do tell."

He unlocked his phone in his grip and scrolled, but the screen was angled so that I couldn't see it. "I tried a few different searches. His mother's name, his father's name, Astro Agencies—"

"How did you get all that information? I never told you his mother's name."

"You told me about the company," he replied without missing a beat, blinking. "Astro Agencies. At the diner. I searched backward from there."

Had I told him? I must've, though I didn't remember it. I drained the final traces of my wine and set it on the glass coffee table. "Well, what did you find about him, then?"

Sumner shifted so that inch of space between us vanished once more, our legs pressing together as he offered his phone screen closer for viewing. An article with blocky text popped up on the screen. "So, this article is about male heirs of businesses that are on the rise," Sumner said, pointing with his finger. "The Astor sons are number seven."

"Male," I scoffed. I didn't take the phone from him, but laid my hand over the back of his, steadying the grip. My fingers were cold against his. "Someone created a male *and* female list before. The Astro sons weren't on it, but I was. Number four, to be exact."

"That doesn't surprise me. You should've been number one."

He was giving me that same puppy dog smile when I glanced over. Our faces were close, and I became all too aware of the way his fingers curved underneath mine as I held his hand in place. It reminded me of how he'd laid his hand over mine in the car on the way to brunch, and the backs of his fingers were just as soft as the other side.

"It's too small of text," I decided, letting go of his hand and sitting back into the couch. "Read it to me."

"It talks about his three older brothers first," Sumner summarized. "The eldest is ten years older than him, and the article talks about how he'll most likely inherit the company. The other three also currently are holding positions at the company. Aaron, though—" Sumner cleared his throat. "'After obtaining his degree at Stanford University, the youngest of the Astor sons has decided to stay out of the spotlight and stay under the radar of business holdings. However, sources state he's dedicated much of his time to community service and brightening his community, an admirable path for someone who desires no credit for the work he gives. He refuses photographs of himself, wishing to pursue his good deeds behind the scenes, a truly humble decision—'"

"Wow, this writer is an Aaron Astor fanboy, aren't they," I muttered.

From the corner of my eye, I caught Sumner's attention flick over at me, and then away. "No pictures, but it does sound like he's got decent character."

I folded one leg over the other and crossed my arms, staring at our reflection in the mirror across from us. "He doesn't work at his family's company?" I asked, trying to recall what he'd said.

"They all do. It doesn't say positions, though." He scrolled a bit. "The only other thing it says about him is that he seems to be the son that's the least interested in shares of the company. Which makes sense, since he doesn't have a chance of inheriting it."

Interesting. Though the bits of information were just crumbs, nothing substantial, but I mulled them over anyway, a bit of my hunger satiated with them.

"He's never reached out to you?" Sumner asked hesitantly, as if he could gauge my mood already. "Aaron?"

"I never said that."

"You said you haven't met him."

"And I haven't."

Sumner shifted on the sofa, jostling against my side. I wondered if his patience was wearing thin with my short answers. "Have *you* ever reached out to *him*?"

"I'm meeting him tomorrow, as it turns out."

"Wait, meeting him," Sumner echoed, lowering his phone and blinking in confusion. "What? How? I thought you said he was on the west coast?"

"Good listener," I complimented, leaning against his arm as I tipped my head against the couch. The wine had left me feeling a little lightheaded. "I'm not sure if you've heard of it, though, but there has been this invention called a video chat."

"And he said yes to it?"

I tilted my head to the side to peer at Sumner. "You seem surprised."

Sumner quickly shook his head. "No, no. You just said he's a private person, that's all. But that's exciting. Makes sense to get a new suit for the occasion. Hopefully the Wi-Fi is good so you get a clear view of him." He looked down at his phone, but the screen was now inky black.

A part of me wondered how Destelle would've responded to the news. I knew, though. Destelle, who pushed me away from the idea that was Aaron Astor, would've been dismayed at the idea of us meeting. She'd be afraid that if I met him, it'd be that much harder to pull myself out of the sinking whirlpool I'd fallen into.

I wondered what my expression looked like. I was about to look toward the mirror when Sumner turned back to me, our faces suddenly inches apart.

I stilled. When I'd studied him before, I'd very much so been in the position over him—now, though, his face was the one hovering over mine. I took my time looking over the new angle of him. The bright lights of Gilfman's waiting room reflected like sparkles in Sumner's eyes as he looked down at me. His lashes were a deep brown, not black, framing his crystal blue eyes. There were freckles just underneath his right one.

How pretty, I thought, realizing that'd been the word he'd used with me the day prior. *Pretty*. Pretty from afar. Prettier up close.

"What did you mean?" I asked him suddenly, though faintly, in a tone one could've called a whisper.

Sumner's lashes fluttered as he blinked, but he, too, didn't pull back. "When?"

"At brunch. *'They ate you up.'* What did you mean?"

I wondered if he remembered that. I wondered if he expected *me* not to remember that, or to not have put any thought into it. The truth was that it'd been all I'd thought of last night as I stretched out in bed, going back and forth between the compliment and the puzzling statement that followed.

His expression, if possible, became more serious. "I could see why you might've not felt like a happy person," he answered. "Because everyone around you enjoyed making sure you weren't."

"They ate it," I echoed with a shake of my head, still not understanding the phrasing. "Like a main course at a meal?"

"Like a paper shredder. Taking something that was whole and tearing it apart."

My first instinct was to roll my eyes at him, because of the grandness of his metaphor, and because I didn't feel shredded. It didn't feel like there were ribbons of me, tattered and scattered around. I felt whole.

He continued, "The fact that you don't think you're pretty tells me that."

"I wear suits. Women who wear suits aren't *pretty*." Not in the way women who wore dresses were.

"Clothes don't make you pretty, and whoever convinced you of that can shove that thought up their ass."

I wasn't sure if it was the curse word or the blunt way he'd said, but I tipped my head back against the couch and laughed. It broke apart the serious moment that'd been building, shattering it. My laugh wasn't a lovely one; it was sharp and abrupt, one that caused my eyes to close. My lips tilted up in a way that almost felt uncomfortable, but I couldn't fight them back to their normal position.

"You," I breathed, giving my head a little shake. "You're definitely not from around here."

Sumner didn't reply. His serious expression had vanished, replaced with an emotion I couldn't place. His stare was intense on me, almost as if I'd just stripped naked in front of him. Whatever it was, it tightened his brow as he looked at me, but his parted lips held zero tension. *Stunned*. He looked stunned.

"What?" I asked, self-conscious under the attention of his strange expression. "Now *you're* staring."

The accusation did nothing to snap Sumner back to the present. He didn't pull back and apologize for gaping so openly, didn't rush to explain. In fact, it was almost as if I hadn't spoken. Whatever caught his attention distracting him too much to form a response.

"Here we are, Miss Margot," Jordan said as he entered the changing area in a rush, gasping at a realization he made as he crossed the threshold. "Oh, I forgot the wine! Hopefully you weren't waiting for it this entire time."

I sat up from the couch and swayed for a moment, warmth kissing at my cheeks. Jordan couldn't have cared less about the strange sight he walked in on, but I couldn't stop picturing what it might've looked like. What it felt like. Clearing my throat, I wiped my features clear of any and all emotion, shrugging back on the air of unaffectedness. "That's quite all right, Jordan. It seems I've had more than I should've, anyway. Let's try on the vest, shall we?"

Chapter 8

The chair I sat in was stiff and uncomfortable Friday morning. Though the Alderton-Du Ponte Country Club had many meeting and conference rooms, the one we resided in now wasn't one that had extravagant views. There were no windows that exposed rolling hills or puffy clouds. There wasn't even a picture on the wall. I had nothing to distract but the staff who fluttered about setting up the computer and webcam.

I sat back and watched, rhythmically tapping my finger on the arm of my chair. "You've got five minutes," I reminded the staff member. The clock was inching closer and closer to noon, and it caused the back of my neck to prickle.

The girl, who looked younger than me, tapped the keypad as if in distress. "The Wi-Fi... It's connecting in here, for some reason."

Hopefully the Wi-Fi is good so you get a clear view of him, Sumner had said yesterday. He jinxed it. My eyes flicked up. "What kind of business doesn't have Wi-Fi in a conference room?"

My father, who sat across from me at the table,

frowned, the array of his wrinkles reflecting his irritation. "Everyone's internet flickers from time to time. It's not something I can control."

"Interesting that it's flickering *now* when it was working perfectly fine five minutes ago."

My father had no response to that.

Could he really be messing with the internet connection? I wouldn't put it past him. I glanced at the clock on the wall. Four minutes left until the top of the hour. Four minutes until Aaron Astor popped up on the other side of the screen, and I'd finally be able to put a face to the dreaded name. Both of my feet were planted on the ground, because I knew that if I crossed my legs, I'd no doubt bounce them.

With a pit in my stomach, I wished Sumner was here. Which was a ridiculous thought. I absolutely did not know him well enough to have him present for such an important moment. No, he was far better off working in whatever department my mother put him in, or sitting in his hotel room, or whatever he was doing this morning. I didn't check in with him.

But he would've said something that lightened the weight on my shoulders. I didn't need to know him well to know that.

Three minutes. Now that I was sitting down, the suit I'd had tailored the day before was far too constricting. It was as if I'd bloated overnight, the material stretching over me in a way that felt two sizes too small. I shouldn't have let Jordan take the vest in. I should've kept it the way it was.

My finger tapping against the chair's arm, besides the

rapid clicking of the keyboard, was the only sound in the room. Two minutes left. Against my will, my leg began bouncing.

I shouldn't care if Aaron thought me to be unpunctual. In fact, didn't this work toward my benefit? Maybe he would be unimpressed with my tardiness, and that could've been the straw that broke the camel's back for him.

The beat in which my finger tapped to sped up.

"Ah!" the staff member exclaimed as the webpage loaded. "It's working now!"

Right as the clock on the wall struck noon, my father's ringtone pierced the air of the small conference room. It caused the poor girl in front of the computer to let out a yelp in surprise, but even with as on edge as I was, I didn't even blink.

My thought was immediate: he hadn't turned his ringer off, despite us stepping into a meeting with someone as important as Aaron Astor.

My father drew his phone from his breast pocket and pressed it to his ear. "Hello?" His eyes rested on me as whoever on the other end of the call answered. I could hear the faint murmuring of a male voice, but it wasn't loud enough to make out specific words. "Ah, yes, thank you for calling. Just on time. We completely understand."

I didn't miss the "we." It was most likely intentional, from the way he stared at me.

The phone call ended as abruptly as it came, and my father repocketed the cell. "You can pack up," he told the girl who'd been fiddling with the laptop. "We won't be video chatting today after all."

I didn't move. "And why's that?"

"A schedule conflict with Aaron," he said, rising from his chair with a creak from his knees. "We sprang this on them quite last minute."

"Then why didn't you reschedule?" My father ignored me as he walked around the boardroom table, and when he came close enough, I shoved my rolling chair out and into his path. It was inches away from rolling over his toes. "Why did you not reschedule?"

"Aaron isn't interested in a video call."

"Isn't interested in a video call," I echoed. Again, it was another curious thing that hadn't come up earlier. "We'll schedule a phone call, then."

"He said he'd much rather meet in person, where there are no internet goofs or awkward silences."

"He said that on the phone?"

"His secretary did."

So, Aaron couldn't even be bothered to call and cancel himself, resorting to letting his staff take care of it. It wasn't outrageous—my parents would've done the same had something come up on our end, though they surely wouldn't have had Sumner make the call. Truth be told, I couldn't even explain why it rubbed me the wrong way— probably because I'd become very accustomed to thinking anything done by Aaron Astor was equivalent to heresy. Everything he did it just irked me.

Aaron isn't interested in a video call. He wasn't interested in hearing my voice at least once. "*Smitten*" with me, was he? No, he'd much rather remain faceless and wait until we were in person, and put off meeting as long as possible.

He really must've been hideous.

My father pushed the back of my chair to move me out of his path, nearly knocking me into the girl who'd begun packing up the computer. He walked out of the conference room without another word.

For a moment, I sat still while the staff member packed up the laptop with fumbling hands. "Tell me honestly," I said to her, holding her still with my gaze. "Was there truly an internet issue?"

"Y-Yes, it wasn't loading—and I—I don't—"

I held up my hand to cut her off as I pushed to my feet. All at once, the suit fit perfectly again, hanging from my body in a way that was comforting rather than constricting. I'd made the right decision yesterday, asking Jordan to alter it. I shouldn't have second guessed myself. "Thank you for trying," I said to her before leaving the room.

I walked down the country club's hallway with no true destination in mind. Before, I'd wished Sumner had been present, and now I was glad he wasn't. Later, though, I'd have to explain that the meeting fell apart before it could even happen, and I'd have to listen to his puppy-dog positivity. I didn't want to be assured. I didn't want platitudes. I wanted someone to say *wow, he couldn't even be bothered to take a phone call?*

No one would say that about Aaron Astor, though, except Destelle. But if I called her, I'd also hear other words I didn't want to. *You shouldn't marry him if you don't want to.*

I passed a few staff members in the country club who avoided eye contact, pretending to be busy with the carts they were pushing or the papers they held. No one looked at me as I meandered through the hall. Instead of heading back to my room, my feet carried me toward the wing that let out onto the tennis and pickleball courts. Alderton-Du Ponte had two of both, and they were often fully booked, even during the weekday. Today, a bright and sunny Sunday afternoon, made for no exception.

Even though I lived a stone's throw from the property for the past four years, I'd never once played here. In fact, many of the club's amenities had gone unused by me. Despite the membership fee being outrageously high, the occupancy of Alderton-Du Ponte never wavered, which meant the pools, the tennis courts, the gyms—they were all always full, and I avoided people like the plague.

Which was why it was annoying I'd unconsciously come here now.

A four-person team on the tennis court swapped out as their time was up, walking off as new wannabe athletes with tennis rackets stepped on. I didn't look at them, keeping my gaze straight ahead, but for once, I was seen. "Margot!"

Though I recognized the voice, I debated not turning. Ultimately, though, my feet once again moved of their own accord, pivoting me to face the group of four approaching.

Ms. Jennings, Yvette Conan, Alice Fontaine— Destelle's mother—and Yvette's daughter, Grace, all dripped with sweat in their tennis outfits, rackets tucked underneath their arms.

Ms. Jennings was the one who'd called out to me. "You've come to play?" she asked, reaching up and swiping at the sweat on her forehead with the back of her hand. "You're not quite dressed for it, dear."

"Then it would seem I am *not* here to play." I kept my voice pleasant enough, which meant I kept it flat. "I feel like I need a shower just looking at you all."

"Sweating is good for you, dear. You'll regret it when your metabolism slows down."

I eyed her. "Indeed."

"What are you doing out here, then?" Alice asked, and she, unlike the others, was all right enough. She was a woman with just as much poise as my mother, an air that demanded respect, which made her stuffy. She complimented me on my suits sometimes, though, so there was some saving grace for her. "Enjoying some fresh air?"

"Mm," I hummed with a slight nod, taking a step back. "If you'll excuse me—"

"Margot," Ms. Jennings said before I could make a retreat, repositioning her racket case underneath her arm. She was trying to appease to my good side now, offering me a plastic smile and adding ooze to her words. "I heard you have a video call with Aaron Astor coming up. Is that true?"

Aaron was inescapable. I knew nothing about him, and yet everyone came to me looking for answers. They came for him, never for me. It was all I was good for, it seemed.

"Don't act as if you didn't hear the rumor from the source," I told her with no affection. "I know you and my mother get tea on Wednesdays."

"Well, we just wanted to talk to *you* about it," Yvette piped in, annoyance quivering in her voice. "Your mother said it was happening today sometime. Surely you aren't wearing that for it, right? Maybe Grace can go through your closet and help you pick out something more...feminine."

I dropped my gaze to the youngest. Grace, at seventeen—or was she eighteen? I didn't particularly care—looked too much like her mother in the way she stared at me. With animosity. Disdain. She'd been around the elders too long, their hostility for me already having rubbed off.

"A man doesn't want a woman who looks like another man," Yvette went on, flapping her hand. There was no diamond bracelet to show off this time, just her sweat coated arm. "And really, dear, you *want* him to desire you, don't you? Men like cleavage, curves..." Her eyes not-so-subtly dropped to my vest. "You *do* have those, don't you?"

Grace snickered as Alice smacked Yvette's arm with a gasp. Ms. Jennings loosely swung her tennis racket as she soaked up the entertainment. I considered the situation, the dozens of eyes from the surrounding courts that'd paused their games to look in our direction. Calculated chaos—that was what I considered. What would be worth it, what would be too far.

Ultimately, I shrugged off my suit jacket and, even though it was sacrilegious, dropped it to the ground. "Is that your way of asking to see?"

Yvette's bully of a smile faltered. "See—what, exactly?"

"My cleavage." I began undoing the buttons on my vest. "My curves."

Now her smile vanished entirely. "I—absolutely not!"

Hers may have vanished, but a wicked curve took to my lips; I could feel it. "My breasts may not be as large—nor as sagging—as yours, but if you really want to compare, we can." My vest fell open, revealing my white dress shirt underneath. I reached for the first button at my collar. Alice took a large step back while Yvette's hand went to cover Grace's eyes. "If my *lack of femininity* really bothers you all *so much*—"

Two large hands closed over mine as I got the first two buttons of my shirt undone, ceasing the stripping before it went past baring my collarbones. I looked up, half expecting to find security restricting me, but it was Sumner, who'd appeared out of nowhere.

His expression was tense, his grip on my fingers firm. His eyes trailed along the skin of my throat, as if on their own accord, before sharply averting to the sky. "That's enough."

My temper flared. I tried to fight the grip, to undo another button, but he rendered me immobile. "Is it?" I returned with a voice full of venom.

"It is."

This was Sumner's first true act he'd been employed for, wasn't it? What had my parents said? *We're hiring someone who can stop you from making poor decisions.* My mother would be pleased to know her hired hand was doing exactly as he was supposed to. It enraged me. Sumner choosing my mother's side over mine, even after spending time together and getting to know each other, left me almost irrationally incensed.

He isn't a friend, a bitter voice hissed. *Instead, yet another handcuff.*

I wrenched my hands out of Sumner's as Yvette stepped back toward me. "The scenes you make are disgusting and childish, Margot," she all but growled, her own cheeks flushed. "Grace is more mature than you. Aren't you at all embarrassed of yourself?"

"Not in the slightest," I returned with my shirt half undone. The summer breeze brushed against the smooth skin just above the tops of my breasts, and I made no effort to button it up. "I'd have to care what any of you think to be embarrassed, wouldn't you say?"

Ms. Jennings looked at Yvette from the corner of her eye, enjoying this moment. Despite her uncharacteristic silence, she irked me too. I wanted to smack the smile off her face.

"You're so draining, Margot." Yvette reached down and grabbed Grace's arm. "It's like you suck the life from anyone you're around. This is why no one likes to talk to you, dear. If you've ever been at all curious."

I couldn't tell if her intention had been to wound or if she just stated something she saw as fact. For some reason, the thought of the latter was like ice in my veins, dousing some of my raging fire. Sumner was still at my side, and after he picked up my suit jacket, I felt him brush my arm, fingertips pinching the fabric of my shirt as if to hold me back.

"I'm sure one day, eventually, it'll occur to you that that is my intention." I looked over Yvette's face. "Especially if the ones talking to me were the likes of you."

While I hadn't been sure if her words were meant to

cause a reaction, mine were, and they did. Yvette's mouth dropped into an offended O, Grace's following suit. Alice looked like she wanted to intervene again, but words were failing her.

Sumner, with his fingertip grip, tugged me. "Come on," he said softly, as if to coax me into a quietness of my own. I allowed him to draw me a step away from them, and then another, until my back was to them. I was the one with the final period of the conversation.

Until Yvette called after me. "I wouldn't be in a rush to meet Aaron Astor if I were you." Her words were shrill, but I continued to walk. "Unless you're looking forward to the embarrassment of having a high-class family realize you aren't good enough."

"It's not as if he's pursuing Margot because he loves her," Grace, who'd been silent the entire time, interjected. Her voice was quieter, but I still heard it. "No one would. He just wants to inherit her parents' company."

I wasn't sure who hissed at Grace in response, whether it was Alice or Ms. Jennings, but it definitely wasn't Yvette; I could hear her chuckle. And it wasn't me who froze mid-step, but Sumner.

I didn't realize until I'd begun to take another step, but the pinch he held on my sleeve held me back. When I looked at his expression, I found something I'd never expected from him: a fire of his own. The normally calm, soft blue eyes of his were stormy with something dark, lit from within.

So, Mr. Unflappable has his limits, I thought as he dropped his hand from me. He turned around. "I don't know who taught you to talk like that," Sumner said to

Grace. "But you should lose the nasty habit of saying garbage things because other people are doing it, too."

Grace's face flushed as bright as a tomato, and Yvette's pleased smile at her devil spawn's words vanished. "Excuse me, but you do not talk to my daughter that way—"

"So, it was you?" Sumner had less patience with her mother than he had with Grace; it was audible in his tone and the way he clutched my suit jacket until his knuckles were white. "You taught her it was okay to be hateful toward people? You didn't teach her that the uglier you speak, the uglier you are? Aren't *you* embarrassed?"

"Who do you think you are?"

"Someone who doesn't like it when someone thinks they're bigger because they make other people small. Someone who doesn't like ugliness." Sumner's gaze gave her a once over. "But sees a lot of it."

Yvette's mouth popped open, and I was sure I looked a whole lot like Ms. Jennings in that moment—like someone could've given me a bucket of popcorn. I could've kissed Sumner. I'd done it before; I knew how easy it was, and in that moment, I could've done it again.

After she sputtered, Yvette finally got out, "I will have your job!"

"Try it. Let's see who wins with that."

I wasn't sure if Sumner didn't know who he was talking to or if his anger made him overly confident, because harassing Yvette Conan, who sat on the country club's board of directors, would easily be grounds for my parents to replace him. Ms. Jennings looked at him with hearts in her eyes, Grace with horror, and Alice with all

117

the uncertainty of what she should do about the situation.

I had to agree—the way he stared her down was undoubtedly, incredibly hot.

"Let's hope nothing happens when Margot meets the Astors," Sumner went on. "Since she's going to be meeting them at *your* daughter's wedding, after all, right?"

The realization flashed in Yvette's eyes, and I watched her process the veiled threat that it was. I didn't bother trying to hide the mirth in my eyes.

And in hers, I saw what I'd been waiting for—a sliver of fear.

Sumner's response had effectively stunned everyone into silence. Our cue. And Sumner seemed to pick up on it, too; he turned around and grabbed me by the wrist with his free hand, drawing us away from the crowd of onlookers we'd amassed.

I couldn't keep the smile off my face as he pulled me after him, away from the country club building. My heart stumbled to keep up in my chest. I'd never had someone defend me so earnestly before, upset on my behalf. Even when my mother's friends muttered snotty things regarding me to her face, my mother rarely quipped back in response.

Sumner, though, had stepped up to bat and swung even against the likes of Yvette Conan, and, in my book, he hit a home run.

Like I said—incredibly hot.

Sumner released me when we were out of view of the tennis courts and halfway to the east pool, finally coming to a halt on the cobblestoned pathway behind the country club. I watched his back as his shoulders rose and fell with his breath, eyes coasting over where his hair brushed the collar of his teal uniform polo. He still clutched my suit jacket, wrinkled from his anger.

"I didn't know you had it in you," I said, allowing myself to show the barest tinge of amusement. "I didn't know your puppy dog self could do more than just show your belly."

Except teasing was not something Sumner wanted to hear. He whirled on me, eyes still flaming. "What is wrong with you?"

"*Me?*"

"You were going to *strip*? Right there in front of everyone? Really, Margot?" He blinked several times, at an obvious loss with his parted lips and livid gaze. "This is exactly what your mother hired me for, isn't it? To keep you from making impulsive decisions like taking your clothes off in the middle of the tennis court? Do you truly not think *anything* through?"

The attraction that'd momentarily reared its head disappeared. "I wasn't stripping."

Sumner lifted my discarded jacket and looked pointedly at my unbuttoned vest and my dress shirt that still bared all the skin of my décolleté area.

"For your information, I *do* think things through." I began buttoning back up, feeling warm. "The second I undid the fourth button, they would've scattered. The lace of the top of my bra would've sent them running into the arms of their therapist. You cut in too quickly."

Sumner shut his eyes. I stood there as he fought for

that unflappability, trying to console his frustration that'd brimmed over. It was clear he wasn't familiar with giving into that feeling often, judging by the way tried to shake it off. I stared at him through it all, watching the livid line above his brow and the pinch of his eyes as they eventually softened.

His eyes opened, and he reached out, folding the distance between us in half as he draped my jacket over his shoulder. "I want to understand you," Sumner murmured as he picked the jacquard fabric of my vest up, fingers beginning to button it back up. The heat behind my neck flared hotter. "Help me to understand you."

This is why no one likes to talk to you, dear. Yvette's voice was an ugly one in my head, and it circled relentlessly, paired with the sarcastic tone of her daughter's. *He just wants to inherit her parents' company.* Neither statement was new to me by any means, but neither had ever been stated so bluntly before. The words stacked upon everything else in my mind, causing the tower to teeter.

"Yvette said a man only wants a woman that looks like one," I said, holding still as his attention was fully focused on his task. "I was going to show her how woman-like I am."

"I thought you didn't care about her opinion of you," he returned. "That's what you told her."

Something in my chest hummed as he delicately fastened the final button of my vest, something that felt dangerous and new and quiet. "I guess I just wanted to prove to her what someone once told me. That it's not clothes that make you ugly or pretty."

Sumner dropped his hands but didn't step away

from me. I wondered if he regretted ever saying such a thing to me. "And to see the look on her face," he added.

My mouth quirked, just a little. "And to see the look on her face."

Sumner's eyes dropped to my lips as he noted the tiny lift, and a corner of his own raised in return. A ripple of something unknown stirred in my chest. He stepped back and replaced the distance between us, drawing a hand through his wind-tousled hair. Only then could I breathe again, lungs aching.

I looked around for the first time. We'd found ourselves truly off the beaten path, a long way to the east pool. Even though it was the beginning of summer, with temperatures that caused the water to beckon, most of the clubgoers opted for the pool on the westside of the facility. The eastside's pool was smaller, and the kitchen didn't deliver meals out to this wing.

"What department are you working in?" I asked, eyeing Sumner's uniform as I took my suit jacket down from his shoulder. As my eyes roamed lower, I locked onto something sticking out of the front of his khaki's pockets. "Is that sunscreen?"

He looked down as if just remembering and pulled out a small tube of sunscreen. "I stepped outside to make a phone call, and this lady..." Sumner trailed off, and for the first time, I noticed the hint of distress on *his* face as he turned the sunblock over in his hands. "She was heading to the pool, and told me she wants me to put sunscreen on her back."

The audacity of it, as well as the absurdity, nearly had

my jaw dropping. "Did you tell her that the staff doesn't do that?"

"She said she's had people do it for her before." Sumner, gazing down at the sunscreen, appeared like a little kid who dreaded something they had to do. It reminded me of all the times I'd been forced in that same position before, not given a choice, not wanting to get in trouble for saying no.

The switch inside me flipped once more. "Where is she?"

Sumner became even more distressed. "It's okay, Margot, seriously."

I wadded the jacket up, fingers digging into the ball and, if it'd been flesh, they would've cut deep. "You are my secretary, not anyone else's. *Mine*. You're not going to rub sunscreen on some middle-aged lady because she wants to get felt up by a hot guy in his twenties."

I'd begun walking toward the pool, but Sumner caught my upper arm, fingers firm against the paper-thin material of my shirt, and pulled me to him. His golden eyes were filled with a complicated emotion. "This is probably the sort of thing I was hired for," he said. "Keeping you from ripping some old lady's head off."

"We're still on country club grounds, which means you're not my babysitter right now."

"I don't need you to fight my battles—"

"If you can fight mine, I can fight yours." I pulled my arm from his grip. "And I'll fight yours because, apparently, you won't fight them yourself."

I unbuttoned my shirt sleeves and rolled them up to my elbows as I walked toward the pool. Whoever bordered on sexual harassment had chosen a poor day to get on my bad side. I'd been far too ready to rip into anyone who crossed my path, and unfortunately for them, they'd stumbled into it.

There was only one person at the pool when I opened the gate, sitting on one of the lounge chairs. Her polka dot swimsuit ducked down in a U at the back that exposed her wrinkled skin. She sat waiting patiently for Sumner to return, and even from here, I could see the eagerness on her profile. There was a wheelchair parked beside her.

All traces of my anger vanished, replaced by an over-whelming urge to sigh. So, I did. The woman turned at the sound, taking in the two newcomers. "Oh, good," Nancy said as she focused on Sumner. "You found some sunscreen. Margot, have you checked out this boy's tush? It's *divine*, isn't it?"

Chapter 9

"You ruin a poor old girl's fun, you know that?" Nancy grumbled, the pool lounge chair creaking underneath her as it shifted.

"I'm just a horrible person," I agreed, slathering her wrinkled back with thick SPF. The U in her polka dot swimsuit dipped far lower than it should've on a ninety-year-old "Putting sunscreen on you so you don't burn to a crisp. Just a downright mean soul, I am."

"I didn't want *you* to do it. That handsome fellow—"

"You can't ask the staff to rub sunscreen on you."

Nancy puffed out a breath. "Before, that nice boy, Trevor, did—"

"Yes, and he stole four-hundred dollars from your purse while you were distracted. We caught him on the security footage."

"I was just paying him for the wonderful service he performed, that's all."

My features twisted on their own accord at her words, unable to stop the instant disgust. "Just ask me to do it next time. Or better yet, ask my mother." Or Yvette.

"I'm half-tempted to," she said, turning her head as far

as she could to look at me as I recapped the sunscreen. "Those ladies will do whatever I ask to just get on my good side."

Tossing the sunscreen on the empty chair beside Nancy, I sat down on its edge, linking my fingers between my knees. "Is that how you convinced Mrs. Holland to bring you here today?"

Nancy gave me a wide smile, showing off her pearly dentures. "I might've dangled a little carrot. I suppose the charity for the dying bees doesn't need the beach house in Florida."

I didn't smile back. "I heard about how weak you've been lately. How weak your heart is. This is too much for you."

"Do you want me to die alone at home, then?" she demanded, finally showing the barb beneath her flippant words as she glared at me. "With Yvette sobbing at her soaps or Ally calling whichever flavor of the week, and where time passes in a crawl? Tell me, Margot, which would you prefer?"

I gave her a look. "Nancy, I just—"

She twisted away from me to glower at the pool. "The others are too gushy, and you're too suffocating."

I stared at her pouting figure as her words shifted into my heart like a dagger. *This is why no one likes to talk to you, dear.*

"Sorry, I hope that didn't take too long," Sumner said in a breathless voice as he approached with a tray of two drinks. Much like how he'd been doing it when I first saw him, he held the tray incorrectly, its center of gravity tipping more to one side than it should've. If I were to have picked the glass up, everything would've toppled. "The girl at the drink station was chatty."

I wondered what girl was working the drink station today, and whether or not I could fire her for being *chatty*.

"Oh, dear, I'm glad you're back," Nancy said as Sumner set the tray down at the foot of my lounger. "Help a little lady into the pool, would you?"

He paused in offering the pink drink out to Nancy, blinking. "I—I'm not a lifeguard," he insisted. "I really think we should move to the other pool, where they're on the clock—"

"Surely a strong man like you can save me." Nancy squeezed his bicep, making a face at it. "Well, we can work on this, hmm?"

Everything in me rebelled at the idea of allowing her to get into the pool. It would exhaust her ninety-year-old body, and all she had to do was lose strength in her legs, or slip, or *anything*, and she'd submerge like a stone. Nancy wasn't a light little thing, and the pool's shallowest footage was four feet. It would take both Sumner and me to pick her up if she fell. Letting her get in was an idea that practically made my skin crawl.

But instead of voicing any of those concerns, I simply said, "Drown if you want."

"Maybe I will," Nancy replied in her crotchety tone, and without waiting for Sumner to make up his mind, she pushed to her feet. She swayed enough that he reached out and caught at her arms, holding her steady. "There'll be a conspiracy theory after that, you know. *Margot drowned Nancy.* Maybe I'll do it just to spite you, so no one talks to you again."

Sumner looked back and forth between us with an increasingly worried expression. I felt a bit bad for him, caught in the crossfire of yet another pissing match of mine. However, it was clear that this one was different from the one with Yvette, and he picked up on it. "Ms. Nancy," he said in a gentle voice, giving a sheepish smile. "No offense, but I'm actually trying to work on this with her." He tipped his head at me.

"What's that?"

"Trying to help her be a little bit happier. Looking at life a bit more positively. Not worrying about people accusing her of murder."

Nancy squinted at him closer before turning to me. "Is this the waiter you macked on?"

I didn't even blink. "Yes."

"You said he was *passably* handsome. Margot, get your eyes checked, this is more than just *passably*!"

"*Passably?*" Sumner asked me with mild offense.

I ignored him. "You heard him. He's trying to make my life more positive. Stop being such a batty old lady."

"I will as soon as you stop being such a brat," she replied, but she sat back down on the lounger. Her breathing had worsened in the brief moments standing, though it was clear she struggled to hide it. "Summer, was it?

He sat on the end of her lounger and allowed her to continue to hold his hand, offering her a smile. "Sum-*ner*, ma'am. It's okay, though, everyone mishears it at first."

"Sumner. Is there a story behind it?"

I tried to not look at him with interest, though my curiosity over the same question piqued. Sumner nodded with affection. "My mom thought she was having a girl her entire pregnancy. When she had me, and found out I was a boy, she changed it to Sumner." He looked at me. "I'm glad she didn't decide to try and make Summer a boy's name."

"We can still try," I insisted. "*Summer.*"

He rolled his eyes.

Nancy patted Sumner's hand to draw his attention back, clearly bothered by sharing it with me. "You do know she's engaged, right?"

He hesitated before answering. "Yes, I know."

I picked up the other drink Sumner had brought off the tray, the grapefruit and lemon taste causing my tongue to wither. Non-alcoholic. Boring.

Nancy leaned into Sumner and lowered her voice. "Do you have any plans to steal her away from her fiancé?"

He jerked back, eyes going wide at the same time that the apples of his cheeks reddened. "No! Definitely not. No plans at all—none. You don't have to worry about that, truly."

Such a quick and fierce denial, I wanted to say. I might've, if his response hadn't knocked a quivering blow to my already teetering ego. He could've denied it, but did he need to deny it so vehemently?

Nancy still gave him a knowing smile. "I'm rooting for you over that stuffy boy. I've always told Margot she needs to get out of this toxic circle. A working-class boy as yourself would do just the trick!"

I raised my eyebrow at her. "Did you just tell me to marry him because he's poor?"

"I didn't say poor, I said *working-class.*"

"It's still rude."

She copied me in raising her eyebrow. "Since when have you ever cared about being rude?"

"I take it you two know each other well?" Sumner asked, cutting between our bickering once more, clearly amused as he glanced back and forth. He leaned closer to Nancy. "Got any good gossip about Margot?"

Nancy, never one to pass up gossip, sat up a bit straighter. "She used to smoke."

"Smoke? Like cigarettes?"

Nancy waved her hand. "A teenager's desperation for her parents' attention, that's all."

I gave her a flat stare. "Don't forget to tell him that *you* were the one who gave me my first pack."

"You weren't supposed to actually smoke them." Nancy patted Sumner on the shoulder to draw his attention back to her. "I thought she'd look cooler carrying them around. She had a hard time fitting in around here, so she should at least have looked tough, don't you think?"

Sumner didn't look inclined to agree, but he at least knew better than to argue. If there was one thing Nancy loved more than gossip, it was a debate. "Anything else?"

"She loves mashed potatoes, but hates it when there's garlic butter on them. Loves avocado toast, too. Don't keep her from her avocado toast."

"He's done that one already," I said.

"She went to boarding school for those younger years," Nancy went on unprompted, reaching deeper into the pot of Margot's Secrets. They weren't necessarily anything scandalous, nothing embarrassing, so I let her go

129

on. Anything to distract her from the pool. "She came back to Addison just before she started high school."

Sumner looked at me in surprise. "Boarding school?"

"Can't you tell from my manners?"

This time, he nearly laughed.

It was as if Nancy didn't hear our side conversations. "Margot's never had a boyfriend. With the way she dresses, I think everyone around here thought she swung the other way—"

I, in fact, shouldn't have let her go on. "Nancy."

"—but I caught her looking at *quite indecent* photos of men on my computer once, so I think it's safe to say she's into your team, Sumner—"

"*Nancy.*"

She huffed a little and took a drink of her lemonade while Sumner pressed his lips together, fighting a smile that still sparkled in his eyes. The sun was hot on my back, leeching into the black material of my vest.

"Oh, and she got into some fancy fashion school in New York out of high school," Nancy added. "But her parents wouldn't let her go."

I stiffened with the words. Even more than me looking up inappropriate pictures on her computer, I wished she'd kept *that* to herself. It felt contradictory, hypocritical, for the truth of it to come to light.

"Fashion school?" Sumner turned to me again, but I refused to meet his gaze this time.

"In New York," Nancy explained. "One of those big expensive ones that don't accept a lot of people, but she got in. Her parents wouldn't let her go, though. Wouldn't pay the ungodly amount of tuition, and made her major in business instead, even though they have no intention to let her take over their company unless she's married—"

"Alright, that's—" I began, at the same time a new voice called, "Nancy!"

The three of us turned to find Mrs. Holland rushing out of the country club's doors while waving her arms in the air. She was a woman in her mid-sixties and had large sunglasses on her head to push her gray hair back, and despite her swimsuit, she had on a full face of makeup that sunk into her wrinkles. "We were supposed to meet at the west pool—" She faltered at the sight of Sumner, batting her lashes. "O-Oh, hello."

Sumner inclined his head in hello, offering her the country club's signature smile.

"I know you," Mrs. Holland exclaimed, pointing a finger at him. "You're the waiter Margot kissed at the fundraiser!" Her eyes scanned him up and down, lingering on his chest. "So, are you Margot's gigolo now?"

Sumner cleared his throat quite uncomfortably, while Nancy just looked tickled at the prospect. "Uh, no—no, they hired me as her secretary." His eyes cut to mine, and he lowered his voice. "People say that unironically?" His lips echoed the word *gigolo*.

I sipped my lemonade. "Only the rich."

"And Aaron Astor doesn't mind that such a...*fine* young man is hanging around you, Margot?"

Truthfully, I didn't know how Aaron felt about it all. Perhaps that was why Aaron ditched the videocall today, because he was more put off by the whole kiss than my parents told me. It made sense they'd keep his reaction from me—they were afraid that if I knew it'd caused a scene, I'd do something like it again.

When she realized I wasn't about to answer, she turned her sights to the little old lady before me. "Nancy." Mrs. Holland's voice carried a whining sound to it, the same one she had initially come over with. "I told you, the *westside* pool, where there's the kitchens and—"

"It's too crowded there, too many screaming kids. If I wanted to be around kids, I would've had my own."

Mrs. Holland sidled up close to Nancy on the pool lounger, waggling her eyebrows. "I scoped out the joint, and the hot lifeguards are on duty today."

It was the perfect thing to say in order to get Nancy moving. "Well, you should've checked earlier. Let's go."

Both Sumner and Mrs. Holland helped her into her wheelchair—I suspected she played helpless in order to have him touch her again.

"I'll see you the next time you drop by without announcing it," she told me as Mrs. Holland wheeled her around. She gestured at Sumner. "Make sure you bring him, too. As a *friend*."

I hummed a soft noise under my breath in reply, and with that, Mrs. Holland wheeled Nancy away from the pool area.

Sumner sat back down on the lounger opposite of me, our knees bumping with how close the two chairs were. "That's your frenemy who asked about my butt, huh?" he asked as he picked up my drink, taking a sip of it. I watched where his lips met the glass. "She's nice. Sort of gives off that fun grandma vibe you can bicker with—"

"Don't you have to get back to work?"

132

He blinked at my tone. "I'm hanging out with you. If my manager says anything, I'll just say you asked for me."

"You shouldn't lie. It's a bad testament of character."

"Haven't you ever told a white lie?"

"Of course. But my character has already been called into question."

We fell quiet for a moment. Sumner shook the drink just enough for the ice to clatter. I could feel his eyes on me, but I was too busy looking at the pool. "Fashion school, huh?"

In the grand scheme of things, it was a ridiculous thing to be embarrassed about, but this was Sumner. He'd thrown away his degree to pursue something else, to find something he was passionate about, something I didn't have the guts to do. I felt naked with the knowledge out in the open, like the façade I'd donned had been shattered to pieces that scattered around me. "I don't want to talk about it."

"You told me you didn't want to pursue fashion."

"I also said I don't want to talk about it."

Sumner laid his hand on my knee, and I dropped my attention to it. His fingers were long, his knuckles a shade darker than the rest of his skin, and I could trace the tendons on the back of his hand with my eyes. He gave my knee a shake to draw my attention. "Why not?"

I smacked his hand off. "Because I don't want to."

"You do realize you sound like a little kid, right?" He waited for me to argue. "You applied to art school, got in, but your parents made you major in business instead? Why? Because it was more practical? That tends to be the go-to argument, doesn't it?"

"I don't know why," I told him honestly. "I never asked."

"You gave up on your dream and never asked why?"

Something uncomfortable tickled the back of my throat. I swallowed it. "You make it sound so dramatic. I was seventeen. It makes sense to pursue something practical over fashion. Especially when I'm going to be inheriting the family business."

They were the words my parents had implanted in my head. I didn't mean them. I just didn't want him to see the resentment underneath. Though I'd said it to him earlier, I was really the one who was a tiny little Maltipoo who rolled over and showed her belly when I tried so hard to give off a Doberman demeanor. Unbothered. Uncaring. I refused to let him—anyone—see me any other way. Sumner could call me his friend all he wanted, but there were some sides I would never let him see.

Sumner took another sip of his drink as he watched me, and I watched him watching me. With the sun glaring down, I felt far too hot in the material of my suit, even with the jacket off. "How did it go with Aaron?" Sumner asked.

Yet another side I wanted nothing more than to bury. Yvette, my father, Aaron—all of it came creeping back like a dark fog rolling over me. *He isn't interested in a video call.* They didn't matter; it didn't matter. Perhaps Aaron was right—perhaps it *was* a better idea to meet in person, to be able to play off each other's energies face to face. Perhaps...perhaps...

I turned to face the pool, focusing on the soft ripples on the surface. It needed skimming; there was far too much debris floating along the surface. My mother would've had a heart attack if she saw, sending any staff within a ten-mile radius into the pool to fish it out with their own hands.

"Margot."

I still didn't look. *It didn't happen*, I knew I should say. *He was too busy.* The admission, though, seemed too humiliating, which was ridiculous. Sumner would say something absurdly supportive; it was why I hadn't sought him out to begin with.

"I don't want to talk about him with you," I said, digging my fingers into the material of my pants. "He's all anyone ever wants to talk to me about. No one ever asks about *me*; they ask about *him*. I want you to be my one person I don't talk about him with. The one person who doesn't ask."

And at first, it almost looked as if Sumner wasn't going to agree. His lips parted in what must've been surprise, lashes fluttering as he blinked. Ultimately, though, he nodded. "All right."

Discomfort settled on me once more at the thought that I could've offended him—he'd only been trying to make conversation. Maybe it was because I shut the conversation down so rudely, refused to answer his question. *This is why no one likes to talk to you, dear.*

"So." Sumner drew the word out, linking his fingers between his knees as he leaned forward, his bubble of space pressing against my own. The sun glimmered in his hair, reflecting in his eyes. "You thought I was handsome, huh?"

"I said *passably*."

"You also said *hot*." I opened my mouth to object when Sumner cut me off. "When I told you a woman wanted help with her sunscreen, you said that she shouldn't get felt up by a 'hot guy in his twenties.'"

I resented the way he said it. When I'd first seen Sumner, one of my initial thoughts had been that he was handsome. Handsome in a way that he could've fit into the diamond life perfectly. I remember thinking it, and I remember it being a throwaway thought. One I would've admitted aloud, easily, without a second thought.

Now, saying those words felt far more charged.

Clearing my throat, I got to my feet. Sumner tipped his head back to peer up at me. "Hey, I called you pretty the other day. You're allowed to compliment me, too."

"I'm not complimenting you." I scooped my jacket up from the pool lounger and threaded my arms through, despite the fact that I already felt close to passing out from heatstroke.

"So, I'm not hot?"

"No."

"I'm not handsome?"

I didn't like how he was looking at me, like he'd somehow discovered the upper hand. I didn't like it one bit, but my mind blanked on any ways to tip the situation back into my favor. My beautiful mind, one that could come up with ways to best anyone at the drop of the hat, was a well that had run completely dry. "Passably," I muttered, and walked toward the country club, once more fidgeting with the stupid vest buttons. Sumner laughed as he caught up behind me.

Chapter 10

One Saturday every month, Alderton-Du Ponte hosted their Mimosa Morning, where members gathered and mingled. It was an excuse to meet and gossip, of course. Getting a bunch of people drunk before noon wasn't a classy look, but they were of the mind that as long as their drinks had at least a drop of orange juice in it, it was fine.

A Mimosa Morning never passed without someone either picking a fight or sobbing so hard they passed out. I still waited for either to happen.

The one disappointing thing about Mimosa Mornings was that everyone had tables to sit at, which meant I couldn't stand in the corner and watch everything unfold from afar. No, instead, I had to be squished between Ms. Jennings, who was on her fourth mimosa, and Grace, whose drink was straight orange juice.

"Ally," Yvette said to Ms. Jennings. The way the circle table was set up had my mother straight across from me, Yvette at her left, Ms. Jennings at *her* left. With the champagne flute in her hand, Yvette gestured at Ms. Jennings, nearly sloshing her half-drunk mimosa onto the latter's dress. "Just give me the casserole recipe, would you?"

Ms. Jennings tossed her napkin from her lap onto the table. "Would you quit pestering me about it? I said no."

"You're acting as if it's some Michelin star recipe. Don't be selfish—share it with us."

"Well, it must be something special if you're going to berate me like this for it."

"This isn't me berating you." Yvette's words ran together as she slammed her champagne flute down on the table, and, if it'd been glass, it would've broken. My mother had learned after the first Mimosa Morning to use plastic flutes. "But I can, if you'd like."

My eyes followed Sumner as he navigated around the tables, delivering drinks and removing dirty dishes. My mother asked him to help serve instead of standing on my guard, though he was asked to keep his eye on me all the while. It at least meant while I waited for the drama to unfold, I had something else to look at. He was far more interesting to watch than the gossip at my table, mostly because I was waiting for his tray to tip over. He still hadn't learned to hold it.

No one had asked about Aaron Astor yet, a small mercy. That, much like the monthly fight or sob session, most definitely was impending.

We were getting close to one of them happening.

"Ms. Nancy shared it with *me*," Ms. Jennings insisted, taking a long drink of her mimosa. "You're just jealous I'm the one she gave it to. Guess someone hasn't impressed Nancy enough, huh? Hurry—you're running out of time."

Most of the table gasped at Ms. Jennings' lack of

politeness, but that was to be expected as she drained her fourth drink. "You're no better, Ally. She just gave it to you because you bribe her with cigarettes."

"And *you* bother and bother about her will, so she says. Apparently, I'm not the only one you berate."

I slipped deeper into my seat, getting ready.

Yvette's mimosa sloshed again as she leaned forward, and this time, it was pure luck that it hadn't gotten on the tablecloth. I then realized that if Yvette did get furious enough to throw her drink, being at Ms. Jennings's other side, I sat in the splash zone. That would not do. I took that as my cue and shoved my chair back. It screamed over the floor, cutting through the conversation at the table, and everyone turned toward me.

"Margot," my mother began, watching as I stood. "Where are you going?"

"The bathroom. Did I need to ask for permission?"

The group gasped again, because while I might not have used vulgar language, I *had* disrespected the supreme authority, and both carried the same severity. At least, in their eyes. My mother looked at me with tired eyes, drawing up her mimosa. "Go, go," she insisted, already turning toward Yvette to change the subject. "How are Annalise's wedding preparations coming along?"

Of course, I wasn't going to the bathroom. Sumner was at a far table bussing it, smiling at the ladies who chatted him up. They seemed far more interested in him than they've ever been in any of the other staff members, but it was understandable—Sumner *was* one of the few male faces among the women on the serving rotation.

I caught his eye as he straightened from the table, his tray half-loaded full of dishes and empty champagne flutes. With a subtle tip of my chin, I beckoned him out into the corridor, to which he gave me a less-than-subtle nod.

Though the chatter followed me into the hallway, there wasn't a soul in sight. Everyone who normally traversed through here already was in the grand room. The husbands of the women who drank their morning away were no doubt all on the golf course, or, if they'd already finished their rounds, having their own drinks or cigars in the outdoor bar. Everything moved like clockwork around here, not a single surprise or thing out of place.

Sumner slipped out of the event hall and into the corridor, holding his now empty tray. "Is it hot in there or is it just me?" he asked me as he tugged on the collar of his shirt. "How're you doing in there? Surviving?"

"Barely," I deadpanned, all at once stilling. "We're getting to the fun part of the morning, though, when everyone gets tipsy and starts saying nasty things."

A corner of his lips tipped up. "Nasty?"

"Last time, Mrs. Holland started talking about the latest sex position she discovered, and accidentally said a name that wasn't her husband's."

Sumner fully laughed now, looking away from me and then looking back. This was another reason why Sumner was a breath of fresh air to be around; anyone else would've gasped, scandalized. Instead, he only gave a musical laugh. "Is that why I haven't seen you drinking much? To avoid spilling your own secrets?"

"More like I need to be sober to remember everything for blackmail later."

"Ah, right, right." Sumner shifted on his feet, and I wondered if he was about to excuse himself to get back to work. "Is that new?" Sumner asked, eyeing what I wore.

The suit was a Malstoni design from years ago, custom made and one of a kind. It was loosely based on one of his runway designs, though he'd made it more feminine. The jacket was long and cream colored, with pearl buttons and silver stitching. I wore a tight lace shirt underneath, one with a nude lining that almost gave it the illusion of sheer material. It looped low on my chest, and I'd layered silver jewelry to make up for the empty real estate.

"I've had it a while." I reached down and tugged on the end of my sleeve, straightening the fabric. "If you see someone about to throw their mimosa at me, be sure to use your body as a shield."

He still hadn't lost his amusement. "Oh yeah? And why should I?"

"Because this suit cost four thousand dollars, while your shirt looks like something I could buy in a pack of three-for-five at Walmart."

Now some of that amusement was replaced. "The country club provided this shirt, thank you very much," he said in defense, tugging at his collar again, and muttered under his breath, "*Three-for-five.*"

Now it was my turn to don a small smirk, effectively pushing his buttons. "It'll happen," I promised him as I moved to lean against the far wall. "Just you wait."

"You know, there's something I don't understand,"

Sumner said, taking a few steps closer to stand before me. "Your mother is afraid of you acting out, and yet she still wants you to come to these events?"

"Ah, you've discovered the conundrum of it all." I tapped the heel of my shoe against the ground. The loafers were Claire Haute, which I normally would've never paired with something as classy as a Malstoni suit, but the pearls that were sewn into the top of the shoe accentuated the pearl stitching of the suit too nicely to pass up. "There are few things my parents consider more than *optics*."

"Optics," he echoed, almost as if he didn't know what the word meant.

"'What would everyone think? What would everyone say?'" I was sure these two questions ran through my parents' thoughts on a daily basis. "If my mother were to tell me not to attend, everyone would be nosy about the *why*. '*Margot lives in the hotel; why isn't she here?*' Or '*What else does your daughter have to do on a Saturday morning?*' Rumors start when someone isn't present, because everyone loves to talk behind someone else's back."

"You make it sound so cutthroat."

I gave a languid shrug. "You haven't been around long enough, but you'll see. People do the most horrible things all for the sake of climbing to the top of the elitist pyramid."

Something in Sumner's gaze flickered then, a faint response that I wouldn't have caught if I wasn't staring. He always accused me of having a problem, but this was why—the longer one stared, the more they saw. "But not you?"

"I'd rather sit back and watch everyone's downfall. It's far more fun."

"Remind me not to get on your bad side."

"Don't worry; I won't let you forget it."

Sumner's eyes dipped to my mouth, and it was only then that I realized I was smiling. It was a small curl to my lips, one that pinched the apples of my cheeks. The moment I noticed, it slipped from my face, and I forced my lips back to their neutral position.

"You're not holding your tray correctly," I told him, straightening from the wall.

Sumner took his tray out from underneath his arm. "I'm not?"

"You're holding it too much in front of you. It's much harder to maintain balance when something is sticking off *in front* of you, rather than at your side." I reached around him and pressed his arm to his side, and bent his elbow so that the point of it dug into his side. Nancy hadn't been lying when she said there was more squish to his arm than I'd been expecting, and it nearly made me smile again. "Your arm will be able to leverage the weight easier with your side supporting it, and your forearm will help you balance the tray. You can load your tray up more and it won't be as straining."

Sumner allowed me to move him like a puppet, not fighting as my fingers grabbed his arm to reposition, brushing against his skin. "I'm surprised you know this, given—" He abruptly stopped.

"Given what?" I came around to his side. "Given that I probably haven't worked a day in my life?"

"I wasn't going to say it like that."

It was true, though, at least not in the way these servers worked. The staff at the country club was hard-working, dedicated, and that was one of the biggest things I'd noticed over the years. "I got used to watching and learning," I told him. "You do a lot of observing at these parties when no one comes up to talk to you."

Sumner watched me with a muted expression. He lowered the tray so it wasn't between us anymore.

"I didn't say that so you would pity me," I said when he remained wordless, wishing I'd kept my mouth shut.

"I'm not."

"Tell that to your face."

He tilted his head to the side. "What about yours?"

To that, I simply raised an eyebrow.

"Why don't you smile more?" And then he quickly shook his head. "Don't give me that look. I'm not *telling* you to smile more. I'm asking why you don't. There are times I can actually *see* you keep yourself from smiling. Why do you do that?"

He was like me, it seemed. Didn't miss anything. "You look too close."

"I like looking close. I like it when you smile."

He said it too factually for it to sound flirty, but I still donned a teasing expression. "Am I pretty when I smile?"

"You're pretty when you don't," Sumner said, looking down at me. "You're beautiful when you do."

Again, his words sounded factual, as nonchalant as informing me that his shirt was blue, but they licked up my skin like a flame anyway. I became all too aware of how close I stood to him, how close we stood together. We fell into a brief silence again, and this time, and I should've taken it as my cue to let us go back into the hall.

I didn't move. I didn't want to. "I've told you before; I'm not a happy person," I replied in a low voice. "Not much makes me smile."

"You've smiled around me. So, I'm the only person who can make you smile?"

"It appears so."

He chuckled at that, and the sound wormed its way to the center of my chest, the vibration creating a strange pressure. I wanted to make him laugh again, but I didn't know how. I hadn't been trying to do so.

Footfalls on the marble floors sounded, interrupting the bubble of space the two of us had created in the hall-way. They weren't coming from in the event hall, but from the rounding south wing, most likely a late joiner to the party. I didn't bother looking, inwardly sighing. Hope-fully it wasn't Annalise. If she came, the wedding prepa-rations would be all anyone wanted to talk about, and that would've eventually led to *me*, and I was exhausted by the mere thought.

From my peripheral, a pair of people stepped around the corner, and that was when Sumner grabbed my upper arm and dragged me to the side. He pulled me into an alcove in the hallway, pressing me against the wall and out of sight from whoever had begun walking down it. I'd allowed myself to be pulled by his whirlwind of move-ment, but when we came to a halt, so did everything else.

Sumner's eyes were wide as he focused off to the side,

as if trying to listen for whoever had been approaching, but not focused on me. It allowed me to focus on him.

He stood close enough that I could smell the scent of his woody cologne, close enough that I could feel the body heat radiating through his blue polo. The barest hints of sweat had gathered along his temples from a morning of bussing tables, and it tamped some of his golden hair down, turning it brown. My gaze traced down from his temple to his sharp cheekbone, from there to his jaw, from his jaw down the curve of his throat.

He met my gaze and swallowed, and my heart jumped in response. Despite the fog in my mind, I had enough wherewithal to raise an eyebrow at him.

"It's your father," he said, breathless as he dropped my arms. It was then that I noticed his chest rose and fell fast. "I—I'm supposed to be working, not chatting with you."

"I take priority over you bussing tables," I whispered back. "We don't have to hide from anyone."

Sumner didn't answer, and his gaze had fallen from mine. The footfalls were louder now as they approached, but the conversation was too hushed to be able to pick out individual words.

It was ridiculous, the pair of us pressed in a hallway like we were caught doing something wrong, but still, I didn't move. I truly didn't understand his fear. Sure, my mother might've asked him to bus a table, but she also asked him to keep an eye on me—I didn't understand why he was alarmed enough to scuttle into a corner.

Being this close had the memory of last week rising up in my mind, unbidden. We'd stood much like this when I batted the tray of drinks out of his hands and took his face in my hands. A week ago, I'd kissed him without thinking about it. A complete stranger. Now, the idea of doing the same—of reaching up, laying my hands on his cheeks, and bringing his mouth to mine—seemed far, far more forbidden.

It'd mean something now if I kissed him. It hadn't meant anything before, but it would mean something now.

A bead of sweat had formed and slid down the side of his throat now, and without thinking, I reached up and swiped it away with the pad of my thumb, my fingers curving lightly around his neck. Sumner jumped at the touch, eyes widening. I watched myself in the reflection of his pupils, and the black depths expanded ever so slightly. The rapid rise and fall of his chest paused.

I pressed my hand a bit firmer against his throat, and underneath my fingertips, the pulse in his throat pounded. Rapid. Stuttering. A captive bird, desperately fluttering around its cage. Because of my father? Or because of me?

I smiled, another small one that pinched my cheeks. "Breathe, Sumner Pennington," I whispered, and without another word, I slid out from the space between his body and the wall and stepped into view of the approaching pair.

My father, dressed in one of his most expensive suits, walked down the hall with a tall woman at his side. I walked toward the event archway, intending to go straight inside without interacting with them at all, until I realized my father was grinning like a madman as he approached.

His attitude was far, far different from how it normally was around me alone, much more animated and lively.

"What luck!" he exclaimed as he and the woman came to a halt in front of me. "It's almost as if you were waiting for us. This is my daughter, Margot."

I gave the middle-aged woman a less than subtle appraising look, stunned. Her pantsuit was a deep emerald color, velvet, with a coat that dipped in at the waist and pants that had a small flare at her ankles. "That's a Malstoni from one of his first collections," I said with a little bit of awe, stunned for more reasons than one. Malstoni's earlier pantsuit collections were no longer being made, which meant the woman was wearing a small fortune on her body.

That, and she was actually *wearing* it. I didn't think I'd ever seen another woman opt for Malstoni's pantsuits, only ever his dresses.

The woman smiled, her mauve lips accentuating her perfectly white teeth. "Beautiful taste," she told me, a slight English accent clinging to her words. "You knew that in ten seconds, mmm? I'm quite impressed."

"More like five," I corrected. "I knew it as soon as I saw the pick stitching at your collar. But not the stitching at the lapel—it's clear that was altered up by a different tailor, most likely done with a machine."

My father's happy little smile disappeared. "*Margot*, this is—"

"Old pieces such as these pull a stitch a time or two," the woman said, appearing unbothered. She regarded me as if my father wasn't even there. "I surely wouldn't walk around with the collar coming undone."

"Why not just replace it?" It was a foolish question, of course. I, myself, had pointed out its uniqueness. This wasn't a suit you could just *replace*.

"Why replace something when it's perfectly beautiful otherwise?" The woman leaned in a little and lowered her voice to a conspiratorial tone. "And I could've requested Malstoni to fix it himself, if I wanted to pay out of price. I like to view this piece as a one-of-a-kind collaboration, you know. Malstoni, my tailor, and me. Quite the unique combination."

It took me only a moment of regarding her to decide. "I like the way you think," I said, offering my hand. "As my father said, I'm Margot. Margot Massey."

She gave me a strong handshake back, but didn't immediately let go, eyes bouncing all over me. I didn't realize it until she spoke, but she was the surprise. The one thing that broke the clockwork, that threw everything into an uproar. I'd been waiting for it, and she'd manifested before my very eyes. "It's a very big pleasure to meet you, Margot. I'm Vivienne Astor." And, in case it hadn't sunk in, she generously added, "Of Astro Agencies. Aaron Astor's mother."

Chapter 11

Apparently, Vivienne had not planned ahead to drop in on Mimosa Mornings, if the look on my mother's face when the tall woman walked in was any sign. My father must not have had the opportunity to warn her, either. I wasn't sure the last time I'd seen my mother so frazzled, though, to her credit, she tried to hide it. She didn't do a good job. I wondered if Vivienne picked up on my mother's nervousness—then again, she had the rest of the mimosa-goers hounding at her heels to prove an effective enough distraction.

"My, you're so beautiful!" Mrs. Holland exclaimed, rubbing Vivienne's hand as if it were a lamp and she was trying to draw out a genie. "Look at that skin!"

"What moisturizer do you use?" This was Ms. Jennings, her worry wrinkles standing out prominently.

"Oh, that perfume!" Yvette exclaimed, all but gripping Vivienne's suit jacket like a child with their mother. "So beautiful! So—so—rich! I mean, rich, as in *deep*, of course, though it smells expensive as well!"

It was almost amusing, watching them make fools of themselves in front of Mrs. Astor with alcohol on their breath. I wondered how many of them would regret their behavior later, sober. Another reason I knew Vivienne's visit was unannounced—my mother absolutely wouldn't have drunk any champagne. She also would've forbidden anyone else to drink it. Especially Ms. Jennings. She would've canceled Mimosa Morning entirely.

"So flattering, so kind," Vivienne would say to everyone's compliments, taking the overwhelming hoard of rich ladies in stride. Almost as if she'd had to handle it many times before, and perhaps she had. "You're all lovelier than I expected. Very welcoming."

"Is that an English accent I hear?" someone asked. "I thought you lived in California!"

"Oh, yes," Vivienne said with a laugh, giving a good-natured nod. "My family and I spent our early years in England, but Malcolm, my husband—he moved us back to his hometown on the west coast after Aaron turned ten, I believe. My accent is slowly fading, but I'm delighted it's still somewhat recognizable."

She had a way of saying these compliments without them falling flat, and I wasn't sure if it was because of the lilt to her words or the gentle way she looked at everyone. It almost felt like she was a mother hen and everyone were her chicks.

Except for me, who stood separate from it all. It was only a matter of time now. The topic I'd successfully dodged all morning... It was only a matter of time.

"Why are you here so early?" Yvette asked, and I was sure she'd meant to sound happier about the prospect, but her voice came out almost accusing. "I thought you weren't coming in until next month, for the wedding."

"I had a few things to do in New York, and it's only an hour's flight to come by here before heading back home." Vivienne looked at me with a fond smile. "I wanted to meet Margot as well, though I'm sure Aaron will be very disappointed I met her first. I'll have to rub his nose in it."

He had the chance to meet me and declined, I wanted to tell her, to hear what she'd say in an excuse. A woman like her, so poised and perfect, would have an excuse for her son's behavior—and probably a great one.

At the mention of Aaron, an *oohh* sound worked through the crowd like a wave. "You'll have to go back to him and sing the praises of our fair Margot," Yvette said, turning around to beam at me.

I stared at her with a flat expression, remembering precisely what she'd said about me meeting the Astors. I wasn't living up to her expectations.

"Oh, show us a photo of him, would you?" Ms. Jennings asked, pressing her palms together. "We've all done our digging—ahem, to make sure Margot isn't getting the short end of the stick—not that your son is the short end of the stick, of course, but—"

"What she's saying," my mother cut in, "is that we haven't been able to find pictures of Aaron online."

"We were very careful about my sons' privacy," Vivienne said with a nod, bringing her orange juice to her lips. "We gave each of them the choice to remain behind the camera or in the spotlight. We tease that Aaron is a bit of a recluse sometimes—he values his privacy, you see."

Everyone in the group gave a reverent nod.

"But... I suppose I can show you a picture, if you were to keep it between us."

And just like that, the group squealed like they were teenage girls.

My pulse had sped up as Vivienne pulled her phone from her pocket, everyone crowding around her to get a good view. I scanned the hall for Sumner, but I hadn't seen him since he'd pulled me aside in the hallway. He must've ducked into the kitchen to help with cleanup, nowhere in sight.

They're all going to see him before me, I thought, staring as Vivienne's thumb swiped through her photos. There was no room for me to press into the group, stuck on the outskirts, as always. *They're all going to know what the man I'm going to marry looks like before I do.*

I took a sharp step backward, feeling as though there suddenly wasn't enough air in the event hall. Surely there were too many people crammed in one space; it had to be a fire hazard. Surely we shouldn't all be huddled together.

Surely this couldn't be happening.

Everyone around me got first dibs on my life... but me. My parents, the deciders. The country club members, the gossipers. Me, the afterthought. Just as with every other choice in my life, I was the last person consulted with. And I couldn't let it happen.

Without thinking it through in its entirety, I shoved into Yvette's back hard, and with how many mimosas she consumed, she had too delayed of a reaction to right herself. She pitched forward, heels stumbling, and the force sent her and her mimosa sprawling all over Vivienne and her one-of-a-kind suit.

Everyone shrieked.

Yvette ricocheted off of Vivienne's lap and onto the

ground, her plastic champagne flute bouncing harmlessly on the floor. Staff workers rushed toward Vivienne with napkins while Mrs. Holland tried swatting the mimosa off of the expensive clothing. As if it would've helped. The liquid seeped into the velvet material, creating a darkened stain on the front of Vivienne's pants. She blinked, stunned, mimosa dripping off her chin.

I leaned to the side, hiding behind Ms. Jennings. If the ladies hadn't been so tipsy, I'm sure I would've been found out immediately, my evil deed witnessed and condemned. But when Yvette looked up from the floor, she zeroed straight in on Ms. Jennings, and didn't look at me at all.

"I've *had* it with you, you tramp!" Yvette screeched, completely forgetting time and place, and all hell broke loose from there.

Yvette launched from the marble and grabbed an entire fistful of Ms. Jennings's auburn curls, snapping Ms. Jennings's head back. Someone's mimosa flute fell to the ground, which sent more specks of liquid flying up. My mother called out Yvette's name and rushed toward the dueling duo, and Ms. Jennings didn't even question why Yvette sprung at her—she grabbed Yvette's own hair, the two locked in a vicious embrace.

"You're just jealous!" Ms. Jennings shouted, unfazed by the grip on her head. "I'm *so sorry* that your husband likes my company better!"

"It isn't your company he likes," Yvette fired back, eyes blazing. "Which is why he only ever stays an hour!"

Scandalized gasps cut through the group, and Vivienne covered her mouth with her hand. I pressed my lips together, but not to fight off a smile. It was a situation that I would've normally looked on with amusement, sipping at my own drink while the dramatics unfolded, but I simply stood there, a buzzing sound filling my head.

I hadn't thought it through, not thoroughly enough the way I normally did. When I pushed Yvette, I wasn't sure what I'd been expecting, but it escalated far further than I thought. I looked at the stain on Vivienne's front. I was the reason it was ruined, all because I hadn't wanted anyone to see Aaron's picture before me.

Grace tried to tug Yvette's hands out of Ms. Jennings's hair, her own expression twisted and flushed with embarrassment. "Mom—Mom, *please.*"

My mother attempted to untangle Ms. Jennings, and while thick in the fray, she turned to me. Her eyes flashed. "*Margot.*"

Security came in then, escorting the two huffing and puffing—and blushing—ladies out of the room. It was too late, though. The damage had been done. The liquid had set into Vivienne's suit, and she'd stopped dabbing at it. Or, really, stopped allowing Mrs. Holland to dab at it, and lifted her hand to ward the napkin off. I couldn't bring myself to study her expression.

"Vivienne, I am so, so sorry," my mother rushed out, fretting with her palms opening and closing over the murder of the fine cloth. "I'll—I'll have it cleaned, replaced—"

"It's an original Malstoni," I found myself saying when I should've kept my mouth shut. "You can't replace it."

My mother looked at me sharply, the realization

rolling like a wave in her eyes. In a split second, I saw it all —the promise of her wrath.

But she had to placate first. She rushed in with more flowery words, more platitudes, expressing her deepest apologies. Vivienne stood up from the chair they'd ushered her into and excused herself to the bathroom, waving off when anyone tried to follow her.

The gossip ensued. "Her poor outfit."

"I can't believe that was our first impression!"

"She must hate us..."

"No, she must hate Yvette. Could you blame her?"

My mother came at me and picked up my arm. Her fingers tightened. "A word," she said in a very pleasant tone, one that would've fooled anyone except me. She escorted me into the kitchen, where the staff was working to clean up behind the scenes. They gave us space, no doubt reading the room my mother created. "You did that, didn't you? I'll never stop being amazed at the lengths you go to, behaving like a spoiled brat, you know that? Ruining her suit, Margot Massey?"

"I would've done it even if it hadn't been an expensive suit," I said, as if it made my actions remotely better. The truth was I was just as horrified as my mother was, appalled I could've done such a thing. If I'd been wearing the suit Vivienne had on, I would've lost my mind if someone spilled something on it. The security would've been hauling *me* out—for murdering the person who'd tripped.

"You knew it was. You knew, and you did it anyway." My mother raised her hand as if to smack me, but when I didn't flinch, she let out a sharp, harsh breath instead.

"You try to ruin everything, don't you? I don't know where I went so wrong to have a daughter like you. I truly don't."

She was a master swordsman, my mother, because she knew just the right words to say to make sure they cut deep.

It was then that she seemed to notice there were other eyes in the kitchen. My mother straightened, smoothing a hand down her sundress. Her tone was a tad bit more controlled. "I hope you can keep a closer eye on her."

It took me until a new voice answered in reply before I realized she wasn't speaking to me. "It won't happen again," Sumner said in a low voice, directly behind me.

"It had better not." With the statement hanging in the air, my mother stalked off back toward the event hall.

I stared at the spot in the kitchen where my mother stood long after she left. The staff continued cleaning around me as if I were a fixed pillar. I squeezed my hands into fists until my fingers bit into my palm, forcing my breathing to stay even.

I had grown used to the thinly veiled comments, the indirect insults, so to have it laid out in such a blatant way slammed into me like a blow. Maybe it was because it was coming so quickly off of Yvette's harsh comments yesterday, or because it was my own mother saying it, or perhaps it was because even I knew I was in the wrong—whatever the reason, it stung to the point that my eyes threatened to fill like a child's. *I don't know where I went so wrong to have a daughter like you.*

And another thing that made it worse: Sumner

witnessed it. "Margot," he began tentatively, laying his hand on my shoulder.

I slapped it off before I could think about it, the gentle pressure enough to make me snap. "Would you stop touching me?" I demanded, smacking at my shoulder again even though his hand had already fallen. "I'm not some little kid you have to comfort. I don't like to be touched; don't touch me."

Sumner raised his palms level with his shoulders, pressing his lips together. He wasn't fighting a smile; I didn't know what the expression was. I didn't look closely. Like every other staff in the kitchen, he became faceless, just like the day I'd first met him.

I was a bad daughter? No one liked to talk to me? As if I cared. As if I didn't actively seek to isolate myself. As if I even *tried* to be a good daughter—my mother didn't deserve one.

Drawing in a sudden breath, I turned on my heel and exited the kitchen through the door to the hallway, bypassing the people still clutching to the remains of Mimosa Morning, ignoring the staff who were lingering for any threads of gossip, and leaving Sumner and his puppy dog eyes behind.

Chapter 12

What did it mean to be an adult? Was it age? Independence? Did one magically turn into an adult at eighteen, or when something adultish happened to them? I often wondered. There were times I still felt like a teenager in an adult's body, like I was still seventeen instead of twenty-two. There were times I felt passable as an adult, though. Moving in here. Graduating college.

Sitting in my hotel room all day Sunday and Monday, though, waiting for my mother or father to come charging in, had me feeling very much so like a child grounded to her room, slowly going insane.

Neither of them ever came.

I wanted to go see Nancy, but I didn't feel up to batting back and forth with her yet. I wanted to go out for a drive, but didn't want to call on Sumner in order to do so. Sumner, in general, was someone I tried not to think about. After spending time with someone nearly every day, it felt strange to not see him at all for two days straight, like something was missing.

The sound my hand made when it smacked his hand

off my shoulder echoed in my head all weekend—probably because my hotel room was otherwise silent. I shouldn't have done it. *I'm not some little kid you have to comfort,* I'd told him, but I'd been acting like one. And the humiliating fact of it was enough to keep me from emerging from my room.

To occupy my mind as the clock ticked down Monday night, I sketched in my art book. I'd begun keeping one in the later days of middle school, when fashion had just start piquing my interest, and had since filled so many pages with designs of suits and outfits. They weren't anything spectacular, given that I was all self-taught, but the general idea could still be pulled off the paper. I was at least good enough to guide the clothiers at Gilfman.

Sometimes, in the quiet moments that I sketched a new piece, I wondered what life would've looked like if I *had* ended up going to one of the fashion schools in New York. The truth I rarely faced was that I could've gone. I had been eighteen, a legal adult. My parents might've wanted me to get a degree in business, but nothing said I *had* to. They might not have paid my tuition for fashion school, but I was sure that if I'd asked Nancy to invest her money in the degree to send me to New York, she would've. I could've been like Destelle and taken the first-class ticket out of this town when it'd been offered to me.

I hadn't done that, though. I'd been too much of a coward, too much of a child afraid to lose the remaining respect of her parents. I was doing the same thing now, agreeing to marry a man because I was afraid.

I knew that. And I did nothing about it.

With a sigh, I sat back in my chair and dropped my

pencil. The sketch I worked on now looked far too much like my last one, and the one before that. It seemed I only knew how to create one silhouette, one pattern. I'd never learn how to advance, but remain stuck sketching the same suit over and over again.

Needing a new distraction, I picked up my phone and typed 'Aaron Astor' into the search, hoping to find the article Sumner had read the other day. I doubted there'd be any more information, but I had the urge to see it with my own eyes rather than letting Sumner read it aloud to me.

I scrolled and scrolled, changed the keywords and search terms, but never came across the article again. Figured.

A soft double knock came at my door, pulling me from the depths of my wandering mind. I would've assumed it was my mother coming to check and make sure I was in my room, except it was after seven o'clock in the evening. Surely she'd gone home by now. My father, too. I hadn't ordered dinner yet, and housekeeping had already stopped by to freshen up my room earlier. It left one person.

And sure enough, when I got up to peer through the peephole, I found Sumner standing in the hall. He had his hands in the front pockets of his light wash denim jeans, his loose-fitted shirt rolled up to his elbows and tucked into his waistband. His gaze was cast away from the door, but he rocked forward onto his toes as he waited.

The strongest desire to not open surfaced. In fact, that feeling was accompanied by another strong desire to never see Sumner Pennington again. After Saturday, the idea of facing him built to be something akin to meeting Aaron Astor in my head—*awkward*. I couldn't think of the last time I'd formed an apology, but for the way I snapped at him, Sumner deserved one.

Sumner knocked again, firmer this time, startling me into unlatching the door.

"This is a surprise." I launched into a greeting, clearing my expression. "Did you run out of things to do on your days off?"

Not an apology. Not even close.

He tried to be quick about it, but I watched as Sumner's gaze scanned my body, as if on their own accord. "Wow. Is this the first time I'm seeing you in something other than a suit?"

I looked down at the loose floral lounge shorts and the dark long-sleeved shirt I wore. My legs were pale, ghostly, since rarely did I ever expose them to the sun. The long sleeves were tight, a shirt with a higher percentage of spandex so that it stuck to my figure. Most definitely not a suit. In fact, he was seeing more of the shape of my body than he ever has.

I had the overwhelming urge to shut the door between us. "What are you doing here?"

Sumner's hands were still in his pockets, and he still rocked on his heels. "I thought I'd stop by."

"I don't need to go anywhere."

"Not as your secretary," he replied. "As your friend."

It was the most beautiful chance for me to apologize, wasn't it? *Speaking of being friends, I was a bad one on Saturday, lashing out at you when it wasn't your fault. I'm sorry.* My ego wouldn't form the words. "You've grown attached in all the time we've spent around each other, hmm?"

"I'm bored out of my mind," he admitted without shame. "Who knew you were my main source of entertainment?"

I could've said the same. Since the housekeeping and room service rarely spoke more than five words to me when they stopped up to my room, even this brief interaction with Sumner felt like I was a dry sponge and just the briefest conversation with him poured water back into me.

I stepped backward into my room, offering the door open. "Want to come in? I can have room service bring us up something to eat."

Sumner peered past me and into the interior of the hotel room for only the briefest moment. His eyes snapped back up to mine, as if he was embarrassed about something he'd seen. "Let's go for a walk instead. After being cooped up for the past two days, I'm sure you're ready for some fresh air."

"How did you know I stayed in my hotel room?"

Sumner opened his mouth to speak but wavered, as if he knew the excuse he'd been about to give wouldn't hold water. "Yeah, fine, I was listening for your door to open. I was going to 'bump' into you in the hallway, but since apparently you were never going to come out, I figured I'd take matters into my own hands."

I drew in the slightest breath at the words. He'd been keeping tabs on me. Giving me space until he couldn't stand it anymore. How I treated him on Saturday hadn't sent him running. He hadn't thrown his hands up in annoyance, in exasperation, and walked away from me. He'd just been giving me space, but never planned to leave.

A warm feeling unfurled in me, near painful. "Let me grab my hotel key."

I let the door fall shut between us as I retreated to retrieve the key. Before heading back out, though, I looked at myself in the mirror beside the door. My eyes were wide and dark, and my hair looked a bit rucked up, as if I hadn't run a brush through it. I combed my fingers through it, smoothing it down against my collarbones as best as possible.

It's just Sumner, I reminded myself. *There is no one here to impress.*

I smoothed my hand down my hair once more, and when I thought it looked good enough, I opened my hotel room door.

We walked down the hallway in silence, and when we came up to it, I reached for the button to summon the elevator at the same time Sumner did. Our fingers brushed an inch from it. It was a millisecond of contact, but enough that the warmth of his skin jumped to mine. We both jerked back, and Sumner curled his hand into a fist as I cleared my throat.

Awkward. I pressed the button. "So, what did you do yesterday?"

"Caught up on sleep. Called a few friends back home. Watched bad TV. You should tell your parents they need to invest in getting Netflix for the rooms or something."

"I'll share my password with you."

"Ah, we're that close now, are we?"

His words were teasing, but they only aided in increasing the awkward tension in the air. I wasn't sure if I should've laughed at it, but by the time I decided yes, it was a joke, I should've laughed, the moment passed.

The elevator arrived then with a blessed ding. "What did you do?" Sumner asked me as we stepped on, putting a respectable space between us.

"Nothing." I kept my gaze on my feet to avoid Sumner in the elevator's mirrored doors. My fingertips fluttered at the hem of my shorts, and I half wished I'd changed into pants so it covered more skin. "Sketched. Read my horoscope. Stared out the window. Exciting times."

"Your horoscope say anything good?"

"*You will not die of boredom, but it will feel like it.*"

"So, I'm your main source of entertainment, too, huh?"

I lifted my chin. "Maybe a little."

Sumner smiled, and my own threatened to tip up in response. *Am I pretty when I smile?*

You're pretty when you don't, Sumner had said. *You're beautiful when you do.*

The elevator opened on the fifth floor, where a group of four men stood waiting to get on. Sumner stepped closer to me, our shoulders brushing once before he shifted to stand slightly in front of me. I had the perfect view of where his golden hair curled against the back of his tanned neck, where the fabric of his shirt lay against his skin. I thought about when I'd pressed my thumb to the side of his neck on Saturday, about how he'd jumped in response. In disgust? Something else?

If I reached out now, he'd surely jump again. My gaze slipped to his shoulders, ones that seemed stiff even through the fabric of his loose shirt. If I traced the tension, he'd be sure to stiffen further. A part of me wanted to test it. It was an impulsive sort of want.

The doors to the ground floor opened before I had a chance to, and the elevator unloaded its occupants. "Did you have a lot of friends back home?" I asked him as I headed off to the left of the hallway, toward the lobby, feeling almost shy.

"A few. Only two that I was close-close with." Sumner tipped his head one way, and then the other. "These past few months were really busy for us all, though. One got engaged, started wedding planning, and the other was busy with work most of the time."

"People grow apart," I murmured with a nod. "I know what that's like."

"Yeah. We talk often, though. One of them, I've known since, like, pre-school. I talk to him practically every day."

I scrunched my nose. "The beans on toast guy?"

"That very one." He smirked at the disgust on my face. "He's the busy one. We both started working for the same company right out of college, but he took on a posi-tion...higher up. Good guy—a little socially awkward, drinks too much sometimes, but I think he's finally ready to settle down."

I listened to his fondness for his friend quietly. The words seemed somewhat of a ramble, but it was rare for Sumner to reveal anything about himself, and I soaked it up. "He's ready to settle down...and you?"

He shrugged. "If I ever meet someone."

"You haven't met anyone yet?"

"I haven't really had time to." We made it to the lobby then, and in a wordless agreement, we turned down the passageway that'd lead us to the country club. There weren't many people about; the country club itself closed at eight on weeknights, so it'd be ghostly soon. "High school, college, work, moving here—maybe one day."

It all sounded very normal, ordinary. I liked the simplicity of it. I also liked knowing that there wasn't someone back in California waiting for him to come home, but I didn't let myself think about it long.

Sumner glanced at me, an obvious attempt to be casual. "So... How did you and Aaron—well, *meet* isn't the right word, is it?"

"We were at the same social event this past December. Apparently, he saw me and fell in love, but not enough to walk over and introduce himself. He's either more of a social outcast than I am, or the ugliest man alive."

Sumner seemed offended for him. "Maybe he's just socially awkward, too. Shy."

"Too shy to talk to me, but not shy enough to reach out to my parents and ask them to 'save me for him.'"

"He didn't say that."

I sighed. "Fine, he didn't, but it was probably along those lines. He did reach out after that event, though, and ever since, my parents have been full steam ahead for an Astor-Massey collaboration."

The lobby of the country club was empty, not even a staff worker seated at the desk. I started down the left corridor, and Sumner followed along after me. "You said yes, though. You talk as if you didn't have a say in marrying Aaron."

I looked at him and realized that he didn't know that I hadn't had a say. Of course, he wouldn't have known, since I'd never told him, but it was still a shock to realize he assumed I was excited about being set up with Aaron Astor.

My silence must've made him suspicious. "You *do* want to marry him, don't you?"

I answered immediately. "Of course."

It was another one of those things where I said it, but I wasn't sure if I meant it. In a way, it was truthful. I wanted to marry Aaron Astor, because marrying him meant keeping all the things I held dear. My suits, my car, my financial status. I'd rather marry him than lose it all.

"I don't want to go for a walk," I decided suddenly, taking a left when we entered the country club and continuing down the empty hallway, knowing Sumner would follow. "I want to go to the golf course."

I hated golfing. My father, in his desperate attempt to pretend I was a son instead of a daughter, took me out with his friends once when I was little. The businessmen had a wonderful time instructing their sons how to line up a swing, how to aim with the wind, the perfect posture. When it'd gotten to my turn, my father hadn't even wanted to touch me to adjust how I held the golf club.

Golfing wasn't a fond memory, but taking the carts for a joyride was right up my alley.

It wasn't hard to procure a golf cart, even though rentals were supposed to have stopped at six. One glimpse of Margot Massey, and everyone jumped to accommodate. I'd gotten lucky, though, and the staff member renting out the carts was a new hire, which made the whole process even easier. Sumner had simply followed my lead, much as he always did.

The sun crept closer and closer to setting on the horizon, which meant that almost all the straggling golfers had packed it in. Meaning we had free rein over the entire course.

Sumner insisted on driving, though I quickly regretted letting him. "Can't you go any faster?" I asked him as we drove away from the first hole. *Crept* away, really. "You're going ten miles per hour."

"It's a golf cart, not your sports car."

"This wasn't what I had in mind when I said I wanted to take it out."

Sumner acquiesced to my complaints by setting his foot down a bit firmer on the gas pedal. The speedometer didn't even raise by five. "Now is it more fun?"

At least there was finally enough wind to pick up my hair. I folded my arms across my chest. "Slightly."

We meandered through the next four holes in silence, though it was the comfortable sort. I could hear the softness of Sumner's breathing mixing with the musical tones drifting through the speakers. He'd picked a playlist that had soft instrumental music, and it fit the tone of the evening perfectly. Nothing loud, nothing harsh. Just simple and comforting, just like his presence.

The longer the quiet stretched between us, though, I knew I needed to bring up Saturday. I needed to apologize and actually clear the air instead of just pretending it was clear. I wasn't sure why it was so hard for me; perhaps because I had little experience in crafting apologies. I didn't have much experience in hearing them, either—it'd been a while since I'd received an apology that didn't have a hidden motive behind it.

I cleared my throat again. "I still can't believe you missed the hair-pulling match on Saturday," I said in a deadpan voice. "I told you there'd be one, didn't I?"

"Oh, I heard about it. Someone asked me to take out the trash. Maybe I can bribe the guys at security to let me watch the CCTV."

"So that's why you got in trouble with my mother, hmm? For being on trash duty instead of keeping an eye on Miss Margot?" My mother would've argued he should've been taking care of the trash—of me.

Sumner's hands flexed a little over the golf cart's steering wheel, tightening, and then loosening. "Does your mother talk to you like that often?"

"Only when I go too far in testing her patience."

Bringing her up soured my mood. My mother had resorted to giving me the silent treatment. Even back in New York, her cold shoulders were frequent. We did always work better when we never spoke to each other. Either she didn't tell my father about the whole incident —doubtful—or he couldn't bring himself to waste any more energy on scolding me—probable—because he hadn't approached me over the whole incident.

I picked at the hem of my shorts again. "About Saturday—"

"Why did you do it? Why spill a drink all over Mrs. Astor?" Before I had a chance to say anything, Sumner clarified, "The other servers were talking about who the woman in the fancy suit was when I was collecting the garbage. The staff *does* talk, you know. Maybe not as much as the people in your circles, but there's also gossip behind the scenes."

Of course there was. I couldn't imagine that there wouldn't be. "You're just assuming it was on purpose?"

"You said to your mother that it was."

I looked out over the green, the sunset turning the world a beautiful shade of yellow. I hadn't realized he'd been there for the *entire* conversation.

"I don't get you sometimes." Sumner did sound confused, and in a way, maybe even a little exasperated. The sound of his voice took whatever warmth that'd been trapped in my chest and froze it cold. "You want to marry Aaron, so why do something that could sabotage it?"

"My mother told you—I'm impulsive."

"And yet, in the short time I've known you, I learned that you don't do anything without a reason. Even if it seems like the opposite."

I said nothing in response to that, and Sumner didn't probe again. Perhaps he was waiting for me to cave. *I ruined her ten-thousand-dollar outfit because she was about to show everyone a photo of her son.* It didn't quite give off the sophisticated vibes I was going for. Then again, spilling a drink on someone wasn't sophisticated in the slightest, either. I wasn't sure why it bothered me so much, the idea of Sumner thinking negatively toward me, but it was all I could think.

Sumner had quickly become almost like a depressant for me, settling my mind and calming my nerves just by being around. Whereas people drained me, sucked me dry, Sumner was different. I found myself wanting to share my mind more with him, even though it went against everything I'd ever done.

So even though it wasn't sophisticated, or classy, or remotely adultish, I was honest. "Mrs. Astor said she had a photo of him and was about to show everyone his picture. Aaron's."

"You say about to—so I'm assuming she didn't?"

"No, a rogue mimosa stopped her." I shifted on the bench of the golf cart. "With the way everyone was crowding around her, they were going to see him first. I wasn't trying to sabotage the whole thing, I just... I truly did just act on impulse."

The defensiveness in my tone was clear, though I wasn't certain the desperation was. *Please don't judge me too harshly*. I would've accepted that he couldn't understand it, but I didn't want this to change how he thought of me. I wanted it so badly that it almost made me feel sick.

"I want to see him before they do," I went on when Sumner didn't interject. "And it felt... wrong, I suppose, to see him through a photo."

"I get that, I guess." Sumner turned the steering wheel to bank us around the seventh hole, where the flag waved in the wind. With how absent his gaze was, he got close enough that I could've reached out and grabbed it. "If he wanted you to know what he looked like, he wouldn't have canceled the video chat."

I'd begun nodding, since that was where my thoughts had been as well, but paused. "How did you know he didn't show?" I asked. "I didn't tell you about it."

He blinked. "I just assumed. You weren't in the meeting long enough, and you seemed upset after—"

"I wasn't upset," I argued, but my posture deflated a little. "About *that*, anyway."

An uncomfortable current ran underneath my skin. Perhaps it was the mere mention of Aaron to begin with, bringing him up even though Sumner was supposed to be my safe place from the topic. "It's strange, not knowing what he looks like, though. I've never even spoken with him. He could be anyone in the world, and I'd never know."

Sumner nodded. "I could be Aaron."

It was such a nonchalant way he'd said it. *I could be Aaron*. It was a thought that made no sense at first, a harmless joke, but it slowly sank in further. He was the same age as Aaron Astor. He was from California...like Aaron Astor. He'd garnered my parents' approval. Saturday, at Mimosa Morning—what if he hadn't been hiding from Mr. Roberts, but from Vivienne? Because it was his mother?

On a slow pivot, I turned my head toward him, staring. The uneasy feeling once again reared its head in full force.

Feeling the intensity of my gaze, Sumner shifted uneasily in his seat. "I just meant, like, since you don't know what he looks like, I could be him for all you know. I'm not, though."

I continued to stare.

"No, seriously, I'm not. It was a joke."

173

"If you're him, I'll kill you." My tone left no room for negotiation. "I really will."

Sumner held one hand up from the steering wheel, leveling it with his shoulders. "You can even look at my license. I'm not Aaron."

His insistence calmed me a little. As logic set in, I realized Sumner couldn't have been Aaron Astor, for many reasons. He told me about not wanting to walk a path that others had set out for him—that wasn't something a rich man like Aaron Astor would say. My mother had even snapped at him Saturday morning. Him being my secretary alone seemed to be the biggest reason. I couldn't imagine Aaron Astor hired to follow me around for...what? Undercover recon on his future fiancée?

Except that sort of sounded like something the rich would do.

His golden hair was quite a bit darker than Vivienne's, but from what I remembered from photos, Mr. Astor had blond hair. Sumner's nose—did it look like Vivienne's?

I held out my hand, palm up.

Sumner blinked at it in confusion for only a moment. "What?"

"Your license."

He sighed before braking completely, putting the golf cart into park. Once we were still, he leaned backward so he could fish his wallet from his front pocket. "You're a little ridiculous, you know that?" His voice held no heat, though. He pried out his license, offering it over to me.

The first thing I looked at on the piece of Californian plastic wasn't the name, but the ID photo. It was a photograph of Sumner, of course. His hair was shorter, cropped closer to his head, which made him look younger. He didn't smile at the camera, but there was still an undercurrent of happiness that was evident in the photo. Apparently, he'd always been perpetually cheerful.

"See?" he said, expectant. "Not Aaron Astor."

My eyes drifted over to the name, and sure enough, *Sumner Pennington* was written in blocky letters. "This could be a fake ID," I said.

"Do you have any idea what a fake ID looks like?"

Admittedly, no. And if this was a fake, it'd have to be a really good one. Trying to seem as nonchalant as possible, I passed the card back.

"You're a conspiracy theorist, aren't you?" he asked as he tucked the license back in. "I bet you believe the earth is flat."

"It is."

He gave a louder sigh.

Sumner had parked beside one of the many ponds the golf course had, and I looked out at the rippling water. It reminded of Nancy and the pond in her yard. This was what I wished hers looked like—serene, calm, clean. If I could've swapped the water out and gave the country club the algae filled depths, I would've.

"I shouldn't have..." I began, and trailed off. I wanted nothing more than to stop, to sweep everything under the rug. Sumner seemed like he was able to easily move on; I wanted to, too. "I shouldn't have snapped at you Saturday."

"You've still been thinking about that?"

"I don't often worry about hurting people's feelings," I

went on, pinching my shorts tighter. "It doesn't matter, really, because it's not like I have anyone I want to keep close to me, anyway."

Sumner leaned forward to catch my eye, smugness filling his expression. "But...? You want to keep me in your life, is that it? Are you finally acknowledging our friendship, Margot Massey?"

His voice was full of amusement, and it lightened the weight on my shoulders a bit. "I don't have many friends, and it would've sucked to lose one."

"Don't worry. I don't know enough about you yet to walk away."

"Meaning once you learn more about me, you'll stop being my friend?"

"The jury's still out."

I sat in the lightheartedness for a moment, allowing the barest tug of my lips. "I want a turn," I said, standing up as best I could underneath the cramped golf cart top. Sumner looked up at me where my neck was craned against the roof as if stunned by my sudden movement. I waved my hand at him. "Slide over."

There wasn't enough space for him to slide across the seat without touching me, and his knees brushed the bare backs of mine in the process. My skin felt far too hot given how quickly the night was cooling off, that fire already simmering underneath my skin.

I fell behind the wheel with a little huff, flexing my hands across the smooth leather. "I should tell you," I said, reaching for the parking brake. "I'm not technically allowed to be driving one of these."

From the corner of my eye, I caught him looking at me. "What? Why not?"

"I've crashed...three? Four?"

His hand shot to the handle on the side of the cart. "*What?*"

"We got lucky with the person at the rental earlier—I don't think they realized I was on the 'do not rent' list. Either that, or they were too afraid to tell me no."

Alarm filled his voice. "Wait—"

But I didn't let him finish before slamming my foot on the gas pedal, causing the tires to tear up the green as we launched forward. I had to twist the wheel to avoid going into the pond, the tires slipping as they got a bit too close to the edge. Not close enough to dump us in, of course, but enough to feel the cart think about it.

Sumner braced his other hand on the dash, peering over the side as if considering jumping. "We're going to die, aren't we?"

The wind tearing through my hair, the sunset surrounding us, the speedometer on the golf cart tipping higher and higher, Sumner's palpable anxiety—I couldn't help but laugh at it all. It arose like a wave in my chest, undammable. Ridiculous, of course, to be laughing at the meager speed of a golf cart tearing through a course, but the little things always did bring me joy.

Sumner gaped, probably thinking I'd lost my mind. Probably worrying that I'd lost my mind and was sitting behind the wheel.

When I tried to look over, he yelled out, "Eyes on the road!"

"The road?" I snorted. "You mean the green?"

"Whatever—just—eyes—" He gestured frantically in front of us. "—*forward.*"

I took a hard left around a sand dune on hole twelve, the cart bouncing with the acceleration. Instead of continuing bracing himself on the dash, he reached his arm around and lined it against the seats, his hand gripping the back of my headrest. "See, *this* is how fast you're supposed to go," I said, looking down at the speedometer with a proud smirk.

"I completely disagree."

The holes from thirteen on were larger, giving us a lot of ground to cover. I took another sharp turn around the deep grass, and Sumner slid in the seat, his shoulder colliding into mine. Even after I straightened out, he didn't move away. In the pocket of my pants, my phone began vibrating with a call. I fished it out and glanced at the screen. *Destelle.*

"You are *not* going to—" Sumner began, but I already answered and put the call on speaker.

"Hi, Destelle," I greeted, holding the wheel with one hand and my phone with the other. "I was beginning to think you lost this number."

"I know, I'm the worst," Destelle groaned. "In my defense, it's been crazy."

Sumner pried my phone out of my hand, grabbing my wrist and forcing my fingers to curl back around the steering wheel. "I can multitask," I whispered to him, low enough for Destelle not to pick up. Sumner vehemently shook his head.

"What's that noise? Are you driving?"

"A golf cart."

"How'd you get one? I thought you were on the ban list."

Sumner had an expression that said *oh, so everyone knows but me.* I slowed down so the engine of the cart wouldn't be as loud, and so Sumner wouldn't have a heart attack and drop my phone. "I'm offended you doubt me."

Destelle laughed on the other end of the phone, but it was riddled with tension. "Listen," she began in a hesitating voice and then paused again, which raised my guard. Disappointment set in even before she spoke. "They added one last show to the tour. One of the bigger venues in San Bernadino had a spot open up, and the band booked it."

I lifted my foot off the gas pedal, the golf cart slowing in a relieved response. Even with preparing for her guilty tone, it hadn't softened the blow. "So, you *won't* be home for Annalise's wedding." It was a statement.

"I know, I know," Destelle rushed, and I could imagine her rubbing her hands into her features. "Their manager didn't check with everyone before they agreed, and they—"

"You could still come home. You don't have to be there for every show." Immediately, I wanted to suck the whining words back in, especially since it wasn't just Destelle who'd heard them.

"I know, I just—it's the last show, and everyone will want to celebrate, and I really wish I could—"

I hated everything about this moment. I hated the fact that I made Destelle stumble over her words in defense, making her feel guilty for living her life. I hated the fact that the call was on speaker and Sumner could hear all of it. I hated the sunset and the golf cart and myself. "Don't give yourself premature wrinkles," I told her, affecting a firmer, nonchalant tone to replace the childlike plaintive one. "Save those for your thirties."

"I'd totally rather be there for the wedding," Destelle said, though we both could hear the lie. She was just trying to make me feel better.

It made me even more pathetic. "Please, even I'd rather be at a concert than the wedding, and that's saying something. Enjoy listening to your boyfriend perform." ... *the same songs they've been playing for the past month and a half.*

"I'll still be coming the day after. I can meet Aaron then—if you're still going through with it, that is."

I'd never gotten a chance to tell her about the video call that didn't happen. At the mention of Aaron, though, Sumner returned his gaze back to me. I refused to look over. "Yes, I am."

"You're always so independent and strong, I have no doubt it's going to go just fine. Have Nancy give you a pep talk beforehand, then, okay? Or call me—I should be free in the morning if you need someone to talk you out of it."

"I'll keep that in mind."

Destelle and I hemmed and hawed on the phone for a few more moments before we hung up. Even after the call ended, Sumner and I sat still in silence, thoughts brewing like a storm in my mind.

It was more than Destelle not being able to show up for a wedding. A wedding didn't matter. But she was going to be by my side and get me through one of my first encounters with Aaron, and that was the most important thing. Disappointment welled, causing the back of my throat to tighten.

"Margot," Sumner began.

"Don't," I warned, but the word came out tired.

He didn't. Instead, Sumner set my phone down on the seat between us, pulling his hand back to rest on his knee. Only for a second, though. When I reached for my phone, to tuck it back into my pocket so we could drive back to the country club, Sumner's hand shifted back over and grabbed mine. A comforting warmth spread from his fingers as they gently wrapped around my palm, thawing the icy chill in my skin. The contact was like a spark, jumpstarting my heart.

I looked at our combined hands and then up to him.

"I figured your apology earlier meant I could touch you again," he said, and then he must've seen the question in my eyes. "It's meant to be comforting. Like a '*I'm here with you*' touch. No one's held your hand in comfort before?"

That was what this was meant to be? Our palms pressing together, holding hands for the first time ever. *Comfort?* Granted, it felt as if his warmth thawed out a bit of my frost, but in a way that left me feeling uneven, like an ice sculpture out in the sun. Comforting would've been the last way I'd describe it.

"I know what you're thinking," he murmured. His fingers readjusted with mine, pressing our palms firmer together. "And Destelle not making it home for the wedding doesn't mean you're not important."

"Of course not," I returned, speaking past my aching throat. "It just means she's busy."

"You say that, but I want you to believe it, too."

The words irked me. "Why are you treating me like I'm fragile?" I looked down at our hands, but not pulling away. "I'm not a little kid who needs to be comforted because they're disappointed. Life is full of disappointments. I don't need someone to pat my back and tell me it'll be okay."

"Just because you don't need it doesn't mean you can't have it. It doesn't mean it's wrong to want it."

It was a comeback that left no room for arguing, too, which made everything even more frustrating. I was used to having the last word; how could he end the conversation every time?

Sumner seemed to grasp the fact that he'd won the upper hand, because he dipped his head down to try and catch my gaze. "It's nice, isn't it?" he asked, squeezing my hand. "Comforting?"

I didn't want to give him the win. Like a stubborn child, I turned away from the puppy-dog look on his face. "Marginally."

Sumner gave me a wide, close-mouthed smile, one that crinkled the corners of his eyes. "Aaron," Sumner began, startling me once more. "Destelle doesn't like him?"

"She doesn't like the idea of everyone pushing me toward a man I've never met. Never even spoken with. She found her true love and thinks I need to find mine."

"What do you think?"

"I think love causes more problems than it's worth. When you grow up around here, you learn that quick." I let out a sigh. "I'd rather have stability than something wildly unpredictable."

The setting sun threw its reddish-yellow rays onto the planes of his face and the strands of his hair, casting him in a warm glow that almost looked like something from a magazine shoot. I couldn't read his expression, whether he thought my take was interesting or sad. I doubted we shared the same views, though. When he'd talked about love, he'd said *one day*. For me, I was quite all right if it never came my way.

At least, I thought so.

The *what if* from earlier surfaced in my mind again like a whisper. *What if...he was Aaron Astor?* What if he'd come here to see me in person, to get to know me, and that was why he hadn't showed up to the video call? What would that be like? A life with Sumner...a romance? I'd never been interested in the latter before, but what if I'd gotten to do it with him?

I let my own gaze drop to his lips, where they still had a little upturn to the corners. Lips I'd kissed once upon a time. Almost on their own accord, my fingers curled over the back of his hand, returning the firm pressure. As if they were connected, my heart skipped a beat.

It did me no good to hold on to useless thoughts. No good at all.

"Okay, that's enough," I said as I pulled my hand away, laying it back on the steering wheel. I had to grip the leather to keep the shaking concealed. "I told you bitterness is one of my better qualities. I can't let you thaw my frozen heart too much."

Sumner laid his arm over the back of the bench seat, his hand brushing my back. "And like I said before." He turned his head to look at me. His eyes were warm, and they flicked to my mouth as if to wait for my smile in return for his. There was something strange about the way he smiled while looking at my lips, something about it that triggered a tumbling feeling in my stomach. "Happiness is better."

Without warning, I slammed my foot back down on the gas pedal, lurching us back into our seats, and the sound Sumner made in response was distinctly not a happy one.

Chapter 13

I prided myself on being a person who was hard to ruffle. My skin was steel, near impossible to get under. Growing up in the elitist atmosphere, it was almost a necessity to have thick skin. Even when bad things happened, I rarely let it bother me. In fact, more often than not, I laughed.

Right now, though, I felt effectively ruffled.

I stared at the phone in my hand Wednesday morning, but the contents on the screen hadn't changed in the past five minutes I'd been staring at it. The sender hadn't changed, nor had the message.

Sender: Aaron Astor
Subject: Greetings

Hello Margot,
I hope this email finds you well. I know this is coming very delayed, but I wanted to reach regarding the meeting we had to cancel last week and express my deepest apologies. I can see, upon reflection, how that might look. While I don't

have room in my schedule to plan another meeting, I do hope we can continue communication
like this until I arrive on the east coast. I should've
reached out earlier, but I fear you will find that
thoughtfulness isn't my strong suit.
Thank you for being patient with me.
I look forward to your reply.

Fondly,
Aaron

I wasn't sure what about the message bothered me
most. That he'd written it as a business email, that he was
just *now* reaching out, that he just assumed I'd give him a
free pass for the radio silence until now, or the way he'd
signed off.

Fondly. *Fondly?*

"He already is unbearable," I said to Nancy. She sat
across from me at the oak table, her teacup sitting
untouched in front of her. She focused on her biscuits and
how terribly overbaked they were. "'*Thank you for being
patient*'—it isn't as if I had a choice."

Nancy grunted in response.

"An email, Nancy? The first time he reaches out to
me, he sends a godforsaken email? And signs it off with
fondly?"

She knocked a frail knuckle against the top of her
biscuit. "Are they trying to break their customer's teeth?"

I sat back in my seat. The tearoom at the country club
was empty this time of day, mostly because this was when
they hosted hot yoga down in the workout wing. It left

Nancy and me to enjoy our tea in peace, and that was all that mattered to me.

Since Mimosa Morning, my parents had implemented a new rule: now, I could no longer go anywhere without Sumner Pennington, not even going to Nancy's alone. So, due to the addendum, Sumner had accompanied Nancy and me for tea, though he wasn't present at the moment.

He'd gone out into the hallway to answer a phone call, though I could still see him pass in front of the doorway from time to time, no doubt checking to make sure I hadn't done anything to get us both into trouble.

Now, I turned the contents of the email, which had arrived in my inbox shortly after Sumner stepped out into the hall, over and over in my mind, unable to stop one line of thought from surfacing. I never considered myself a conspiracy theorist, like Sumner had said, but I couldn't help from wandering down that path. What if...what if Sumner *was* Aaron Astor? What if that was why "Aaron" was finally sending an email—because I'd told Sumner I wanted to speak to him.

No. It didn't make sense.

But...

I looked over my shoulder once more, but Sumner was still in the hall. I leaned forward, lowered my voice. "Aaron Astor wouldn't go undercover to meet me first... would he?"

Nancy raised a gray eyebrow at me. "Why would he go to all that trouble?"

"To get an idea of the woman he's going to marry?"

"He hasn't seemed at all interested in the woman he

was going to marry before, has he? Hasn't called, hasn't reached out to you personally?"

"Well, no, but—"

"I doubt he'd go through all that trouble for you, dearie."

"Right?" I picked up my tea and drew in a breath of the floral scent before taking a sip. I made a face. Steeped far too long. "Right. That stuff only happens in movies."

Nancy picked up her tea biscuit and made a face at it, hitting it onto the table. Not even a crumb fell off. "Then again, it isn't too often you see an arranged marriage in this day and age, either."

I looked at my phone again, though the words on the email hadn't changed. "*Fondly,*" I scoffed. My anger grew each time the word echoed in my head. "I met my future mother-in-law last weekend. It's funny, isn't it? I met Mrs. Astor before I ever even spoke with her son."

Nancy pursed her lips at me, crumbs from her biscuit dotting at the corner of her mouth. "It isn't funny."

"Not funny ha-ha."

The server came over and replaced our biscuit plates with the brunch we ordered. For Nancy, it'd been a simple platter—eggs, sourdough toast, roasted potatoes. For me, avocado toast. Not nearly as brilliant as the toast at Pierre's, but close. Sumner had ordered their pot roast hash. Thank God they didn't serve beans on toast.

I picked up my fork in my right hand and grabbed my knife with my left. "Sumner hid from her, did I tell you that? Mrs. Astor, I mean. Well, he says he was hiding from my father, but—"

"Sumner, Sumner," Nancy said in a chiding voice.

She, too, followed my movements and picked up her fork in her right hand. Holding the silverware this way, against the "proper" table manners, was a habit I'd learned from her, a small show of rebellion against the strict rules of etiquette. "You talk about him an awful lot."

"I do not. You just only listen to me when I bring up his name. And besides, he's my friend. I can talk about him."

"You can't be friends."

I stabbed a piece of my toast with my fork, making sure it had an ample amount of salmon, but paused before taking a bite. "Stuck in the dinosaur age, are you? Men and women can be friends."

"It's not that men and women can't be friends." Nancy pointed her fork at me. "It's that *you two* can't be friends."

"And why not?"

She began cutting up her eggs. "You can't be friends with someone you kissed."

Sometimes it slipped my mind I'd ever kissed Sumner, because in that moment, he hadn't been my focus—my mother's reaction had. I still sometimes found myself wishing I'd paid more attention when I'd pressed my lips to his, lingered against them just a bit longer. "You were the one to told me to be his friend first," I reminded her. "Are you forgetting that in your old age?"

"That was before I saw how you act around him."

"And how do I act?"

"Like you're thawing on the inside."

Thawing. Me? Because of *Sumner*? "Perhaps you

189

need to get your eyes checked," I grumbled, trying to shake off the thought.

"Sorry," Sumner said as he approached, smoothing his hand down the front of his dark buttoned shirt. I jumped at his sudden appearance, but he didn't look like he heard what Nancy had said.

"Anyone important on the phone?" Nancy asked, curbing no corners as he settled back into his seat.

"Just a friend from back home," he replied, picking up his silverware to cut into his pot roast hash. He picked it up the correct way—knife in his right hand and his fork in his left. "I told him I'd call him back later."

"Do you talk to your friends back home much?" Nancy pressed. The question might've seemed innocent enough to anyone else, but I saw through her and the shifty way she looked at him. "Do you miss them much?"

"I text them here and there," Sumner replied good-naturedly. "I didn't really have many friends back in Cali, honestly. I worked most of the time, and it kept me busy."

"One must have a good balance of work and play," Nancy said with a sage nod. "What did you do? Margot said you worked at a company after graduation—what did you do there?"

He raised up his teacup, holding it the refined way I'd see at tea parties. "I started from the bottom at a company as a secretary."

Nancy had all but abandoned her food now to play inquisitor. "What company?"

"A small startup."

"In what field?"

190

"Nancy," I said calmly, though all but glaring at her from across the table. "Let the poor man eat."

"A secretary," Nancy mused. "Makes sense why Margot's parents were so willing to hire you, then. At least, to some extent. I *am* still perplexed by that. Aren't you, Margot?"

"They hired him because they needed someone to babysit me while they prepped for Annalise's wedding."

"Yes, but why *him*? A man, and a young one at that."

That, honestly, made a bit less sense. If my parents were to hire a secretary for me, I would have expected it to be a woman. If not a woman, then a man in his fifties or older. Not near enough in age to me that someone could've thought we were dating. We both turned to Sumner, since only he knew the answer.

"I think your parents might've thought I'd be able to understand you better," he said slowly, turning his attention to his plate. "Since we're close in age."

My parents wouldn't have wanted anyone who might've understood me. The purpose of hiring Sumner wasn't to find me a playmate, but to be their warden in the interim. They'd done a wonderful job at isolating me nearly my entire life. They wouldn't have started being thoughtful now. "That's what they told you?" I asked.

He blinked. "Yeah, I think it was something like that."

Growing up in the social circles I had, I'd gotten very good at hearing a lie when spoken. Usually, there were other tells to aid in the deception hunting. Rapid blinking —check. No eye contact—check. Fiddling hands, forced smiles, fake laughs. It was more common to hear a lie than it was to hear the truth, and perhaps that was why

Sumner had been so refreshing. When he spoke, I never had to worry about hearing a lie in his voice.

Until now.

Nancy caught my eye as she reached for her own cup of tea. It was clear; she heard it too.

When it came to my parents, the waters grew muddied with Sumner, for whatever reason. And perhaps it was time to get to the bottom of it.

"Margot."

Sumner looked up before I did; I didn't even flinch at the unexpected voice calling my name directly behind me. Instead, I sawed off a piece of my avocado toast. "Good morning. Fancy meeting you here."

"Ms. Nancy," my father greeted luxuriously, donning a tone that he used with no one else but her. He had to butter her up, after all, if he wanted the property his hotel sat on to be left to him in the will. "It's been far too long since our paths have crossed."

"It has, hasn't it?" Nancy's tone held no affection as she picked up her water. She didn't even spare him a look. "Took you long enough. I certainly wasn't about to seek you out."

"Margot has been keeping up appearances, hasn't she? She's my proxy." My father said it like a joke.

No one laughed.

My father laid his hand on my shoulder, causing me to still at once. His hand was firm, and even through the material of the shoulder pad stitched into my suit jacket, it weighed heavy. "Margot, there's someone who would like to speak with you."

That "someone" was most likely him, and he was only

trying to be polite about it in front of my companions. I'd been wondering when he'd approach me regarding what happened on Saturday. "Can't I finish my meal first?"

My father hesitated, and if I looked, I'd probably have found him looking from Sumner to Nancy. He knew he had to be tactful. "This is a guest we cannot keep waiting."

I set my silverware down and turned. My father stood as an imposing figure behind me, taking up my view with the broad frame of his own shoulders. His expression was flat and clear, though it was one he normally donned around me. I would've been far more uncomfortable if I could've been able to tell what he was feeling—though there was something in his eyes that still put me on edge.

"Keep Nancy company," I told Sumner as I pushed my chair back. He wasn't looking at me, though, but at my father. "Nancy, don't grill him for information."

"Hurry back, now," Nancy said, finally regarding my father. Her features always held a bit of a frown, but it seemed more prominent now. "Your tea will get cold."

My father was silent as he escorted me from the room, which didn't bode well. I wondered if he'd take me all the way back to his office in the hotel or if we could talk this out in one of the meeting rooms. I at least had more time to think of what to say than I'd had with my mother, giving me more time to figure out what could appease him.

But as we stepped into the lobby of the country club, I realized there really *was* someone waiting to speak with me, and it was Vivienne Astor.

Today, instead of a suit, she wore a flowy sundress

and a lightweight cardigan, one that fit well with the higher temperatures of the day. Her brown hair was back out of her face up by a pair of sunglasses, and she had a pale yellow Claire-Haute purse nestled at the crook of her elbow. She looked different from the authoritative, sure women I'd seen at Mimosa Morning in her Malstoni suit, but her presence wasn't any less prominent. It made me wonder, briefly, what I'd look like in a sundress.

Whereas I stiffened upon seeing her, her features softened at the sight of me, almost in a welcoming expression. "Margot," she greeted as I came close. "Lovely to see you."

Lovely. It wasn't the word I expected her to use, but then again, she must've still thought it was Yvette who caused the commotion on Saturday. My father, discreetly laying his hand on my back, shuffled me forward. "Mrs. Astor, hi," I greeted. When she stuck her hand out, I pressed mine into it.

She hadn't been shaking my hand, though, but captured and held it. Her fingers held a pleasant warmth. "You're a difficult lady to track down."

"I didn't realize you were still in Addison," I said honestly. My parents hadn't said anything at all about her extended stay. "I—I thought you were only here for that day."

"I had a few more things to take care of," she replied, and then lowered her voice. "But I wanted to see you before I left, given what happened Saturday."

I was all too aware of my father's presence, his hand remaining on my back like a warning. "S-Saturday?"

"You thought the little *tumble* was subtle?" A corner

of her lips lifted, and she looked into the mirror to inspect her expression. "Then again, perhaps it was. No one else noticed."

Everyone else was already three mimosas deep, I thought, but took a step closer. "I'll pay for it. I know I can't replace it, but I'll pay for the damage." My eagerness wasn't just due to the fact that my father hadn't moved his hand, nor was it because I wanted to be on her good side. The guilt over damaging the garment was enough to scar me.

"It was a one-of-a-kind," she said, still holding my hand. "And still is. A little stain doesn't change that."

I frowned at her, wondering if her nonchalance was coming just before she snapped at me. "But...but it's ruined."

"Besides, it's just orange juice and vodka. I could probably remove the stain myself at home. Why does a spill ruin a garment? Why does a stitch by a different tailor make it less valuable?" Vivienne pursed her lips a little. "I see you're a woman of great taste, with that Gilfman you're wearing now, but who taught you these things? That if something isn't perfect, it deserves to be thrown out?"

I felt a little ashamed under the directness of her stare, at the way she phrased the question. Ashamed of myself for unconsciously thinking that way, ashamed that it was something that someone had to point out to me— someone as elegant as her.

Vivienne folded her hands in front of her and gave me a passive expression. "Tell me why you spilled, Margot, and I'll consider what I want in repayment."

I wished she could've been like any of the other club members, so suffocating with a stick up her ass and a chip on her shoulder, so I could lie to her. Though the excuse was childish, there wasn't a different one I could give. "She asked you a question, Margot," my father told me, as if I was a child and needed prompting.

Vivienne looked at him, but said nothing.

"I didn't want the others to see what Aaron looked like before I did." I winced after I confessed it.

Vivienne took it in with a soft head nod. "So, you caused that woman to spill her drink to stop me?"

I could feel my cheeks burn. "I—I don't know what I was thinking. I did it on impulse."

"I see." Her voice gave nothing away. I held my breath as I stared at the tiled ground, waiting for her decision. "Would you like to see him? Aaron? I'll show you a picture first, before anyone else."

When I looked at her, her expression was light, almost caring, an expression I rarely saw. Especially not at the country club. She had her phone pulled out in her hand already, though her screen was still black. I stared at it, at her offer, the meaning of it slowly breaking through my surprise of it. This was my opportunity to finally see my fiancé. To see if he truly was a frog or a prince. To see him first.

To see if he was Sumner or not.

What does it change? The thought surfaced like a buoy breaching the water. *Seeing him now or seeing him in a few weeks. What will it change? What if it makes you feel worse?*

And that, ultimately, caused my stomach to sink.

"No," I managed to get out, listening to the thoughts even though I wasn't sure I should've trusted them. "Thank you, but if he prefers to wait until we see each other in person, I'll wait."

Vivienne nodded, pocketing her phone. "Then I won't show anyone else, then, either. Your respect, Margot, is what I seek more than anyone else's." With this, she gave a not-so-discreet glance once more at my father.

His hand at my back pressed in deeper, though I tried to ignore it. "Mine?"

"Why should I worry about what anyone else thinks? They aren't the one my son has his eye on." Vivienne came close enough to touch me lightly on the shoulder, her expression as gentle as ever. She drew me close, just enough that it forced my father's hand off my back. "If you change your mind, just let me know. Bit of advice, though. Next time, words go a long way."

The scolding felt very motherly—at least, in the way a mother was supposed to scold. The intention was there, but soft, in a way that made me feel guilty, but not weighed down. It wasn't anything like the tone my mother used. *I don't know where I went so wrong to have a daughter like you.*

"I will be taking Mrs. Astor to the airport to fly back to California," my father informed me, his hand falling onto my shoulder. "Then she'll be back for Annalise and Michael's wedding at the end of the month."

"Exciting times, seeing Aaron's best friend getting married," she murmured, pressing her hands together.

"And it won't be long until we have another wedding to prepare for, hopefully."

My father squeezed my shoulder again until I smiled.

"You'll be riding with us, right?" Vivienne asked me. "I'd love to talk more on the car ride to the airport."

My initial reaction was to decline, thinking of Sumner and Nancy waiting in the tearoom. Strangely, though, a part of me didn't want to decline. While I wanted to go back and enjoy my avocado toast, I, too, wanted to get to know Vivienne better, even if it was with the ears of my father listening in. "Of course," I replied without my father's prompting, offering her a genuine smile. "I'd love to."

As we wheeled her suitcase toward the entrance, I replayed the conversation over and over in my head. Kindness was such a rarity, so much so that it seemed wrong to blindly accept it. Especially coming from her. The players in this game never stopped surprising me, much like how a rug being ripped from under my feet would surprise me. Vivienne, the woman my parents had done a fine job of building up as a daunting figure in my head, turned out to be lovelier than I thought. Could someone as influential to my life as her really be that kind? Had I really gotten that lucky?

I reached up and touched my shoulder where her hand had been, swallowing hard. Perhaps I had.

Chapter 14

I sat in the middle of my bed that night with my knees drawn to my chest, the silk of my nightgown pooling around me. I had my arms wrapped around my legs and my chin resting on top, staring out the window even though I could only see my reflection in the black. My dark hair hung over my one shoulder, but it only stretched down a smidge past my collarbones. If someone were to have stumbled into my hotel room, they would've thought a ghost sat atop of the bed instead of a young woman.

I suppose, really, I *felt* like a ghost. It was one of the pitfalls of living in the hotel, the loneliness. Surrounded by people at all times, but ones I'd never interact with. Ones who didn't know I existed. Except for one.

Sumner was on the other side of the wall, but I couldn't hear him. I wondered if he was asleep.

Airport traffic was hell, which meant my father and I hadn't gotten back to the estate until a little after five. My mother, who'd stayed back at the country club due to a meeting, told me that Sumner had driven Nancy home before working a short shift in the pool area. I hadn't sought him out once I returned, needing to decompress.

I'd known going into the drive that I liked Vivienne Astor, but I came out of it loving her. She had such a warm and endearing sort of personality; like Sumner, the way she spoke left me feeling seen. She'd asked me about college, about my hobbies, about my likes and dislikes. The attention had been fully on me as we chatted in the backseat of my father's car. And when she'd finished asking me questions, it was my turn to ask a few of my own—about her son.

"He's insecure," she'd told me. "Almost to a detriment. His brothers are a bit older than him, and seeing them achieve big things has left him nervous to branch out, I think. He's very good at keeping it to himself, but he never puts himself out there. That's why, I think, he's so nervous to meet you. It's sweet, really. Or, well, I think so —I am his mother, after all." She'd laughed then.

Insecure. Nervous. They weren't words I'd ever associated with Aaron Astor before. Arrogant had been one, uncaring another. I'd asked her then what had him so smitten with me, if she knew.

Vivienne had lowered her voice and shifted closer in her seat to me. "He was feeling quite shy at the event, and wanted to escape to get some fresh air, but saw you out on the balcony," she'd replied, a lovely smile on her face. "The way he describes it... You were standing in a corner by yourself, and he said he couldn't stop thinking about you since."

I couldn't help but think how lonely you looked,

Sumner had told me once upon a time. *That's why I'm being nice. Because I know what it's like to feel alone in a room full of people.*

I fell back on my bed and stared up at the ceiling, seeing shapes in the plaster. A useless thought. A childish one. Him and his stupid boyish smiles and endless positivity. His ridiculous ways of comfort and attempts at amusement. Him and his stupid mouth. I wasn't sure I'd ever in my life thought twice about someone like this, but then again, had I ever been close to someone like this before? Destelle, maybe, but I'd never even held her hand. I'd definitely never kissed her.

I curled my hand into a fist, attempting to banish thoughts of his hand on mine. The thought of his mouth—

Useless.

I sat up and grabbed my phone from my bed, loading up a social media site. Sumner had to be a unique enough name that I'd easily be able to find it, right? Except when the search loaded, I was met with a few women named Sumner, a few profiles with no picture, or profiles that didn't belong to the man sleeping next door. I tried a different app, but again ended up with nothing.

In the age where everything was online, how was it that the only two men in my life didn't have profiles I could stalk?

Three knocks on my hotel room door pulled me from the depths of my spiral, along with a soft voice through the wall. "Room service."

"Finally," I all but exclaimed. Pushing up from my bed, I shoved my feet into my slippers and stalked across the room. Most of the lights in my hotel room were off save for the lamp near my bed, and it threw odd shadows on the walls. "Nearly an hour for a bottle of wine." With that, I hauled the door open.

A staff member stood outside with a cart that held the chilling bottle of wine, and he greeted me with the signature Massey Suites smile. He must've heard my muttered remark through the door, because he replied, "We didn't have what you requested in stock, Miss Margot, so we had someone run to the store."

I peered closer at the label on the wine. "I didn't ask anyone to make a special trip."

He had his shoulders hunched like he was afraid of a scolding. "Only the best for our best."

I actually cringed at the motto.

The door to Sumner's hotel room ripped inward, much like it had the very first time I'd discovered him to be my neighbor, but this time, it only startled the staff member. Sumner stumbled into the hall in his bare feet, as if ready to catch me sneaking from my room, but halted at the sight of the room service deliverer and their cart.

"You weren't sleeping?" I asked him in mild surprise. It was clear that he'd planned on it soon. He wore navy pajama bottoms and a loose-fitting gray T-shirt. His golden hair was loose in waves over his forehead, eyes bright.

I became aware of my attire, and all the bared skin on display. There was no time, no chance, to cover it up this time.

Sumner didn't focus on me, though. He zeroed in on the staff with immediate suspicion. "What's this?"

"He's delivering wine, clearly."

"At eleven o'clock at night?"

The man butted back in, "We deliver whenever someone orders it."

"Helpful, thank you," Sumner muttered, and turned to me with his eyebrows raised.

I, however, was no longer willing to continue the conversation in the hall. I stepped out of the path of the door and held it open. "Into the living room, please," I told the staff.

Sumner immediately laid his hand on the service cart, refusing to allow it to move even an inch. "She doesn't need you to bring it in," he said. "Having a man in your room is exactly what your parents are against."

"He's a staff member."

"So was I when you kissed me."

The man, after a moment of deliberation, seemed to decide it was in his best interests to abandon the cart. "H-Have a good evening." With a little bow, he excused himself, and Sumner turned back to me.

I leaned my hip against the door. "You scared him off."

It was almost as if Sumner didn't notice what I wore until that exact moment. The vintage inspired piece was nothing scandalous by any means. The silk gown was white, but perfectly opaque. The top was lower cut, but not so much that cleavage was visible. The lace hem fell just below my knees, and the sleeves were long, cinched at my wrists. Not anything scandalous at all.

And yet Sumner looked sharply away, as if he'd seen a

plethora of my skin and not the silk material. "What—what are you wearing?"

"Pajamas."

"It's—it's a *dress*."

I tilted my head to see him clearer. Even though he turned his face away, I could see a flush to his cheeks. "More specifically, it's a nightgown."

"You don't wear dresses."

I stepped back out of the doorway. "Come in and we can argue about my clothing attire over a glass of wine. Or at least out of the hallway."

He was hesitant, but ultimately complied. The dark room cast a strange mood as Sumner steered the cart deeper in, coming to a pause near the sofa. "I can't stay," he said as I shut the door. "I'm not staying."

"Doth protest too much," I quipped as I walked up to him, picking the bottle of wine from the chiller. I offered the bottle out to Sumner, expression expectant.

He picked up the wine opener and began attempting to uncork the bottle. He twisted the spiral into the cork, but struggled to pull it out, working the wine opener back and forth. He looked like a little kid trying—and failing. I watched him through it all, fighting a smile.

"You're probably the worst waiter I've seen," I said as a minute ticked by.

Sumner still fought to uncork the wine. "I'll get it."

"Here, give it, I'll do it."

"I've—" Sumner finally ripped the cork from the bottle with a small pop, a victorious smile working over his lips. "—got it." He flipped one of the glasses over, but before he began to pour, I grabbed his wrist.

"One glass," I said, attempting to persuade him. "You don't have to drink. Just sit with me for one glass."

Sumner's eyes skirted around my living area. "I don't think that's—"

"I was thinking to myself how lonely I was, and then you came out into the hall. Coincidence?" I attempted to give him a sort of puppy dog look of my own underneath my lashes. "Fate, isn't it?"

He regarded me and my neediness with a tired sort of amusement. "Fate," he echoed with a soft scoff. "Sit. I'll pour you a glass—a *small one*, because I can't be long. It's not... appropriate."

Appropriate. *Psh.* It was my turn, though, to don a triumphant smile. I sat down on the edge of the settee in the living area and crossed my legs, watching as he poured the sweet wine into its glass. This movement, though, was expert, not a quiver to his grip. Didn't know how to open a bottle of wine, but knew how to pour it. Interesting.

"Any reason for wine on a random Wednesday night?" Sumner asked as he passed me the glass.

I peered at the pinky-colored liquid, taking a whiff. I relished in the peachy scent, my tongue anticipating the first sip. "I already said."

"Because you were lonely?" Sumner moved to sit on the couch across from me, stiff at first. He stretched his pajama-clad legs out in front of him, underneath the glass coffee table. "Terrible reason to be drinking."

"Are there any good reasons?"

"Touché." He watched as I touched the glass to my lips, sloping it back to have my first drink. *Divine.* "If you're so lonely here, why don't you move back home? With your parents?"

"It was more suitable for all of us if I were to stay here," I said dismissively. "I supposed I'd be lonely at home as well." Perhaps lonelier, knowing my parents were a few rooms away but unwilling to visit. I raised my glass to my lips, peering at Sumner over the rim. "At least here I can order room service."

He looked at the room service cart in question. "True."

Sumner was only in the living room of the suite—I even had the door leading to my bedroom closed—but having him in here introduced a strange tone that hung between us. I'd ordered the wine to help me fall asleep, but his presence in a room no one had stepped in except for housekeeping left me wide awake. A shot of espresso, a second wind. I tried to remember if I'd ever felt this way when Destelle was around, but it was different.

Sumner nodded his chin at me. "You're drinking too slow."

"I'm savoring it," I replied, tilting my glass. "One does not *chug* wine, Sumner Pennington."

He let out a small breath through his nose, another scoffing sort of chuckle, as he leaned back further into the couch. It was strange to see him in his pajamas; he no doubt thought the same about me. That this was some personal gap we'd bridged together. It was small, but it felt significant... intimate.

"You didn't come back to tea," Sumner pointed out after a moment. "Your mother came and told us. Nancy was worried you'd gotten kidnapped."

"Oh, I went willingly. We drove Vivienne Astor to the airport." I sipped at my wine again as I studied him, my thoughts going back to the merry-go-round of the Aaron Astor train track, and I decided to test those murky waters. "She's how I want to be when I'm older. Sophisticated, but still down to earth. I never expected it from her."

"What *did* you expect?"

"Snotty. Stuck-up. Entitled. Really, pick any woman from the country club and use them as a model. Use my mother as an example, if you want."

"That's good, then," Sumner said. "That your future mother-in-law is nice."

I still couldn't get a good read on him. I picked another angle. "Did I tell you Aaron Astor emailed me?"

"He did?" Sumner sounded surprised enough, somewhat curious. Nothing off-putting. "What'd he say?"

"He felt bad for having to cancel our virtual meeting, but he wants to talk more over email until he comes into town for the wedding. Interesting that he's ready for conversation now, isn't it?" *After I had told you that I wished we could've talked more.*

If Sumner picked up on my insinuation, he didn't make it clear. "Isn't it a good thing?"

"Of course. I am going to be meeting him in two weeks when he comes for the wedding. Maybe I can coerce him into sending a picture of himself. Of his hands, even."

"His *hands*?"

"I've recently discovered I'm a hands girl."

Sumner's gaze dipped a little to my wine glass. "No way you're already tipsy from that small pour."

I ignored him. "You have nice hands," I mused, looking down into the depths of the peach. One more sip and it'd be gone; one more sip and so would he. "I noticed that the other day, on the golf course. Very lovely hands, indeed."

Very lovely hands, with slim, long fingers that had wrapped so easily around my own.

"As far as compliments go, I think that's the strangest one I've gotten. Even Nancy saying my *tush* looked *squishable* was more normal."

"I'd argue me liking your hands is far more appropriate than talking about your butt."

"Yeah, I guess as far as things go, I'd rather you check out the former than the latter." Sumner spread his palms before him, studying his fingertips. I could practically see the question on his face. *Do I have nice hands?*

I rose from the couch and walked around the coffee table, pausing just before him. "Admit it," I mused, swirling the final drops of wine in my glass. "Following around a rich girl isn't half as bad as you thought it'd be."

Sumner didn't look intimidated by my sudden proximity; in fact, an unfamiliar emotion bloomed in his eyes. "I shouldn't have said that."

"Why not? Is it not true?"

"No. It's not."

"I'm not rich? Or, when you said it, did you not mean rich? Did you mean to say *spoiled*?" I took a theatrical look around my grand hotel room. A few lamps were on, giving a glimpse of its illustrious wallpaper and the sleek fixtures. "Is a penthouse suite not a sign someone is spoiled?"

"Placated. You're being placated by it. Even I can see that."

Placated. I felt my brow crease. His own expression was just so...*compassionate,* and in that moment, it irked me. I took a half step closer to grow more imposing, the toe of my slipper brushing his. "Will you stop?" I demanded, glaring down above him. "Stop looking at me with your 'poor little bird' eyes. Why do you look at me that way? I'm not someone to look down on."

"I'm not looking down on you, Margot," Sumner insisted. It was ironic, given the fact that he had to tilt his head back to meet my stare. "You live in a penthouse suite, yes, but you don't *want* to. You said yourself, you're lonely here."

"So what?" My voice was flat. "I have everything I could ever want. Clothes, cars, a future paved in a golden path. Am I lonely here? Does it matter? Being alone is a choice," I echoed Nancy's words, "and I've chosen it. I'd much rather be alone than surrounded by a million people speaking a language I'll never understand."

Things were always a give and take with Sumner. When he was there, I enjoyed his company. It was when he stared a bit closer, when he attempted to peel back the layers I very much so enjoyed leaving sealed, that I was ready to throw him away like a child growing bored with a toy. I wanted him as a distraction, not as my therapist.

I tipped my glass back and drained the remainder of the wine, the punch of peach causing my throat to ache as I swallowed. "You can leave now."

Sumner caught my wrist before I could take a full step away from him. He sat up on the couch, but didn't rise. "Margot."

"I can think of myself as the most pitiful person in the world, but I refuse to allow anyone else to even consider it." I looked down at him, pulse fluttering. "Especially not you, Mr. Pennington."

As I wrenched my hand out of his grip, the open back of my slipper caught on the leg of the coffee table, and I tripped over it. Quite the opposite of the calm and collected image I'd tried to portray, I nearly tumbled back onto the coffee table itself, which would've caused the glass to shatter, but Sumner grabbed my wrist again and pulled me back forward. Too hard. My knee crashed against his as I tried to find my balance again, which sent me stumbling—oh-so gracefully—into Sumner's lap.

All at once, everything stilled. One of my hands had curved over Sumner's shoulder, steadying my fall. Sumner's hand still gripped my wrist, the one that held my wine glass, and his other braced against my waist. The fabric of my nightgown bunched under his touch, exposing the bottom of my thigh as my knee dug into the couch on the other side of his hip.

The position was accidental, but undeniably intimate, our faces only inches apart.

My heart had fluttered before, but it completely stopped now.

Sumner didn't breathe underneath me. His gaze didn't stray from my eyes, either, locked on as if they were his lifeline. And his were so, so pretty. Up close, I once more got a full view of his deep brown lashes, of his trail of freckles underneath his right eye. I wanted to trace them with my fingertip. His irises were blue, but they looked so dark now, almost as if the pupil had bled into the color.

Almost imperceptibly, his hand squeezed my hip. "I don't—" Sumner drew in a shaky breath. "I don't find you pitiful." His voice was a whisper.

I should've climbed off him then, but instead, my grip tightened on his shoulder. I brought my other hand down his fingers braceleting my wrist, lowering with it, as I set the empty wine glass on the cushion beside us. "Then how do you feel about me?" I asked in a low voice, never breaking eye contact. I didn't want to miss even a fraction of a moment in his expression.

Summer, of course, didn't answer, but I hadn't been expecting him to. I hadn't wanted him to. I'd asked the question, but I had a sudden and intense fear of hearing the answer either way.

In a slow movement, I lifted the tip of my finger to trace the freckles underneath his eye with a delicate touch. Sumner didn't even flinch, but held perfectly still, almost statuesque. His hand hung off mine almost heavily, but my touch was steady. My fingertip trailed from the freckles over the curve of his cheekbone, finding its path all the way down to the top of his cupid's bow.

Once more, my thoughts traveled back to the night that I'd kissed him in the ballroom. I hadn't been paying enough attention then, hadn't memorized the sensation enough. A greedy need rose within me now, the faint drops of wine I'd sipped spurring it on. Sumner's lashes fluttered as I shifted forward in his lap, ready to find out just what would happen if I were to kiss him again.

I waited, but just like the time before, Sumner did not push me away now. He watched me loom closer, closer—

A sudden, hard knock on my hotel room door caused us both to jump a second before our lips met. Sumner's hand spasmed on my hip before I tumbled from his lap, my feet barely getting underneath me on the floor. We both turned toward the door, but we didn't have to wonder for long. "Open up, Margot." My father's voice was a clear call.

It was after eleven. It was a bad sign. A very bad sign.

Now it was my turn to grab Sumner's wrist, hauling him to his feet. "Go into my bedroom," I ordered in a rushed whisper.

His eyes widened. "Your bedroom—"

I slapped a hand over his mouth, because even though this was a penthouse, I was afraid the walls were still thin. Thankfully, Sumner didn't fight me as I tugged open my bedroom door and shoved him inside. Without wasting time, I snapped the door shut.

"Margot." My father knocked again, harder this time. "I know you just had room service delivered, so I know you're up. Open the door."

I scanned the living area, but there were no traces of Sumner Pennington left. My empty wine glass still sat on the couch, though tipped over due to our movements. Nothing suspicious.

Even though he'd announced his presence, I looked through the peephole to find my father. He wore the same clothes from when we'd taken Vivienne to the airport, though he didn't have his suit jacket now, and his tie was loose at his collar. The sight was unsettling, almost to where I didn't unlatch the door.

I did, though, because there was no true alternative. "To what do I owe the pleasure?" I asked my father as he stumbled inside, barely a second after I had the door open. As he passed by me, I caught a strong whiff of brandy. Another bad sign.

My father looked out of place in my hotel room. In the shadows of the room, he was a monstrous figure, one that brought nothing but bad feelings.

"Wine?" he asked as he peered at the cart. He was clearly displeased with it, which was ironic, given the slur of his own speech. "Did you have another person in here?"

I did not look in the direction of my closed bedroom door. "No."

"There are two glasses."

"One is untouched, as you see. Room service just brought me up two."

My father turned and stared me down, and it was then that I got a full view of just how unsettled he looked up close. A hollowness clung to his eyes, leeching the skin underneath, accompanied by something like desperation. It made him look older than his sixty-one years, like that monstrous figure slowly morphed into a pitiful old man. "Margot, tell it to me straight—you'll be a good girl about this, won't you?"

"What do you mean?"

"What can I give you?" My father brought his palm down on the cart as if to catch his balance. The wine bottle and the remaining glass trembled, but nothing fell. "Do you want a check? A new car? I can give you that. A house of your own, so you don't have to live at the hotel? Be a good girl about this, and I'll buy you whatever you want."

Bribery—my parents hadn't resorted to it since the mention of Aaron. Guilt tripping and manipulation, yes, but never bribery. "What makes you think I want anything?"

"Everyone wants something," he said with his head still bowed, speaking to the wine glass. "These past few years, it's like we stalled out, Margot. Like we've hit a plateau with growing as an empire. But this deal with the Astors—can you picture it? How much grander things will be? How much more room we'll have to *breathe*?"

My father spoke as if I knew about the business side of Massey Suites. I didn't. Despite being his only heir, he never shared any business talk with me, most likely because he never intended to allow me to take it over.

"You've had it so easy, so good," he went on. "And this one thing that I ask of you—this *one thing*—you just make it so difficult."

"I thought I did a good job with Mrs. Astor in the car today."

"I'm talking about insulting your mother's friends, kissing that waiter boy, spilling your drink on Vivienne. I find you a good, *suitable* match, and you're doing every-thing to get rid of him?"

I'd never seen my father like this before. He drank, and drank often, but he never drank enough to lose control of propriety. My father was a tougher one to navigate in general, but with alcohol in him—enough to trip his steps—I didn't know how to respond. An unsettling weight rolled onto my chest. "Suitable for *you*," I murmured, keeping my voice even. "Suitable enough to deepen your pockets."

My father traced his fingertip over the base of the glass I hadn't touched, still leaning on the cart. "Your mother told me that it was Ally Jennings who was responsible for Vivienne Astor's suit being ruined," he began, the turn of the conversation one I barely followed. "That it was Ally was being billed the *ten thousand dollars* for Mrs. Astor's suit. But it was *your* fault?"

I thought of the conversation with Vivienne earlier this morning, of my father's hand at my back. I quickly tried to figure out how to navigate the situation. "I'll pay for it."

"You'll pay for it?" he echoed, and now, the soft demeanor of his voice was gone. A harshness began seeping through. "With what money? With my money, you mean? Just like you buy all your clothes with *my money*."

I had to think of the right thing to say to appease him, but I came up with no rebuttal. Discreetly, I took a glance over my shoulder to make sure that the bedroom door was still closed. I was all too aware of Sumner in the next room. The door remained shut, and my father's voice was still quiet, so perhaps Sumner couldn't hear.

"I refuse to do this song and dance with you, Margot," my father said. "My patience has reached its peak for your spitefulness. You *will* behave, or it will be over."

Horror and embarrassment were two separate threads

in a braid, weaving together in a noose around my neck. I fought the urge to swallow hard. "Ominous," I said as lightly as I could. "You've been watching too many action movies."

It was the wrong thing to say. My father, a man who rarely raised his voice, was a dangerous creature now with enough brandy in him to stink his breath. I should've thought of that. I should've calculated that, but I didn't.

He picked up the empty wine glass and dashed it to the floor in front of my feet. It shattered apart with a scream, shards scraping across the exposed skin of my ankles, and, on instinct, my arms rose to cover my face.

"Everything is a joke to you," he said through clenched teeth, crossing the room in brisk steps. Glass crunched underneath his Hefman & Italia dress shoes. I had my slippers on, but the bottoms were soft, thin; I was too afraid to take a step. I couldn't help but check the distance that still stretched between us. "Will it be a joke when you have no place to go? No one in your life? Do you want to be alone?"

"I've been alone my entire life," I returned with a steely gaze of my own, gritting my teeth. "And I will be alone, even if I do what you want and marry someone I don't know. Don't pretend you care when we both know you don't."

My father suddenly wrapped his hands around my upper arms and squeezed. Tightly. So tightly that I scrunched my shoulders against the grip, attempting to lessen the force. I tried to stay silent, but a gasp slipped through. "It isn't just your dignity you're throwing in the trash, you know. Mine, your mother's, Aaron's—you're bringing down everyone who associates themselves with you." His eyes were wide, glassy, and almost crazed. "That is why no one does. Why Destelle even left you behind. Kissing the waiter boy, spilling your drink on the most influential person Alderton-Du Ponte has had in its walls. You're not just embarrassing yourself, Margot, but everyone around you. You're right, I don't care that you're alone. You've done it to yourself."

It was clear my father and my mother were both cut from the same cloth. My mother, who grabbed my chin thinking it'd get me to straighten up. My father, gripping my arms, thinking I'd bow into submission. They never learned that it didn't work with me.

"You act as if you've ever said no to this marriage," he ranted on. "As if you wouldn't benefit at all from this marriage. Once you're married, once we join hands with the Astors, we'll have everything we could ever want."

The pressure in my throat was almost too tight to speak around. "Sure, because it's only my happiness that's the sacrifice you'll make."

My father looked at me strangely, as if this was the first time he was being confronted with the plain and simple words. *I don't want to.* He looked like such a stranger at that moment, and I wondered if he thought the same of me. He gripped me, but it was like neither of us knew each other. "Happiness," he echoed. "It's subjective. You won't be happy marrying Aaron, but you won't be happy being disowned either, would you?"

My father released me, and I swayed from the withdrawal almost as if a breeze in the room threatened to knock me over. He and my mother could grab me, hit me, bruise me, and none of it would hurt more than the way their words were expertly designed to cut. I stared up at him still, but my vision blurred, the specific features of his expression warping.

"I know you know the pros outweigh the cons," my father said, almost softly now. The brandy on his breath choked me as he leaned in. "Think about what you want, Margot. Be a good girl about this." He patted my head, and with that, he crunched over the glass to step away.

For a long moment, there was nothing. No ache in my arms, no thoughts in my head—nothing but the compressing numbness that seemed to grow tighter and tighter around my rib cage. The nothingness yawned like a black hole inside me, consuming everything, tugging it all into its depths.

Something small in me snapped, like a rubber band splitting. That was the feeling; a thousand rubber bands squeezing my insides, holding me together. Another snapped, bringing a flicker of pain through the blissful deadness.

When my hotel room door fell shut, that was when I heard my bedroom door creak open, the slight sound just enough to pull me back from the edge. I looked down at the floor, at the shards all around me, sparkling on the floor near my white slippers. Facing Sumner was the last thing I wanted to do. It was one thing to tell him not to pity me when I'd been able to keep everything at bay. Now, with my façade in ruins at my feet, there was no keeping it hidden.

I waited for Sumner's touch, his hand on my shoulder, his fingers brushing my palm, *something*—but it didn't come. Instead, Sumner walked past me and moved to where the phone sat on the credenza by the sofa, picking up the receiver and pressing a button. I watched numbly, wondering, in a distant way, if he was about to call the police. "Hi," he said into the phone, turning to look at me. His eyes were profoundly sad. "I'm calling from the penthouse suite. I know it's a bit late, but can we have housekeeping come up, please?"

Chapter 15

$\mathcal{A}$n emotion I didn't feel very often was embarrassment. To be embarrassed, one had to care about the thoughts of others around them, and I rarely ever did. Second-hand embarrassment was one I knew often—God only knew how many times someone had made a fool of themselves at all the parties and fundraisers and galas over the years—but feeling it first-hand was a rarity. So much so that I truly had no knowledge of how to navigate it, aside from pretending absolutely nothing happened.

I sat on the edge of my bed, listening to Sumner chatter with the housekeeping staff in the main room. My door was closed, but their muffled voices still seeped through. Sumner explained how he'd tripped, dropped the glass. I wondered if he knew how much he implicated himself; this gossip would spread like wildfire by tomorrow morning. *Sumner was in the Ice Queen's hotel room late at night. They were even drinking together. What else did they do?*

If he wasn't outcast before, he would be now.

Part of me wished my bedroom door would never

open. The other part wished Sumner would stop talking to the staff and come hold my hand. *Comfort*, he'd called it. I wanted it now.

And then, as if he heard my thoughts, Sumner opened my bedroom door and stepped inside. Only my bedside lamps were on, and it was clear from the way he hesitated on the threshold that it took him a moment to adjust. Sumner's eyes were soft at first until they zeroed in on my feet. Then his gaze sharpened. "Margot, you're bleeding."

I looked down. A cut lanced into the skin of my shin, and blood trickled from it in a dark trail. A piece of glass must've nicked it. It'd been bleeding long enough that it dotted the top of my white slipper. "I didn't notice."

Sumner muttered a curse as he ducked into my bathroom, and a moment later, the faucet was running. I had no time to worry about the state of my bathroom—if there were any of my hairs on the sink or underwear on the ground—before Sumner was already coming back into my bedroom, kneeling before me at my feet.

In his hands, he held a white washcloth, and with the gentlest touch, he began dabbing the drying blood off my leg. The warm water he'd dampened it with felt good on my skin. "Housekeeping is going to vacuum up the glass," he told me as he wiped. "They brought up extra cups if you wanted another drink."

I didn't, but I wished I'd drank more wine earlier, for no other reason but to numb the sheer humiliation of it all. Sumner wiped at where my skin was sliced, and with the blood cleaned, it was clear that the cut was no bigger than the size of my pinky nail. It'd just been bleeding for a while, unnoticed.

"Don't listen to him," Sumner said in a falsely cheerful voice. "He was just drunk. I doubt he meant any of what he said."

I held still during his ministrations, throat tight. "What makes you an expert on my father?"

Sumner peered up at me from his crouched position with an almost haunted shadow over his face, one that matched with the darkness of the bedroom. "Don't... don't take any of what he said to heart."

"Which part?" I gave a slow blink. "That I'm spiteful? Lacking in dignity? How I'm an embarrassment to everyone around me?"

"You are none of those things."

"You aren't a very good liar."

Sumner let out a small breath and broke his gaze, only for a moment. "You are." When he spoke next, his words almost bordered on a whisper, as if he hadn't wanted to ask the question. "Did you mean it?"

For some reason, the softness of his voice made me unreasonably annoyed. "Mean *what*?"

"That you didn't want to marry Aaron."

I let out a slow, rattling breath, exhausted to my core. I didn't want to talk about it. I didn't want to talk at all. The comfort I wanted didn't include him asking questions. "I wouldn't have said it if I hadn't meant it."

"This entire time," Sumner said, almost as if he were talking to himself. His forehead creased with his sad frown. "This entire time, I thought you wanted to marry him. You kissing me, spilling a drink on Mrs. Astor—this entire time, I thought it was just because you were impulsive. You *said* it was because you were impulsive. You said it *wasn't* that you didn't want to marry Aaron. But you did those things because you *didn't* want to."

I found myself unable to look away from the oddity of his expression. His unease summoned a weird feeling inside me, one that made me feel like I needed to apologize. For what, though, I wasn't sure.

He sat back on his heels and looked at the wadded washcloth in his hands, a smear of red visible. "When I asked you if you wanted to marry him, you said yes. You said *of course.*"

My head swam with pressure, and it made my chest feel as though it was vibrating.

"Why would I have assumed you were lying? That you were *marrying* someone when you didn't want to?" he demanded, incredulous. He did, indeed, look at me like I'd lost my mind. "No one just lets themselves be forced into marriage. Except you, apparently."

"What did it matter? Telling you that everyone wanted me to do something that I didn't want—what would it have done? It's not like you have any control over it." Looking at him, it was almost embarrassing thinking he could've ever been Aaron Astor. The childish thought was ridiculous now. "But come on, Sumner. No one would let themselves be forced into marriage? What, but people would marry someone they've never even spoken to? *Really?*"

"You're playing the martyr, then." The distraught expression on his face morphed into something else, something that was reminiscent of the expression he wore when he stopped me from unbuttoning my shirt. "God,

Margot, you—you're like the definition of a self-fulfilling prophecy. Why are you even doing this, then?"

I stared down at where he kneeled in front of me, warmth building underneath my skin, but worlds different from the previous moment between us. This time it was hot, suffocating, a wave of irritation that washed away the numbness. "I want you to leave. I'm tired."

"No." Sumner didn't even miss a beat, his stony stare matching mine. "What your dad said isn't true—people aren't *embarrassed* to be around you. You're the one pushing me away because I'm asking a question you don't want to answer. You want me to leave? Call security. Because if I walk out now, I'm just giving you more ammo. You *aren't* pitiful, Margot, so why are you acting like you are?"

I'd never felt such potent anger before, all channeled toward one specific person. I got to my feet and towered over him, hands curling into fists at my sides. I'd never hit anyone in my life, but I wanted to hit Sumner Pennington now. If this was what Yvette felt after I shoved Ms. Jennings into her, I understood her rage. I trembled with it now. "Get. Out."

Sumner did not rise from his kneeling position. "Make me."

I dug my hands into his upper arms, and if I'd been able to get at skin instead of his shirtsleeves, my nails would've cut. Of course, though, with Sumner as unwilling, there was no moving him more than an inch.

I tugged again, straining against the grown man on the ground, before falling to my own knees beside him.

"Fine," I gasped out, chest heaving with painful pressure. Fire flamed in my eyes, but Sumner didn't melt with it. He remained still, solid beneath my grip. "I can't call myself pitiful if I'm practically asking for it, right? But you heard my father. If I refused to marry Aaron, they'd *disown* me. They'd have no more use for me. They'd throw me out and never look back."

As I spoke, incensed tears began to burn, and I blinked at them furiously. Sumner's expression softened when he saw them.

"I'm crazy for marrying someone I don't want to? As if it's *easy* to just throw away everything I've ever known, huh? Tell me, when you moved here, did you move here broke? Not a single dollar to your name? Or did you have a savings account to fall back on?"

His voice was quiet. "I had something to fall back on."

"Then you have *no right* to tell me what to do in this situation." An angry tear slid down my cheek. "I may not want to marry Aaron, but I'd much rather avoid being homeless without a penny to my name."

And that was the epitome of it all. I didn't want to do it, any of it. Marry Aaron Astor, inherit the Massey Suites empire, spend the rest of my life attending the revolving events the Alderton-Du Ponte Country Club always hosted. The future of it all yawned wide before me, dark and gloomy and suffocating, but I still marched forward toward it. The paralyzing fear of turning away was far, far greater. As frightening as walking up to a precipice and jumping off with no knowledge of how far the drop was.

I'd rather not jump. I'd rather be stuck in hell than jump. I was too afraid to jump.

I was messed up beyond saving because I couldn't be bothered to save myself.

"Why don't you ask Nancy for help? I'm sure she'd lend you something to help get you settled—"

"Contrary to what my father says, I do have some dignity left." I let my hands fall from his arms, weighing like pieces of lead in my lap. "If I'm too much of a coward to leave without her help, I don't deserve her money." Even the idea of asking made me sick to my stomach. It made me hate myself even more for ever considering it. "And you know what, Sumner? Have you ever thought that maybe I'd be embarrassed to admit to you the truth about marrying Aaron? Embarrassed to admit that my life isn't unfolding how I wanted it to—how I *dreamed* for it to." My words ran together rapidly, chest feeling as though it was cracking apart. "And I *hate* it. But the only thing I can do is to throw it all away, and I can't, I can't—"

Before I could get another word out, Sumner leaned forward and wrapped his arms around me, drawing me into him. Our kneeling knees pressed together as he tucked me close, one hand wrapped around my lower back while the other reached up and rubbed between my shoulder blades. "Shh," Sumner murmured in my ear, his cheek pressing against the side of my head. "Shh, it's all right, Margot. Take a breath."

I trembled in Sumner's warm embrace, unable to reign in my shaking. I knotted my fingers into the loose fabric of his shirt, my knuckles brushing the firmness of his stomach underneath. I could smell the scent of his laundry detergent and hear the pulse of his heart, and I focused on those things, allowing them to pull me back from the brink.

"I'd be alone," I whispered into his shoulder, my lips brushing the material of his shirt. The wetness on my cheeks had to be transferring onto him, but I didn't pull away. "If I were to back out of the agreement with Aaron, if my parents were to throw me away—I'd be truly alone. And I don't want to be."

Sumner continued to rub circles on my back, sealing the cracks that'd begun to form within me. I felt so small in his arms, like a child finding true comfort for the first time. This was more than holding my hand. And it *was* the first time someone held me like this. I'd told Sumner I wasn't fragile, but in that moment, I felt as though the slightest breeze could've broken me.

Tension began unwinding within me with each cycle of Sumner's palm. For the first time, I allowed myself to let my guard down, and let him bear more and more of my weight. He never wavered, never shifted; his arms remained steadfast around me. "What if it's better?" Sumner murmured. "That other life."

Could it have been? Was being disowned by my parents better? A life without my Malstoni and Gilfman suits, without my Pierre's avocado toast, without my Chateau Miselle Sauternes wine. A life without a home, without money. Shallow things, perhaps, but would I be happy without them? Could I be? All alone?

The vacuum from the living room kicked off, which only deepened the quiet.

Earlier in the night, when we'd been this close, I'd been about to kiss him. That magical sort of moment was gone now, shattered along with the wine glass out in the living room. But this one... this moment was simultaneously painful and comforting, tightening my chest with tension while also easing it. It made no sense, but it was the first time such a feeling arose within me.

It was comforting because I felt safe, and it was painful because it wouldn't last.

Comforting because it was Sumner. Painful because it was Sumner.

But I wanted it to. I wanted to stay in Sumner's embrace, where I was thawing and sheltered and held tight. "Sumner," I whispered. "I—"

"We've finished cleaning up all the glass," housekeeping spoke through the door.

The sudden voice caused us both to pull away from each other—Sumner released me first, and I forced myself to relinquish the grip on his shirt. "Thank you," he called to them. After a beat, Sumner slid the pad of his thumb along my cheekbone, swiping away the tear that had fallen, the gentleness chasing away its path of frustration. The action caused my throat to tighten, and in spite of the horrible night, a fragment of the fluttering feeling from earlier resurfaced in my chest.

He'd been hired to be my secretary, my babysitter, but over the past few weeks, Sumner had become more important to me than I'd realized. If he hadn't been here tonight, I'd be bearing the aftermath of my father's anger alone. I wouldn't have called housekeeping. I wouldn't have cleaned up my cut. I would've been alone. And he didn't leave when I told him to. He stayed, and he held me tight.

I wondered if my parents realized how much they were giving me when they hired him. How much of a risk it was.

It almost hurt how much my heart swelled with the realization. I didn't like Sumner Pennington as my secretary. I didn't like Sumner Pennington as my friend. I liked him in the way I never, ever should've.

But it was too late.

"You should go, too," I said, though my voice was far more exhausted than it'd been a moment ago. I reached up and withdrew his hand, holding it for a moment before setting it back into his lap. I wondered if he noticed that mine shook. "It's late."

This time, he didn't immediately fire back a retort, refusing to leave. Any argument he had died on his parted lips. I knew I sounded exhausted, but I must've looked it too—my eyes already felt near impossible to keep open.

Sumner didn't fight me this time. With my drained order in the air, he rose to his feet, but instead of turning away, he grabbed my hands and drew me to stand, too. "Let's get you into bed," he said, and led me over. "If you need anything, just call me. Or bang on the wall—I'll know it's not the air conditioner this time."

If I hadn't been so drained, so overwhelmed with my realization, I might've smiled.

Sumner pulled back the duvet so I could crawl under the covers, and he laid them over me when I settled in. I watched as he did so with slow but deliberate movements, and when he was finished tucking me in, he curled his hands into fists at his sides.

"You're a good secretary," I said to him, and even just

laying down, I could feel my eyelids grow heavy. My pulse thudded in my ears. "And a good friend."

A surprised emotion flickered across his gaze. "You're acknowledging it now, huh? That we're friends?"

Now, I did smile. It was small, but it was there. I knew Sumner was looking at it, just as he always did. "Don't get used to it."

His hand coasted from the top of my head to the side, the touch barely there but comforting. The gentleness of it, despite everything, caused the breath in my lungs to quiver. I swallowed hard against the sudden pressure in my throat, shutting my eyes.

At first, I didn't think I'd be able to sleep, that despite my tiredness, the night's events would prove too horrifying to even fathom closing my eyes. But the second I closed them, the numbness from before sunk back in now, teeth sinking into my skin.

Sumner's hand still eased the hair off my face, but darkness swept in fast. *I'm in trouble*, I thought, just before I fell asleep.

Chapter 16

Sender: Aaron Astor
Subject: Touching Base

Hello Margot,
I hope you've been well since my last email. I'm
sure your schedule has kept you busy, as has
mine. Can you believe that in just two weeks, we
will meet face to face? I confess, when I think
about it, I get a little nervous. You'll find me much
less eloquent in person, I'm afraid. I hope you can
forgive me for that.
I've gone ahead and sent my flight information to
your father. I'm looking forward to meeting you.
Please let me know where our meeting location
will be, and I'll be there.

Fondly,
Aaron

*H*aving any meal with my parents was a rare occasion, much less breakfast. My parents were two busy workaholics who prided themselves in having no time for anything outside of their scheduled meetings. Their lunches always related to business. Their dinners, if not also under the pretense of business, were held in the private of their homes with not even their daughter bearing witness. Before today, I had been convinced they didn't eat breakfast.

Perhaps that was why their eight o'clock invitation the next morning had been so jarring.

No, I knew why. It had been the invitation itself.

"Oh, I haven't been here in years," my mother said as she cut into her chive and smoked cheddar pancakes of Pierre's. "The atmosphere is different from how I remember."

My father, who wasn't known for his creative palate, played it safe and ordered the bacon topped porridge with soft-boiled eggs. He stirred his spoon through the mixture before deciding he needed more cracked pepper. "Isn't it?" he asked with obvious disinterest. He hadn't looked at me once.

I'd barely been able to take my eyes off him. I'd thought seeing him again, in the broad daylight, would invoke rage, but it didn't. No fear, either. Instead, all I felt was unease.

My mother hadn't been speaking to either of us in particular, it seemed. She just spoke to hear her own voice. "A bit stuffier, isn't it? Ironic, given the view of the bay, but the dated furniture most certainly isn't helping the atmosphere."

This time, my father simply hummed as he lifted a spoonful of porridge to his mouth. He seemed quite well for how much he drank last night.

My parents sat across from me at the square table at Pierre's, their shoulders near touching from how close the chairs were. We were hours before my avocado toast would be served, so I settled with eggs Benedict with a side of grapefruit, though the dish sat untouched in front of me. It was impossible to have an appetite in their presence, especially since we'd been here thirty minutes and they hadn't announced the reason for the impromptu family meal.

I had a few guesses, though. My father's arrival to my hotel room was one of them.

"How's Ms. Nancy doing?" my mother asked me after she chewed through her bite of pancake.

"She's still kicking."

I'd been watching my mother's expression, and saw her lips quirk unpleasantly before she brought her water to her lips. "Has she mentioned anything about...well, you know."

I played dumb. "Mentioned anything about what?"

My mother cleared her throat once. "Never mind."

Being at Pierre's instead of the country club's dining hall meant Sumner was not present to catch the eye of. The thought of him caused something in my lower stomach to shift.

He'd left me in bed last night, but when I'd woken this morning, I'd been in my suite fully alone. At least, until I'd walked out into the living area and found Sumner asleep on my couch.

He had covered himself with one of my suit jackets I'd left out, his legs curled up to strain to fit on the small sofa. I'd allowed myself only a moment to gaze at him, knowing the soft feeling that'd unfurled in my stomach was too dangerous to let bloom further.

Sumner's lips had been parted as he slept, unflinching even as I laid a throw blanket over him. I should've woken him, but I couldn't. At that moment, I couldn't bring myself to face him.

"We're hosting an event next Saturday evening," my mother told me. "Plan to attend. And, Margot—I heard about your most recent *escapade* at the tennis courts the other day. Things always get back to me, you know, even if they take time."

Honestly, I was shocked it'd taken this long for her to bring it up.

"I'll be sending something to your room. Wear it for the event."

It wasn't the first time my mother attempted to dress me, attempted to steer me clear of my Gilfmans and Malstonis. I wasn't sure why she thought I'd agree this time. "I have enough suits of my own to choose from."

"If you don't wear what I send, I'll cancel your credit card." She tilted her head with almost sadness at the fact that she was proposing such a thing. "Don't make me be the bad guy. Please, just this once, wear what I send you. Maybe then Yvette and Ally will keep their mouths shut, hmm?"

I stared at her, knowing that whatever she wanted to

dress me in would not be something I liked. She must truly be desperate to shut her friends up before word traveled back to the Astors about my *unfemininity*.

"Aren't you going to eat?" my father asked, grumbling around his mouthful of food.

Admittedly, my mouth was practically watering, but I didn't want to wave my white flag yet, not before discerning whether this was their attempt at raising one or sneaking in on a Trojan Horse. "I'm feeling a bit sick," I said, and it wasn't quite a lie.

The next time my mother spoke, I recognized her tone—damage control. It was the tone she'd used when I kissed Sumner the first time we met. "We realized we've been going about this in the wrong way. Forcing you to do something without properly discussing it with you first. Without hearing your concerns and figuring out how to mitigate them."

"Is this about last night?" I asked, eyes flicking toward my father.

Yes, my mother must've known, because she didn't ask me what I was talking about. "It's about us wanting to make sure you're comfortable moving forward."

Proceed with caution, my thoughts were telling me. *This is a trap*. "Comfortable marrying Aaron Astor?"

"Let's hear your concerns," my father said, picking his napkin off his lap and using it to dot at the porridge at the corner of his lips. "You don't love him, is that it?"

"Is love something you're interested in?" my mother asked in a gentler tone, shooting my father a side eye. "Of course, love won't bloom when you haven't interacted before. It comes with time. Time, Margot, *is* something we have. We're not marrying you off next week. We haven't even begun any wedding planning. In fact, as you know, Aaron hasn't even proposed yet."

"You pick my suitor, you plan my wedding," I murmured, dragging my nail over my knuckles now. "Will you pick out my dress as well? What's next, picking in what position we consummate the marriage?"

My father choked on his porridge.

My mother's composure remained. "You will have a say in the planning, of course. I don't know why you think you won't."

"Perhaps because I've had no say until now."

"How haven't you? You agreed to marrying Aaron, have you forgotten? You're the one that requested to meet him privately first; we've arranged that, and he's coming in the day before the wedding to meet you. You were the one that wanted communication beforehand; has he not been emailing you? In what way have you had no say, Margot?"

"You've threatened to disown me if I didn't follow through with the marriage," I said evenly, lifting my chin. "Doesn't exactly sound like I have a choice, now, does it?"

My mother's arm moved under the table, presumedly laying on my father's leg. He'd been sitting forward before he halted. "I'm sorry you're seeing it that way," my mother said, raising her eyebrows in an almost insulted way. "If that's the impression we gave you, we're sorry about that."

The impression they gave. More like they'd said as much to my face. It was clear now, though, that there *was* a motive to this breakfast. A motive that'd led my mother to believe she could lie to my face and get away with it. It wasn't just my father who "gave me that impression"—my mother had said it herself. She was trying to change history, which meant there was a bigger reason for it.

Why butter me up now? Though she tried to play it off, I noticed the tremble in my mother's left hand as it gripped her fork. *What changed?*

"Vivienne Astor was quite smitten with you," she murmured, interrupting my train of thought. "Your father told me how you two chatted all the way to the airport yesterday, and she's even emailed me, asking if she can get on your schedule when she's in town for the wedding. She wants to have a meal with you. She gushed about you, about how you seem to be the perfect fit for her son."

"I am quite impressive," I replied, eyes dropping to my plate. "At least someone noticed."

"Despite the fact that you ruined her ten-thousand-dollar suit," my father muttered around yet another spoonful of porridge. It was as if he thought shoveling it quicker and quicker into his mouth would get this breakfast over with quicker.

My mother gripped his leg again, but I simply tilted my head at him. "If it can be cleaned, it isn't ruined," I said, echoing what Vivienne had said.

My father huffed.

Without looking at me, my mother began sawing into her pancakes, and in the most conversational voice she could muster, she asked, "Did you ever meet Vivienne privately and talk to her, Margot? Before taking her to the airport? When would you have gotten into her good graces?"

It was the puzzle piece I'd been waiting for, searching

for, and I'd been able to find it before my mother. All at once, the anxiety I'd been knotted with loosened, the oxygen in my lungs reappearing. "Ah," I murmured, sitting up in my seat and picking up my silverware. "I see."

"See what?" my father demanded with a frown.

I began cutting into my eggs Benedict, gripping my fork in my right hand. "You're afraid that I could win Vivienne Astor's approval without you." A little smile fluttered to my lips. "You've finally realized I'm the one with the better hand of cards. Took you long enough."

Both of my parents stopped eating, the atmosphere changing in an instant. I chewed with a small smirk on my lips. "Margot," my mother began in a low tone, all pretense of pleasantness fading away. "This isn't a joke."

It reminded me of last night, my father saying I took everything as a joke. "It is a bit funny, though, isn't it?" I asked with a mouthful. The eggs were heavenly, the hollandaise sauce perfect. "When did it occur to you? When Mrs. Astor spoke about how lovely I was? When you realized she might like me more than you? Is that why you stormed in last night, throwing wine glasses around like a caveman? *Hmm*." I picked up my water. "I wonder what the Astors would say about *that* behavior."

My parents had no response. The rush of power I felt due to having the upper hand was almost addicting, making me near dizzy like a glass of wine. Striking them speechless didn't happen often, and I relished in it.

"You were hoping you'd meet Mrs. Astor first and spin the situation in your favor, weren't you?" I went on, stabbing a piece of grapefruit. "A fine line you'd have to balance, making me sound like a rebellious daughter while simultaneously a good wife. How were you going to do it? Say that, while I was a little impulsive, I'd make a nice and *obedient* daughter-in-law?"

Again, their silence was louder than any other sound in the restaurant.

"What are you afraid I'll say?" I asked them. "That you threatened me to marry their son? Manipulated me into doing it? Are you afraid they'll throw your business deal out, and me along with it?"

"We're not afraid," my father said firmly, resuming stirring the remaining spoonfuls of porridge. "Because you won't say a thing."

I raised an eyebrow. "I won't?"

"You know what will happen if this deal falls through."

My smile stretched wider as I laid my fork down on my plate. "You need to pick which angle to attack from. You can't say you never threatened me in one breath and bring up disowning again in the next."

"You won't say anything," my mother cut in, "because we'll give you whatever you want. Because, yes, we do realize we should've listened to you more. That we should've cared more... about what you're feeling."

She had to practically choke the words out, but I would give her points for trying. "So, what? What are you offering me to tell the Astors you're amazing parents?"

"Whatever you want," my mother repeated. "More shares in the business, a larger inheritance, a house of your own while you're waiting on the wedding. We're here to negotiate, Margot."

As I listened to her pitch the monetary things at me, the eggs began to settle wrongly in my stomach. It was their fix for everything, of course, as it was the go-to solution to anyone with a thick wallet. But my parents didn't know me enough to realize I didn't care about a larger inheritance or a fancy house. They didn't know me in the slightest, and that was what turned my stomach. "Father already offered."

My mother looked at my father, and for the first time, I saw disdain in her gaze. "I'm offering in a far more civilized manner than he did."

Not marrying Aaron Astor wasn't an option on their list, of course. That went without saying. "There isn't anything I want from you," I said at last.

My father laid his hand on the table's surface hard enough for the plates to clatter, and to draw the eye of those at surrounding tables. "So, what, you plan to lord it over our heads? We won't have you threatening us, Margot."

"What about fashion school?" My mom spoke the words as if they were game-changing. "Your dream of being a designer in fashion is within reach, Margot. You wanted to go to fashion school? Aaron is your opportunity. Agree to his engagement, without fighting us, and we'll pay your full tuition to return to school."

She thought it was her trump card, but it was the wrong thing to bring up. Her mentioning it took me back to the very day they told me that I wouldn't be going to New York City for fashion, but for business. To the very first day they took any dreams of mine and shattered them. The Margot that would've been tempted by my mother's offer was in shards in my body, too broken up to be properly enticed.

As my father had, I pulled my napkin from my lap and used it to wipe my mouth, trying to wipe away the soured expression. "My, how the tables have turned."

With that, I shoved my chair back and rose to my feet, buttoning my suit jacket as I did so. "Where are you going?" my mother demanded, eyes wide. "We aren't finished discussing—"

"There isn't anything to discuss," I cut her off. "I've always had to wait for you to decide my fate. I suppose it's your turn to wait now, isn't it?"

The server had chosen that moment to come and check on us, stealing my parents' attention just long enough. They scrambled to appear sophisticated and refined while I made my getaway. "The meal was delicious," I said as I slid past the server's shoulder. "Give my compliments to the chef."

I walked out of the front of the restaurant and to the elevators at the back of the building. Staring at the closed metal doors, I waited. My reflection was a blur in the shine, too fuzzy to pick out my expression. I could make out my hands, fists at my sides.

I waited, but neither parent came after me.

They were a book I'd memorized; one I could easily predict. Too many eyes, they must've decided. Tonight, when I was in my hotel room, they could ambush me then. However, the knot of unease from earlier came back with a vengeance, the oxygen thinning as I reached out and pressed the call button.

The elevator doors opened to reveal an empty chamber, and I stepped inside, giving it one last moment. Even now, when they had something to risk, it wasn't worth it to them. I wasn't worth it.

With a sniff, I pressed the button for the lobby, and as the elevator plummeted, my mood fell right along with it. I pulled my phone out and sent a text. *Come pick me up?*

Chapter 17

Sender: Margot Massey
Subject: RE: Touching Base

Hello Aaron,
I have been well, and busy, which I believe is
evident by my lack of response. I've been navigating rough waters on this side of the internet, so
I will not be checking my email often. We'll speak
more in person at the wedding, as you initially
wished.

Safe travels when you do,
M.M.

*I*n the passenger's seat of my car, I typed the
email with no emotion, knowing it probably
read abrupt and blunt, but not bringing myself to care. If
Aaron Astor was wowed by just a glimpse of me, as Vivienne had claimed, I doubted a brusque email would
change his mind.

The seat's heater warmed up the leather, one of the

only comforts. Sumner sat behind the wheel beside me, one hand gripping the leather. We didn't speak; in fact, neither of us said a word since he pulled up at the curb of the hotel and I climbed in. The atmosphere had immediately turned tense when I shut the door and sealed myself in.

For me, it was because in the light of day, my feelings for him felt too obvious. Now that I realized them, I had no idea how to hide them. For him... I didn't know why he was so quiet. It made me nervous.

"Take a right up here," I told him. I sent the email off, and I hated how I waited to hear Sumner's phone chime with a notification. It didn't. "Her driveway is the gravel one between the trees."

Sumner obeyed. The gravel popped over the tires as Sumner eased into Nancy's driveway. He parked in front of her rusting car, shutting off the engine. The air was still and calm, and from here, I could see a small glimpse of the pond in her backyard.

When he didn't open his door, I looked over at him. He, too, stared out the windshield, but almost like he wasn't seeing. I thought about cracking a joke as I normally would, but my mind was blank of anything other than concern. "Are you okay?"

He made a soft affirmative sound, but still didn't meet my gaze. "I'll wait here while you go visit."

When Sumner had picked me up from Pierre's, instead of going back to the hotel, I asked him to take me to Nancy's. It'd been a few days since I visited her, and after everything with my parents, I needed her biting banter to take my mind off it. "You can come in,"

I said softly, squeezing my phone in my lap. "If you want."

"Nancy's was your one safe place. I don't need to come in."

"That was back when you were just my babysitter. Not my friend."

He finally turned to look at me, and it was then that I noticed how *tired* he looked. The sparkle in his blue eyes seemed duller than normal, like an overcast sky instead of a sunny one. *Gloomy*. That was the perfect word for it. Something *was* wrong.

"Nancy would be happy to see you," I added, unable to stop picking at the case of my phone.

Sumner reached over and laid his hand on top of mine, ceasing my movements. His fingers were soft, stilling my own. *I like your hands*, I'd told him the night prior. My cheeks flamed at the confession now, as true as it was. "You're fidgeting."

I wanted to turn my hand over, to press our palms together. I didn't need comforting...but I wanted to hold his hand anyway. "You're on Nancy's property this time, though. Instead of grabbing your bicep this time, she might grab your *tush*."

My lame attempt worked; Sumner's lips tipped up at one corner ever so slightly. A small shot of victory lanced through me at the tiniest crack in his expression. "Yeah, she wasn't too impressed with my bicep, was she?"

That's enough for now, I told myself, and pulled my hand out from his to pop my door open. "But I'm sure she'll have different feelings toward your back end."

As I shut the car door behind me, I realized something

wasn't quite right about the sight of Nancy's driveway, though, and it took me a moment to place what it was.

I frowned. "That's weird."

"What is?"

"No one's here. I thought they said someone was with her at all times." There was no car parked beside Nancy's rusting one. "I swear, if they took her to the country club again..."

Sumner rounded the front of the car. "Let's check it out, hmm?"

The door was unlocked when we got to it, which increased my apprehension. It swung in easily, revealing a silent house. There was no sound of the TV, no sound of someone speaking, and not even the small clattering of Nancy's wheelchair rolling over the hardwood floors.

I didn't want to call out. It seemed wrong to raise my voice in such a silent house.

There was a slippery slope in my mind, and my thoughts began falling down it. *What if something happened? What if whoever was here had to rush her to the hospital? What if no one came today, and she had an accident? What if I find her...?*

Sumner's hand wound around mine, wedging its way through my semi-closed fist and grabbing on. He didn't say anything, but gave me a slow nod. *I'm here*, his expression said. *Whatever we walk in on, I'm here.*

I returned the grip, and despite my anxiety snowballing out of control, that was the tiniest bit of comfort.

Nancy's bedroom door was shut when we got to it, and I raised my fist to the wood. "Nancy?"

No answer. Sumner reached for the knob for me,

positioning himself in front of the door. He glanced at me as if for permission before pushing it open, its hinges creaking as if we were in a scene straight out of a horror movie. The bedroom was empty, though, and I drew in a breath that gave my lungs no relief.

"She isn't supposed to be out of the house so often," I said in a rough voice, fishing my phone out of my pocket. "That's too many days in a row. She knows this. Everyone knows this."

"Maybe she had a doctor's appointment?" he offered as I scrolled through my contacts. I had just found hers when Sumner placed his hands on my shoulders and pivoted me toward the far wall in Nancy's bedroom, facing the window. "Margot. Look."

For a wild moment, I thought I'd look outside and find Nancy lifeless on the ground. The view from her room was half obscured by the giant hedges she had outside, but through the bristles of green, I could see what he made out. Barely. The worry replaced with a fiery annoyance that bloomed in its wake. Letting out a sharp breath, I ducked out of her bedroom and started toward the back door.

And there Nancy was, parked in her wheelchair by the pond, just as she'd been the first day I came to see her. The only difference was that there was no one here at all to make sure she was okay.

"What are you doing?" I demanded as soon as I pulled open the sliding door, voice a snap that carried its way to where she was sitting. I could tell, because she lifted her head ever so slightly. "You know you shouldn't be out here by yourself."

"Oh, I know that, do I?" she asked with a sigh, one that turned into a crackling cough. "Ally went to the store to get more pain relievers. I ran out."

"You shouldn't be outside when no one's home to watch you, Nancy. It's too hot—"

"I'm old. I'm always cold."

"Just because you *feel* cold doesn't mean you can't get heatstroke," I shot back. I came up behind her now, grabbing onto the handlebars of her wheelchair. "Or slide down the slope into the lake."

I tried to tug her, but the wheelchair wouldn't budge. "That's what brakes are for, Margot," she said in a voice that lacked all energy.

"Do you at least have your phone on you if you needed help?" I asked while looking for the clips on her brakes.

"It's in the house."

I closed my eyes. "Nancy—"

"I'm not feeling too good today," she mumbled. "Everything hurts."

With my grip on the handlebars, I stopped. There wasn't a breeze today, so the water in the pond was very still, algae blooming on the stagnant surface. Her words sounded more like a confession than anything else, one I selfishly wished she'd kept to herself. I couldn't see her face, but I could see her hands where they were folded in her lap. The backs of her hands looked bruised, veiny, weak. I was surprised they could wheel her all the way out here. Surely, they wouldn't have been able to wheel her back inside.

It was only then that I noticed that Sumner hadn't

followed me out to the pond, but still lingered by the back door by the house. "If you're not feeling good, why did you come out here?" I asked.

Nancy coughed again, this time the hacking, body-wracking sound only lasted a moment. "I figured if I keel over, might as well have a nice view."

This time, I thought she was joking. The words were designed in her normal ornery way; she was just lacking the strength in her voice. "I suppose you're right," I said, trying to be as lighthearted as I knew she wanted me to be. "Better out here than your bathroom."

"What, you thought I keeled over in the bathroom?"

"I considered it."

She gave a wheezing laugh. "What a sight you'd find. Hopefully I don't go out that way—or, if I do, that Yvette is the one that finds me naked on the floor."

I allowed myself to smile, but it withered away when what we were talking about sank in. The jokes and banter attempted to keep the truth at bay, but the reality broke through as Nancy's laughs turned into labored wheezing. "You can't leave me, you know." I left no room for argument.

It could've been a shift in the wind if there'd been any, but following my words, all lightheartedness between us disappeared. I'd known Nancy Du Pont since before I could remember. As co-founder of the country club, everyone pressed close, but especially my parents. She was the one who allowed them to build the very first Massey Suites on the property beside Alderton-Du Ponte, allowed them to build grand dreams. They paid more attention to currying her favor than they did to me, but it was me that had captured Nancy's attention. At every gala, every fundraiser, every event, she'd make sure she sat beside me. We were a pair of thieves, snickering at everything together.

In my world, there was no life before Nancy Du Pont. I couldn't even begin to picture a world after.

"I can't very well live forever, Margot," she said.

My hands clutched the handles of her wheelchair tighter, the grooves in the plastic handles digging into my skin. "You could try. You're stubborn enough."

"I don't want to be stubborn anymore. I'm...I'm tired, Margot."

There was a ripple in the pond then, as if something stirred just underneath the surface. *I don't want to be standing here anymore*, I thought, feet aching, throat aching. *I wish I hadn't come. I wish I could unhear this.*

Nancy lifted her hand from her lap and held it up to me, wrinkled fingers outstretched to me. I stared at the hand, puzzled about what she was reaching for when it was as if Sumner spoke into my ear. *Comfort.*

I wanted to knock it away. I wanted to laugh at it, because it was an absurd thing, Nancy offering her hand out to me. Nothing about Nancy was warm and fuzzy, but prickly, like a cactus. She didn't offer her hand out without pricking your finger. Her reaching out was a silent admission following the verbal one I'd tried to push past. *I'm not feeling too good today.*

An invisible grip tightened around my throat as I placed my hand in hers.

We stood there for the longest time, watching the water that hardly moved, wondering when it had lost its charm. Neither one of us spoke, and we didn't look at each other. My eyes burned, and the pond grew blurry, but my cheeks remained dry.

I didn't know how much time passed before my phone in my jacket pocket buzzed. I was going to ignore it at first, but eventually ended up pulling it out just to check the notification.

Aaron Astor.

Before even reading the email, I turned around and searched for Sumner on the back deck. He leaned against the side of the railing, not facing us, but it was still clear to see the phone in his hand.

Sender: Aaron Astor
Subject: RE: Touching Base

Hello Margot,
I completely understand what you mean about being busy. I hope nothing too negative is keeping your schedule booked. Perhaps when I come, it will be a nice reprieve—a vacation of sorts—and I can take your mind off anything that's bothering you.
Sending you my best wishes.

Fondly,
Aaron

"Anyone important?" Nancy asked. I hadn't realized she would've been able to hear the notification buzz.

The question of it all continued to swirl in my mind,

but I didn't want to say anything to Nancy. Not yet. "We'll see," I replied to Nancy, all while typing out a quick email in my right hand.

Sender: Margot Massey
Subject: RE: Touching Base

Aaron,
I just realized, I never said where we should meet.
There's a restaurant in Bayview called Pierre's.
I'll attach the address to the email. Wear something red so I can see you.

See you then,
M.M.

Chapter 18

The next week passed by in another slow montage, where I spent my days either walking the grounds with Sumner or going to Nancy's with Sumner. Either way, he and I spent nearly every moment of the day at each other's sides, so much so that when we parted for the day, it felt... strange. Him stopping at his own hotel room door, me continuing to mine. He would wait until I had my own door unlocked before entering his room.

A time or two, we ordered room service and ate it in one of the common rooms. Another time, Sumner even coerced me to play a round of tennis with him on the court, which we were both quite terrible at. I'd thought that the night my father came into my room, and he realized the truth behind the mask of Margot Massey, that our friendship would crumble. It was almost like the opposite happened. It felt like his whole life had begun to revolve around mine—or, rather, my whole life had begun to revolve around Sumner Pennington.

I wasn't sure if I was the sun or he was, but either

way, spending time with him left me warm, an Ice Queen with a melting heart.

A dangerous thing.

I knew I enjoyed spending time with him more than I should've, but I kept it all to myself. The fluttering that appeared each time he touched my hand, the tingling that surfaced whenever his eyes traced my smile. I tucked it all away, relishing it in secret. It was enough, for now.

Saturday night, less than an hour before the event my mother was hosting began, I was having an existential crisis as I stared in the mirror. I'd thrown a slight curl into my hair and applied a bit of makeup, like how I used to do in high school, but it wasn't the hair or makeup that left me feeling like a fish out of water.

It was the white cocktail dress that currently stretched out on my bed. I could see it in the reflection of my bathroom mirror. I'd known my mother was sending an outfit for tonight, and I'd figured it would be a dress, but it wasn't what I'd been expecting. Which, in hindsight, was ridiculous.

It was beautiful, to be fair. It was a Malstoni, with an elastic-shirred bodice that shrunk at the waist to illuminate the wearer's silhouette, with little bows that tied at the top of the thin straps. Up close, the fabric had an almost shimmer to it, one that would look lovely in direct sunlight. I dragged the tip of my finger along it, wondering when my mother would've bought this.

When I put it on, the Malstoni draped over my body perfectly, almost as if my mother had used my exact specifications. The material was soft against my skin and flowing, the hemline falling an inch above my knobby knees, exposing the pale skin of my legs. The white, of course, was to give Aaron "bride vibes," I was sure. It was strappy, showing off my arms, my chest, far, far more skin than I normally ever showed. I craved the comfort of a suit jacket, the security of the fabric.

My phone, which I'd left lying on my bathroom counter, chimed. when I retrieved it, I found a text from my mother, demanding to know where I was.

My stomach clenched, but I smoothed my palm down the front of my dress, imagining that I was smoothing a palm down my nerves. I quickly typed back that I'd retrieve Sumner and then be down.

It was utterly ridiculous how nervous I felt to walk into the event. I didn't care in the slightest if these people thought me ugly, pretty, *whatever*—so why did I feel as though I could've thrown up? All over the beautiful white gown. My mother would've been furious.

Drawing a breath and lifting my chin, I headed out to get my shoes. *You've got this.*

Sumner's room was only a few feet away from my door, and I stopped in front of his. I hadn't seen him since last night, and eagerness bubbled in my chest, so much so that I held myself back for a moment. After Mimosa Morning, my mother had made it clear that instead of trying to multitask for events, Sumner was to be my shadow.

That should've been the case from the start, but I liked that I'd made her regret a decision.

You've got this, I thought again, and knocked.

When the door swept inward, the air in my lungs went with it.

Though I knew Sumner was attending tonight's event and not working it, I'd still been foolishly expecting him to greet me in his Alderton-Du Ponte uniform. There wasn't a trace of teal or khaki in sight, nor any denim. When he opened the door, I found Sumner wearing a deep navy suit. He had the perfect frame to wear a suit but not appear swallowed by or stuffed into it, the dark color flattering his complexion and the golden brown of his hair. Ungelled, as always, and tousled over his forehead. His jacket was unbuttoned, but his white dress shirt underneath was fastened up to his throat, missing its necktie.

Sumner in a suit tailored to him was exactly as I'd always expected: breathtaking.

"I know," Sumner said with a smug air, eyes closed as he grabbed his suit jacket by the lapels and giving the fabric a tug. "Don't I clean up—" He'd opened his eyes, and when he saw me, his words cut off.

"You clean up very well," I agreed.

But Sumner didn't look as though he heard me. His lips parted as his eyes roamed from my face down my body, somewhat mimicking the roving gaze he'd had the night he found me in my nightgown. This time, though, instead of looking away in embarrassment—and flushing —Sumner swallowed hard. I nearly shivered under his stare, the intensity of it enough to feel like a physical touch on my skin.

"What are you wearing?" he demanded, almost sounding accusatory.

I lifted my chin. "What does it look like?"

"Why aren't you wearing a suit?"

"What's wrong with the dress?"

"It's not you."

Of course it wasn't. It wasn't as if it mattered anyway, though, whether or not I was myself for one night. "My mom wanted me to wear it." I ran my fingers over the bumps in the dress's fabric, the material soft. It still almost felt like I wasn't wearing anything, though, like I was going out of the house half dressed. "Mrs. Astor wore a dress the last day I saw her. Even though it wasn't another suit, I thought she looked stylish. Maybe it's okay to wear both. Dresses can be pretty, too."

Sumner didn't reply, still taken aback by my appearance.

"Unless you think I look hideous."

"You look beautiful." He spoke without hesitation, the words almost compelled out of him. An emotion I didn't recognize knotted in his eyes, and he swallowed hard. "Just like you always do."

The compliment wasn't anything world-shaking, but it still warmed me. I had to stop looking at him, stop thinking about how he looked with the expensive fabric stretching over his body. His golden hair was a bit more styled than usual, but he hadn't seemed to have mastered gelling it back, because some pieces fell over his forehead and into his eyes.

"You're missing your tie," I mused with a smile I couldn't fight; I could feel it light up my face, all because of the man before me.

"I was in the middle of picking one out when you knocked." Sumner shook his head, almost as if to clear it.

"Your mother brought over a whole suitcase full. It's something I would've expected you to do, honestly."

A suitcase full of neckties? "This I have to see," I said, brushing past Sumner and entering his hotel room without further permission.

"Wait," he called after me, but didn't attempt to stop me.

Sumner's hotel room was different from mine. Though his was a suite, it was more of a studio style, with only a half wall separating his bedroom from the rest of the space. His bed, though, mirrored mine. No wonder his alarm was loud every morning; our beds were practically back-to-back. From here, I could see the white hotel stock duvet laid neatly over his bed, but in a way that it was clear he'd done it himself, not housekeeping. His seating area looked much like mine, though with less square footage.

The room itself was clean and completely lacking personal touch, but then again, did Sumner really have time to decorate, what with playing cater waiter/secretary/babysitter?

Not that I had room to talk. The most I'd decorated is my closet.

Though his one point of decoration was a suitcase open on his glass coffee table. "She sent this today?" I asked as I stepped closer to it.

"Yesterday."

The suitcase was more of a carry-on size, but it was indeed filled with rolled neckties. They were all Gilfman, judging by the faint motif most of them sported in the fabric. Some were a flat color, some were silk, and there was even one from their limited watercolor-inspired collection they did a few years ago.

"My mother is responsible for dressing you?" I asked, trying to hide my interest among the neckties.

"To a point. When she hired me, she told me I'd need at least one suit for situations like this, but left me to pick it out on my own."

It seemed like quite the present, luggage full of name brand neckties. Their cheaper ones could easily go for a hundred dollars a pop, and for her to gift at least twenty of them to a staff member was beyond strange. My suspicion of it all prickled once more.

"And you got a suit tailored without me?" I picked up a burgundy silk tie with a paisley motif that was only a shade or two lighter than the fabric itself. I admired its sheen in the hotel room light, lifting to examine it against Sumner's suit. "Me, the suit queen?"

"Because I thought about this moment." When I looked past the necktie to Sumner's eyes, I found them shimmering just as delicately as the fabric. "I wanted to surprise you."

I leaned forward and reached the silk tie around his neck, thinking about which I would've preferred. As fun as it might've been to see Sumner try on different fabrics and silhouettes, I preferred this moment, too. "I'm probably the only person who would be pleasantly surprised by a suit."

Sumner held perfectly still. "You're the only person I'd want to surprise with one."

My hold on the tie fumbled.

Sumner looked down at me as my fingers knotted his

tie, though my actions were slow. Something about the way the silk fabric glided in my fingertips seemed delicate...intimate. Maybe it was how closely I stood to him; close enough to smell the aftershave that seeped from his warm skin. I held the front of his tie loosely between my fingers, passing the wide end through the knot I created. My pulse stirred as I tightened the knot, easing it up toward the collar of his shirt and adjusting the length. I smoothed the dark tie flat down the front of his shirt, trying to ignore the firmness of his chest beneath the fabric.

I swallowed, hoping it was only obvious to me.

Nancy would laugh. Of course, tying a necktie was a turn on.

"Lovely," I said as I folded the collar of his shirt down, making sure it was symmetrical. My knuckles brushed his throat. "Don't let anyone whisk you away tonight—and trust me, with how expensive you look, someone will try. More than likely, Ms. Jennings. You belong to me."

Sumner drew in a quiet breath. "Yes, ma'am."

Wouldn't it be a dream? I found myself thinking as my hands lingered on his collar. I pictured laying them flat on his shoulders, to feel their curve that was hidden beneath the thin material of his dress shirt. I pictured my hands moving from his shoulders to underneath his suit jacket. I pictured taking that half step closer. *Wouldn't just be lovely like champagne?*

If he was Aaron Astor?

It was a thought I hadn't been able to rid myself of, even as I tried. The possibility of it, while outlandish, was too sweet. It was a dream I let myself envision, only briefly. If Sumner was Aaron, it would mean that he came here intentionally to get to know me. He asked my parents to get close to me, learned information about me, tried to sway me toward him. On one hand, it should've felt like a betrayal, sneaking close under the disguise of someone else.

But, in that dream, I didn't feel betrayed at all. If Sumner was Aaron...I wouldn't have been hurt. I would've been *relieved*.

I dropped my hands, stepping back.

Sumner offered his arm to me. "Shall we?"

It was a fairytale moment, a princess in a beautiful gown entering a social event on the arm of a prince. I felt like an imposter, wearing the white dress, thinking the thoughts I was, but I allowed myself to think them anyway. For tonight, just this once, and I would take it to my grave, but I'd let myself feel like a princess with Prince Charming.

Curving my hand on the inside of his jacket sleeve, I held on, trying to ignore the flutter that tickled my chest once more. "We shall."

You can do this, I told myself as we stepped into the hallway and headed for the elevator doors. My footsteps in my sandals only clacked a little, like little ticks of a clock. *You can do this. You never care what anyone else thinks of you.*

My stomach dipped as the elevator doors slipped shut, a shiver working its way across my skin. Without thinking, I reached out and took ahold of Sumner's hand, which hung at his side, pressing my palm against his and wrapping my fingers tight.

Sumner lifted his chin ever so slightly, but didn't look down at me. Instead, he just returned the grip. *Comfort.* "What is this event for again?" Sumner asked as the elevator descended. Our reflections were thrown around the space, all glitz and glamour.

It was hard to keep my eyes off his figure, but I forced myself to look at my own. "I don't remember." I wasn't even sure my mother even told me. "It was last minute. It wasn't on the social calendar at the beginning of the month, I didn't think." Which was strange, given the fact that Annalise's wedding was next weekend. I would've thought they'd keep from booking anything last minute.

Sumner made a soft humming noise. Both of our hands were back at our sides when the elevator doors opened, and good thing too, because when they parted, they revealed my mother waiting on the other side. She'd been poised toward the elevator, but slouched back onto her heels as if who'd she'd been expecting hadn't been on.

And then she blinked. "*Margot,*" she gasped in realization, her eyes widening near saucer wide. "Oh, my heavens, you look *beautiful*! More than I'd imagined!"

I looked down at the way the dress fell against my figure, down at my Claire-Haute sandals. In a pathetic way, my mother's compliment affected me more than I should've let it. I couldn't remember the last time she'd called me beautiful, and even though I was wearing a face full of makeup, and even though she only wanted me to be beautiful to impress a man, it still felt good.

And I hated that it felt good.

She fluffed her own hand down the front of my dress, smoothing out a nonexistent wrinkle. She then went from studying the dress to the jewelry that draped against my throat. One dipped down into the dress's neckline, drawing the eye to my cleavage. Satisfied with that, she looked to my earrings, and then to my hair. Every inch of me was analyzed, scrutinized, and ultimately passed her test. "Margot," she whispered, speaking to me without looking in my eyes. "You are very beautiful."

The compliment once more felt like a balm to something prickly inside me, even though I knew her motives behind it. "The women at the country club wouldn't recognize me."

"Of course not." My mother gently brought a section of my curls around my shoulder, laying them delicately against my collarbone. "You're dressing like a woman for once."

The comforting balm became like ice.

"And you, Sumner—very handsome." My mother's eyes, though, flicked to Sumner, a slight curve to them. "The suit is very striking on you."

His expression was unreadable. "Thank you."

"Well, come on, come on!" My mother grabbed my hand, and I couldn't help but wonder when the last time that happened. "Let's go show you off."

I pulled my hand from her grip, though, and settled back onto Sumner's arm. I felt far more comfortable with his touch than hers. He settled into the embrace easily, tucking my arm close against his side. My mother didn't seem too bothered by my brush off, but instead whisked us toward the country club.

I had to hold myself back from trembling as we walked nearer and nearer to the entrance of the grand ballroom. I could already hear the music trickle from the open doors, the soft and beautiful piano that people were no doubt dancing and chattering to.

My mother scanned the grand ballroom before setting off somewhere, but I didn't see where she'd set her sights. I was far too concerned with staring at my shoes.

"Clothes don't change who you are," Sumner reminded me softly, and with his other hand, he patted where I gripped his jacket sleeve. "You're still you, Margot Massey."

"I don't feel like me."

"Well, you look like you. Just you in a dress."

"Margot?" Mrs. Holland exclaimed as she passed by the ballroom's doorway, stumbling upon me first with a champagne glass in her hands. A spark of unease shot through my chest. "Oh, why don't you look lovely! Wow. I wouldn't have recognized you if it weren't for your gigolo there." She looked at him with flirty eyes.

For once, I had no idea what to say in response. It was as if my confidence were embedded in the fabric of my suits, in the stitching—without it, I was at a loss.

Sumner chuckled good-naturedly at her tipsy joke. "Good to see you again."

Mrs. Holland flushed, tickled with the attention. "Don't stand in the doorway," she insisted, urging us forward with her free hand. "Come, come. You'll want to come in, trust me."

Sumner took a small step forward, allowing me to decide if I'd continue or book it back into the safety of the hallway. I allowed him to lure me inside, a death grip on his arm. It was almost comical how sick to my stomach I felt over the thought of walking in wearing a dress. I was too busy considering my knobby knees, my pale skin.

"Everyone's staring at me," I whispered to Sumner, the anxiety behind my ribs tightening.

He leaned in, his lips brushing the hair above my ear. "Maybe they're staring at me."

I turned to look at him, to give a tense laugh, but he hadn't leaned back, and I'd brought my face directly to his. Only an inch separated our mouths for a moment, energy causing me to still.

Until Sumner straightened, pulling away with a subtle clearing of his throat. "Want to dance?"

"No." I didn't even hesitate. "I want champagne."

"Come on, dance with me first and fulfill my Prince Charming dreams before I turn back into a pumpkin."

"The *carriage* turns back into a pumpkin," I said, trying to ignore the fact that we'd shared the same thought, Sumner being a prince. My prince. I tried to shove the thought down. "You'd turn back into a cater waiter."

"The horror." Sumner picked up my hand, though, his long fingers curving underneath mine. "Dance with me before it happens."

My feet instinctively dug in at first, sandals slipping over the shiny ground. "I've attended hundreds of these events, and I've never once danced at them," I said almost desperately as he led me out onto the floor, pulse fluttering. *Faceless, become faceless,* I willed the crowd, but I couldn't quite seem to dodge the eyes. "It—I won't be any good."

"Well, I've attended two of these Alderton-Du Ponte

events now, and I, too, have never danced at them." Sumner's teasing demeanor was designed to calm me, I knew, just from the way he peered into my eyes. His blue irises were an almost ooey-gooey sort of color, pupils large. "Just focus on me."

I grumbled, but still allowed him to pick up my left hand and lay it on his shoulder, and allowed him to pick my right hand up. His other hand slid around my body and rested at a respectable spot on my lower back.

Though Sumner didn't know how to hold a serving tray, he knew the dancing form for an event like this.

His hand pressed me a bit closer, and from there, he took a step, leading me into it. "Not too bad," he murmured with a smug smile, gazing down at me. "Not terrible."

I choked on a laugh, because even though the nerves were still there, being in Sumner's arms felt like a safe haven, a light that chased away the darkness. We'd formed our own little bubble, and I focused on the way he looked at me. I couldn't have cared less about the people around us, about where my mother ran off to. Nothing but the way we seemed to move together like magnets.

I'd rather do things I don't want to than find out what that other life looks like, I'd said to Sumner the night my father had come into my room.

What if it's better? Sumner had asked. *That other life.*

What if this was what that other life looked like? Sumner Pennington, in all his golden-haired, puppy dog-eyed glory, on the other side. His hand in mine as if it'd always belonged there, as if it were the other half of my own.

Or what if...what if he belonged in *this* life? What if the universe, just this once, let me have both worlds? I would've given anything for my conspiracy theory to be right, that the man I looked up to now was, by some miracle, Aaron Astor. In that moment, I would've given anything for Sumner Pennington. Given up anything.

I looked up at him, and for one final, foolish moment as our eyes locked, I hoped. I hoped that the wish turned out to be true, that maybe, just maybe, the universe would tip its hat in my favor just this once. I'd done everything requested of me, and this was going to be my ultimate reward.

I lingered in the arms of the golden-haired man, relishing in that foolish hope for one last time.

Sumner's hand around the small of my back pressed me just a fraction of an inch closer, and a delirious sort of heat swamped my skin. *Wouldn't it be just champagne?*

A new voice broke my thoughts apart, chasing away the dream with reality. "Mind if I cut in?"

I didn't recognize the male voice, and when I looked over, I didn't recognize his face, either. The man seemed in his mid-to-late twenties, dark hair was cut short off the back of his neck, styled and kept out of his eyes. He wasn't ugly, but he wasn't devastatingly handsome either. Just...average, with a wide nose and a curved jaw.

His megawatt smile was full of pearly white teeth, as if waiting for me to jump into his arms. "I do mind, actually," I replied, tightening my grip on Sumner's hand and shoulder. It was then that I realized he'd gone stiff.

Sumner's voice was low. "Margot—"

"I don't make a habit of dancing with strangers." Or

dancing period. I was relieved, though, that some of my old attitude surfaced at the audacity of some random man. It left me feeling a bit more grounded in Sumner's arms, at least until they fell away from me. I looked at him, finding his face pale.

"Sorry, sorry, I guess I am being rude," the man said a little awkwardly, and when he brushed his hands down the front of his suit jacket, I saw they were shaking. "Rude of me to just waltz up to you and assume you'd know who I was. Silly of me."

Unease seeped further into me, a sinking feeling weighing me down. "Should I know you?" I asked, still holding onto Sumner's shoulder despite his own hands now hanging at his sides.

I did not want to hear the answer. My gut knew before I did.

The stranger outstretched his hand to mine, and as I looked at it, the first thing I noticed was how small it was compared to Sumner's. It looked even smaller than mine. "It's a pleasure to finally meet you, Margot," he said with that same megawatt smile, leaning in. "I'm Aaron Astor. Your fiancé."

And just like that, reality shattered that hope around me like glass.

Chapter 19

I thought I heard him wrong. That there was no way the man before me said any of the words that came from his mouth. *I'm Aaron Astor. Your fiancé.*

"Or, well, not fiancé yet," the man—Aaron Astor—fumbled in his recovery, cheeks flushing as he dropped his untouched hand. "That—that was a slip of the tongue, forgive me."

I blinked at him as if he spoke another language, the words registering, but distantly. Instead, reality took more importance. I could've laughed, because this obviously wasn't a random impromptu event, like my mother had made it sound. No wonder there weren't many people in attendance—she'd no doubt culled the guest list, keeping it to the professional ones in her friend group. It was planned, all for Aaron Astor's arrival.

Our meeting wasn't supposed to happen yet. It wasn't supposed to be until next week, the day before the wedding. I hadn't prepared for it yet. But that was why my mother laid out a dress for me. A *white* dress. She'd laid the trap, such a painfully obvious one, and I all but waltzed into it. Her gushing over my appearance hadn't been because her friends would see me, but because Aaron Astor would.

My mother made that even clearer when she joined our bubble. "Oh, good, you've found Margot!" she said with an exuberant voice I hadn't heard her use in a while. "Doesn't she look absolutely stunning, Aaron?"

"Indeed," he returned, beaming that pearly smile now at my mother. "I was told she had an affinity for suits."

"Oh, well, here and there, I suppose," my mother tried to cover. "But she knows when to dress up."

They were speaking about me as if I wasn't standing two feet from them, eyeing me like a painting that hung in a museum. It only heightened the urge to laugh, and the one thing keeping me from doing so was how sick to my stomach I felt.

"I will say, Margot," Aaron said, returning his attention to me. His eyes roamed me in a polite way, but I was suddenly all too aware of how much of my skin was on display in this dress. "You're much more beautiful up close than you were from afar."

If I hadn't been fully knocked off-kilter, I might've had a comeback for his words. Here or California, there was no escaping the flowery, empty compliments that came with the rich. But I stood there staring at the man who'd been an ominous figure in my head for the past few months, feeling as though I'd woken from a dream.

Aaron's eyes slid from me, who struggled to find her words, to the equally silent man at my side. "Hopefully you aren't her date," Aaron said to Sumner in greeting, his voice a forced sort of light; I could hear it immediately. Aaron stepped closer, offering his hand out once more.

"That would make things very awkward. Good to meet you."

It seemed to take a whole beat for Sumner to draw his hand from his side and take Aaron's—enough of a hesitation that I caught it. Sumner didn't look him in the eye, but inclined his head. "Sumner Pennington."

The sound of his voice caused something in me to tighten. Sumner... There was no way he hadn't known, right? Thinking back, it was obvious. My mother gifted him a suitcase of ties. Told him to get a suit tailored. Asked him to keep me on my best behavior for tonight. He'd known, and he'd let me walk into the ambush.

My mother looked between the two of them, clearly wondering if Sumner's presence was preventing the sparks from flying. Everyone in our group—in the room— seemed to await my move. *Would she lash out with her impulsivity and ruin everything?* my mother's eyes seemed to question as she watched me. *Or will she step into the role I've lured her into?*

Looking at Aaron now caused something in me to flatline. It was that *what if* bubble—it had burst apart the second he'd spoken his name, and all the barest hints of hope withered with those pieces.

I gave one more humorless chuckle before lifting my chin. "Go fetch me a drink, would you?" I told Sumner while barely turning my head toward him. My voice was bitter, the way it would've been if I'd spoken to any other staff member. I focused on Aaron, my full attention on his ordinary face. "You asked to dance?"

Aaron resumed his beam, offering his hand once more to me. This time, with no hesitation, I took it.

He, thankfully, led us away from my mother and Sumner, toward the middle of the dancefloor instead of the outskirts. As I left them behind, I built a wall around me, lifting my chin and squaring my shoulders. This was no different than any of the other times I went to a gala or a dinner. Aaron Astor was just another person in the realm I wanted nothing to do with. *I can do this.*

He halted us just underneath the grand chandelier light, picking my body into his arms much like Sumner had, with his hand at my back and his other grasping mine.

"You truly are more stunning in person," he gushed. Close to him like this, I could smell his spiced cologne, a scent that didn't seem to mix well with his body's natural odor. At least, it didn't interest me. Not in the way—*stop.* "The first time I saw you, it was only a glimpse, but to see you now—the glimpse didn't do you justice, darling."

Darling. The endearment made him sound old. Seeing Aaron in real life, putting a face to the elusive creature who'd been ruling my mind, somewhat took away the fear of it all. He certainly wasn't ugly. Certainly, wasn't anything like how I imagined him. He at least had hair. He was shorter, maybe an inch shorter than me, but nothing about him was horrifying enough to warrant removing all traces of himself from the internet. "I do look better under chandelier light," I said graciously.

"Indeed." His eyes did a slow cast back to where we'd walked over from, though I refused to follow. "I really do hope that man wasn't your date."

"And why's that?"

"He's quite handsome." He hadn't managed to keep the worry from his voice.

It was interesting to see a man as rich and affluential as Aaron Astor, with pockets as deep as the Pacific Ocean, be intimated by someone like Sumner, who bought his shirts from the local supermarket. "He's my secretary."

"Interesting," he mused instead, seeming to absorb the words and mull them over in his head. "So, are you close with him?"

"Why?"

"Just trying to see how I should go about this, that's all. If I have any competition."

I readjusted my fingers and how they laid on his stiff suit jacket. The embrace alone was far different than it'd been with Sumner. We stood close, but no magnetic energy lured me in nearer. "You think you have to compete with my *staff*?"

"Only him." Aaron gave a small, almost boyish smile. "Though if all your staff is as handsome as he is, I'm in trouble."

A corner of my lips rose, and instead of fighting it back, I allowed the small smile to remain. "A little competition is healthy now and again, isn't it?"

Aaron's dark eyes dipped to my mouth. "And here I heard it was difficult to make you smile."

"Who told you that? My mother?" It didn't quite seem like an endearing quality for her to brag about.

Aaron gave his head a small shake. "I have little birds everywhere."

He'd said it in a playful tone, but it left me irritatingly curious over who had been telling him things about me.

What sort of gossip chain reached him all the way into California? And then I realized. "Annalise?"

"You're a quick one," he said with affection. "Yes, I know her through her fiancé. I'm sure I don't have to remind you, but he and I have been friends since childhood. I'm his best man. I may have asked her a thing or two about you. I hope that doesn't bother you too much."

I didn't blame him for trying to dig up information on me, but what did bother me were the unknowns of what Annalise could've told him. She didn't know me well, but her judgment of me was like everyone else at Alderton-Du Ponte: nearsighted. They only saw what they wanted, never bothering to look further.

I didn't want to care about what Aaron Astor thought about me, but the curiosity needled me anyway.

"I'd love to get lunch with you," Aaron said as he dipped his head closer to me, his words tickling the skin of my throat. "Learn more about each other, talk about... our future. I hope I didn't scare you off by calling myself your fiancé prematurely. I guess I was just hoping... we'd end up there."

Straightforward. I almost said as much when a flute of champagne appeared at my side, and I traced the bubbling glass up to find Sumner holding it out to me. His blue eyes focused solely on me, almost as if I wasn't in Aaron's arms at all. "Your champagne."

I dropped Aaron's hand mid-sway, extracting myself from his loose grip. "Would you excuse me?" I asked him as I took the champagne flute. "I'm going to get a bit of air."

"I could come with you—"

I gave him a smile. "Let my mother talk your ear off. I won't be long."

When I glanced over, Sumner was looking at my lips and the way they tipped up, his own expression complicated and hard to read in the chandelier light. I didn't examine it too closely.

When I headed toward the ballroom's doors, I was relieved to hear Sumner's footfalls following behind me. We both got out into the hallway, and without a word, I grabbed Sumner by the lapel and dragged him down the hall. As I walked, I tipped my champagne flute to my lips and drained the alcohol in three drinks, the bubbles burning the back of my throat.

"Margot," he said as he stumbled along. "Where are you—"

A girl in her late twenties manned the coat check counter and blinked at me when I approached the desk. "Miss Margot, can I—"

I shoved my empty champagne flute into her hand, and she fumbled to catch it before it slipped from her grip. "Excuse us."

"No one's supposed to go back there—" the girl didn't reach out to stop me, but cut herself off when I took no care in brushing past her, dragging Sumner into the large closet, where coat hangers lined the walls. Most hung empty—the burgeoning summer heat didn't leave one needing a coat—and gave the room an empty feel.

I let go of Sumner's lapel and turned on him, leveling him with a stare. "Did you know?" I demanded in a low voice, the words a tremble. "Did you know Aaron Astor would be here?"

Sumner slowly shook his head, but he wouldn't look me in the eye. "I didn't know."

"You expect me to believe that? That my parents didn't warn you?" The frustration I'd shoved down earlier began fighting its way back to the surface. "You and my mother knew that if you told me, I'd—I'd sabotage it. I'd run away, I'd do something—"

"No. You would've *wanted* to, but you wouldn't have." Sumner's chest gave a shaky rise and fall. "You said so yourself you never wanted to find out what a life outside of your parents' wishes was like. You wouldn't have wanted to come down here and meet him, but you would've anyway."

My fingers curled into a fist at my side at how factually he spoke, and my resentment brewing only grew because he was most likely right. But he didn't need to point it out. "You knew," I repeated. "And you didn't tell me."

"I didn't know, Margot. If I had—" He stopped.

"If you had?"

In a sort of resigned way, Sumner lifted his gaze from the floor to mine. "I would've told you."

I wanted to latch onto anger, since it was a safer emotion to feel, but the way he stared at me with his sad puppy-dog eyes, I couldn't hold on to it. It hadn't been that long since our last argument, but Sumner was vastly different now than he'd been then, kneeling on my floor with eyes snapping his own fire. He looked uncomfortable, as if being in this closet—at Alderton-Du Ponte—was the last place he wanted to be.

I stood still, trying to pinpoint and lock down the

emotion in my chest. The pressure was suffocating, like how it felt when I wore a vest tailored too tightly, but the chiffon fabric of my dress wasn't restricting now.

"You weren't Aaron," I said.

I didn't want to look at Sumner to perceive his reaction, but I couldn't turn away. Confusion swamped his already tense expression. "What do you mean?" Then the realization struck, because shock flooded in. "I—I told you I wasn't. This whole time—this *entire* time, you thought I was Aaron?"

"No." And it was honest for the most part. The errant thought had popped up now and then, like a mosquito buzzing around me, but my rationale had always been quick to chase it off. I looked into Sumner's eyes, the next words slipping out. "But I was hoping you were."

Sumner's lips parted as he drew in a silent breath. The country club's air conditioning was on, but not high enough—my skin seemed warm, too warm, as if I was growing feverish. I *felt* feverish. My thoughts weren't clear in the slightest. Sumner's expression was far too guarded for me to tell if the confession made him uncomfortable. His eyes, though, were still very wide. "Margot—"

"It's just me, right?" I asked, my soft words threatening to get lost in the space between us. I thought about it all in a sort of clinical way, with no emotions attached other than curiosity. My stomach felt tight, as if someone reached into me and squeezed, but that was it. Just curiosity. "That feels this way?"

After meeting with Aaron, it felt important to clarify. The newfound festering collection of emotions that bloomed each time Sumner smiled at me, the ones that'd been ever-present in the seconds before Aaron came up to us. The look of fascination that always seemed to grace his expression whenever I laughed. The charged energy that ran in a gentle current underneath my skin, a TV turned on but muted. No sound, just feeling.

Sumner didn't answer, but he closed his eyes. It gave me another selfish moment to study him, the slight curve to his shoulders as his head ducked down. He'd been all smiles moments before, on the dancefloor, almost awestruck in the way he looked at me.

Was this change because of Aaron's sudden appearance?

By some chance, was it *not* just me who felt this way?

With his eyes closed, Sumner didn't see me take a step toward him. "I liked dancing with you more."

He let out a slow breath. "Margot."

I took another step. "I like the way you smell more."

"*Margot.*"

"I like your hands more."

Sumner's eyes popped open, and he found me standing before him. He didn't react at first, nothing beyond repeating my name in quiet desperation. "Margot."

Much like I'd grappled to hang onto my anger to not entertain the sort of helpless feeling, Sumner saying my name sounded like he, too, was wrestling with an emotion. A warning, whether to me or himself.

"I need to know." I scanned his face as if the answer would be there. My eyes traced the freckles underneath his right eye, the curve of his cheek, down to the rosy bow of his upper lip. "I thought I didn't need to—I've *thought* it for a while—but in there, I realized...I can't *not* know."

With Sumner, I'd never been nervous. Even from the beginning. It was almost as if Sumner was a long-lost friend, and we fell into a routine. In the weeks we'd spent nearly every day together, his presence had become somewhat of a haven to me, a vacation house, a place I could go when I wanted to feel like myself. I'd smiled more in the past few weeks than I had in years. He proved to me, time and time again, that there was no reason to worry about how I seemed or how I acted around him. *There's nothing wrong with you.* That sort of acceptance was new for me, and it'd undone all the hard strides I'd made over the years of hardening my heart. I couldn't tell if it meant more.

I needed to know.

A pained sort of wariness filled Sumner's eyes and stormed the blue further. "Know *what?*"

Without an ounce of warning or hesitation, I reached up and laid my hands on either side of Sumner's neck, using the touch to draw his mouth to mine.

Since it'd happened, I'd thought about my first kiss with Sumner plenty, though my mind could never truly provide a satisfying memory of it. I'd been too preoccupied, too busy gloating over the shock of it all, to really put it to memory. I made sure not to make the same mistake now.

My lips took Sumner's without hesitation, and the second they connected, something burst through me. I'd thought my skin was warm, but Sumner's throat was blazing with heat, warming my fingers as I held him to me. I felt girlish for the first time in my life as I rose to my tiptoes, kissing him in the increasingly stuffy air of the closet. With my eyes closed, I relished in the moment.

Sumner's hands reached up and grasped my wrists, but hesitated there, not pulling me closer nor pushing me away. His lips were soft against mine, yielding, and through the blood pounding in my head and in my heart, I finally realized—Sumner was not kissing me back.

I jerked my head away, an almost painful pins-and-needles feeling crawling along the back of my neck. I waited for a moment, as if expecting him to chase the distance I created and initiate the kiss himself this time, but he didn't. Instead, Sumner just swallowed hard and continued to hold my wrists, not quite looking at me. "You —you don't like me, Margot," he whispered, breathless. "I don't belong in your world."

"I like that you don't belong in my world." My voice was softer than I meant for it to be. "I don't belong in it either."

"But you—you *do*." Sumner pinched his eyes shut as he took a step back from me, releasing my hands. He shook his head a little, as if attempting to clear it. "You're *engaged*—or about to be. Aaron—he's going to propose."

"What if I didn't accept?"

"Margot, what—" He cut himself off to run a hand across his features, at a total loss. "What are you talking about? You said yourself that refusing Aaron meant your parents would throw you out. I don't—I don't understand you right now." When he lowered his hands, he looked so stressed, regarding me. "Was it that bad? In there, with Aaron? Did he say something? Do something?"

"No," I answered immediately. "I could settle for Aaron Astor. It would be easy. Settling for him would mean my parents' approval, the approval from everyone in the club; it would mean an easy rest of my life. I'd never have to give up my Malstoni or my Gilfman or my wine. I'd be comfortable...but you wouldn't be there."

I might not have fought for my choices before, never considered my happiness before. I'd sat back, allowed the world to make the decisions for me, and complained about them each time. Sumner was right; I couldn't be a martyr about my life when I allowed others to direct it for me. I'd take decisions into my own hands now, and wait for whatever consequences that came with it. I wouldn't roll over anymore. If I got bit, so be it.

"You said so yourself," I murmured, "that choosing happiness is better."

"Your parents," Sumner began, picking another angle. "The reason they chose me to watch you was to keep this from happening. They—"

"This isn't about my parents." I could deal with Sumner not liking me romantically, but I couldn't take it if this was yet another thing that my parents could ruin. Their claws sunk deep into every single aspect of my life, it seemed.

"It *is*, though," he said in a small, exasperated, a crease deep between his eyebrows. "They hired me to keep you out of trouble. They *trusted* me. I can't just—I *can't*. I may not belong in your world, but Aaron does. He's a better fit for you."

"I don't want Aaron," I said simply. "I want you."

The words stunned him for a moment, and in that

moment, the warmth that crossed over his eyes came in a fleeting flash. If I hadn't been watching, I would've missed it entirely. I'd think about that warmth later and convince myself that I'd imagined it, misinterpreted it, but for that brief moment, I thought he was about to say what I wanted to hear.

"Margot." Sumner let out a breath, and when he spoke again, there was no budging in his voice. "You don't like me. You just like the way I make you feel."

"Isn't...isn't that why you like someone?" I blinked, not understanding. "Because you like how they make you feel?"

"You're forgetting." He looked at me with a flat expression, wiping away the wariness and the confusion, giving me a poker face that would've made anyone in the ballroom jealous. "I was only hired to make you feel that way."

I let out a soft breath, as if he'd knocked it out of me. My fingers instinctively went to my torso, as if to fiddle with my vest's buttons, but it found nothing but the chiffon material of the cocktail dress. I'd walked up to that precipice of the unknown, just nearly about to jump off, but his words yanked me back. It was such an obvious truth that it almost felt like a slap to the face when Sumner said it.

But he wasn't finished. "Your parents hired me to keep you from doing anything impulsive. I was paid to be at your side. I wouldn't be here...if not for that."

Sumner's tone wasn't harsh, but it left no room for misunderstanding. My parents had hired him to be my secretary; that was why Sumner stuck around. Not because he liked me, not because he craved my company, but because he was getting paid.

"You wanted to be my friend instead of just my secretary," I pointed out slowly, my voice small. "I thought—"

"I thought it'd make it easier on the both of us. Not because... Not because I had feelings for you."

Having to follow around a rich girl because she can't keep herself from causing trouble isn't really ideal.

I couldn't even be angry. Sumner was right; I'd just forgotten. It was just that, somewhere along the way, I thought it'd changed for him just as it'd changed for me. That him holding my hand, calling me pretty, and giving awestruck expression at my smiles were more than a hired reaction. That him holding me while I cried, while I let my guard down, had been more than just simple empathy.

I felt like an idiot. Margot Massey wasn't the sweet and bubbly woman men fell for—there was no ounce of bubbliness in me. I was bitter and cruel and had more baggage than any one person would bother dealing with. It wasn't that Aaron was a better fit for me, but rather that *I* wasn't a good fit for *Sumner*. I knew it, and he knew it. I couldn't blame him at all.

Along with embarrassment, something ickier worked its way up my throat, something darker. I took a step back from him. "Well, this is awkward, then."

Sumner inhaled like he was about to speak, but stopped short. I wondered if he thought I'd fight him more on it, to challenge him and his nonexistent feelings. I didn't look at his expression anymore; he became faceless as I focused on the walls, just as he'd been the first day I met him.

"I'd appreciate it if you didn't hang off my arm for the rest of the night," I said stiffly, stepping back into the role I'd allowed myself to forget the second I stepped into the closet. "Be like the rest of the staff—seen and not heard. I have my soon to be fiancé to focus on, after all."

I didn't wait for Sumner to respond, but turned on my heel and left the coat closet. Olivia still held my champagne flute, not even trying to hide the fact that she'd been eavesdropping. I couldn't have cared less about her. Later, I might be embarrassed—maybe more so at the fact that I'd experienced my first rejected confession—but right now, my heart hardened back to how it'd been, closing down and returning to its normal Ice Queen state.

Once more, I was on my own, and I remembered that life was a lot simpler that way.

Chapter 20

The lobby of the country club was bustling today, a Sunday afternoon. I felt ghostly sitting in the plush chair, watching everyone mill about. Workers carrying towels, mothers pulling the hands of their children toward the daycare, men chattering with their golf gloves hanging out of their back pockets. I watched it all silently, waiting for someone to glance over at me and make eye contact. No one did.

I flipped a page in my fashion magazine, studying the fabrics and textiles used in the pictures to avoid thinking about the world around me. I picked at the sleeve of my black long-sleeved shirt in a self-soothing comfort, my cool-toned floral-printed vest keeping my posture straight. My navy dress pants, despite the heat, were a loose wool fabric, flowy in a way that they seemed more casual than business.

I forced myself to recount my outfit from top to bottom, over and over again, reminding myself that I *was* put together. I *was* refined. I *did* belong here.

Last night had passed in a blur after I'd returned from the coat closet without Sumner in tow. It'd been a whirlwind of bouncing from person to person, introducing them to Aaron and allowing them to gush over the newness of a fresh face. My mother accompanied us the entire time, and the short dance we'd shared had been the only time we'd been left alone.

Which prompted Aaron, when we parted ways at the elevator, to ask if we could meet the next morning. "I'd love to do something with you tomorrow," he'd said. "Shall we meet in the lobby in the morning?"

I'd agreed, though I hadn't really had a choice—my mother had been standing there when he asked. She had been disappointed that the night had ended without a ring on my finger. My parents had swept into my room to debrief, picking apart every scant piece of conversation we'd been able to share alone. They also came up with a plan of attack for the next afternoon—what I would say to Aaron, how I would act, to lock down his heart.

They'd been speaking and speaking, but I couldn't focus on them until I'd heard Sumner's hotel room door open, and it'd been well after midnight.

What he'd been doing for the two hours since we'd left the ballroom, I had no idea. I told myself not to be curious.

That didn't work. Despite everything, I was awake all night, straining to hear the slightest sound through the walls. I listened and listened until Sumner's alarm began blaring in its wake-up call, and I realized I'd spent the entire night thinking about someone who was not thinking about me.

Now, I flipped another page in my fashion magazine, turning my head to the side, trying to fight off a cringe.

Even just thinking his name caused discomfort to bloom in my chest, following by the rushing sting of embarrassment.

While crushes weren't things I entertained, rejection was not an unfamiliar notion. I never did much to put myself out on a limb, but I'd spent most of my life on the outskirts of the in-crowd, scorned and spurned for not conforming. Sumner's rejection, though, hit me differently. Hurt me differently. I didn't realize just how much I wanted him to tell me to drop everything to be with him until he didn't say it. Until he pulled me away. *I was paid to be at your side. I wouldn't be here...if not for that.*

I closed my eyes and winced again.

Sumner's laugh suddenly floated down the hallway, and I heard him before he stepped into view from where I sat. He came from one of the main country club hallways with two women at his heel, all three of them wearing matching Alderton-Du Ponte teal polos and smiles. I recognized two of the women as servers from past events, similar to my age. Blonde. Tall. Pretty. Prettier when they smiled.

I turned back around in my chair and slumped low, though the low-backed seat would do nothing to fully obscure me. If I got up and tried to escape back into the hotel now, he'd surely see me. Him and his gaggle of little groupies, apparently.

The rise of my ire was ridiculous, of course. I wouldn't have felt so strongly if Sumner had been laughing with two other guys on the staff. Maybe I would've. Maybe I would've resented anyone he smiled at, when I'd grown comfortable with the thought that he saved it only for me.

But he hadn't. He never smiled at me for anything more than politeness. Friendship. Because he was paid to smile at me.

"Your life is just *so* interesting," one of the girls gushed. "You're so well-traveled. I haven't ever left Addison."

"Same here," the other one replied. "California, England, Spain—it's all quite the adventure."

I frowned a little as I eavesdropped, certain I had locked onto the wrong conversation until Sumner replied. "It's been quite the jam-packed life, that's for sure." The smile in his voice was practically audible. "It's nice to slow down for a change."

England and Spain? Sumner had been to those places? He'd never mentioned it to me before. A different thought occurred to me, in a bitter way; Sumner had traveled more than I ever had? When? I thought him making his way into Addison after quitting his job was the first time traveling outside of California. He'd traveled the world?

My heart hardened further. Apparently, he'd been right. I didn't really know him much at all.

"Margot?"

For half a second, I debated on ignoring him. Bracing myself, I lifted my head to where he stood ten feet away, and even though I didn't want to, I forced myself to meet his gaze. "Mr. Pennington," I greeted, closing my fashion magazine and sitting up straighter. "You were working today?"

I had to be horrifyingly transparent.

The two girls who stood beside Sumner lost their smiles at the sight of me, a reaction I was long since used to. They even looked as if they wanted to turn and walk in the opposite direction, but it was too late; I'd already risen from the chair and sauntered over. "You seem awfully relaxed to be on the clock."

"W-We were just coming back from break," one girl got out, struggling to maintain her even tone. "We ran into Sumner in the hallway."

I tilted my stare toward her, not saying a word. It made her nearly cower.

"What are you doing in the lobby?" Sumner asked at once, oblivious to the tension, taking in my suit. He had a frown on his features now, worlds different from the smile on his face moments ago. "You're supposed to call me when you leave your room."

He couldn't have thought I'd call him after last night. Confessing my feelings was bad enough, but the fact that I kissed him just made his presence more unbearable. "To Gilfman's," I replied flatly, slipping a hand into my pocket. "I have a fitting for the wedding next Saturday. You left my car at the country club's valet, if you remember."

"You didn't say anything yesterday."

"I had other things on my mind yesterday."

At that, I could've sworn Sumner flushed.

The two other staff members had been bouncing back and forth between us as if we were a tennis match, their expressions growing increasingly shocked. Perhaps because Sumner wasn't cowering beneath the imposing stare of Margot Massey. Perhaps because no one was being turned to stone with just one glance at me. Perhaps because I hadn't fired anyone on the spot yet.

"We—we can tell Mr. Massey that Miss Margot needs your assistance," one of the staff members said, the one who'd spoken a moment ago. She was the one that stood the closest to Sumner. The one who'd had her hand on his back as they'd walked into the lobby.

Maybe she was the reason he turned me down. Maybe he preferred this bubbly blonde over me, who contained nothing but ire.

Sumner shook his head "No, I can go tell him—"

"You aren't coming."

My tone was blunt and unmissable, and it caused Sumner to blink. The way he stared at me was almost like we were the only two in the conversation, the other girls forgotten. "You're not supposed to go anywhere by yourself."

"She won't be alone," a voice cut in as a shadow fell over my shoulder. "I'm going with her."

The group we'd gathered all turned to find Aaron Astor sauntering up from the direction of the elevator, a half-smile smirking his lips. His outfit was summery, with a striped buttonless polo, a pair of chinos that hemmed high on his ankle, expensive boat shoes to top it off. He looked like the epitome of someone who would be wandering about the Alderton-Du Ponte Country Club. He fit in perfectly.

"Wow," Aaron exclaimed, his eyes roaming my figure. "The rumors about the way you dress were true, apparently. Lovely. Reminds me of my mother a little."

How my stock Gilfman design could compare to his mother's original Malstoni was beyond me, but I didn't comment on it. "She has good taste, your mother."

"And so do I, apparently." Aaron turned his attention to Sumner, mirth entering his eyes. "Mr. Pennington."

Sumner, though, held no amusement in his expression. "Mr. Astor."

The two other girls who'd been sticking around chose then to titter off with polite smiles, and Aaron tipped his head at their departure. It left the three of us alone, though not truly; a quick scan of the lobby proved that eyes of those in the space were on us, trying to soak it all in to gossip about later.

The only word that could describe the way I felt, with Aaron and Sumner looking at each other, was *awkward*. I tried not to let it show as I turned to Aaron. "You ready?"

Aaron brightened. "I am. I'm excited to explore your quaint little area a bit more."

"You'll be majorly unimpressed," I promised him. I took a step forward, but instead of just Aaron following, Sumner also moved.

Aaron raised an eyebrow. "You aren't coming along as well, are you?"

"I'm to accompany Margot any time she leaves the grounds," Sumner said in a formal voice. "She's not supposed to go anywhere without me."

"Your services are probably no longer required, Mr. Pennington. Now that I'm here."

"Her parents didn't say my presence was conditional on yours."

Aaron turned to look at Sumner head on. "Maybe we

should call her parents, then." While Aaron was an inch shorter than me, he was several shorter than Sumner, facing off in a power struggle I was already done with. "I'd hate for you to be a third wheel."

"Or are you worried you'll be the awkward one left out?" It was ironic how much Sumner combated Aaron, given how he reacted in the coat closet the night prior. "Because she knows me better than you."

Sumner, trying so hard to show up Aaron, irked me more than the other man. "I doubt my mother would want you tagging along," I told Sumner. "Aaron and I would get to know each other far easier without a chaperone."

I'd said the words as if they'd hurt Sumner, as if they were salt that I could rub into a wound, but it wasn't his skin that was broken. It was mine. My words did nothing but prove to be a reminder of the way we left things yesterday; they did nothing but remind me that I was alone in the way I felt. *I was paid to be at your side. I wouldn't be here…if not for that.*

I didn't look at him as I offered my fashion magazine out. "Take this to my room, would you?"

Wordlessly, Sumner took the magazine, freeing up my hand to slip around Aaron's arm. Aaron tipped his head in an almost smug manner before escorting me away, toward the front doors. I forced myself to stare straight and told myself I'd rather die than look back. I refused to look to see if Sumner stood staring after us. I'd rather die.

I'd made it to the automatic doors that greeted Aaron and me with warm summer air before impulse took control. Almost as if my body was hijacked, I glanced over my shoulder, wanting to see Sumner's expression, wondering what it looked like.

He was nowhere in sight. Thirty seconds had passed, and he wasn't standing there anymore, already having left to run my errand and get back to work.

My fist of a heart hardened further.

Aaron was less than impressed by the view of the bay, but then again, coming from the grandness of living ocean side, it most likely was like looking at a pond to him. One not nearly as expansive and blue. The tailoring session at Gilfman Clothier went off without a hitch, and Jordan had successfully helped bring another design of mine to life.

Aaron, though, seemed tickled by my choice. "Cream for a wedding?" he'd asked when I'd stepped out from behind the curtain, his eyes roaming over my figure. It had been similar to the way Sumner had the time I'd brought him; and then I'd scolded myself for thinking about Sumner. "A little close to white, no?"

"It's beige," I'd corrected, but felt a little smug looking in the mirror. "Though if anyone gets confused, maybe they'll think Annalise and I got married."

Aaron had lifted his maple whisky to his lips, his smile distorted by the glass.

Once we finished at the fitting, instead of going to Pierre's for lunch—because I was more likely to win the lottery than to win last-minute reservations for a Sunday afternoon—we returned to the country club to dine at their outdoor restaurant.

"I will say, I am a little surprised." Aaron came around and pulled out the chair for me, gesturing me to sit. "I'd meant it mostly as a joke earlier, but this area *is* quaint. You don't strike me as the quaint sort."

In the orchestrated dance, I sat down, and Aaron pushed in the chair as I did so. "I only just finished college. I'm sure I'll branch out sometime."

"Like California?"

I took in his hopeful expression. "Perhaps."

He rounded the small table and sat across from me, the intrigue clear on his face. "You know, I've been debating asking about it all day. About your secretary. He's a bit young, no?"

"There's an age limit to secretaries?" I said in a voice that made it clear I wasn't interested in pursuing the conversation further.

"No, no, just is...interesting."

It was clear he was hoping for a nonchalant expression now, but his insecurity shined through in the constant shifting of his eyes, bouncing around. It was another interesting thing about Aaron Astor that I hadn't been expecting. Though I hadn't had high hopes for his looks, I still expected a man with more confidence, used to getting what he wanted. Why else assume I'd be yapping at his heels the second he showed up, even though he hadn't ever bothered speaking to me directly? But the man before me definitely didn't possess the sort of confidence I'd been expecting, though he tried to prove otherwise.

The waitress came over then and delivered us menus and waters, fluttering off to give us a moment. "You drank that maple whisky at the clothier," I said to Aaron, crossing my legs underneath the table. "Do you drink often?"

"Not too often," he replied leisurely, mimicking my posture and reclining further into his seat. When he did it, though, he couldn't quite abandon all of his stiffness. "Mostly whisky here and there, and the occasional wine. Red, of course. The correct answer is always red."

I disagreed, and normally would've voiced my opinion, but I kept it to myself. Pulling my punches to start might've been the correct way to play this. "I prefer water over wine,"

I said, picking up the sweating glass to punctuate this.

Aaron picked up his own glass. "Cheers, then."

The server came back over then, asking if we were ready to order. Aaron went first, ordering the braised salmon for himself, and when the server turned to me, he cut back in. "She'll have the chicken giardiniera," he said, eyes on the menu. "With the mashed potatoes and grilled asparagus. Do the potatoes come with garlic butter?"

The server nodded.

"None on them, then, please. For hers and for mine." To me, Aaron gave a breathy laugh. "Can't have garlic breath, can we?"

It was strange, listening to him order for me. Normally, someone did it out of a show of dominance—that was how my parents were—but with Aaron, his voice lacked the authoritative tone that I expected in this sort of situation. It was almost hesitant, as if he'd been waiting for me to cut him off.

When the waitstaff departed to put in our orders, Aaron swirled his water in his glass as if it were wine, voice delicate as he said, "I've heard you're a straightforward person, Margot Massey. I like to think I am as well. Shall we jump straight into the thick of things?"

"By all means."

"I've heard you're not too interested in pursuing anything with me."

If I'd been taking a sip of water, I would've choked on it. It'd quite possibly been the last thing I'd expected to come from his mouth, but he'd said it with no hesitation. My parents had gone to great lengths to keep my personal feelings of it under wraps. Who would've known? More specifically, who would've known that had contact with the Astors? Yvette? "Where did you hear that?"

Aaron fluttered his hand by his ear. "A little bird, is all. I'd like to hear those concerns of yours, if you're willing to open yourself to me."

I made a face, both at the horrendous phrasing and the fact that he unknowingly echoed what my parents had done the week prior. Brought me to Pierre's, sat me down, and asked me to "voice my concerns." Now, though, it was much more awkward since the person I was voicing my concerns to coexisted with the root of the problem.

"I think you and I are in a very unique position," he went on when I took too long to answer. "Both of us are going into this with no preconceived notions. I, Margot, am not looking for love, and I've got a feeling you aren't either."

A frown formed on my brow. "I was under the impression that you were," I replied. "That you saw me at the Christmas party in New York and fell in love."

"I *did* see you there, and was immediately intrigued."

"Intrigued, but not enough to come over and talk to me."

"I'm a bit of an introvert," he said with a chuckle. "And you do have an intimidating air to you, darling, you must admit. But when I heard your story, and—well. It intrigued me further. Only child of two self-made parents who were more dedicated to building their career than creating a warm environment for their daughter. Parents who, despite only having one heir, had no intention of leaving the business to their daughter."

He spoke in such a matter-of-fact way, so nonchalantly, that I almost didn't even realize what he was saying. My eyes narrowed. "What, did you have a background check run on me?"

"Oh, no, no, I'd never do such a thing. The people around here do enjoy their gossip, you know. My best friend is marrying the daughter of someone who's on the board of directors for Alderton-Du Ponte's Country Club. I've heard a lot of things. Besides, I'm from this world, too. If there's one thing I've learned, it's to read between the lines."

It was funny—I couldn't care less about Aaron knowing about the tumultuous relationship between my parents and me, but I had practically crumpled from the embarrassment when Sumner found out. Interesting. "And my sad upbringing was *intriguing* to you?"

"Your isolation intrigued me."

I couldn't help but think how lonely you looked. So it hadn't just been Sumner who had noticed. How was it that complete strangers could see but no one else? "That sounds vaguely offensive."

"I, too, have lived much of my life feeling on the outskirts of things. No one bothers to talk about business holdings with the bottom of the pyramid, you know? I've always felt like an outcast, too." Aaron leaned forward across the table and laid his elbow on the surface. "My parents think I'm in this because I fell head over heels for you. My friends, too. The only one who knows the truth now, Margot, is you."

"Why tell me? Why not attempt to woo me?"

"I've learned, in the very brief time that I've known you, you aren't one easily wooed." He gave a little smile. "And since arriving here, I've discovered it might be in more of my interest to appeal to your mind than your heart. I'm sure I don't have to tell you how positively this will impact both of our parents' companies, merging our families and our business ventures. Massey Hotels with Astro Agencies is a beautiful marriage itself."

The spiel he gave me sounded like my father, as if he were presenting a business proposal at a meeting. I was almost surprised he hadn't broken out a PowerPoint. The evening, perhaps, was still young. "That's why you were never interested in getting to know me. You just want to marry me because your family's business will benefit."

"I don't care about my family's business," Aaron

replied in a candid manner. "I'm fifth in line to receive anything from it. No," he went on with a shake of his head. "I don't care about Astro Agencies. What I care about, Margot, is Massey Suites."

Despite the sheer audacity of it all, a slow, understanding smile spread across my lips. "You want to marry me to inherit my parents' company."

Aaron Astor looked like a child given the number one present from their wish list. "You understand me."

The gall this man could muster, and to wield it so boldly, was almost impressive.

My mother must've warned the waitstaff to give us their prime service, because they served our plates in record time. The smile remained on my face as I watched them set everything out, and if the tension hadn't completely dissolved before, it did now. The importance of this meeting, the importance of impressing the infamous Aaron Astor, was pretty much void now. I could've let out a sigh of relief as I reached for my silverware, picking up my fork and knife and beginning to transfer them to the other sides of the plate.

Aaron's hand shot out and covered my right hand. "That's correct," he said, gently, as if he was afraid of embarrassing me. "The way they have it placed. It's correct."

"I know," I returned in a soft voice that mimicked his, holding my fork in my right hand.

"You learned how to hold silverware incorrectly?"

"No."

We stared at each other for a moment. Aaron seemed perplexed, but instead of pushing the issue, he seemed to force himself to segue back into the conversation. "It is scary, I suppose," he continued. "Tying our lives together when we barely know each other. I can see why you might be hesitant about it. That's why I came out a week before the wedding—so we could spend more time together. I also had some documents drafted up."

Oh, my mother definitely had been in contact with the staff, or at least Aaron had, because when he turned around, a man—whom I hadn't noticed until that moment —stepped out from where he'd been at the bar. The man handed Aaron a leatherbound file holder. It was all very pretentious.

Aaron laid it down on the side of the table where our plates didn't touch. Not a PowerPoint, but close.

I stared at it, and though my curiosity overwhelmed me, I didn't reach for it. Toward him, I only arched a brow.

"An unofficial prenup. Not of business holdings, of course, as that will go through our parents' lawyers, but one in the more personal sense. What we can expect from each other as we move forward in this venture."

No wonder he had trouble finding a partner, if he talked to women like this. It was a good thing he wasn't attempting to woo me; this would've been a poor start.

Upon opening the file, it was immediately obvious he'd made this with his business account, since the company's logo was at the top and their watermark embedded into the paper at the bottom. The paragraphs were blocky, written in the way a legal text would, and I scanned it slowly. "And you want me to sign to this?"

"Not now, of course," he said, picking back up his

water glass. "I want you to marinate on it, of course. Mull it all over. See if there are any points you'd like added or tweaked."

I closed the folder and fixed him with my most serious stare, the poker face of all poker faces. "What if I were to tell you I wanted to go to fashion school?" I asked him. "That I wanted to live separate from you?"

"If pursuing fashion is a dream of yours, I'd support it. And if you'd prefer separate houses, we can look into that. Or we could style our own wings in a home—I'd get the east, you'd get the west. I'm willing to make compromises, darling." He leaned forward across the table, his boyish grin resurfacing. "From what I know about you, Margot, I like you. I like how our worlds are aligning. We're cut from the same cloth after all, you and I."

My mind was still stuck on his offer of a compromise, surprised by it. "Are we now?"

"Raised in the same atmosphere, heading in the same direction in life. We would make quite a good fit. Hold each other up, keep each other on task. And isn't that a quality of a suitable partner? You can have love, but a partner who can't match your pace will not be able to keep up with you in the long run. And I think we'd keep up well with each other."

The words did, in fact, belong on a PowerPoint slide. They seemed meaningful, beautiful, and if he'd spoken them under the pretense of romance, they might've someone else swoon. No, they *would've*. The words were perfectly designed for it. Sitting there, though, I couldn't help but wonder if he'd rehearsed them, had them written on the inside of his wrist and reread them before we sat down.

I felt for him, in a way—his desperation to make this work was clear. Less intense than my parents, but more prominent than I expected. My parents made it sound like impressing Aaron Astor would be the make it or break it moment, but I had a feeling I could've insulted the man to his face and he still would've been on his knees asking for my hand in marriage.

It was a strange thing to know I held all the power.

Aaron was waiting for my answer, blinking his dark eyes at me expectantly. "You're not what I expected," I told him, turning to my plate. "Not in the slightest."

"And just how did you expect me?" he asked with a boyish smile.

I stared at him and the glint in his eye, thinking about just how well he'd fit in with the Alderton-Du Ponte society. He was charming, straightforward, and seemed to have everything planned out. He was not some man infatuated with me, nor a man uninterested in me. No, he was calculated—just as I was. He knew what he wanted, and he went for it, but unlike my parents, he wanted this to be a partnership rather than a dictatorship. It was interesting.

"I thought you'd be suffocating," I said, and began eating my meal.

Aaron spent the rest of the dinner talking about himself, which I appreciated in a way, since I had been the one to go into this blind. He'd gone to an all-boy's high school, studied abroad in London with a group of friends for his senior year, volunteered in Spain during a few of his summers. Whatever article Sumner had found on Aaron had been accurate.

As he spoke, I waited for the red flags to appear, but they didn't pop up. Sure, it wasn't normal to want to marry someone you didn't love, but for Aaron, he was quite content with the idea. He told me how he'd never been interested in love in the first place, wasn't sure he believed in it, and would much rather settle down without such a complicated emotion getting in the way.

It was all very interesting. While I never relished in the idea of marrying someone I didn't love, I, too, had never been sure I'd ever felt it before. What I thought had been budding with Sumner hadn't been that at all. *You don't like me. You just like the way I make you feel.*

Perhaps Aaron Astor could make me feel that way, given time.

Spending just an hour or two with Aaron as he talked, and my lack of sleep the previous night, left me eager to go back to my hotel room. I wasn't one for midday naps, but I wanted to take a long one now, to just fall down and sleep and sleep and sleep.

The second we walked into the country club's lobby, I spotted Nancy with Ms. Jennings waiting in the same seating area I'd been earlier that day. Ms. Jennings spotted me first, and nudged Nancy, who'd been dozing off in her wheelchair. Ms. Jennings had to shake her shoulder, and the elderly woman startled awake, looking as if she'd forgotten where she was.

And then her gaze settled on me. "There you are!" she complained, drawing her knitted blanket further up her lap. "Making an old lady wait all this time. The world revolves around you, does it? And no one in this godfor-saken place could find Hot Stuff, either. What'd you do, convince him to quit?"

Aaron looked between her and me with alarm. "Do—do you know this woman?"

He no doubt thought Nancy was a dementia patient with the way she was rambling, and a part of me wanted to allow him to continue assuming. "Nancy Du Ponte," I said in a withering tone, gesturing toward her. "Owner of the Alderton-Du Ponte Country Club."

Nancy regarded him with a twist to her lips, one that wasn't happy. "And who might you be,

Ms. Jennings, though, had locked onto Aaron the moment she'd risen to her feet, and everything finally clicked into place for her. "Oh my!" she exclaimed loudly enough for her words to echo in the broad lobby. Her eyes sparkled with the swell of gossip, one she was the first to hear. "Is this handsome thing *the* Aaron Astor?"

I sighed, and the sound was most definitely a death rattle. It seemed my day wasn't over yet after all.

Chapter 21

*D*espite the fact that Aaron and I ate not even ten minutes ago, Ms. Jennings had grabbed Nancy's wheelchair and set us on a course to the restaurant, not waiting for anyone to argue. "You can at least have a drink," she'd insisted. "Nancy would love your company."

Nancy had one condition, though—only if Sumner came along too.

He'd been out caddying on the golf course, which was why no one could find him earlier, but they tracked him down fast when I'd inquired. Sumner sat to my right on, with Aaron on my left, and it was a suffocating position. Ms. Jennings, seated on Aaron's other side, talked animatedly, and had been the entire walk from the hotel to the club. We sat at a round table in the restaurant at the country club, waiting for our late lunch to be served.

And I would've rather been anywhere in the entire world than here.

"Your life just sounds so fascinating," Ms. Jennings said as Aaron finished the same resume-like details he'd given me. She batted her mascara-coated lashes at him, tucking her hands underneath her chin like a schoolgirl. "So much accomplished at just twenty-five! I find it admirable...and very impressive."

Ms. Jennings truly had no shame, given that Aaron, at half her age, could've been her son. Then again, *shame* and *Ms. Jennings* didn't really fit in the same sentence.

Aaron lapped up all the attention, though his nervousness seeped through ever so slightly. "Yes, well, it's been quite an adventurous one, bouncing around from city to city. Experiencing it all while I'm young has been something to remember." He picked up his water glass, casting a glance to me. "I still can't believe you haven't traveled much, darling."

"Margot's parents don't like her traveling without them," Ms. Jennings cut in, giving her head a small shake. "I agree with your philosophy, Aaron. You should travel when you're young."

"Perhaps I can take you somewhere and impress you," Aaron said to me. His expression was so simple and kind. "Fashion week, perhaps? Milan? You should really see more that the world has to offer."

I regarded him curiously. "How did you know I was into fashion?"

"My mother mentioned it to me. She said you talked about it on the way to the airport." His lips quirked. "Besides, judging by your clothing, I thought it was clear. A woman who wears sophisticated clothing can't be *uninterested* in fashion, at the very least."

"We have always loved Margot's affinity for her suits," Ms. Jennings enthused, giving a dramatic nod, as if to convince herself. "She's just so unique."

I wasn't sure who the "we" she was referring to was, but given the fact that she'd told me I dressed like a man at the last fundraiser, I doubted that "we" included herself.

"Can you believe the wedding is this weekend?" Ms. Jennings asked, pressing her palms together. She looked at Nancy. "I can just remember when Annalise was a young little thing, toddling around, and now she's getting married."

Nancy didn't reply. In fact, since her greeting Sumner when he joined us for lunch, she hadn't spoken once.

With my attention on Nancy now, it was clear she didn't look well in the slightest. She wasn't strong enough to transfer from her wheelchair to a dining chair, even though Sumner offered to help, and she somewhat slumped in her seat. Her skin was paler than usual, almost gray-looking, but I tried to tell myself it was just the lighting. I wanted to ask if she was feeling okay, but I didn't want to draw attention to it, knowing she wouldn't have been honest, anyway. Instead, I took a sip of my water, swallowing hard.

"And yours and Margot's wedding is following soon after!" Ms. Jennings said, her segue not smooth in the slightest. She leaned toward Aaron with a bright look in her eye, laying her hand on his forearm. "That is...if you've proposed yet."

Her interest charmed Aaron—then again, he seemed the type to be charmed by anyone's slightest interest in him. Perhaps it was because he was the youngest of five. "Things are still a bit up in the air." He glanced over at me. "Margot seems to enjoy playing hard to get."

"And here I thought I was being subtle," I replied before sipping my water. I didn't look at Sumner, who had also been silent the entire time.

"Aaron," Ms. Jennings began with intrigue, once more leaning forward. "Why aren't there any photos of you online? Us ladies at the club have been *very* curious. And you're handsome—why not show it off!"

He tucked his head in an almost sheepish expression. "I've never been a fan of posting everything online. Never been a fan of that sort of limelight. I prefer to wait for people to see me in person to form a judgement of me. I'm sorry I left you in suspense for so long—I hope you weren't disappointed."

Ms. Jennings giggled. "Not in the slightest."

Nancy silently reached for her water glass on the table. When she grabbed it, it tipped toward her in her weak grip, and it nearly upended all over her and the table. Sumner caught it in time, his hand covering hers. "Oh, careful, careful," he said, though his voice was light. "It was just out of reach."

Nancy grunted, but when she took the water from him, it was a gentle movement.

Aaron leaned closer to me and lowered his voice. "I know earlier you said she owned the country club, but is this your grandmother?"

"No."

"She's practically her grandmother," Ms. Jennings joined our whispering. "She was there for all the big events in Margot's life."

"I'm old," Nancy snapped, lowering her water glass in

her shaking hand. "Not deaf. If you have any questions, you can ask me yourself, young man."

"I wasn't meaning to offend," he quickly assured. "Just trying to piece the puzzle together, that's all."

Nancy grumbled something, but it was around the rim of her water glass, and she ended up swallowing the words.

Another near silent member ever since we entered the restaurant had been Sumner. He hadn't attempted to chime in a conversation, and with Nancy seeming under the weather, she didn't try to pull him into one. He just sat quietly, listening. I should've included him somehow, but the thought of trying to spark a conversation with him, of looking him in the eye, caused my throat to feel too constricted.

"Speaking of puzzle pieces," Ms. Jennings said, and this time, her focus fell on Sumner. "You knew that Mr. Pennington is Margot's babysitter, right?"

"I do know that, yes." Aaron laid his arm over the back of my chair, claiming me like a caveman. The look he gave Sumner was nothing short of challenging. "Now that I've arrived, I do believe I could fill your shoes, Mr. Pennington. Your services may no longer be needed."

Sumner, though, despite his normally good-natured self, didn't back down to Aaron's stare. "It's up to the Masseys how long they need me for."

Aaron gave an empty smile. "It seems like an odd thing, though, doesn't it? Hiring a man to get close to their daughter? Doesn't seem like something they'd do."

Sumner was calm. "I came highly recommended."

Aaron's smile, at some point, had twisted into a sneer. "Oh, I bet you did."

Ms. Jennings watched them bicker with an invested smile on her face, eating up the sight of two boys fighting. I should've cut in then, said something to stop the display of testosterone, but she beat me to the jump. "It *is* odd that they hired him," she agreed. "Especially given the fact that the two of them kissed."

I closed my eyes and let out a slow breath through my nose, because if there was anything I didn't want brought up, it was this.

But Aaron's reaction wasn't one I'd been expecting. I just wanted to avoid the topic being awkwardly brought to the surface, especially after yesterday, but Aaron—he tensed all over. He gaped not at me but at Sumner, the crease between his brows livid. "You *kissed* her? When?"

"Oh, about a month ago now," Ms. Jennings answered him, ever and always helpful. "Right in front of everyone, too. It was his first day on the job—"

My parents said Aaron had been made aware of the situation, but this was clearly a man who had no idea. "You *kissed her*," he repeated, and on the table, his fist clenched. "Really?"

"If we're going to get technical, I kissed him." I picked my water back up, but my glass was empty. "And before you ask, I kissed him because I wanted to. Because I could. My parents hired him, despite that fact, because he made it crystal clear he had no feelings for me. So there you go."

For the first time, the expression on Aaron's face was not warm nor charming. The look reminded me of the night my father came into my room, thinly veiled anger about to burst into the open. *There it is*, I found myself thinking. *There's the red flag.* "It's funny that I never heard about it."

"When would you have?" I returned. "You refused to speak with me beforehand. Unless, of course, you're wondering why your spies didn't tell you." It was curious that Yvette hadn't blabbed *that* particular detail; it was the most scandalous one.

"Indeed." Aaron went back and forth between Sumner and me, staring us down. "They seem to have gone rogue."

I couldn't break away, almost as if there was a challenge in his stare. Was he really that bothered by the idea of me kissing another man? Bothered enough to throw me and my parents' company away, or just bothered enough to throw a tantrum?

Ms. Jennings leaned back in her chair with an amused grin, tapping her fingers together. At that moment, the waitstaff *finally* began bringing out everyone's entrees, breaking through the tension that'd been building to an unbearable degree. "Did you have to catch her salmon yourself?" I snapped, and then inwardly kicked myself for taking the frustration on them.

The server stuttered out apologies as she began placing the plates down, starting with Yvette. Throughout everything, Sumner stared down at his place setting with his jaw locked. Since I sat beside him, I could see his hands clenched underneath the table, resting on his thighs.

Silent through practically the entire conversation,

Nancy took in a sharp, shuddering breath. While everyone had been talking, she'd grown paler, to the point where the bags underneath her eyes looked as dark as a bruise.

"Nancy," I said, my heart stuttering on a beat. "Are you okay?"

Not yet, not yet, not yet. The thought was on a repeating loop in my head, a desperate echo that I was too afraid to think about what it meant.

Nancy never answered. Instead, she collapsed forward, her frail body falling onto the table. Sumner barely caught her before her head slammed onto the oak, and after that, everything had become a loud, roaring blur.

Chapter 22

*I*n the daytime, the hospital almost seemed pleasant with its grand windows letting streams of warm summer sunlight into the lobby, soft, upbeat music playing over the speakers, and staff chattering at the lobby's desk. Nothing about the atmosphere felt like a hospital at all.

No one ever would've guessed that this was the place people came to die.

After Nancy collapsed, eyes rolling back into her head, everything blurred with only snapshots of focus. Sumner easing her off the table and into his arms, keeping her from falling out of her seat. Ms. Jennings giving a shrill, theatrical wail. Aaron sipping his water as if nothing were happening.

I didn't remember how I reacted; it all blended together like splotches of paint, creating the ugliest shade of brown.

The sunlight in the hospital windows seemed somewhat low, but I had no concept of time. I knew I left my hotel room earlier this morning around nine, but after that, I knew nothing else. My phone was in my pocket, but it weighed far too heavy for me to pull it out. There was no clock on the walls.

Suddenly, a figure appeared before me, crouching down and coming into my frame of sight. He'd pushed his golden hair out of his eyes, which glowed with concern. "Here," Sumner said, offering something out to me. "Have something to snack on. It's been a while since you've eaten."

It took my sluggish mind several moments to catch up that he held an unopened bag of salt and vinegar potato chips. I didn't even realize he'd moved from sitting beside me, let alone went off to find food. "Nutritious." My voice was flat.

"The vending machine was slim pickings, and the food court closes at six on Sundays."

So it was after six. It didn't feel like it should've been that late in the day; it didn't feel like I'd been sitting in this hard chair that long.

When I didn't take the bag, Sumner ripped the top open, ducked his hand in, and pulled out a chip. He stretched it out to me, the worry flaring in his eyes and thawing just a bit of my numbness.

I took it. "Where's Aaron?"

"He...didn't come with us. You remember that?"

I did. I don't know why I even asked; I knew Aaron hadn't come with us. In the hectic confusion of it all, he'd asked if I wanted him to stay behind and out of the way. I'd barely batted an eye twice at him, my non-answer answer enough.

My eyes flicked to the hospital desk. "I should see if they have any more information they can give me."

When we'd arrived at the ER, the paramedics transferred Nancy off to a collection of doctors and nurses, and despite the fact that I'd come in with her, they restricted me. *"Are you family?"* one of them had asked, in a far rougher tone than necessary. *"If you're not family, please move to the waiting room."*

Sometime since the ER and me moving to the lobby, Dr. Conan, who'd begun his shift, had come to find me. It was mostly to get information on what happened, and I couldn't tell if it was for medical purposes or because he was just being nosy. Dr. Conan, despite my insistence, was tight-lipped about anything to do with Nancy's condition. It seemed he took his doctoral vows more seriously than his marriage ones.

"I can go see," Sumner said, rubbing his free palm over my knee. "I want half that bag gone by the time I get back, okay?"

Sumner shifted as he was about to stand up, but I grabbed his wrist, holding his hand to my leg and holding him in his crouched position. His fingers were slender, and I couldn't help but remember the countless of times they'd curved over my own, a comforting grip. "Not yet." My voice was as small as a child's. "Not yet."

He fell back firmer into his heels, continuing to peer up at me, returning to rub my knee. The touch was grounding, the slight massage giving me something to focus on. In this moment, I could pretend that his concern was because he cared about me—*really* cared about me. It was a delusional sort of thought, but it brought me the barest comfort. *Comfort.*

With his free hand, Sumner held the bag of chips out to me again.

"It's true Nancy fashion," I said as I dipped my hand in, pulling out a few chips and scattering them in my palm. "Making a scene when she's meeting my fiancé for the first time."

Sumner let out a soft breath, a laugh adjacent. "She really doesn't want you to choose him, does she?"

"That's one thing about Nancy—she does have good taste."

"I thought you liked Aaron."

Despite being weary, I raised an eyebrow at him. "I thought *you* liked Aaron. The entire time I've known you, you were always pro Aaron Astor. The way you were bickering with him earlier, it didn't seem like you liked him much at all. Is this an enemies-to-lovers thing?"

"Who knows? Maybe I'll be the one running off with him at the end."

"My parents would be very upset."

Sumner smiled, which caused my lips to tip up in a mirrored response. His eyes dropped to it, and the knowledge that he looked at my mouth stalled the breath in my lungs, even in a situation such as this. It felt like a lifetime ago that I kissed him in the coat check closet, not just yesterday. A lifetime ago that I met Aaron Astor. It almost made my head hurt how much things could change in just twenty-four hours.

I let go of his wrist and my hand fell back into my lap. "It's funny," I murmured in a flat voice. "That no one from the country club is here. I would've thought everyone would be nosing their way in, desperate to try and get on Nancy's will before she croaks. They couldn't be bothered, I guess."

"Who would've told them?"

"Ms. Jennings surely would've blabbed."

"She's here," Sumner said. "Ms. Jennings. She came about an hour or two after we got here. You didn't see her?"

I really *had* zoned out. "No."

"She said she was going to see Dr. Conan. She didn't come back."

Ms. Jennings came to the hospital *now* to see Dr. Conan? She didn't ride in the ambulance with Nancy and me, but came separately to see the doctor? It wasn't that surprising, given their adulterous relationship, but for her to come visit him at work seemed strange. Unless...

I laughed once, a hollow sound. "She used him to sneak back to Nancy." No wonder the rest of the ladies from the club hadn't come rushing in; if Ms. Jennings spilled the beans, she would've had to fight for Nancy's attention. When Nancy should've been resting, recuperating from whatever had her passing out to begin with, Ms. Jennings had weaseled her way in.

I shoved to my feet, dots flooding my vision from the sudden movement. "I'm going to kill her," I declared, feeling as if I could've meant it.

Sumner rose to his feet, too, and this time, he was the one to grab my wrist. "Margot—"

"It's ridiculous!" My voice echoed in the hospital's lobby. One of the ladies at the reception desk looked up, but discreetly, as if she, too, tried to pick up on the gossip. "Even in a situation like this, it's all anyone thinks about.

Nancy's money, Nancy's estate, Nancy's financial hold-ings. They're—they're vultures. She's *dying*, and they—"

I stopped. The one word sucked all the air from my lungs and from the room, leaving me with nothing to draw on. *Dying*. All at once, the picture of her slumping forward at the table filled my vision, and the few chips I'd munched felt as if they'd gotten stuck in my throat.

Sumner's hand slipped from braceleting my wrist to holding my hand, fingers curving around my palm. For one brief instant, I allowed myself to be lulled by the touch, to pretend it meant more than it did. I pulled back, severing the connection. "Don't. Even if it's to be comfort-ing, don't." *Don't confuse me. Don't make my heart flutter.* Straightening my spine, I started toward the reception desk and the peeping woman behind it.

I only got a few steps away, though, before Nancy, Dr. Conan, and Ms. Jennings all came around the corner of the hallway. Dr. Conan was behind her manning the handles, directing her toward us with a phony smile on his face, and Ms. Jennings walked at his side. Nancy's expression was in its usual stony grimace. She had on a pair of scrubs with a plastic bag of her clothes in her lap, the knitted blanket long gone.

"Here's our lovely lady," Dr. Conan said as he wheeled her closer.

"You're discharging her?" I demanded.

"Leave it, Margot," Nancy snapped, finally strength in her voice. She *looked* better; at least, she didn't look so gray. Her eyes still drooped, though, like she could fall asleep and rest for a long while. "Quit fussing."

"Yes, Margot, don't be so fussy," Ms. Jennings piped

in, laying her hand on Nancy's bony shoulder. "She doesn't need the stress.

I squared my jaw at her tone, clenching my teeth around a frustrated sound. "You passed out at dinner."

"I was a little tired, that's all."

"The paramedics couldn't wake you. Your blood pressure was—"

"Hot stuff, can you wheel me to the car?" Nancy asked Sumner, cutting me off as cleanly as if I weren't speaking. "I've already signed all the paperwork."

Sumner looked around all of us before reaching a hand into the pocket of his khakis to pull out the key fob. "I'll go bring it around." He looked prepared for me to argue, but I remained stonily silent.

Nancy watched Sumner's retreating figure, and even though her eyes had been slow to blink, they were certainly fixated on one thing. "You think he does squats?"

"Definitely," Ms. Jennings murmured, also gawking.

They both ignored my burning glare completely, but of course they did. I switched focus. "Dr. Conan." I let his name hang in the air, my clear questioning of his license hanging along with it.

He pressed his lips into a line and shrugged. "It's what she wants, Margot."

"So, she's leaving against medical advice?"

Nancy turned her head ever so slightly, threatening with her side eye, and Dr. Conan straightened his shoulders. "I can't answer that."

The bag of chips crumpled in my ruthless grip, but it was either the plastic or the doctor's neck. He must've seen the dark look on my face, because he suddenly claimed he was being paged and bid us both a rushed farewell. He gave Ms. Jennings a look that said *I'll call you*.

"Where'd your other lover boy go?" Nancy asked, readjusting the bag in her lap. "Couldn't bother to accompany a poor little old lady to the hospital?"

"Why would he?" I asked coldly. "If you were just *a little tired*?"

Nancy smacked her lips. "I don't care for your tone."

"Oh, you don't care for it? I should change my tone, then, shouldn't I? Because it only ever matters what you want."

"Stop throwing a tantrum like a child." Nancy stopped playing with the plastic of her bag and reached for the guards on her wheels. Her grouchy expression matched her voice. "It's irritating."

Before she had a chance to wheel more than an inch, my hand slammed down on the arm rest of her wheelchair, jolting her to a halt. "*You're* irritating," I said, repeating her insult like the child she accused me of being. "You're acting like your blood pressure dropping that low is *normal*. That it's *normal* to just pass out at a dinner table. That it's *normal* to have to be rushed to the hospital."

"It's a good thing they hadn't served the food yet, or else I'd have fallen face-first into my baked potato."

"You think all this is *funny*?"

Nancy glared at me. "What, you think I actually dropped dead at the table?"

I didn't reply. Instead, the image of her falling over in

her wheelchair, as gray as a corpse, flashed through my mind. The words that'd been screaming on repeat followed. *Not yet, not yet, not yet.* My eyes burned.

Nancy smacked her lips again. "Margot," she began, huffing at what she probably decided was an overreaction. "I'm old. I'm going to drop dead sometime. You'll have to get over it."

"At least have the decency not to do it while I'm watching."

"If you're going to act like a crybaby like this, I won't." Nancy swatted my hand off her wheelchair, but didn't reach for the rails again. "If you were this invested in other people, they might like you more."

Her words were a lash against my skin, biting and painful. It was hardly any different than the barking way we normally spoke to each other, but in that moment, I could've screamed. It built in my throat, the pressure about to explode.

Nancy turned up to look at Ms. Jennings. "Ally, drive me home, would you? At least I know *you* won't be sniveling the entire ride. Let's stop by the gift shop first, hmm?"

Ms. Jennings was all too happy to oblige, stepping behind Nancy's wheelchair and pushing her forward. When I turned around to watch them go, Sumner was there, a few feet away, awkwardly inching closer to the tense conversation. His expression oozed concern and worry and it made the compression in my throat worse.

Anger consumed me, so inexplicable but *hot*. Unthinkable around. I couldn't remember the last time rage had consumed me so fully; not even my parents had elicited it in all their demands and patronizing. "And you wonder why I'm not a happy person," I muttered, only half wanting him to hear. "Tell me, Sumner—what's there to be *happy* about?"

For once, I'd struck the ever-witty Sumner Pennington speechless. He pressed his lips together, at a loss.

As I stormed outside, my body trembled with the anger, and the hot summer air didn't help. My car was waiting on the curb, and I had a brief, exhilarating thought of taking it. Of climbing into the driver's seat and leaving Sumner behind. I'd top out the speedometer, race away as far and as fast as I could. It wouldn't matter where I ended up; Bayview, New York, a ditch—as long as I got away from here.

Instead, I ripped open the passenger door and fell into the seat, slamming it shut with a force that shook the car.

I wiped my cheek, my fingers coming away wet, and it only incensed me further. Emotions *were* stupid. Pointless. And I refused to give into them again.

Chapter 23

$\mathcal{A}$fter word had spread that Nancy had taken a trip to the hospital, it seemed everyone was making their rounds to her house. Everyone but me, of course. I only knew the We Care About Nancy campaign when my mother had told me she was going to be taking over a fruit basket the next day, and had asked me if Nancy preferred strawberries or blueberries.

I'd told my mother blackberries. Nancy hated those.

The black cloud that'd fallen over me Sunday lingered beyond the walls of the hospital. Irritability had sunk its teeth into me, becoming hard to shake. My mother wanted me to go visit her, but she had others that could keep her company. I hope they all asked her if she'd finalized her will yet, just so it pissed her off.

Normally, when restlessness gripped me, I wandered around the grounds like a ghost. For the past two days, though, I didn't leave my hotel room. I ordered room service and sat on the couch while housekeeping tidied up my room. And since I didn't leave the hotel, I didn't see Sumner.

Even though Sumner didn't have any romantic feelings toward me, I couldn't keep myself from craving his company. In the past few weeks, when my days had been filled with his companionship, I didn't realize how much I'd begun to lean on it. And even if he didn't like me, I wanted to just ask him to do *something* with me—go for a drive, go to Gilfman's, watch a movie. But I couldn't. I would not cross the lines of professionalism again.

I wouldn't put him in an uncomfortable position again. I missed him, and I hated that I missed him, and then I hated that I was being like this to begin with.

Tuesday night, a little after nine o'clock, there was a soft knock on my hotel room door. When neither voice of my parents followed, my pulse jumped alive, and it was embarrassing how quickly I jumped up from the settee. I peered through the peephole, hoping for a certain someone, finding another instead.

I fought the urge to groan, hauling open the door to showcase Aaron Astor standing in the carpeted hall. "Hi, darling," he greeted, and the first thing he did, as he always did, was allow his eyes to rake over my figure. "Ah, no suit today?"

The black long-sleeve shirt and loose dark green pants were far more casual than I ever would've left my room wearing, more casual than I would've wanted anyone other than Sumner seeing me in. They weren't pajamas, but I felt so self-conscious in about relaxed I looked that they might as well have been. "Would you put on a five-piece if you weren't going to leave your room?" I returned, keeping the door close to me to prevent him from getting a clear glance inside. "How did you know my room number?"

"A little birdie," he replied, and at the twist in my features, he quickly followed up with an amused, "Your mother. I asked her for your room number so I could call you."

"So, you lied to her."

He gave an awkward smile. "Ah, well, I decided why only hear your voice when I could see your face?"

"Where was that mindset when I wanted to videocall you weeks ago?"

His sheepishness only deepened as he slipped his hands into his pockets. "I did say that I preferred us to meet for the first time in person."

"It's getting late," I told him, already backing up. "Let's meet tomorrow."

Aaron caught the door handle before I could close it. "It's been two days since I've seen you. Are you really going to make me chase after your parents to make you meet me?"

Already, he knew of their hold over me. I wasn't sure if he was perceptive or if their control was just so blatantly obvious. "You should've come earlier. It's after nine, and I've already had my dinner."

"Let's get a drink, then. The hotel has a bar, doesn't it? On the ground floor?"

I let out a little breath, knowing I didn't have much of a choice. I glanced towards Sumner's door, the one that always seemed to pull open when mine did, but it remained closed. I wondered if he was inside. "Fine. Give me a moment to change."

Again, Aaron caught the door. "No, no, I like this look

on you. Almost as much as your dress. This is very...*informal*."

I debated on whether fighting him on it, but ultimately conceded. My lack of backbone with him was concerning, but it seemed better to give into than to fight. I grabbed my hotel key and begrudgingly followed him out into the hallway.

The hotel lounge wasn't one I frequented too often, mostly because I wasn't incredibly drawn to middle-aged men traveling on business looking for a pretty, young thing to take up to their hotel room. It'd happened three times before I started to order my wine to my room.

"Oh, it's quite lovely in here, isn't it?" Aaron asked as we stepped into the space.

It was empty for a weeknight, when the businessmen usually were on the prowl. That meant there wouldn't be as many distractions.

Aaron ordered a whisky neat while I requested a cola —plain cola. He frowned at my choice before he started off the conversation with pleasantries—asking me how I was, asking how Nancy was, which I humored him with. I knew he didn't really care. If he'd cared, he would've come to see me that night.

Eventually, though, the main reason Aaron had come knocking surfaced. "So," he began languidly, tilting his head at me. "Have you thought more about my offer?"

I peered at my glass, using the tips of my fingers to stir the straw around the ice. "About marrying you?"

"Unless there was another offer on the table," he said, and I couldn't quite tell if he was intending to be flirty. His alcohol already seemed to be hitting. "I'll be honest,

Margot, I didn't expect you to give me so much pushback."

"You thought I'd fall to your feet at the idea of a proposal?"

"At the very least, I didn't expect so much hesitation."

"I live for nothing except knocking down egos," I murmured, taking the straw between my lips. "I know you said I'd be hard to woo, but I didn't expect you wouldn't try at all. I at least thought you'd have a ring to offer me."

Aaron began reaching for the pocket on the inside of his jacket.

"You have a ring?" I asked, startled.

"Of course."

"*On you?*" He slipped his hand into the pocket, but I threw a hand toward him, catching his arm. "No, no, don't pull it out."

He seemed amused with me, but when he withdrew his hand, it was thankfully empty. "You don't care for those trivial things." Aaron swirled the whisky in his glass, but didn't look at the amber liquid as he did so, trusting he wouldn't let even a drop spill out. "Besides, it isn't your heart I'm after, remember?"

I watched the bartender wipe down the bar and wondered if he was eavesdropping. He didn't quite appear to be, but I was sure he must've mastered the art of secretively listening in by now. Trick of the trade. "I haven't made my decision yet."

Aaron let out a breath, one that was probably intended to be a chuckle, but the impatience bled through the sound. He laid his hand on the back of my bar stool's seat, leaning in. "I'm needed home right after the wedding on Saturday. I was hoping I could bring you with me."

"My, you *do* move fast."

"Do you want me to woo you?" he asked, entering my personal space. In an instant, the scent of his cologne filled my nose, along with the smell of the whiskey on his breath. "Do you want to be wooed, Margot Massey? I can do that."

His face was a foot from mine, and instead of pulling away, I met the stare and looked deep into his dark eyes. They were so vastly different from Sumner's, nearly black compared to Sumner's brilliant blue. Pretty, but like the way the scales on a snake could be pretty. The alcohol seemed to have made him bolder, given him the confidence he'd lacked sober.

His hand was still on the back of my seat, and he still leaned close enough that the whisky on his breath began to turn my stomach. "I know that it's him. Your babysitter. You like him—that's why you're resisting me."

I stared into his gaze, unflinching. "And if that was the case?"

He rested his elbow on the countertop and then resting his chin on his fist, peering at me with a light expression. "If it's a lover you want, you can take one. I won't mind."

"You make it sound like we're in a historical movie. I can *take a lover*. Who even says that?" I took a sip from my soda, wrinkling my nose. "I'm glad I have your permission, of course, to take another man to bed."

"I'm nothing if not generous."

Despite everything, I smirked around my straw. It was

a dark sort of amusement as I pictured the life Aaron painted for me. He gave me permission to kiss Sumner in the closets of fundraisers all I wanted, so long as Aaron was the one to take me home.

The eloquently crafted life of the rich. History seemed doomed to repeat itself after all.

Aaron seemed to be lost in thought. "What do you like about him?"

"What I like about him isn't anything you can be."

"You say that as if you know me."

"These past few days, I've learned plenty about you."

Truth be told, while Aaron didn't distinctly rub me the wrong way, there was something that held me back now. Perhaps because of all the negative quirks he'd accumulated since I first heard his name. Perhaps because he was unfortunately tied to my parents. Perhaps it was the alcohol bolstering him now. Perhaps it was just because he wasn't Sumner. Whatever the reason, though, I'd crossed him out in my mind, leaving him on the side of *do not touch.*

"What do you even know about him, hmm?" Aaron asked me, his own impatience beginning to betray his voice. The muscles in his arm grew tense as he gripped my chair harder. "What was his childhood like? What are his parents like? His sister?"

I blinked. "How do you know if he has a sister?"

"The question is, do *you* know if he has a sister? Or a brother? Or is he an only child? It seems to me you hardly know him at all, but it makes sense, doesn't it? If you've only known him for a month?" Aaron seemed encouraged by my silence. "He was hired to be close to you, darling. It wasn't *real*. What you feel for him isn't real."

"And you?" I demanded, irritation biting down in me. "My parents might've hired Sumner, but how is why you're here any different?"

"Because you and I are the same, Margot." His own voice grew with passion. "You're a selfish person, Margot. No, no, I don't mean that as an insult. You're very focused on what *you* like. I can see that about you just from what I've observed so far. But selfishness in a relationship...it's the worst kind. Some people just aren't meant for the love in movies, you know?"

I just stared at him, thinking of how much better it would've been if I'd ordered an alcoholic drink before he spoke. I was sober, but a witty comeback to his bluntness eluded me, and so did the ability to laugh off what he said. "You're saying I don't deserve love?"

"Not that you don't deserve it, but I'm saying you're better off letting it go." Aaron gave me a sympathetic expression. "What happens when Sumner doesn't make you feel good anymore? What happens when your disdain and unhappiness ebbs away at his charm? When it drains him? Will you grow to resent him? Will he grow to resent *you*?"

You're so draining. Words that had somewhat fallen into the never-ending roar of my mind came back in full force now, a repeating loop. *This is why no one likes to talk to you, dear.*

My lips parted, but there wasn't any other thought in my head. *You're so draining.*

"People like us...we are not meant to be the main

leads in rom-coms, Margot." Aaron shook his head. "Not everyone is meant for love. You have to see that. You might not be meant for love, but that doesn't mean you have to be alone. We can be—"

Suddenly, Aaron jerked away from me, and it took me several moments to see that a hand had him by the shoulder, fisting in the loose material of his shirt. I traced the arm up to find Sumner there, his face shadowed in the low light of the bar. When he spoke, Sumner's voice was low; lower than I'd ever heard it. He stared straight into Aaron's eyes, into his soul. "You don't talk to her like that."

"I was wondering when you'd pop up," Aaron said in a grand manner, not at all bothered by the hand at his collar. "Took you longer than I expected, I'll admit."

"What the hell is your problem?" Sumner demanded, the exasperation in his voice snapping in the bar. If there'd been any other patrons, they would've grumbled in complaint. But it was only me, and I stared on in shocked silence. "How could you say any of that to someone you care about?"

"Because he doesn't care about me," I murmured, twisting my straw between my fingers. "He cares about the company I'll inherit."

It seemed to take a moment for it to sink into Sumner, what my words meant. The hard anger that'd been in his gaze before seemed to melt into magma, blazing hot. "You...you were going to marry her just for *their business*?" I'd never heard him sound more incredulous. "You never liked her? You were going to *marry her*, and you didn't *like her*?"

Aaron cast his gaze around the lounge, unwilling to look at Sumner. "She was about to do the same thing, wasn't she?"

It was so clear that Sumner didn't belong in this world, given the look of absolute horror on his face. I wondered what, specifically, about this situation left him so upset. He'd been the one to tell me to marry Aaron despite knowing how I felt—why did it matter if Aaron felt the same as me? Not invested romantically, but monetarily. Perhaps Sumner thought we were all insane, and only just then realized the true depths of our madness.

"That's how you're playing it, then?" Sumner demanded, fingers tightening in the fabric. "Manipulate her to think she doesn't deserve love, so she'll settle for you?"

"Is it manipulation when I'm just stating facts?" Aaron gestured aimlessly with his hand, though I could see his arm shake when he did so. "Margot's like a pet that's been ignored too long. She just likes the attention. If I'd met her first—"

"You didn't want to." Sumner's voice was ice. "Don't forget that."

While it was mostly the women at the country club who were catty, I was no stranger to male egos butting heads. Even the most civilized could lose their mind in the right circumstance, and with alcohol involved. My father was one example. Dr. Conan getting into a pissing match with Mr. Holland over investment strategies was another. If it was in a safe environment, it was always amusing to me to see a man who prided himself in maintaining an air of importance fall prey to childish temper tantrums.

But seeing Sumner, calm and patient Sumner whose eyes rarely lost their puppy dog shine, with his fingers twisted around Aaron's collar and the muscles in his forearm flexing, I didn't think it was amusing.

I thought it was hot.

Perhaps I *was* twisted.

"It's funny," Aaron murmured, only focusing on Sumner. "How this situation unfolded. Truly. Not quite how I'd been expecting."

It was then that the delayed realization of this being a precarious situation hit me—Sumner gripping a multi-millionaire's collar in a hotel bar. It didn't fully shock me from my thoughts, but it pulled me to the present enough that I slid off the barstool. "Okay, caveman," I said loftily, laying my hand on Sumner's back. "Walk me back to my room?"

It was clear Sumner didn't want to let go, that relaxing his grip took all his effort, but he did it. He dropped Aaron's collar and took a step back, ready to follow me wherever I went, just like always.

"Tomorrow," Aaron called after us. "We'll talk more tomorrow."

I regarded him for a moment, because there wasn't really a way I could say no. Aaron had made it clear that if he couldn't coax me from my room, he'd get my parents' help. I'd been backed into a corner with him without realizing it.

Ultimately, without a word, I walked out of the lounge.

The hallway was so bright compared to the lounge that it almost was shocking stepping out into it, as if it'd been night but suddenly turned into day. I looked down at where Sumner's hand balled into a fist at his side, wondering what it'd be like if I tried to pry his fingers apart. *Comfort.* He preoccupied with striding down the corridor, his focus internal. The elevator already rested on the ground level when he pressed the button, and we both stepped on.

There were so many things I could've asked him; how he knew to come down to the lounge, being one. I stared at my reflection in the mirror, though she looked different going back up to the eighth floor than she had coming down. She looked like a shell. In the reflection beside me, Sumner was the opposite—filled, but with clear agitation. I wanted to bask in Sumner's anger, as it was my first time seeing the fuming side of him truly come out.

Except I couldn't look at the frown on his face without thinking about what Aaron said—*what happens when your disdain and unhappiness ebbs away at his charm?* Sumner was already changing, right before my eyes.

In that moment, Sumner's eyes met mine in the reflection, and he pivoted immediately. In a flash, he laid his palms on either side of my face and forced me to look at him. The blue eyes were filled with intensity, and the only place I could look. "Don't."

My heart stuttered in my chest at the sudden closeness, at the heat radiating from his palms. "Don't what?"

"Don't let a single word of what he said into your head." While frustration radiated from him from every pore, his touch was gentle on me, the stark contrast making this moment stranger. "Don't even think about it."

The air stalled in my lungs. "Why...why did what he said make you so upset?"

"You're *not* a human vacuum that sucks the happiness out of people. You *do* deserve love, and to be loved. This entire time, I've been trying to get that garbage out of your head, and that *idiot*—"

The elevator chimed as it stopped at our floor, and the sound broke Sumner from his train of thought, at least for a moment. His hands fell from my face, and he pressed his fingers into his eyes. I hesitated for only a moment watching him, but stepped off the elevator before the doors could close.

"Did you know?" Sumner demanded, coming up from behind me. "When you met him the other day, did he tell you he wasn't interested in a romantic relationship?"

I fished my room key from my pocket. "Yes, I knew."

"You didn't tell me," he murmured, half to himself. "God, Margot, why do you never tell me *anything* important?"

"I didn't see why it would've mattered to you. Since you were only *paid* to be around me, anyway."

"Jeez, you're so—" He cut himself off with a sharp breath. "Because it's one thing for me to let you go to a guy who called dibs first, it's another when—"

"Dibs." I scoffed, pressing my hotel key to the lock. "What are we, twelve?" It unbolted with a click, but as I grabbed the handle, Sumner's unfinished sentence registered. *It's one thing to let you go.* I frowned up at him. "It's another thing when what?"

Sumner let out a small breath through his parted lips, and when he spoke, his voice was low. "When he doesn't like you like I do."

I was certain I'd heard him wrong. I was certain that the words didn't mean what I wanted them to. Sumner looked stunned at his own confession, lips parted, but earnestness in his eyes. The small, stupid part of me wanted to jump in excitement, but it was too far buried underneath the mountain of something darker.

"Oh, you like me now, do you?" I asked emphatically, and shoved in my hotel room door. It flung into the wall as I stalked in and slapped on the lights, but it didn't swing shut; Sumner propped it open to follow in after me. "You didn't like me before, but you like me now, when you know Aaron doesn't?"

"That's not—"

"How Aaron feels is more important than how I feel, right? I told you that I liked you, but what *Aaron* wanted was more important?" I whirled around, staring at him as he stood in the entryway, the door to the hallway now closed. "Why? Why are you so loyal to him? Because he's rich? Because—"

"Him liking you was *perfect*." The words were strained, almost as if they were painful as they were ripped from him. "Your parents wanted him, his parents loved you, and you could've gone the rest of your life living it *exactly* the way you have been, without ever wondering what something different looked like. It was my fault, coming here and introducing you to the what

336

if. Aaron is the perfect pick. Me wanting you...is a disaster."

His voice trailed off into a weak sound at the end, eyes wrought with ache. It caused something in me to twinge in tandem, the latter half of his words, his confession, bouncing around in my head. "I thought you were only hanging out with me because it was a part of your job description." I tried to pack snark in my voice, but it came out off-kilter. "That you weren't here because you wanted to be."

"It was just a job at first, yes." Sumner closed his eyes briefly, as if he couldn't believe what he was about to say. "After that first event, after what happened, after talking to you—it felt like I *had* to get to know you. I told you before that I know what it feels like to be in a room full of people, but to feel like you don't even exist." A serious shadow covered Sumner's expression. "It was the first time I'd ever seen the exact way I felt reflected back at me. And I couldn't walk away without getting to know you."

The intensity in his stare was almost too much to stand under, but I couldn't bring myself to look away, either. I could do nothing more than scarcely breathe. His confession took mine from a few days ago and blew it out of the water, his words each weighted with sincerity and seriousness. There was no wavering in his voice, no hesitance—after keeping the thoughts to himself, Sumner had no qualms about bringing it all to light.

"You're snarky and pessimistic, and you don't smile often, but when you do—when you do—" Sumner's chest rose and fell once, as if just the image in his head was enough to take his breath away, and he took a step

337

forward. "I've never seen anything more beautiful in my entire life. And the only thing I can think about after is how I'm going to make you smile again."

Ten feet of space stretched between us, and it felt dangerous, like if either one of us crossed the distance, there'd be no turning back. I could picture each time he'd donned the awestruck expression when I smiled, each time it'd struck him speechless. *Am I pretty when I smile?*

You're pretty when you don't, Sumner had replied. *You're beautiful when you do.*

"I didn't push you away for Aaron's sake, but for yours." Sumner advanced a step, and then another, and patted his pockets, a helpless crease forming at his brow. "I'm not even close to the level of Aaron, Margot. You know that. I don't own a multi-million-dollar business; I don't have influential parents. I couldn't tell you the difference between silk and satin, and the watch I wear is probably one you could find at the bottom of a cereal box. I am quite possibly the worst choice for you."

When I spoke, I was surprised with how even I sounded despite how furiously I trembled on the inside. "And you're asking me to choose you anyway?"

"If Aaron Astor is not going to treasure you like the gem you are, then I will." Sumner took slow another step. "And I'll do it gladly."

The words unlocked something in me. I could feel them seep their way through my skin and burrow into my chest. Instead of the pain that normally came with words spoken to me from every other person in my life, Sumner's words unwound something tight. Sumner had seen me in an undesirable light plenty of times, and yet, time and time again, he came to me.

Six feet now, close enough to imagine what it'd be like if his arms surrounded me.

"What if you were right before?" My voice was quiet. "What if I only like you because of the way you make me feel?"

"Like me selfishly. I'll let you. Gladly. I've been liking you selfishly all along."

His insistence caused me to simultaneously melt and freeze, mind playing tug-of-war on which emotion to feel. "I'll have nothing," I told him in more of a warning, because though I'd been the one to confess to him first, the one to open this door, it suddenly terrified me. The prospect of it all, the unknowns. It wasn't a gilded road that I would take. There'd be no streetlights to guide me. "If I leave here, I'll have nothing to offer you. No nice car to drive, no upscale penthouse to sleep in. I couldn't even buy your beans on toast. I won't be a gem anymore, but a commonplace stone. *I'll* have nothing to offer *you*."

"It'll be my turn to take care of you." A small smile lifted his lips as he stopped four feet from me. "I'll work to put you through fashion school and then you can be our breadwinner, and then we can eat all the beans on toast we want. I don't want what you *have*, Margot Massey. I want *you*. If you'll have me."

In the world of Addison high society, everyone was used to the world tipping in their favor. Besides, what did they have to resent besides taxes? Money brought good fortune to them like a magnet, multiplying the luck and growing it further. Grander houses, flashier cars, finer clothes. Everyone made bad investments from time to time, but with the devils they'd sold their souls to on their side, bouncing back from them was a given. Their difficulties were champagne problems, inconsequential and frivolous.

The world never tipped in my favor. My choices were never meaningless, never inconsequential, never frivolous. And in the eyes of everyone else, a bad investment stood before me, with blue eyes that were as enticing as the ocean after a hot day in the sun. One never knowingly walked into a bad investment. No one willingly decided to jump off a precipice without knowing what'd catch them underneath.

I once thought I was far too much of a coward to jump. That I'd rather be stuck in hell than jump. Now, though, I didn't mind if I jumped, so long as I had Sumner's hand in mine.

I crossed the remaining distance, standing before him with terror behind the weight of the choice. Up close, I could see everything about Sumner that I loved, from the freckles under his eyes to the curl of his golden hair. His kindness practically shined in his puppy dog eyes, creating a warmth that wrapped around me like a promise. "You're not allowed to change your mind," I whispered.

"Never."

"You'd be stuck with me, with my snark and pessimism."

"I will be a lucky man." Like he had in the elevator, Sumner reached out and laid his palms on either side of my face, his fingers stretching back to delve into my thick hair. He held me gently, reverently, as if it were something precious in his palms. "And we'll find out what that other life is like together."

And with that, he leaned in and kissed me.

My eyes fluttered shut as Sumner's soft lips pressed against mine, sealing the promise between us. My head swam as my heart raced. I lifted my own hands back up and rested on the tops of his shoulders, anchoring myself to him because otherwise, it felt as if I could float away.

His soft lips on mine turned from sweet and soft to something firmer, teasing, testing as if to see if it was okay. He was so *firm*, and I inched my fingers along the quiet muscle hidden beneath his cotton shirt, pressing closer, closer, until the firmness was everywhere, every inch of him against every inch of me. Sumner's hand that wasn't in my hair slipped down to the small of my back, long fingers spanning and urging me nearer. He kissed me deeply, claiming my mouth in a way I'd been aching for. I melted with the intensity of it, with the sureness of his mouth on mine.

It was a promise of a different sort. *I will treasure you,* his kiss said. *I will treat you well. You are mine, and I am yours.*

I'd always thought each moment in my life was inevitable, even if I'd never seen it coming. My parents deciding where I'd attend college. Their attempt at getting me to marry Aaron Astor. What I didn't realize was that this moment was inevitable, too. I'd never known that kissing Sumner Pennington the night at the first fundraiser would lead to this, but it was like fate, if I believed in such a thing.

And maybe, when it came to Sumner, I did.

I matched him kiss for kiss, stroke for stroke, digging my fingers into his skin as if to burrow my own sincerity deep. *I will treat you well*, I thought.

My mouth opened underneath his, my heart pounding harder. *I will treasure you.*

Sumner gasped against my lips, a beautifully low sound stuck in his throat and stuck in my chest. *You are mine.*

Despite the weight of the decision, in that moment and in Sumner's arms, I'd never felt freer in my life. *And I am yours.*

Chapter 24

I woke the next morning slowly, my blackout curtains preventing the sunlight from rousing me. The first thing that broke into my awareness was the heavy warmth that draped over my side, curved along my stomach. My mind traced the warmth, realizing that it wasn't just on my side, but pressing all along my back as well.

And I found I very much so enjoyed the feeling of someone's body pressed against mine.

I opened my eyes, looking down and finding the tanned arm tucked around me, and the hand that rested off my hip.

No, I didn't enjoy the feeling of just anyone's body pressed against mine. Only Sumner's.

The second thing that broke into my awareness: how painfully hard the thin-carpeted floor was.

We lay in my bedroom, but on the ground, and my duvet we'd dragged from my bed did nothing to cushion the makeshift sleeping pad. Despite accepting my request for him to stay the previous night, Sumner refused to even sit on my bed, let alone sleep on it. *You're being ridiculous*, I'd told him as I laid on the mattress, comfortable under my eight-hundred thread count covers.

His reply had wafted up from the floor. *No, I'm being respectful.*

After my failed attempts to entice him to join me on the mattress, I accompanied him on the floor. My hip would thank me for it later.

With the gentlest touch now, I traced the outline of his long fingers as they curled against my stomach, more of a whisper beneath my fingertip than actual contact. I wanted nothing more than to roll over, to see his sleeping face, but was too afraid the movement would wake him. I settled for gazing at his hand, remembering the first time it'd wrapped so easily around mine.

Of course, though, along with wakefulness, the events of the previous night also washed back in like a rising tide. Sumner's mouth against mine, his confession winding around us and tying us together. My choice, and what impending consequences that choice meant. Aaron's words. Last night, what he'd said had felt overwhelming, damning, but now in the light of the morning, I could see the spew for what it was worth.

Aaron wasn't looking out for Sumner's wellbeing, of course. Instead, he was banking on the hope that I would be selfless enough to walk away before I ruined Sumner. That, once pointed out to me, I wouldn't dream of being selfish enough to continue down the path I set on.

I traced the lines on Sumner's knuckles. I couldn't remember when the last time I'd been selfless was, though. Aaron was putting his faith in the wrong place.

Sumner's arm loosened around my waist as he shifted,

making a low sound in his throat as he woke up. I lay still, trying to keep my breathing even, trying not to give away my own wakefulness, feeling him stretch and stir behind me.

A part of me just wanted to stay in this moment forever—albeit I would've preferred to be comfortable on the bed in this moment forever instead—and never move from the safety and contentment of Sumner's arms. I didn't want the rosy haze of lips on mine from last night to wear off, didn't want the coldness of reality to sink in. In this moment, there was nothing to fear. There was no Aaron Astor and no impending proposal and looming disownment. There was just Sumner and me, slowly waking up with cricks in our necks.

Not now. I settled firmer against him. *Later. We'll think about it all later.*

It was a childish move, sinking my head into the sand, but I did it anyway.

Sumner's hand curled into a loose fist against my stomach before flattening once more, tracing the fabric of my shirt. "Good morning," he murmured in the world's most beautiful voice, breathy and rough and still laced with the lingering sleep.

I sighed at his unknowing refusal to stick his head in the sand with me. I reached down and covered his hand with my palm, fingers slipping in between his.

Sumner brought his body even closer to mine, the back of my legs connecting with the front of his. "How long have you been awake?"

"Not long." I felt so small pressed against his chest, and this hadn't been how we fell asleep last night. We'd been facing each other, and Sumner had traced his fingers through my hair until my eyes slipped closed. It hadn't taken that long; I truly had been wiped out. "I think the pain in my hip woke me up."

He gave a ghostly laugh behind me, one that disappeared into my hair as he ducked his head closer. "You could've stayed in your bed."

"You should've joined me." I scowled at the far wall. "What is the difference, anyway? We're laying exactly like we would've up there, except we're laying on dust bunnies instead of a memory foam mattress."

"It's different," he said, but followed it up with no supporting evidence. Instead, his arm just tightened around me, pressing me closer to him. "What are you doing today?"

Staying here all day. "I should..." I drew in a short breath, something in my stomach turning. "I should probably go see Nancy."

"Probably," he agreed. "You haven't seen her since Sunday, right?"

Not since we'd parted ways at the hospital on awful terms. I knew it was a terrible way to leave things, especially given her precarious health, but more than anger, a different emotion kept me away now. I ran my fingertips over his knuckles. "I'm...scared."

Sumner's voice was soft as his nose brushed my ear. "Of what?"

"I'm afraid I'll go, and I'll find her doing worse." I once more scowled at the wall, because a burning sensation had crept into my eyes. "Which I know is stupid—if I thought she was going to be worse, I should've gone to see her as soon as I could, but..."

"It is scary," Sumner agreed, and he pulled his hand out from underneath mine to trace his hand down my arm, starting where my short-sleeve shirt ended all the way to my wrist. it was a different sort of comforting touch, one that distracted me at the same time. "But it'd be worse to regret it later."

The burning in my eyes intensified, and I squeezed them shut. *Later. We'll think about it all later.* "When did you go to Spain?"

"What?"

"I heard your coworkers you'd been to England and Spain." I settled back firmer against his chest, trying to feel his heartbeat. "I want to know more about you. I feel like... there's more I have to learn."

"And I have more to learn about you. We have all the time in the world to work through it." Sumner's fingertips traced their way back up my arm, a lulling, pacing path. "Those were both trips I took after high school, before college. It was the same trip, really—a long one. Fun, but I learned I'm not really a travel bug."

I hummed a little as I took in his words. The ache in my hip was getting too painful to ignore, but I still didn't move. Because *there*, finally—I held still long enough that I could feel the steady *thump-thump* of his heart through his chest. It was enough to ease the worries I'd woken up with from my mind, or at least ease them enough that they didn't seem so heavy.

"I was thinking about what Aaron said," I told

Sumner suddenly, changing the subject. "Before you woke up."

Sumner laid his hand on my arm, trying to roll me over. "Look at me," he said at once.

"No." My voice was resolute. "I haven't brushed my teeth and I refuse to let you smell my morning breath. I wasn't thinking anything bad. I was just... I think it's funny."

"What's funny?"

"How convinced Aaron was that I'd do the right thing. He thought for sure if the choice was having you and ruining you, that I'd go without." I let out a little breath, one that could've sounded like a laugh in different circumstances. "I just find it funny."

Sumner propped himself up, his elbow digging into the pillows. "Why is that funny?"

"Not funny ha-ha. He just called me selfish, told me all those things about resenting you, and expected me to do the selfless thing." I brought Sumner's hand up to my lips, allowing his skin to absorb my words. "Do you think he knows what irony is?"

Sumner didn't reply at first, most likely struggling to gauge my tone without being able to doublecheck my expression.

"I don't know why he expected that to work," I said ultimately. "He claims he knows me so well, but he doesn't know me at all."

Sumner still didn't speak. I let myself roll just a little bit, just enough to look at him over my shoulder. Sleep left Sumner's golden hair mussed, his blue eyes puffy, everything about him just chest-achingly breathtaking.

How many more times? The words were a whisper in my mind. *How many more times will I get to wake up to this?* "So, you're going to be selfish, then?" he asked with a hopeful tone. *Like me selfishly,* Sumner had said last night. *I'll let you.*

"No." I watched his eyes. "I don't like you just because of the way you make me feel. If that were the case, I would've fired you the moment you called me out for being whiny. Or when you said you enjoyed the beans on toast."

A corner of his mouth peeked up.

"I like you because you're kind and funny and have the cutest puppy eyes. And, sure, maybe we still have a lot to learn about each other, but... that's just another reason to keep going, right?"

The way Sumner propped up had him hovering over me, peering down as if I, too, was the most breathtaking thing he'd seen in a while. I couldn't imagine that being the case; my hair had to be a knotted, rumpled mess. "I think we balance each other out well."

"Meaning you balance me out well."

"I meant what I said." He withdrew his hand from mine and reached up to tuck my hair behind my ear, fingers lingering near the pulse point on my neck. "We've both spent our whole lives doing what other people wanted us to do. You're showing me it's okay to stand up for what you want."

I rolled over flat on my back now, raising an eyebrow. "What are you talking about? *You* were the one that showed *me* it's okay to stand up for what you want. Your whole 'happiness is better' mission, remember?"

349

"I never let myself do it before," he confessed, gaze tracing my face. "I never practiced what I preached. You've shown me that I can be my own person and the world won't fall apart."

"Even though my attempts to be my own person have my world falling apart."

"We're talking about me here."

A startled laugh burst from me, and I pressed a hand over my mouth, far too self-conscious about my unbrushed teeth.

Sumner pulled my fingers away. "I love that I get your real smiles," Sumner said, and he moved his hand from my neck to trace his finger along my lips. His fingertip caressed the bow of my top lip, tracing all the way down to the bottom. It was pure electricity, his touch, waking up my insides and causing my blood to sing. "They're mine."

"I'm yours," I murmured, his finger bumping along my mouth as I spoke. His gaze dipped down to my mouth, the blue darkening like the sky as a storm rolled in. Watching the hue shift, morphing into a new color of desire, caused heat to flush through me, warming any of the frost that'd sunk its teeth into me the night before. I lifted my hand to cover my mouth again. "Don't kiss me; I've got morning—"

"Then keep your mouth shut," he said with affection, grabbing my hand once more, but this time, he didn't let go.

So, despite the bedhead and unscrubbed teeth, with his hand holding mine, Sumner kissed me, and I let him.

And yes, indeed, I very much so liked Sumner's body against mine.

Later that morning, I walked from the hotel to the country club, enjoying the sunlight that gazed down. It seemed horribly cliché, and I'd never admit it aloud, but the air seemed fresher today, the sun brighter. For the first time in the longest time, a smile felt like it was constantly resting just underneath the surface of my mouth—the same mouth that'd kissed Sumner Pennington yesterday.

I was a girl smitten. My pessimistic side said *ew*, but I let myself be cheery. Just this once. And I made sure no one was looking.

With Annalise's wedding happening on Saturday, the country club was a flurry of activity as everyone scrambled to prepare for the wedding of the century. It was all hands-on deck, which meant Sumner had a shift this morning. While I technically still had the power to whisk him away, since his babysitter role was more important than his Alderton-Du Ponte role, I continued to talk myself out of seeing Nancy, pushing it off. We could go later tonight. Maybe we could go out to eat together after we left. Our first official date.

My parents were also in peak stress over the fact that Vivienne Astor would be returning, along with her infamous husband. Some of their stress poured over onto me, of course, because the arrival of the Astors also meant that this weekend was D-Day—to decide which route to take my life.

Not that I even considered the alternative, but it was a lot easier to dream about abandoning everything I'd ever known versus actually doing it.

So, of course, there was only one person I could call who had experience with making her own decisions.

"I'm missing *so much*," Destelle groaned on the other end of the phone.

"That's what you get for following your boyfriend around the country." I walked heel to toe around the east pool, where no one was present on a Wednesday afternoon. The sun was bright, and I'd discarded my suit jacket over one of the lounge chairs. It was getting too hot to wear them, but it felt disconcerting walking out of my room without one, as if I was leaving half-dressed. "It's only just become eventful."

"It wasn't that exciting when I visited in February."

"I do bring the party with me wherever I go."

Destelle's comforting, musical laugh traveled through the phone. "So, let me get this straight—there's a boy."

I scrunched my nose. "A *man*, but yes."

"And it's not Aaron Astor?"

"It is not."

"But you like him."

I thought about Sumner's warm arms around me this morning in bed, the effortless way he held himself above me as his lips touched mine. "Yes."

"And *not* Aaron Astor?"

"Correct. Your listening and retention skills have improved."

She made an offended noise on the other end of the line. "You have my full focus, babe," she returned with a playful drawl. Her voice became serious. "It's a pickle you've found yourself in."

"You did it." I came to a halt at the poolside, staring at

my reflection that rippled in the pearly blue water. "You said to hell with what your family wanted and chose your own path."

"I was a teenager. The stakes were a lot lower then." She hesitated. "And my parents...they're not like yours."

"They're not the worst?"

"I was going to say they're not as cutthroat."

Even though Destelle's parents were influential in their own way, it was clear they'd had children because they wanted to start a family, wanted to grow their love for each other. My parents had me for purely transactional reasons, thinking of what I could've provided them in the future. Destelle was right; it wasn't a fair comparison.

"My parents might've threatened to disown me, but they never would've," Destelle went on. "But yours...they would."

They would, and they'd do so swiftly. They'd cancel credit cards, disable my hotel key, have me removed from the premises. My Gilfman filled closet, revoked. It wouldn't have even surprised me if they'd try to take the suit on my back, even.

The problem was that I'd become too accustomed to *that* Margot. The one who lived in the lap of luxury. I had no idea if I could even exist without everything my parents provided. It was purposeful on their part, of course. To create a life so lavish that I'd never feel comfortable leaving it.

"You told me not to choose Aaron," I pointed out.

"I know, but—and I mean this in the most loving way —I never thought you'd listen to me. Not that I regret telling you to do it, though. If he's just after your inheritance, screw him. But, like, not literally."

"What do you think I should do, then?" I asked, both her and the reflection in the pool water.

The reflection didn't respond, but Destelle did, though it was equally unhelpful. "I can't tell you what to do, Margot. I'm in your corner regardless, of course, you know that, but this... this is too big for me to decide for you."

Of course, I understood her reasoning—I wouldn't have wanted to be in the position either—but it didn't keep me from frowning. "I thought you grew a spine, Stella."

Destelle, from nearly a decade of knowing me, could recognize my tone. A smile was in her voice. "Not with you. You know you've always been the decision-maker between us."

"I do have a more straightforward personality."

"More like a *bulldozer* personality."

Now it was my turn to smirk a little, a twinge prickling behind my ribcage. I missed teasing with her. "I'm disappointed you won't be home for the wedding." It was a selfish thing to say, but it slipped out.

"I'm still coming home," she assured me. "Just after the concert."

"But I have to suffer through the wedding all alone."

"It sounds like you have a cutie guy to keep you company, though."

Not really. It wasn't as if Sumner got to sit by me for the ceremony, for the reception. He'd be catering it, his hands busy all night, his attention forced to focus elsewhere. Even if he hadn't been on the waitstaff for the event, it would've been a hard thing to explain away, why I was so interested in my babysitter.

After suffering in the heat for as long as I could, I collected my jacket and headed into the comfort of the air-conditioned country club interior. I chatted with Destelle as I headed to the lobby, and I passed by the double doors that led into the grand ballroom. They were open, which wasn't common when there wasn't an event, but when I glanced in, I saw why.

And the reason, unfortunately, saw me.

"Oh, Margot!" a crystalline voice called. In the room's corner, surrounded by what looked like a camera crew, a young woman waved at me. "I was hoping I'd run into you!"

I groaned into the phone. "I'll have to call you later."

"You'd better," Destelle replied, and I pulled my phone away from my ear as the newcomer approached.

Annalise Conan was known around the country club as the most beautiful woman in Addison, at least when she'd lived here. Her blonde hair was icy and long, natural ringlets that never frizzed a day in their life. She was tall, slender, fair, pleasant. She had a beautiful laugh and inspired the best warm and fuzzy feelings in everyone she interacted with. In a way, she was almost my antithesis, because everything she was, I was the opposite.

I debated on continuing walking down the hallway, but when the people around her turned, I realized it *was* a camera crew, and they pointed the lens at me. It stunned me enough that I didn't move.

"Oh, it's *so* good to see you!" Annalise said as she

hurried to cross the room to me, her high heels snapping across the marbled floor. The four-man camera crew chased after her, attempting to get in front to capture the most ideal angle. "You've grown into yourself, truly!"

The words felt a little like a dig, but I ignored them. "I could say the same for you," I said, as if she hadn't always been so annoyingly perfect.

When Annalise came close enough, she grabbed my hands that'd been hanging at my sides and leaned in, pressing her cheek against mine and making a kissing sound. I jolted at the sudden closeness, but she was already pulling back by the time I attempted to. "How have you been? We're doing last-minute finalizing of the details for the reception. It's going to be just magical, Margot, you have no idea."

The ballroom itself was in the process of being set up, with fabrics draping from the ceiling and string lights halfway lining the room. I eyed the man who held the camera in his hand, feeling my lips twist into a scowl as I stared directly into the lens. "You're making a documentary of your wedding?"

"*Radiant She Magazine* is doing a special feature on it all," Annalise gushed, biting down on her giddy smile. "Have you seen the engagement photos? They paid for the dresses and gowns, and they rented a mansion in Napa for the shoot. It was *stunning*. Would you like to see? I have pictures on my phone—"

"I'm sure I'll see it all in your little video," I muttered. Not that I planned to watch it, of course. I withdrew my hands from hers and slipped them into my pockets so she couldn't grab at them again. "I'll let you get back to it."

"You can take five," Annalise told the crew. "I want to catch up with an old friend, if that's okay."

Friend. I had to keep myself from making a face, at least until the man lowered his camera. Even with the cameras off, though, Annalise's smile didn't change. Even though she was everything I wasn't, she wasn't *unbearable*. Not like the rest of the people at the country club. Annalise would've been the picture-perfect candidate for marrying Aaron, if a different heir to another company hadn't put a rock the size of Jupiter on her finger first.

"It's a little over the top," Annalise said, and without the fish-eyed lens of a camera on her, she seemed to relax a bit more. She didn't lose her poise entirely, but allowed herself to slouch just a little. "The cameras, the gold. I'm sure I don't have to tell you it's all my mom's doing."

"Mm."

"I'd honestly rather just elope," she went on, shaking her head. "Or have a small wedding. But, no, my mother has to do everything to the nines."

I studied her closely. "What a hard life you live."

Annalise snorted a little. "I know, I know. She's paying for it all, so I should be grateful."

I hadn't realized Yvette had also accompanied her daughter until she stepped into the ballroom with another woman in tow. A wedding planner, I assumed, at least from the conversation. "...and make sure the lighting is grand and golden," Yvette was saying to the woman as they approached. "I want her to look like an angel from heaven, all warm and ethereal."

Annalise straightened upon her mother's presence,

once more donning an excited expression over all the final wedding planning.

"Margot," Yvette greeted in a less-than-friendly voice. "Getting ideas for your own wedding?"

I didn't even blink. "No."

"That's right, that has to be coming up," Annalise said, laying her hand on my arm. "Have you met him yet? Aaron? He's handsome, isn't he?"

Good God, he was all anyone ever wanted to talk about. "Where's your fiancé?" I asked, glancing around the empty room. "He isn't helping with the setup?"

"Oh, he doesn't care about the way anything looks," she said with a wave of her hand. "Just as long as I'm happy."

"Which is just how it's supposed to be," the wedding planner said with a wink, causing all three women to laugh.

I didn't. "So, he's got no say in any of the wedding planning?"

"He got to pick where we honeymoon." Annalise squeezed my arm with a waggle of her eyebrows. "I'm sure he's more excited about that, anyway."

Mrs. Holland gave a scandalized gasp and swatted at her daughter's arm, but her words had already sunk in my stomach. Our paths were glaringly different; Annalise was blessed enough that her wedding wasn't an arranged one—she'd managed to find love as naturally as a rom-com. She could enjoy and even tease about her honeymoon. It wasn't the first time I'd thought about a honeymoon of my own, of course, but it was the first time I actually paused and thought about what would happen during it.

If I married Aaron, would he be expecting an *actual* marriage? Surely. Who would agree to a sexless marriage?

Not that I would marry Aaron. I wouldn't. I didn't even know why I was thinking about it.

When I finally extracted myself from the conversation and walked out of the ballroom, I ran straight into Sumner.

"Woah." His hands came up, latching onto my arms and steadying me. He peered down, a surprised smile on his face. "I was just thinking about you."

And I was just thinking about my nonexistent honeymoon with Aaron. "Here I am," I said awkwardly. Aside from my thoughts about Aaron, I felt shy to look in Sumner's eyes after this morning, waking up in his arms and kissing the morning away. I never was shy; I didn't know I had it in me.

Sumner must've thought my awkwardness was cute and endearing, because his smile broadened. He dropped my arms, though, severing our connection. "When did you want to go to Nancy's?"

"This is about the time she takes her midday nap," I lied, starting down the hallway, letting him follow. I fluffed my suit jacket over my arm, shaking off the strangeness. "So maybe later."

He saw through me. "Margot—"

"I was thinking," I said as we approached the lobby. "We should go on an official first date, shouldn't we? I never got a chance to take you to Pierre's to eat—you'll love it."

"You just want your avocado toast."

I cracked a smile. "You do know me."

I reached for him, but Sumner slid just out of reach, eyes shifting around. "Not here."

"Here" meant down the hallway from the elevator, just in front of one of the staff rooms. If we continued down the hallway, we'd get to the lobby. Right here, though, no one was around.

In that moment, a voice floated from the direction of the lobby, just loud enough for the owner to register. "It's great that you flew in early," Aaron Astor said, sounding as if he were walking closer. "We can get a round of golf in before—"

Sumner's reaction was far quicker than mine. He gripped my wrist and tugged me toward him, simultaneously slapping his ID card on the staff only door. He rushed us inside, sealing it quickly and shutting us inside the narrow darkness.

I blinked, but my view didn't change. "So, you can recognize Aaron Astor by his voice now, can you?" I mused as I stared at him in the black. Or, really, stared in his general direction. "I take it back. My parents won't be pissed if you run off into the sunset with him, but I will be."

"I was waiting for him to appear, actually." Sumner flicked the light switch on the wall, and then the small closet brightened with light. It was a storage closet for linen and towels, most likely an area where someone folded them, because there was a long countertop stretching against the back wall. "The bridal party has been helping set up for the wedding all morning. I figured he'd turn up sooner or later, and it had to be the moment I found you."

I hummed a little as I glanced around the space. Sumner stood just in front of the door, blocking any escape, but also blocking anyone from being able to come in. Aaron, even if he had seen us, wouldn't have been able to follow without a key card, so we were safe in here. Most likely, Aaron was already gone, disappeared into the main ballroom. I almost told Sumner this, that we could probably step out now, but in the small space, my thoughts began to tip-toe down a different path. A path that chased away those negative thoughts and feelings of the previous conversation, at least for a moment.

A small smile tipped my lips.

Sumner watched my mouth as it smiled. "What?"

"I'm leaving the hotel today," I said, taking a slight step closer.

"To someplace other than Nancy's?"

With a slight touch, I rested one hand on Sumner's side, feeling the firmness through his polo. "I'm leaving the hotel," I repeated, watching as his breath hitched. "Which means you're going to tell Mr. Roberts you had to come with me. Which means you're mine now."

I loved that Sumner wasn't too much taller than me, so I didn't have to fight to draw his mouth to mine. All I had to do was tip onto my toes and lean in, and that was what I did. With my hand curving around his side, I leaned into him, kissing him without a trace of delicacy in the small space of the closet.

Even if his words had been ever true to his positivity, I hoped this moment could chase away any shadow of a doubt, if it lingered with him. I didn't care about Aaron and my parents and what they wanted. I just wanted Sumner.

"Margot," he murmured against my mouth, but his lips were yielding against mine. "We should—"

"Kiss. We should kiss."

Sumner melted into me, responding to my touch, my lips. And for a moment, the power balance weighed heavily in my favor, the kiss *mine*, under my full control. He let it go on for a few more moments before shifting.

His mouth became a firmer pressure on mine, the confidence building from my encouragement. One of his hands came up to cup just under my jaw, the other falling to the flare of my hip. The two points of contact were the grounding points of electricity, and it hummed through me, sparking each time his lips parted from mine and returned with urgency. With his grip on me firm, he pushed closer.

Sumner walked me backward, backward, until my spine collided with the housekeeping cart that was parked in the corner of the closet. Sumner pressed me firmer against it, the plastic digging into my back, but I could barely feel anything other than his hands as they roamed over my body. The thin linen cloth was a cruel barrier. My own hands were aching to run underneath the polo, to feel the smooth skin of his stomach, but for some reason, wouldn't go any further than pressing against his cloth-covered chest. My mind was brave, but my fingers were shy.

He clasped my waist, and without breaking his mouth from mine, he lifted me up onto the housekeeping cart. At this angle, he had to tip his head back to kiss me, but I was at the perfect angle to taste him deeper. He stepped between my knees, his hands tightening on my hips in a way that caused my heart to race faster and faster.

"Okay, okay," Sumner gasped, pulled back from me, chest heaving. "Let's—let's stop here."

I watched him attempt to recover from the moment, his swollen lips parted as he tried to catch his breath. Something about the sight of him undone lit a warmth inside me, a flame licking along my insides. I locked my legs around his waist, holding him to me. "Not yet," I murmured, reaching my hand around the back of his neck to twine my hands into the ends of his hair. "Not that easily."

"You..." Sumner let out a small breath, and he laid his palm on the surface of the housekeeping cart beside my hip to brace himself. "You're a bad influence."

"Why bad?" I slipped my fingers further into his hair, pressing into his scalp. "You don't like it?"

Sumner's eyelashes fluttered, the blue in his eyes growing stormy. "A bad influence," he repeated, though this time far, far breathier. "Listen, I wanted to tell you before you found out from anyone else—your parents told me I'm not working the wedding."

"Like, not being my babysitter during it?" It made sense he wouldn't be needed, since I'd be either on Aaron's arm all night or with my parents. "Or not catering?"

Sumner sighed. "They asked me to not attend altogether."

My fingers hung limply off his belt loops, my arms suddenly becoming heavy. "Did they say why?"

"Aaron asked for me not to attend. They said...they said that they no longer needed my services with you."

His words broke apart the haze his kiss had settled over me, but I still didn't let him go. He didn't step back either. Of course Aaron asked my parents to not let Sumner attend the wedding; he probably asked them to fire Sumner, too. Anything to separate us. Aaron no doubt thought that was his best chance.

But them firing Sumner as my secretary also meant I was also running out of time before I had to make the big decision. "It doesn't mean we have to stop spending time together," I told him. "Just because you're not my secretary anymore doesn't mean anything."

"There's something else." Nervousness tightened his gaze. "You know... You know how you said it's okay that we don't know everything about each other, that we can get to know each other as we go? Well, there's something I want to tell you. Later tonight. It's nothing bad, but something that will probably be a long conversation."

My frown deepened. "Pass."

Sumner chuckled a little, but it was a tense sound, one that did nothing to ease me. "I'll get you an avocado toast for it."

"That's a brunch food. I can't have it for dinner."

"You're saying no to avocado toast?"

No, I was saying no to whatever serious conversation Sumner wanted to have. It was a bad sign, probably, that we were not even one day into our relationship and I wanted to dodge the important conversations. I was back to sticking my head in the sand, it seemed. "Tonight," I said, readjusting my legs in how they were wrapped around his waist. "But not now."

"Not now," he repeated, eyes falling back once more to my lips.

With my grip on his hair, I angled his head back once more and reclaimed his mouth with mine.

"Oh!"

We'd been so absorbed in each other that we hadn't even heard the whirring click of the locked door unlocking and then opening. At the exclamation, Sumner broke away from me, and this time, I allowed him to untangle himself with ease. A middle-aged woman in the country club's teal polo stood there with her jaw dropped open fully, scandalized—but not looking away.

I hopped off the counter with as much grace as I could muster, thanking my lucky stars that my jelly legs held me up. "Hope we didn't startle you too much," I said to the woman in an unaffected tone, willing my pulse to slow down. Channeling my ice queen self was a lot harder when my blood burned. "We were just making sure everything was...well-stocked."

I looked at Sumner for him to say *something* in support of my lie, but he was absolutely terrible at lying— he choked on his breath, his neck beet red in embarrassment.

"Happy cleaning," I said with false cheer, grabbing Sumner's wrist and tugging him past the woman and out of the closet. He stumbled out after me as I headed toward the lobby. "We *really* need to work on your poker face, Sumner."

"Sumner Pennington!"

Sumner and I both turned sharply toward the new voice, finding a man in a green sweater with ankle-length pants striding over to us from the direction of the lobby. Thankfully, not Aaron, who we seemed to dodge. The man looked about Sumner's age—maybe a few years older —with a speckling of well-groomed facial hair along his jaw. I stared openly at him, because I knew for a fact I'd never seen him before in my life. He wasn't a member at the country club.

Sumner, though, recognized him; that much was clear by the way he drew in a breath. Not quite a gasp, but more of a bracing sound, one filled with surprise.

"It's so good to see you," the man said as he came closer, his grin broadening with each step. He loomed tall, but his smile was too boyish to be imposing. "It's been way too long."

"Too long," Sumner echoed as the man pulled him in for a hug, clasping Sumner hard on the back. I studied the differences in their posture. The man, who looked effort- lessly happy about seeing Sumner again, was a stark contrast to Sumner's visible discomfort. Sumner's blue eyes cut to me, a look of almost panic in them.

I decided to cut in. "And who might you be?" I asked in a dull voice, maintaining an icy cold shoulder to whoever this was who was making Sumner so nervous.

"Michael Huntsly," he replied, pulling off Sumner and offering me a hand. The Rolex on his wrist snuck out from underneath the sleeve of his sweater, a peek-a-boo of expensiveness. "Pleased to meet you."

"Huntsly," I echoed, returning the firm grip. I

couldn't figure out why it sounded so familiar. The situation, the longer it continued, only left me more and more confused. I tried to sort through the pieces, but I couldn't figure out how they fit together. "How do you know Sumner?"

Sumner opened his mouth to answer, but Michael replied, "We were friends back in California."

"Really?" I kept my intrigue to a minimum, at least visibly. Sumner had talked about his friends once before, and I tried to recall what he'd said. One was engaged and one was busy all the time. I thought about asking which one he was, but when I looked at Sumner, he still seemed stiff as a board. He wasn't looking at either of us, his gaze unfocused on Michael's shoes. His face was pale.

I laid a hand on his arm, ready to give us an out of this conversation that was making him so uncomfortable. "Well, we were just on our way—"

"Could you maybe give us a few minutes?" Sumner asked me suddenly, his eyes wide. He attempted a smile, but it was worlds away from his genuine grin that I saw through it immediately. "To catch up?"

"Of course," I replied without pause, giving his arm an affectionate squeeze. *Comfort*, I tried to convey, except I wasn't as good at it as he was. I turned to Michael. "It was nice to meet you."

He had a smirk on his face as he glanced between the two of us, offering his hand out once more. "Hopefully we can get to know each other before I go back home. It was a true pleasure to meet you..." He trailed off expectantly.

I placed my hand in his grip. "Margot."

The easygoing grin he'd had on his face the entire

time faltered then, subtly enough that if I hadn't been looking, I wouldn't have noticed. But I was always looking; I always noticed.

I still gave Sumner the privacy he asked for, though, mind working. If this was the friend who'd introduced him to beans on toast, the one he butted heads with on the phone, maybe Sumner had mentioned me. Maybe Sumner told him more about the selfish rich girl side about Margot Massey in the beginning instead of the version of me now, maybe that was why Michael's expression had faltered. Maybe—

I stopped at the mouth of the lobby. In front of the front desk sat a woman in a wheelchair, her head too low to even see over the top of the mahogany. "Nancy?"

She didn't hear my voice at first, so I called her name again. Nancy seemed to slump back in her wheelchair when she found me, her frail hands reaching for the guards on her wheels. "There you are," she said, her voice breathy as if she were about to cough. She shot a glare to the receptionist. "Wasn't so hard, was it?"

Like she had Sunday, she looked *rough*. Gray. Like keeping her spine upright was taking all her energy. "Why were you looking for me at the country club and not the hotel?"

Nancy did cough this time, a congested sound. "I... thought I was at the hotel."

"Who brought you here?" I didn't recognize anyone in the lobby.

"Ally had hot yoga." Nancy craned her neck, attempting to look around. "I understand why living here isn't a hardship. There are delicious men *everywhere*."

The urge to give her the cold shoulder was strong, especially because she was acting like the last time we parted had been on good terms. Not her being rushed to the hospital and then yelling at me for being concerned. The urge, too, to scold her for yet again leaving the house tugged at me, but I held back.

Nancy picked up my hand before I could say anything. Her fingers were icy cold, and when I looked closer at them, I could see their color was grayish. "Walk me around the grounds, would you?"

"What? Why?"

"It's been too long since I've seen everything."

It wasn't often Nancy asked me for favors, at least not in the direct way as she had. Perhaps this was her way of waving a white flag after the whole hospital incident, attempting to get on my good side so I'd start visiting again. Perhaps she just needed someone to wheel her around and preferred me, who wouldn't be sappy and dramatic like Ms. Jennings or Yvette would be.

I walked around to the backside of her wheelchair and grabbed the handles. "Annalise's setting up in the ballroom."

Nancy coughed, and it morphed into a grumble. "Show me everywhere *but* the ballroom, then."

Despite everything, I allowed myself a small smirk.

Chapter 25

Nancy sat with her hands in her lap as we walked through the building, quiet as she took it all in. We stopped by the indoor rec center, where the daycare had taken the kids to play around in the open space. I paused there, allowing Nancy a few minutes to smile at the children, before we moved onto the indoor pool area. Though it was well-occupied in the winter months, it was empty now, everyone preferring the summer sun than to indoors.

"I remember breaking ground for this and thinking it was ridiculous," Nancy said as we walked past the broad, glass windows where we could see inside. "We had *two pools* outside; why did we need one inside? But Herbert was persistent..."

From the indoor pool, we made our way outside to the west pool. Little kids filled its shallow waters, splashing around, the loungers filled with parents who barely watched and allowed the lifeguard to do all the heavy lifting.

Nancy was quiet for most of the meandering we did, though, taking in the nostalgia in silence. I tried not to think too hard about why she suddenly came to the country club just to tour it, a place she never cared to visit in the previous years. Instead, I, too, remained quiet, focusing on the clicking of my shoes as I walked across the cobblestoned path.

We ended our journey near the beginning of the golf course. Nancy lifted her hand to signal me to stop, and we came to a halt at the crest of the hill that overlooked the visible holes. There were a few carts in the distance, men lining up their shots, and we watched them in uneasy silence.

"It's quite lovely to build something from the ground up," Nancy murmured, her voice almost too soft to hear. I had to lean in, gripping the handles of her wheelchair tighter. "This country club—it's like a child of mine, in a way. No one thinks about that anymore, though. That receptionist in there had no idea who I was."

"You're not royalty, Nancy."

"No," she agreed, lacking the bite and scorn I'd been waiting for. Her tone was too hushed. "I've watched it grow so much, but you know, Margot... I don't care to watch it anymore."

I bit down on the inside of my cheek. "You did a good job," I got out, matching her seriousness despite the slow suffocation in my lungs. "You've built a beautiful place."

"And everyone inside it is rotten."

I didn't argue with her.

"Your fiancé," Nancy began, but had to cough hard enough that it pitched her body forward. I eyed her just to make sure she didn't slide from the wheelchair, much like she had at the dinner table. The visual made me shift on my feet. "Have you gotten any closer with him?"

I thought about last night at the bar, his whisky-coated words foggy now. "No."

Nancy *harrumphed*, but it was a pleased sound.

"You don't like him," I said.

"I don't know him," she returned, voice tired. "I don't care to, either, but that doesn't mean anything. I'm old and grouchy. I don't like anyone I meet."

"You liked Sumner."

Nancy sighed again, but agreed, "I like Sumner."

"I'm thinking about running away with him," I said casually, as if the words weren't ones that could change the entire trajectory of my future. "Sumner, I mean. I think I could make him into a good housewife."

Nancy didn't turn to look at me, but continued to focus on the green. "You'd give up everything for him?" she asked, skeptical. It was far easier to have such a weighted conversation when neither of us looked at each other. "Everything you've ever known for a man you met a month ago?"

Well, I did not like it when she put it that way. "I thought you *wanted* me to end up with Sumner instead of Aaron."

"Love is the first thing to go when you're struggling for money."

I knew that, of course. It was, after all, one of the biggest things holding me to my parents like a chain around my wrist.

"But, if you choose the money path, you may end up like me," Nancy went on, and if I hadn't known any better, I would've thought her voice grew sad. "A widow after a loveless marriage with no children. Enough money to swim in, but nothing to spend it on and no one to spend it with. Now, which sounds better to you?"

It was another example of what life would look like if I chose Aaron, which should've made the answer obvious. I could've married Aaron, but it was a different kind of lonesomeness waiting for me then. The worst kind—being alone when the room is filled with people. But just because I chose Sumner now didn't extinguish that fear. "Do you think I'll ruin him?" A drip of sweat slid down between my shoulder blades, but I felt cold. "That I would be a black hole to his starlight?"

"I think you're giving yourself an awful lot of credit if you think you can ruin him so easily. In fact, since you met him, I rather think it's been the other way around, don't you?"

I didn't respond. It was true that over the course of the past month, I'd smiled more than I had in years. The muscles in my face had only just begun to grow used to it.

"Come here," Nancy said, using her grip on my hand to draw me to the front of her wheelchair.

I knelt down, and for the first time in years, I felt like a little girl before her. I had fierce déjà vu of years past, looking up at Nancy. I could remember her in the different stages of my life, more of a pillar than my own parents were. She attended my graduations, she sat beside me at all the country club functions, she bought me birthday gifts. I remembered her young, when we'd swim in the east side pool together. I remembered her older, when she started having health issues. I remembered when she first was resigned to her wheelchair.

Her wrinkles were deeper now, her hair was whiter, and the life that'd burned in her eyes with the fire of her ire had dimmed. I desperately searched the depths for the flame now, but only found a flicker.

"Whatever you choose, you *will* be okay." Nancy's hand trembled as she held my fingers tighter, or attempted to—I could barely feel her grip. "Choose what you think will make you happy in the long-term. Build something from the ground up. Choose to be happy. You deserve it."

I swallowed hard, lifting my chin. "Why are you being so serious? It's not like you."

"I just want the best things for you." With her other hand, Nancy reached out and touched my cheek, pinching everything inside me tighter. "You're the grand-daughter I never got to have."

"Stop—stop talking like this," I ordered her, sniffing. "Stop being mushy-gushy."

She patted my cheek, but there wasn't enough strength to make it sting. "I'm trying to have a nice moment, you brat."

But I didn't want a nice moment. I didn't want her speaking to me as if she'd never see me again. *Later*, I wanted to say. *We'll think about it all later*. Sumner was right, though, when he said it was better to face something that scared me than to regret it later. I'd never be able to live with myself and if I left regrets with Nancy. Never. So, despite the burn in my eyes and the tension in my throat, I nodded. "I'll choose to be happy," I whispered, squeezing her hand in mine. "Just for you."

Nancy gave me a warm, satisfied smile. Smiles on Nancy were rare and normally were unsettling, but this one was beautiful. It lifted her wrinkles and lightened her eyes, giving me a clearer glimpse once more at who she was when she was young. "Good girl," she said with tired affection, and pulled both hands back into her lap. "Now, enough with that sappiness. Let's go find me some tush to gawk at."

And off we went, leaving the serious moment behind at the cusp of the golf course, a memory trapped within the Alderton-Du Ponte Country Club forever.

Chapter 26

*N*ancy Rose Du Ponte passed peacefully in her sleep that night. I'd gotten the call from Ms. Jennings around seven-forty-five o'clock, answering to sobbing from the other line. Nancy had been tired after her excursion at the country club and had excused herself to her bedroom for a nap before supper. When Ms. Jennings went to wake her, Nancy had been gone. Sumner and I had been driving to Pierre's for a late dinner of our own; it'd been the only reservation I could snag for that day. We'd turned around immediately, rushing to a person we were far too late to be there for.

Margot, I'm old, she'd said once upon a time. *I'm going to drop dead sometime. You'll have to get over it.*

At least have the decency not to do it while I'm watching. The harsh words were ones I'd snapped out of frustration, anger, and yet she'd listened to them. Peaceful in her bed, she'd left with no one to hold her hand when she went. Gone before I could even say goodbye.

The middle-aged pastor at the podium presumedly spoke pleasantly about the woman in the black framed photograph behind him, readjusting his glasses every few moments to peer more closely at his papers. I wasn't sure if the microphone wasn't working or if his voice was too quiet for the equipment to pick up. Either way, I wasn't sure I wanted to hear a single thing out of his mouth. Most likely, he was repeating the same canned cliché sayings one could find on a webpage "How to Preach at a Funeral."

"Nancy lived a good life" and *"she leaves behind a legacy"* and *"she's no longer in pain"* were the only phrases that'd been picked up by the mic that I caught.

They weren't wrong, of course, but empty, as hollow as my chest felt now.

While Nancy Du Ponte had no children, she'd been surrounded by dozens of families she met while helping her late husband establish the very first and only country club in Fenton County. She was gruff at times, enjoyed a good sarcastic remark, but she was someone who attended all the events, the gatherings, and enjoyed seeing life continue around her. Even if she ended up at a table alone, she enjoyed seeing all the hard work pay off. She loved seeing everyone enjoy the country club she helped establish.

And not a single one of them showed up to her funeral.

The vultures that'd been circling her for months, picking at the exposed flesh of a dying woman, scattered when there was no more meat left to peel off. Nancy was gone; there would be no more amendments made to her will. There was no reason to show up at the funeral of an old woman who gave them nothing in the end. Not even

Ms. Jennings showed. I didn't even care to hear her excuse.

It should've enraged me to no end, but it didn't. Staring at the photograph of Nancy near the podium, one taken a few years ago when she still had plumpness to her cheeks, I didn't feel anything. No anger, no sadness. Nothing at all.

There were probably near one hundred chairs, but the funeral hall only consisted of six people. The pastor, two elderly women, me, and Sumner. Sumner sat at my side and held my hand in his, resting both of them on his knee. My fingers were limp in his grip, but I cherished the small warmth.

"Nancy brought joy to the people around her," the pastor said, voice suddenly cutting through the room. The microphone had been the problem, after all. "She was a bright light and always put a smile on others' faces. I can see that from the many—uh, from those who've showed up for her today."

The pastor looked up from his notes with a little bit of horror, realizing his pre-written response made no sense. He looked even sweatier.

I refocused on her portrait. *You chose a crappy pastor, Nancy.* Her smile never changed.

Nancy had known her health was declining fast. Sunday, when she'd collapsed at the table and we took her to the hospital, Dr. Conan had told her that her heart was tired. Her organs were in the process of shutting down. He'd given her something for the pain, but he'd told her it wouldn't be long. And it turned out that Nancy had been preparing for her impending death in the weeks leading up to it. She'd gotten her affairs in order with her lawyers, sat down with the funeral home, picked out a cremation plan. She wanted her funeral three days after her death, and the funeral home arranged it. Apparently, she'd paid for expedited services, given that her urn already sat beside her portrait.

"Nancy chose cremation," the pastor went on, shuffling through his papers. "She shared with me, once upon a time, that she didn't want to be in a cemetery surrounded by people she didn't know. She wanted to be spread at her favorite place on earth: the pond behind her house."

I thought of the last time we were there together, looking at the water. Of all the times I stood there with her, both of us just quietly watching the ripple in the surface as the wind brushed along. It made sense she'd want to be scattered there, at the home she made her own, but I couldn't help but feel like it was such a waste. A waste to lay her to rest in a place no one would ever visit.

"Normally, after a service, we continue onto a luncheon, but, well—the only place Nancy had in her notes is booked today, unfortunately. So, the funeral dinner will be postponed."

My lips twisted, and I tipped my face toward my lap. The only place Nancy requested to have her celebration of life at was the country club, which was rented out for Annalise's wedding. The main ballroom was, at least. The smaller event hall off the back wasn't, but they refused to double rent out the space even though they'd done it dozens of times before. I wasn't sure who'd been in charge of that decision. I didn't care.

It was just ironic. The place she helped grow from the ground up, the place she helped break ground on, the place that wouldn't have been where it was today without her, the last place she wanted to visit before she passed—they wouldn't even open their doors for her ashes.

"I'd like to think Nancy is smiling down at all of you, the warm and bubbly woman she was," the pastor said as he began his closing statements. "Think of her as you go about life, and continue to do the things that would've made her smile."

But Nancy wasn't a smiler, I wanted to tell him. She might've been smiling in the portrait on the podium, but it was rare for her to show her happiness in that way. Quips and barbs and witty remarks—that was Nancy. Even her laugh had a wicked witch sound to it. *Warm* and *bubbly* would never be two words I'd use to describe her.

The funeral director—who was not the man standing watch in the back—took over the microphone from the pastor, sharing his own sentiments, and saying that now the funeral service concluded, there was no other direction for us to go. No dinner, no cemetery. From here, there was nothing left to celebrate Nancy's life other than going home. The old ladies in the row ahead of me walked out first, not bothering to step up to Nancy's urn and pay their respects one more time. One had a tissue pressed into her nose and the other had red-rimmed eyes. Both of their cheeks were dry. I didn't recognize either of them.

I wondered if they were crying for Nancy or because they knew that with their white hair and walking canes that they weren't far off from an urn themselves.

Sumner sat still at my side. He wore the khaki pants

that Nancy had always loved on him, and a black long-sleeve shirt that he had pushed up to his elbows. I wore a black dress pants that tapered at my ankles, with a black shirt and a black vest tight around my midsection. We were a pair of mourners, the only ones left in the funeral hall.

"Well, one thing's for sure," I finally said, my voice low with disuse. "Nancy would've laughed at that trainwreck."

A chuckle burst free from Sumner before he could dam it up, and his mouth twitched as he fought to keep the corners down. "It's not funny."

"It is a little."

Sumner pressed his lips together. "We can't laugh in a funeral hall."

"What are we going to do? Cause a scene? What, will the ghosts be offended?"

Something about that bled some of his humor, and he looked down at where our hands still rested on his knee. He coasted his thumb over the back of mine.

It was almost as if it hadn't hit me yet, Nancy being *gone*. It didn't feel like she was. It felt like she'd be at home, watching her bad TV shows. That if I called her, she'd pick up. That if I pulled into her driveway and stepped into her house, I'd find her sitting in her wheelchair out in the backyard, gazing at her algae-infested pond.

I hadn't cried yet, not even when we arrived at her house to find the funeral home wheeling her bagged body into their hearse; I wasn't sure what that said about me.

I could feel Sumner looking at me, no doubt with

concern in his expression over how flat my voice was. Those were the looks I'd been getting over the past few days. They only increased my unease.

"I wonder what everyone will say as an excuse," I murmured, beginning to pick at the buttons on my vest. "Do you think they'll say they put the wrong date on their calendar? That they were too busy with wedding preparation to come? Not everyone can use that excuse, surely."

Sumner's fingers caught at mine where they'd been plucking at my buttons, saving from ripping the thread loose. "I'm sure you're all she'd have wanted to see."

I stared at the back of the chair in front of me. Focusing on the skin there helped me ignore the pressure that'd wrapped around my throat. "Yeah."

"I think you missed the wedding ceremony, but you'll still make it in plenty time for the reception."

My *generous* parents allowed my absence for Annalise's wedding on the sole condition that I would be present for the reception. They made it clear that if I did not show up, they'd hunt me down. *Sign our name on the guestbook,* they'd told me, as if their names written on a piece of paper no one would ever read was respectful enough.

"A travesty," I said. "I was hoping the pastor ramble about Nancy and her *bubbly personality* longer."

"For a moment there, I thought he'd walked into the wrong funeral."

I smirked a little before standing, squeezing Sumner's hand once more before letting go. "Thank you for coming. For...being with me."

"I knew Nancy, too," he told me, blue eyes bright. He rose to his feet, too, and he laid his hands on my shoulders and forced me to face him. My body responded by swaying closer. "I'm here because I want to be."

The weight of his hands, in reality, was slight, but it felt as though they held me heavily to the floor. I didn't like it. I didn't like feeling grounded to the moment. It'd been this way the past few days, Sumner picking up my hand, offering the little touches here and there. In a distant way, I appreciated it, but each time he looked at me like that—with sympathy swimming in the blue eyes of his—it felt as if I was moments away from drowning myself.

And I hated myself for feeling that way. "Don't look at me like that," I told him.

"Like what?"

"Like I'm going to start crying. That's the only way you've been looking at me."

"It's okay if you do." Sumner's hands shifted from my shoulders to rub down my upper arms, though I couldn't feel his touch through the fabric of my shirt. "Crying isn't a bad thing, Margot. Sleep isn't either, and you haven't been getting nearly enough of it."

I moved away enough that his hands fell off my arms. "You worry too much."

Sumner tilted his head a little, that sad expression deepening. "Don't push me away, Margot."

"I'm not."

"You are, because it's what you do."

Something dark rolled over me, like a cloud blocking sunlight. It left me cold, near shivering. I didn't look at him. I stared at Nancy's portrait. Her smile became creepier the longer I looked. I almost wondered if it was photoshopped.

"Why don't we skip the wedding? I'm sure everyone would understand—"

"I can't." As tempting as it was, I didn't let myself entertain his words for longer than a moment. "I have to meet the Astors."

"Why do they matter? You're not going to marry Aaron."

I hesitated. I didn't know why I hesitated, but the silence in the beat before I spoke was louder than my words. "I don't know."

"You don't know what? You don't know why they matter, or you don't know if you're marrying Aaron?"

I did not want to marry Aaron Astor. I didn't know why I couldn't say that. I should've told him Aaron was a nonissue, that meeting the Astors meant nothing, but I couldn't. The words wouldn't form. I normally loved Sumner's full attention, but it felt almost suffocating now, and I hated that I felt that way. I hated myself for feeling sick when he turned to me with that concerned expression. I hated myself for it.

You like how he makes you feel, but what happens when he doesn't make you feel good anymore? Aaron's words, for no reason, crept back into my mind. *Will you grow to resent him? Will he grow to resent you?*

I closed my eyes now to block out the words, but it didn't work.

We're not meant to be the main leads in rom-coms,

Margot. Not everyone is meant for love. You have to see that.

Panic fluttered through me, the first real emotion I'd felt in days. I couldn't even put a name to the *wanting* in my rib cage, but all I knew was that it felt as I could've collapsed under the pressure. I surely couldn't be made for love, because I couldn't even muster up a single tear at the funeral of the woman I loved more than my own parents.

Without warning, Sumner wrapped his arms around me, tugging me flush to his chest, almost as if he could read my mind. I'd never considered myself a dainty girl who could fall into the arms of someone for comfort, but here I was now. I felt small against him, consumed, and for a moment, I gave into the desire and melted into him. *Sumner, Sumner, Sumner.* The scent of the cologne in the fabric of his shirt calmed me somewhat. I wanted to burrow into his chest and never emerge.

The darkness was still there, but it was like he was trying to extinguish it with the warmth exuding from him. I let him try. "How can I help you, Margot?" The words were just a step above a mumbled whisper, and I could feel them vibrate in his chest. "Tell me, and I'll do it."

I wanted to tell him that he'd done plenty over the past few days, enough to last a lifetime. I appreciated everything he'd done since Nancy's passing—ordering me room service, staying with me until I fell asleep for the night, holding my hand as long as I needed it. Why couldn't I tell him any of that? Why couldn't I just let myself be vulnerable with him?

"Do you have a sister?" I asked into his chest.

I could practically feel Sumner's confusion. "What?"

"Do you have a sister?" I tightened my hold on him. "Tell me."

"I do. She's older—in her thirties." Sumner's hand smoothed up and down my back in slow, lulling movements. "Why?"

Because I want Aaron's voice out of my head. "Any brothers?"

"No. No brothers. I think that's why my mom thought I'd be a girl, since she already had one. Why are you asking?"

"I never ask questions about you," I whispered, a burning popping into my eyes. "I should ask more questions."

Sumner's voice grew gentle, mimicking the touch along my spine. "Stop, Margot."

"Stop what?"

"We learn things about each other *in time.* That's how relationships work." Sumner pulled away enough to tip his head down toward me. "You're not running out of time with me. I'm here. I promised, remember?"

I drew away from his chest and sniffed, though there were still no tears in my eyes. The burning, though, still remained. "You did promise," I said thickly, fingers once more finding their way to my vest's buttons. "I should've asked Nancy more questions."

Sumner once more caught at my fingers and stopped them from ruining the fabric. "I'm sure you asked her plenty, Margot. And besides, Nancy's the kind of woman who only tells you what she wants to. Even if you didn't ask, she'd have told you something if she wanted you to know it."

He was right, of course. And if I asked her about something she didn't want to share, she never would. She'd never be vulnerable unless she chose to be, and even with me, that was rarely.

"Tell me what you need. If you need space—if you need me to call an Uber and let you go back to the hotel alone—I can do that. I don't want to, but if it's what you need, I will."

Alone. If Sumner hadn't been here today, I would've been alone during her service. Mourning one of the most important people in my life...all by myself. I well and truly would've gone insane then; I just knew it. And it wasn't necessarily the fact that I wanted to be alone because I didn't want to be around anyone—I wanted to be alone to keep these feelings from lashing out.

But another small cry echoed in my head. *Please, please, please don't leave me. Don't let me push you away.*

Nancy had never been vulnerable with me, who was one of the most important people in her life, and I didn't want to be that way with Sumner. I realized, much like being alone, it was a choice. A hard choice, because it was easier to push someone away, to run from anything uncomfortable. But Sumner was right. That was how relationships worked.

I twisted my fingers in his hand so that they could squeeze his. I tried to imagine this moment without a hand to hold, without a comfort, and thinking about the alternative helped me realize how grateful I actually was for his presence. Even if I felt like a timebomb about to explode. "I don't want you to leave," I murmured. "Could you go pull the car around, though? I just want a few minutes... with Nancy."

"Of course," he answered with so much tenderness in the two words. With his free hand, he dragged the pad of his thumb along the top of my cheekbone. "Come out to me whenever you're ready."

He waited for me to pull my hand back first, but before I did, I leaned forward and kissed him. It was probably inappropriate, given our location, but I had never cared about propriety. It was a short kiss, an assurance where my words were lacking. A promise, of sorts. *I'm here. I'm not going anywhere either.* I squeezed my eyes shut and pulled back.

I half expected the pastor to remain and speak with anyone who wanted to talk to him, but he must've realized that there was no one to talk *to*. I was sure my stone-faced expression during his sermon left him not really wanting to talk to me, either. But the funeral hall was completely empty now, with no sound to echo off the walls.

I walked up to Nancy's portrait and urn, staring at the wooden lacquered box with her name engraved into it. The date of her birth and death seemed impossibly far apart, nearly a century. And if the birth date was correct, it made her a year older than she always said she was. Ninety-one instead of ninety. An ancient lady. Not anymore.

"You're such a coward, you know that?" I said to her

urn, to the burnt up remains of her just barely hidden from view. "Making me go to Annalise's wedding alone. You were the one I was supposed to sit and talk to."

I stared at her urn, trying to imagine what she'd say in response to that—something snippy, I was sure—but her voice was quiet in my mind.

"Then again, it's totally like you to mar the beautiful day of the Conan wedding. It's something I would've done."

Again, I couldn't imagine what she'd say to that. That was almost more painful, the silence of her voice. I hadn't thought the absence of her would come so quickly, but it was like my brain couldn't recall the timbre of her tone. Not yet. Not yet.

The choking band around my throat squeezed tighter, and I cleared my throat to speak around it. "You want to be spread around that pond?" I asked the urn. "I don't know how bad your eyes were, but it's not as pretty as it once was. I bet all the fish in it are dead. It'd be a drabby spot to be laid to rest, you know."

There was a sound behind me, rustling, and I glanced over my shoulder. They started picking up the chairs. The remembrance of Nancy, rushed to a finish. It felt morbid, but I reached out and traced her name engraving with the tip of my finger, the scripted font elegant and wrong. Everything all felt wrong.

"Margot."

I turned at the sound of my name being called from behind me, finding a lone girl standing at the entrance of the funeral hall.

At first, I didn't recognize her. Her brown hair was pulled back into a low bun, a few curls escaping to frame her face. Her features were sharper than I remembered them, as if she'd lost weight, or maybe it was just that she'd lost her baby fat that'd still lingered in high school. She looked older, as if in the year since we last saw each other, she'd grown five. She looked elegant in her black dress, resembling something like a full adult.

"This was supposed to be a *good* surprise," Destelle Brighton said with her eyebrows scrunched together in the world's saddest expression.

The ache in my chest returned in full force at the sight of my best friend. "I thought you weren't flying in until tomorrow."

"I wanted to surprise you by showing up at Annalise's wedding." She started toward me, her small heels muffled on the carpeted floors. "Mom only *just* told me about Nancy. You should've called me."

I should've. She should've been the first person I called. While Destelle wasn't close with Nancy much at all, not in the way I was, I still should've reached out. Thinking back now, I couldn't believe I hadn't. "These past few days have been a whirlwind."

Destelle was the only one I could stand the pitying expression from, strangely enough. Maybe it was because we'd been so close, had seen each other at our worsts growing up, that it felt okay to let her see that side of me. To bear that burden of my sadness.

Destelle leaned her shoulder against mine and tilted her head close. I could smell her strawberry scented shampoo, and the familiarity of it comforted me. "It doesn't really look like her, does it?"

We peered at Nancy's portrait for another long moment, but it didn't grow any more similar to her. I half expected the funeral director to come up and shoo us out. I wondered what they would do with the portrait then. What they'd do with her ashes. Would they go to the country and spread the ashes themselves? Would they entrust someone else to do it? My stomach clenched at the idea of them reaching out to Yvette or Ms. Jennings, or even my mother.

I allowed myself to lean a bit firmer against Destelle's side. "No one came."

Destelle didn't hesitate. "Bitches."

A corner of my lips tilted up. "Bitches," I agreed. Nancy would've said the same. I could finally, blessedly, hear her voice in my head. *Bitches.* "All of them."

"Are you still going to the wedding?"

Sumner's suggestion about skipping it echoed in my mind. The idea of going, facing everyone happy and laughing on such a miserable day, was exhausting. But then, the idea of facing my parents' wrath for not showing up, for not properly introducing myself to Mr. Astor... it was equally exhausting. Breathing itself just felt so exhausting. I just wanted to close my eyes, to bask in that darkness.

"Of course," I said to Destelle. "My chariot awaits outside. Do you need a ride?"

"Wait, that *was* your car pulled out front? Was the guy inside *him*?" Destelle's expression lit up a little, and she bumped harder into my shoulder. "*The* boy?"

She nudged me again until I smiled, tugging on the hem of my vest to straighten it out. "Yes, that's him. Sumner. Nancy always talked about how he had a nice butt."

Destelle nodded understandingly. "She liked Harry's too. She liked her butts, that's for sure."

Chapter 27

*D*estelle loved Sumner, obviously. She rode in the backseat on our way to the country club, and she asked him many questions about himself, to which he answered good-naturedly. They both were good at that sort of thing, being genuinely curious about others, where I was more so used to sitting in the quiet while others asked the questions. It made me happy, though, that they seemed to immediately click, that the two important people left in my life weren't uncomfortable around each other.

During the car ride, I crept my hand over to Sumner, and he didn't hesitate. Sumner slid his hand into mine, wrapping his fingers around and giving a comforting squeeze. My heart mirrored the pulse, some of the ache from the day dissipating just a little. At least I'd thought so until we pulled up to the country club, and Sumner slid the car into the valet lane.

Both the wedding and the reception were being held at the country club, so no doubt everyone was already in the grand ballroom. It officially would've started ten minutes ago.

We all climbed out, and a valet I didn't recognize slid into the driver's seat. Sumner came to my side and looked into my eyes. "I'm not going to try to persuade you to just order room service and watch a movie in your room," he said, threading his fingers through my hair to push it behind my ear. "But I want to. I really want to."

"I want to, too. But I shouldn't."

Worry stirred in his eyes, increasing the longer he looked at me. I hated that I made that emotion surface. I wanted to be calm and put together, a person he only had to love, not be concerned about. Even if I were to lift my chin now, though, he'd see through the act. He always did. It wasn't only worry in his gaze, the longer I looked. Nervousness twined in the blue depths.

"I'll be on my best behavior," I promised. "And as my reward, you're spending the night with me tonight. And we're not sleeping on the floor this time."

I'd said the words to be teasing, but the anxiety didn't vanish from Sumner's eyes. His hand reached out and picked up mine, gripping it almost as if he was holding me back. "Do you remember," he began in a quiet voice, low enough that I was sure Destelle couldn't hear, "when I told you there was something I needed to tell you the other day?"

I blinked in surprise. We hadn't had the chance to have that long conversation he asked for. I'd forgotten all about that. Granted, everything had hit the fan in that time, but I still felt bad for it having slipped my mind. "You said it was a long conversation."

"It is." He gripped my hand tighter, almost as if he were afraid to let me go. "But it's—it's important."

Destelle had her own worried expression. "I hate to be the bearer of bad news, but you don't *really* have time to talk now."

I couldn't look away from him. "I can make time."

"No, it's because—"

"*Margot Massey!*"

The three of us turned to find my mother striding from the country club, her blue dress hugging her body. Though her appearance was elegant, there was no hiding the tension around her eyes. "Took you long enough," my mother said in an affectionate voice through clenched teeth. She grabbed my arm as if she thought I'd make a break for it. "I thought I was going to have to follow through on my promise."

Destelle gave me a look of *that's why*, glancing to Sumner, who had dropped his gaze to his feet.

"What are you wearing?" She looked down at my attire with wide eyes. "Did you not change from the funeral?"

She needed to make up her mind—if she wanted me to hurry up or take longer.

"Hi, Mrs. Massey," Destelle interjected, attempting to sway my mother's attention.

It didn't work. "Hi, dear. Let's go, Margot. The Astors have been waiting on you." My mother did halt for the man at my side, though, seeming to not have noticed that we'd been holding hands when she came out. Her gaze was fond, and it was a little unsettling. "Thank you for everything, Sumner."

Her tone, too, was far more affectionate than I'd been expecting from her, especially since she technically fired him a few days prior. Destelle picked up on it, frowning a little. Before I had a chance to speculate it further, my mother swept me toward the country club. Destelle's heels clicked on the cobblestones as she hurried after us.

"They're serving the dinner now," my mother said in her stressed tone. "The Astors kept asking where you were, and I kept giving an excuse. Please, for the love of God, don't mention the funeral, okay? I'd hate to bring down the mood."

I almost laughed, though I held no humor.

"I didn't get a chance to ask you." Now, my mother's voice was low so that only I would hear. "Did you find out if Nancy put you in her will?"

I wasn't sure if it was a cruel joke. The buzzing in my head was loud.

"If she did, the first order of business is getting it submitted to probate court," my mother mused, almost manic as she thought of the next steps. "And see what she gave you, of course. Hopefully she left the land the hotel is on to you. Then from there, work on signing it over to your father and I, and—"

So, this is what it feels like, I thought to myself distantly, as if I were on the outside of this moment looking in. *This is what it feels like to be on the brink of snapping.* "I don't get anything," I said, cutting her off. "She left it all to charity."

My mother gasped. "*What?*"

I didn't tell her that I didn't know for a fact, but it'd been what Nancy had told me a few times. *I wish I could see the looks on their faces when they find out I left it all to charity.*

I'll look for you.

"Careful," I said without affection. "You don't want to *bring down the mood.*"

We followed the elaborate signs that directed us toward the reception indoors. The ceremony itself had been held out near the golf course, where the views in the background were as stunning as could be. I'd been able to see them setting up this morning from the view of my hotel room, an abundance of white linen and floral. The camera crew had also been there, capturing every inch of the scene that they could.

I'd found myself wishing it would've rained, just to see what it would've looked like on camera. Just to see everyone's day fall apart, just as my world had.

It hadn't rained. I was sure the wedding went on without a hitch, as magical as Yvette had wanted.

As we walked up to the ballroom, the muted chatter of voices filtered out into the hall, and my mother still didn't slow down. "Destelle, you'll be sitting with your parents," my mother said lightly. Her intention was clear: *do not follow Margot.*

I glanced over my shoulder at my friend, who shot me an apologetic look. "I understand, Mrs. Massey."

Of course, Destelle and I hadn't gotten lucky enough to sit at the same table. Destelle gave me a *good luck* face before heading to her family.

Yvette had wanted the reception to be angelic, with golds and warm lighting, and her design team had delivered. The white linen they'd had at the golf course had been replaced in the ballroom with gold fabrics, draped along the tables and along the free-standing partitions that were sectioned off about. The DJ booth in the corner was also decked out with glittering material and wispy white tulle, as if to give the illusion that it'd been taken from heaven itself. They'd even gone as far as replacing the bulbs in the chandelier with warmer toned ones, and it gave an ethereal glow to the entirety of the ballroom.

Ironic, given that it was my hell. I didn't even look at the bride and groom's table.

"Best behavior," my mother warned, smoothing a hand down my hair. "Understood?"

I didn't bother responding. My father sat there with his focus on his water glass, the socially awkward man he was. Vivienne Astor was there with her husband, undoubtedly, at her side. He was tall and thin but looked much like Aaron in the features. There were four empty seats at the table, one for me, one for Aaron, but I didn't know who the two other ones were for.

"Here she is," my mother announced as we made it to our table. I didn't look at anyone as they lifted their heads. *Faceless.* "Fashionably late, as always."

"Indeed, fashionably," Aaron mused as I sat down in the chair beside him. We hadn't spoken since Tuesday night at the bar; I wasn't sure if that meant he'd given up or had taken time to develop a new strategy. "Don't you look...*dashing* is almost the right word, isn't it?"

I just stared at him.

My mother introduced me to Malcolm Astor, who seemed jovial enough as he paused from cutting into his chicken and stretched his hand to me across the table. In the ten seconds I'd arrived, I realized Sumner was right when he said that the Astors didn't matter, because they didn't. I liked Vivienne well enough, but there was no urge to impress her as I met her this time. There was no reason to anymore.

I took a seat beside Aaron and stared at my plate of food. "Why do we have extra seats?" Mr. Astor asked as we all sat down, glancing at the two chairs that separated him and my father. "Who was supposed to be sitting with us?"

"Margot's godmother, of sorts, Nancy." Aaron reached over and laid his hand on mine underneath the table. His fingers were hot. "She, unfortunately, passed earlier in the week. Her funeral was today."

"Is that why you're wearing such attire?" Mr. Astor raised his bushy eyebrows in surprise. He then cleared his throat noisily when Vivienne shot him a dark look. "Well, Margot, I'm very sorry for your loss."

My father, who sat beside my mother, nodded. "But how fitting, to celebrate loss with something beautiful on the same day, wouldn't you agree?"

Fitting. Nancy's death offsetting Annalise's wedding was *fitting*. I gave a slow blink, a pounding beginning to drum behind my eyes. "Aren't you at all concerned?" I asked my father, gaze flat. "What's going to happen to the land your hotel is on?"

My father blanched at my words and the domino effect they caused. "You don't own the land?" Mr. Astor asked, sounding confused. "I thought you did."

"This is the one plot of our hotels we don't own," my mother supplied, sliding in smoothly as she always did. "Ms. Nancy always held out on selling. To answer your question, Margot." Her voice hardened ever so slightly as she turned to address me. "We plan to buy it from whoever gets it in her will. We have more than enough to purchase at a handsome price."

"Sounds like a stubborn lady," Mr. Astor mused. Vivienne laid a hand on his arm, her gaze cutting to me, and her husband rushed to add, "Oh, I meant no offense, of course. It's just an interesting business move on her part, not agreeing to sell when offered."

"My parents always offered amounts under its value." I stared at the bubbles billowing in the champagne, the image similar to what simmered inside me. "She would've been a fool to sell at the price they proposed."

Underneath the table, my mother discreetly placed her hand on my leg and squeezed. Enough that it hurt. I didn't even flinch. Instead, I smiled. With Aaron's hand on mine and my mother's on my leg, I was being held from both sides, tied in place.

"Vivienne," my mother murmured. She had her gossip tone on and picked up her silverware. "Your son has been such a gentleman to Margot this past week. I've enjoyed getting to know him."

Aaron tried to hide his smug smile by ducking his head, but Vivienne's expression was far more gracious. "Thank you. It's a relief to know we've raised him well enough. It's no simple task, raising a child."

"Oh, Margot was just a breeze." My mom beamed at me. "Never gave us any problems. It was like she wasn't there half the time!"

Probably because I wasn't.

"I think..." My mother gave a girly chuckle. "I think

Aaron would fit in well with our family. I hope I'm not overstepping by saying I think Margot would fit in well with yours, as well. From how much you seem to favor her."

Vivienne's lips parted, whether out of shock from my mother's blunt segue or from something else, I wasn't sure. I didn't care.

Aaron took my hand from my leg to lay ours on the table, showcasing his fingers knitted around mine. "I know I favor her," he said in a grandiose tone that nearly made me gag. "I'm excited for her to come back to California with us. Margot, you'll find the beaches just lovely, I assure you."

"So you've agreed?" Vivienne asked me. "To come back with us on Monday?"

It was the first I'd heard of it, outside of Aaron posing the ridiculous question earlier in the week. He'd said he'd been hoping I'd come back with him to California, but it was almost laughable he stated it now as if fact. However, in the eyes of everyone else, it was. "We have her flight already booked," my mother assured. "It'll be hard to be without her—it's the first time, really!—but I know she'll be in good hands."

So that was why my parents had ended Sumner's employment. I wouldn't need a secretary anymore in California, not when the Astors would be there to watch over me. *I'm not going,* I wanted to tell them, but the words wouldn't come.

Mic feedback cut through the room, startling into our conversation, a blessed reprieve. "Everyone, the bride and groom are getting ready to have their first dance!" a man's voice announced. "Please turn your eyes toward the dance floor."

The camera crew rushed to get the perfect shot as everyone turned in their seats, except for me. As I sat there, poking the dry chicken and the mashed potatoes drenched in garlic butter, I had a thought that shouldn't have been in my head. The white linen, the gold accents, the expensive crowd, the beautiful backdrop—*if I married Aaron, is this what our wedding would've looked like?*

The ceremony itself would've looked similar, surely. Aaron in a tailored tux, standing at the end of the aisle with that signature smile on his face. His parents would be in the aisle before him, mine on the other side, all beaming as their children married—and their businesses, at the same time. The wedding of the century paired with the business partnership of the century. The sun would be shining down on them, the heavens blessing the moment they'd all been preparing so hard for.

At my wedding, I'd be at the top of the aisle, holding the arm of a man I called my father in name only, surrounded by the same sea of faceless people I never looked at. I'd never given much thought before to if I'd want to wear a wedding dress or not, but I'd be in one; I'd only be able to wear a suit over my mother's dead body.

It felt wrong to imagine a wedding with Aaron, having kissed another man not even an hour ago, but as I did, I realized with an almost blinding certainty that I would never do it. Could never do it. Even if I were to take Sumner out of the equation entirely, I couldn't put my entire future into someone else's hands. Going to college for a major I didn't want to pursue was nothing. A blip on the map. But *this*—letting my parents push me into marrying a man I did not want to—was life-altering. Even if divorce was an option down the road, there were too many other variables that could trap me, hold me down.

At this moment, I could still get out relatively unscathed. Disowned and thrown away, but free. The noose had not yet tightened around my throat.

Words in my head felt familiar, as if they'd whispered to me before. *You cannot do this*, it said. *This is something you cannot do.*

Everyone's expressions were so light when I looked around. Ms. Jennings was laughing at something Mr. Holland was saying, laying her arm happily on his. Yvette was grinning at a few ladies who went to the club. People I didn't know were smiling, chattering, everyone having a beautiful time at a beautiful wedding of a beautiful woman. People Nancy knew, people Nancy helped fund, and there wasn't a trace of sadness surrounding them. Not a single one.

This is something you cannot do.

Just as I had the thought, I lifted my gaze to the ballroom's entrance, finding Sumner standing there. He looked like a beacon, standing there, the golden warmth from the room reflecting on him in a way that almost made him look unreal. His eyes trailed across the room, clearly looking for someone, before finding relief when he spotted me.

Then his gaze slid from my face to where Aaron held my hand on the table.

I drew in a sharp breath, ready to jump up from the

table, but before I could, Aaron moved first. "Excuse me," he said suddenly, his chair skidding across the floor as he rose. "I'll—I'll be right back."

His gaze was fixed on Sumner, making it perfectly clear who he was gunning for. I tried to stand up, to go after him, but my mother's hand moved from my leg to my arm, holding it down underneath the table. She gave me a look full of warning, as much as she dared, giving her head a minute shake.

In my head, I contemplated what would happen if I shrugged her off. If I ripped my arm from her grip, went against her wishes, and ran after him. What did it matter, angering her now? When my mind had been made up? Maybe it was a good idea to send myself off with one last act of adult rebellion, one last hurrah.

I was about to do just that, to pull free from my mother for the last time with flourish, when Vivienne Astor asked, in a clear voice, "Was that Sumner Pennington?"

I froze. It almost felt as if time itself froze, and I would've thought it had if Vivienne's eyelashes hadn't swept down in a blink. Sumner's name on her lips made no sense. She shouldn't have known him. They didn't meet the last time she'd been here. She couldn't have known him.

"It looked like him, didn't it?" Malcolm agreed, also turned toward the doors. "I thought Aaron said he wouldn't be able to make it."

"Well, good. I know Hannah was worried, him disappearing for a month and missing Michael's wedding."

Michael. The name tugged my memory back to a few

days prior, and in almost frantic movement, my head whipped toward the dancefloor. The bride and groom were still locked in their embrace, and I finally, finally focused on them for the first time. Annalise's white wedding gown belled out with pools and pools of tulle, her frame standing out daintily in the midst of it. The cut was low on her chest, her pale skin a backdrop for the thick and impressive diamond necklace around her throat. Her blonde curls were pinned up into a beautiful bridal style; she was a woman belonging on a magazine.

The man in her arms was handsome with his hair styled and shaped, clean-shaven and jaw chiseled.

Familiar.

Sumner Pennington! that same man had exclaimed only a few days prior. *It's been too long!*

That was why the Michael Huntsly name had sounded familiar, because I'd heard it before. It was Annalise's fiancé.

The thoughts tipped over like a champagne flute, all the golden sparkles streaming onto the ground, ruined.

Sumner knows Michael. Aaron knows Michael. Vivienne knows Sumner...

I could still remember the day I'd asked Sumner. *Do you have a lot of friends back home?*

A few. Only two, maybe, that I was close-close with. One got engaged, started wedding planning.

"How..." The word had come out barely a sound, and I swallowed hard to start over. "How do know Sumner?"

Vivienne blinked at me in surprise. "*You* know Sumner?"

"He's my secretary." *And so, so much more.*

Vivienne's mouth dropped open as some sort of realization hit her, one that shined in the wideness of her eyes. I thought my heart would be racing in anticipation of her response, but it only seemed to be beating normally, not even skipping a beat.

Good guy, Sumner had said about his other friend. *A little awkward, drinks a bit much sometimes, but I think he's finally ready to settle down.*

It was Malcolm, in the end, who answered. "Why, Sumner is Aaron's best friend."

And then my heart stopped entirely.

Chapter 28

I was nearly positive I was dreaming.

That was the only way to explain the situation, the way I felt. My vest felt too tight around me, stealing my breath and crushing me. *Why, Sumner is Aaron's best friend.*

For a moment, my eyes were unseeing as I stared at the tablecloth. I could feel my mind racing, struggling to absorb the shock of his words. Surely he was mistaken; perhaps there was another man named Sumner. Perhaps —perhaps—

I closed my eyes, my world spinning.

"How did he end up being her secretary?" Malcolm asked with clear confusion. "He—he's supposed to be visiting his father in New York, I thought?"

He'd directed this last bit toward his wife, whose brow knitted. "Who hired him?" she asked.

"We did," my mother responded, her damage control voice on. "Your son—Aaron asked us to hire him, and —well."

Sumner's voice was soft in my head. *I came highly*

recommended. The few peckings I'd taken from my food in front of me threatened to make a reappearance.

Vivienne's accent caused her words to sound sharper. "You hired him to help my son spy on your own daughter?"

"Heavens, no!" my mother rushed in. I wanted to look over and see her expression, because we both knew it was a lie. If there was anything my mother did, it was attempt to brainwash me. "We hired him on Aaron's suggestion, with no other intention in mind."

I tried to keep my breathing calm through it all, the first potent emotion I'd felt in days beginning to seep through the bare numbness: rage. It was the sort of rush of anger that caused my head to swim, and before I knew it, I pushed to my feet.

My mother tried to catch my arm. "Margot, sit back down—"

This time, I followed through on my earlier thought and tore out of her grip. "Do *not* touch me," I snapped at her, my voice loud enough to cause a few heads from surrounding tables to turn. I couldn't care less who eavesdropped. *Faceless.* I stared into her chocolate eyes, and I wondered what she saw. I couldn't quite feel my expression on my cheeks, but I only knew that I felt hollow. It had to be reflected on my face. "You, unfortunately, picked a very bad day to get me to listen to you."

Horror scrawled across her face, predicting my moves before I made them. But still, just a beat too late.

I stalked away from the table and to the hallway, no doubt with murder in my eyes. I found Sumner and Aaron in the hallway, Aaron holding his arm out to keep

Sumner back. "—going to ruin everything, showing up here," Aaron was saying. Sumner looked over Aaron's shoulder, eyes widening when he saw me. "Do you really think it's a good idea—"

I grabbed a fistful of the back of Aaron's dress shirt and turned him around. I relished in the shocked expression in his wide eyes, only for a moment before I slapped him.

I'd packed all of my force into the reel back, so as soon as my palm connected with his cheek, Aaron stumbled sideways like a drunkard. He pitched up against the country club's wall, his shoes screeching against the floor as he caught himself.

"I don't know if it's clear," I told him, ignoring the stinging pain in my hand, "but that's my way of saying you can take your engagement ring and shove it up your ass."

"I'd say she knows," Aaron muttered while he held his cheek. "Margot, listen—"

But I was beyond listening to him ever again. "You should go in there and try to save the situation with your parents."

Aside from the red palm print on his cheek, Aaron blanched. "My—my parents know?"

I just stared at him.

He seemed to debate which took precedence, placating me or his parents, when the latter eventually won out. Aaron, still cradling his cheek, rushed back into the wedding venue, abandoning Sumner and me in the hall.

I was no stranger to being alone with Sumner, but in

this moment, *he* was the one who felt like a stranger before me. Had it even been an hour since I stepped into the ballroom? An hour since I'd stepped from his arms? And yet it felt like it'd happened years ago. I could remember the embrace around me, but couldn't remember the warmth. I only felt cold now.

Sumner took one tentative step toward me after several moments of silence. "Margot—"

"This was the long conversation, wasn't it? Not bad?" My voice shook, but it wasn't with anger. "*Not bad?* You being a spy for Aaron Astor this entire time is *not bad?*"

I memorized the horror in Sumner's expression, the panic of someone caught in their lie, their secrets found out. His beautiful lips parted, lips that I'd kissed earlier today. The pit in my stomach formed into a chasm now, empty and bottomless.

"That's why you felt like you *needed* to get to know me. Because Aaron told you to."

"No—"

"That's why he knew everything about me," I said in a flat voice. "Because you told him. Everything I told you in confidence, you told to Aaron."

"Not—not everything."

"He knew about my relationship with my parents, knew that I used to want to go to fashion school. He even knew I took my mashed potatoes without garlic butter, Sumner. What *didn't* you tell him?"

A pained expression crossed Sumner's face, but for the first time ever, I was hesitant to believe it. All this time, I thought he'd been an open book, when in reality, he'd been written in a different language. I thought of all the times in the past few weeks that I ignored what was right in front of me. Misunderstood.

"If I was Aaron's spy, I wouldn't have fallen for you," Sumner insisted, taking a hesitant step closer. "And I did. You know I did. I—"

"Stop, *stop.*" I held up a hand and was grateful he actually listened. Sumner fell silent, still.

I was so tired. *So tired.* The exhaustion ran deep into my bones. If I closed my eyes, it felt as if I'd instantly fall asleep. I was once more back at all the fundraisers and galas and parties, wishing I could be anywhere else in the world but *here.* The Alderton-Du Ponte Country Club felt cursed, almost laughably so. It was shallow and airless and draining.

Aaron had abandoned pleading his case in favor of appeasing his own parents, which, I knew, was him giving up in a way. It didn't matter in the end, did it? I'd already told the Astors I would not be marrying Aaron. Everything was unraveling like a spool of thread, faster than I could latch onto any of it.

I closed my eyes, wanting nothing more than to sleep. "I have had quite possibly the worst day of my life today. I'm literally *this close* to losing my mind. If you want me to hear you out...you have to wait."

Sumner drew in a shaky breath. "Promise," he whispered, and it wasn't just my voice that shook. "Promise you'll hear me out."

His eyes were red as I studied them. Years and years of being trapped in a life with fake expressions and false smiles always had me looking closely, searching for the truth. In Sumner's eyes, I saw it now. The earnest. The desperation. It reminded me of the night he knelt before me in my bedroom, cleaning the cut on my leg, his worry blooming in his eyes like a flower. It was real.

I closed my eyes once more, not wanting to see it. "I promise."

Whether or not that was a lie, in that moment, I didn't know. I only knew that I couldn't do any of this right now.

Instead of walking away from the ballroom, I returned to it, only to find my parents and the Astors absent from our table. My mother must've coerced them away from the prying eyes. Sumner, for what felt like the first time, did not trail after me, and the absence of him darkened everything around me. He was not my shadow, I realized. He was the light.

I stopped at the entrance of the ballroom, staring at it all for what would probably be the final time, taking in its grandeur and glory. The chandelier, the glass ceiling, the large windows. It screamed money, influence, power. It was a place Nancy had founded, but it lacked all traces of her now. I ventured past the tables and the wedding attendants, toward the open bar, ready to close my time here with one final drink. "A glass of champagne, please," I said to the bartender, grabbing the hem of my vest and tugging it down, away from my chest, trying to lessen the pressure of it against my ribs.

I had no idea what would happen after tonight. It was my final night to sleep in my bed, to pack my things, because surely my parents would throw me out in the morning. I was too tired to speculate.

As I waited for the pour, my ears picked up on words I wished they hadn't. "I wonder if she planned it," someone whispered in a conspiratorial tone. I looked around, but I couldn't tell which moving mouth spoke. "When you're that old, can you *plan* your death?"

Someone else gasped. "What, like an assisted suicide?"

"Could've happened." There was a pause, and though the whisper dropped lower, I could still hear it. "That girl was with her the day she passed. Maybe she gave Nancy something to help her go, if you know what I mean."

My world darkened at the edges of my vision, rage simmering through the numbness that'd been clinging to me all day. As they continued to run their mouths, I imagined turning around and throwing my glass at whatever table the gossips sat at. I imagined marching over and grabbing a fistful of whosever hair and yanking it backward. I pictured it all in my head, relishing in the imaginary screams. My body vibrated from the barely restrained desire to act the fantasy out.

But I couldn't find the source of the voice. It was only the words, ones that felt like they were coming from inside my head. It felt like, in that moment, that I could've screamed at the top of my lungs and no one would've noticed. That they'd assume it was part of the music, if they even heard it at all. How could my life be falling apart and everyone else's be perfectly fine? How could not a single person blink twice on a day like today?

"Your champagne," the bartender said, setting the small flute on the bar. They immediately turned to the next customer, as if I had never existed.

"It's been hanging over our heads for months," a new

voice added to the gossip. "God forgive me, but thank goodness it's finally over with."

"All those trips to and from her house. With nothing to do! Oh, I thought *I* was going to die at times. Of boredom!"

Everyone gave a tittering laugh.

I closed my eyes to shut out the voices, the sounds, but they were everywhere. The words swirled around in my head, a choking fog. The few bits of food I'd choked down twisted in my stomach, as if I was on the verge of throwing it all back up.

"Margot?"

I closed my eyes, as if the action alone could shut out the voice and the impending person accompanying. I had no patience left to stretch; I was a wet towel wrung dry.

A hand curved along my back and up to my shoulder, and when I opened my eyes, I found Yvette coming around to face me. She had a painted smile on her lips, makeup that was far too heavy for her middle-aged features. She looked like a child who'd gotten into their mother's beauty cabinet. "I'm surprised you're here," she said in a deceptively soft voice.

"It must be quite the day for you," I said, swallowing down the bile that had risen in my throat. "Your daughter getting married and your friend's funeral on the same day. Not that you showed up for the latter."

"I'm sure Nancy would've understood," Yvette said as she nodded, reassuring herself. "It's just a whirlwind, getting prepared for a wedding. I'm sure there was quite a turnout without me there."

She'd said it with a twist to her lips, without looking

me in the eye. She knew no one went, and judging by the look in her gaze, she thought it was *funny*. My chest began rising and falling a bit quicker, a tremor working its way through me. "If it was any other day, you would've attended?"

"But it wasn't, was it? And I'm sure you had a hand in the day the funeral was held, didn't you?" Yvette gave an unkind smile. "Out of all the days the funeral could've fallen on, it had to be today? Anything to ruin someone else's happiness."

I had nothing to do with deciding the funeral date, but I didn't tell Yvette that. "I'm sure you're only upset that Nancy couldn't make it to the wedding because you won't get her wedding gift." My fingers dented into my cup more firmly. "What a shame. Your ass kissing didn't even get you a penny in the end."

Yvette lost her smile.

Once I'd started, there was no stopping. My chest rose and fell faster, and so did my words. "I'm sure you're happy she's dead, just like every other pathetic blood-sucker that'd been hanging off her these past few months. Happy you don't have to waste your own time anymore, trying to steal an old lady's fortune. You might not have gotten the money you wanted, but at least you don't have to play nursemaid."

"Give me a break, Margot. You're acting all high and mighty, as if you weren't doing the same." Yvette looked around briefly before taking a half-step closer. "Don't pretend like you cared about Nancy in the slightest. We both know you're just a selfish black hole. Have *you* even cried for Ms. Nancy?"

I didn't even blink, though her words were a strangling blow. I hadn't cried. Not once.

She wrinkled her nose in distaste. "I doubt it. You have to have emotions to cry. So don't pretend as if you're better than me. Better than *any* of us. You aren't. And given the fact that your mother escorted the Astors out, with angry expressions all around, it seems my prediction was true, hmm? You truly *weren't* good enough for a family like them."

The flute of champagne in my hand was slippery, as if it could've fallen from my grip any moment. I let the mental image play out, me tossing its sparkling contents onto Yvette's mother-of-the-bride dress. It'd be an improvement on the ugly blue fabric, that was for sure. She'd screech, and her scream would be one everyone would hear. Everyone would've blocked out mine if I screamed, but they'd answer the call of one of their own.

My parents would be humiliated. It most likely would've gotten caught by the wandering camera crew.

Perhaps this was my opportunity to go out with a bang.

Yvette seemed to realize I had a drink in my hand, because she took a large step away from me, her heels clicking on the floors. She darted away before I could follow through on the fantasy I'd built in my head, taking my opportunity to let everything out.

I wandered away from the bar, feet taking me toward the desserts. The cupcake table, like every other square inch of the ballroom, was elegant, of course. The table itself was draped with a golden satin tablecloth with pearls littering the surface to catch the eye. I wondered if they were real. Probably. The cupcakes themselves had golden frosting with glitter shining atop, stretched in tiers throughout the dessert table. At the center of the table, though, sat the large, seven-tiered wedding cake, all white and gold with icing flowers cascading in a waterfall down the fondant.

I swiped my index finger through a flower, ruining its blooming image. I touched the frosting to my tongue. Sweet. Too sweet. It turned my stomach.

Everyone was too busy dancing, mingling, gossiping, drinking, to notice the lone girl at the table. It was a Margot Massey specialty, being overlooked while she stood in a corner. Perhaps people purposefully ignored me. Perhaps they didn't notice me at all. I didn't know where Destelle was. I didn't care.

I ran my hand along the table's edge, feeling the hard plastic hidden beneath the silk tablecloth. I caressed the edge, lifting ever so slightly, testing the weight. For a seven-tiered cake and dozens of cupcakes, it wasn't as heavy as I thought it'd be. I lifted the table an inch, staring at the flower I'd swiped my finger through.

The day felt like it'd been five years long. Never-ending. Too much to think about. Nancy, Sumner, Aaron, Vivienne, my mother, Yvette, Annalise. I couldn't focus on a single one of them; they were too scattered in my head. Everything from the day bombarded my senses—the funeral, the wedding, the betrayal. My head pounded with it all, a jackknifing pressure that drove me mad.

I pictured lifting the dessert table up by more than an inch. In my pounding mind, I pictured flipping it over, sending decorations and icing and cake everywhere. The pearls would scatter. I pictured the surprised shrieks that would've surely erupted by the sudden sound, and then Yvette's scream as she realized the seven-tiered wedding cake of her dreams—ahem, her *daughter's dreams*—was reduced to something to be scraped into the trash.

The gold icing rose was ruined, and the sugar burned my tongue.

I pictured Yvette's face as she would gasp at what I did. I pictured my mother's face.

And I flipped the table.

Chapter 29

Calculated chaos was my specialty. My mother called me impulsive, but she didn't know that everything that I did, I did for a reason. I thought it all out before acting, watching the events play out in my head so that things would unfold in exactly the way I'd intended them to. It was chaos, but planned—orchestrated to yield the most beautiful results.

Except for tonight. I didn't think about the consequences. I didn't think about anything other than ruining it all.

I'd figured security probably throw me out of the wedding, but I did not realize they'd ban me from the property entirely. Which meant, since the Alderton-Du Ponte Country Club was affiliated with Massey Suites, I was also banned from the hotel. Effective immediately. Security didn't even let me go back to my room and collect my things, not even my wallet. Instead, security escorted me to the valet, where they called a taxi.

I wasn't allowed to take my car; it wasn't in my name, after all.

My parents did not accompany me to the valet, nor

did any of the Astors. The only person who stood with me in the breezy summer night was the bulky security guard while we waited for the car. I had no idea where Sumner was.

Flipping the desserts table at the wedding reception was not properly calculated. It was impulsive. It was reckless.

Reckless, but worth it.

For a moment, I'd sat in the backseat of the taxi, silent. I hadn't known what to do. *If it isn't the consequences of my own actions.*

Really, I only had one place to go.

Nancy's house was warm when I unlocked the front door and stepped inside, in the way a house would be with no air conditioning. The garbage must've been full, because the second I stepped into the entryway, it was all I could smell. For a brief, horrifying moment, I had a delusional thought that Nancy's body was still in her bedroom, left alone—but no. No. I had to swallow back the bile and continue further into the house. As soon as I stepped into the kitchen, the overflowing trash was in plain sight, as were the dishes that were left in the sink. Her weekly pill container was still on the counter, with Thursday, Friday, Saturday, and Sunday untouched.

It was like Nancy's house had been put on pause, waiting for her to return. But she wouldn't. Only the ghost of her traces would remain.

I was a different kind of ghost in this house—a squatter. I wasn't legally allowed to be in here—that right belonged to whoever Nancy left the estate to in her will— but seeing as how the air was stinking and stale, whoever *had* been given the house hadn't come by to check in on it. So, for now, I'd be its caregiver until its new owner returned.

"You should've at least made Yvette or Ms. Jennings clean when they were over," I said to the empty air. "If you weren't going to send them packing, you should've at least put them to work."

The house answered with silence.

Despite the exhaustion that dug into my bones, for the first time in my life, I washed the dishes. I took out the garbage. The outside sky was dark, prolonging the world's longest day even further, but I was lively as I went through the house and emptied every trash can Nancy owned. Once that task was complete, I went to work wiping down the surfaces, dusting the knickknack filled bookshelf, keeping busy in a space that, now with the trash gone, smelled too much like her.

I didn't go into her bedroom. I left that door closed.

I hunted through the house for Nancy's vacuum cleaner, which had been stashed in a random closet in the garage. The thing was ancient, and screeched like a wild animal, but sucked up the dirt that was scattered around her floors with a satisfying proficiency. In fact, watching the room go from disorderly and slumped to clean with pillows fluffed was satisfying.

I even scrubbed her bathroom floors, the tub, the toilet. When I couldn't find anything else left to clean, I finally fell still. I'd discarded my suit jacket somewhere in my manic cleaning session; my suit trousers were wrinkled, my dress shirt smelling like bleach, my hands feeling grimy despite all the disinfectants I'd been using. Sweat clung to my temples and frizzed the hair near it, and when I looked in the mirror, I found my makeup smudged and barely hanging on.

Outside, the birds chirped as they woke up.

I fell onto Nancy's couch and slept like the dead.

~

I woke up to the sound of a car door slamming shut.

For the longest moment, I held still, uncertain why I would've heard it on the eighth floor of the hotel. When I shifted, I remembered that I wasn't on my memory foam mattress at the hotel but cramped on a sofa where the ancient springs practically dug into my back. I grimaced as I shifted, every muscle in my body aching, especially my arms. It felt like I'd pulled a muscle.

Probably from flipping the table yesterday.

It all came back in a flash. The funeral, the wedding, Sumner, the cupcakes. I stared at the ceiling, half wondering if it'd all been a dream.

Nancy's front door began shaking as someone tried opening it, and I could hear the jingle of keys. I shot to my feet and toward the door, uncertain who I'd find on the other side, but hauling the door open.

And then I sighed.

"I figured you'd be here," Ms. Jennings said as she pulled her key out of the lock. She looked bright and chipper, makeup perfectly done. "The only place you could go, really, isn't it? A good choice. Between you and me, I doubt your parents even knew where Nancy lived, so you'll be safe enough here for a while."

I stared at her, wondering if it was the fact that I was still half-asleep or her actually being friendlier than normal. "What are you doing here?"

She seemed to guess my train of thought, because Ms. Jennings smirked. "You were a rockstar last night, you know. Turning over that table. Oh, it was delightful to see. Did you catch a good glimpse of Yvette's face? *Priceless.*"

I was in no mood to entertain her. "You're not taking a thing from this house," I warned her. "You're not coming inside."

Ms. Jennings held her hands up, rolling her eyes. "You act as if the deed is in your name. But don't worry, darling, wouldn't dream of it."

My patience was thinning. "Then why are you here?"

Ms. Jennings pointed her thumb over her shoulder, drawing my attention to her shiny red car as it sat parked beside mine. I didn't know how I hadn't noticed earlier, but someone sat in the passenger's seat, their face partly obscured by the visor as it hung down to shield the sun. I hated how my insides jumped, heart skipping a beat at the potential of who she could've carted out here. *Please*, the word rang in my head as the door popped open. *Please.*

Standing from the car, gaze shielded with black shades, lips turned up in a pleased smirk, stood Aaron Astor.

My pulse returned to normal almost immediately. "He's dedicated," I muttered under my breath. "I'll give him that."

"Are those the same clothes you wore last night?" Aaron asked as he approached, sliding off his sunglasses.

He peered at me closer, expression twisting. "Oh, it is. Did you not brush your hair either?"

I moved to shut the door between the three of us, already eager to finish this conversation.

"Hang on!" Aaron rushed forward, as if he were going to attempt to stop the door from closing if I hadn't paused. Ms. Jennings swung her keys around a finger, as if warning she'd just open it back up. "I just wanted to talk to you for a moment. Five minutes. Ms. Jennings, do you think you could keep the car cool for me?"

She flashed him a smile before leaving us alone on the porch. I absolutely did not want to have a single word exchanged with him, and I resented myself and my curiosity for winning out. I retreated back into the house, but Aaron followed after me, letting the screen door slam shut. "Oh, this is a—cluttered little place, isn't it?"

I stepped into the kitchen, shaking my head. "If you're here to convince me one last time why marrying you would be in my best interest, save it." I pulled a coffee mug down from the cabinet, hunting for her Keurig coffee cups. "My answer is no."

"You think I want to marry you after the spectacle last night?" Even though his words weren't kind, his voice was very shocked, which lightened the mood. "All of my friends saw how impulsive you are. They'd never let you in our circles now."

Despite everything, I smirked down into my empty coffee mug.

"Besides, I doubt after last night your parents are too thrilled with you, either. What's the point in marrying into your family if they're going to disown you?"

My smirk vanished. He was quite possibly the bluntest person I'd ever met, apart from Nancy. "I'm glad we're on the same page, then." I placed my mug underneath the spout and pressed the start button, turning around to lean against the counter. Aaron had helped himself to a seat at Nancy's small kitchen table, his hands folded professionally on its surface. "What do you want?"

Aaron looked very ordinary sitting in Nancy's kitchen. He wore designer, as always, but nothing about him seemed special in a space that used to hold the world's most special woman. He could've blended in with the wallpaper and I wouldn't have noticed. "You might've created quite the spectacle, but you also *missed* one."

"Did I, now?"

"Let me paint the scene," Aaron said, ignoring me. "You're off out in the hallway, listening to Sumner plead his case, but in the ballroom? Chaos. It was quite funny, in a way. in the beginning, anyway, before my parents took their anger out on me."

I ignored him as best as I could as I hunted around for wherever Nancy kept her Keurig cups. It would've been monumentally disappointing if she'd run out of them.

"My mother, in a fit of anger, says—are you paying attention, Margot? Stay with me, this is the fun part. My mom, in front of everyone, goes off on how your mother and I conspired to manipulate you into marrying me for business."

"Which you did."

"Yes, but it was a little amusing to see your parents stutter an excuse." Aaron propped his chin on his hand.

425

"Your mother is a good liar. I almost believed her when she said no."

I squeezed my eyes shut, but the visual pervaded anyway.

"My mother was only interested in the business deal because she thought I liked you," Aaron went on. "So, upon this *unsavory* discovery, she called it off. Loudly. This time, people *did* hear. It was all very embarrassing."

Everything Aaron said made it clear what my parents would say over the phone when I did call them. The phone weighed heavily in my pocket, and I didn't want to pull it out. I wanted to stay in this bubble of Nancy's sanctuary for as long as I could. "Let's hope they *did* catch that for Annalise's video," I said at last, turning back to hunt for coffee grounds. "You deserve to be embarrassed in front of all your friends."

"I suppose." To his credit, he seemed a bit sheepish, back to the nervous self I'd first met. "Have you spoken to Sumner?"

The next drawer I opened had the Keurig cups—thankfully. "I'm not talking to you about him."

"I get it, I'd be pissed at him too. I'm just saying—"

"You two did a good job." I pressed the start button and turned around, giving Aaron the full view of my glare. "Acting like you hated each other. You had me perfectly fooled."

"It wasn't an act so much," he said with a shake of his head. "I was pissed he got so buddy-buddy with you —he was just supposed to find out information, not become your new BFF—and he was pissed that I wouldn't call the whole thing off after finding out you didn't want to marry me. I'd say the tension was quite real."

I eyed the annoyance on his face, and from what I could tell, it was genuine. "He told you that I didn't want to marry you?"

"Yep. Which, honestly, I thought was a good thing—I was able to switch tactics. I had been coming here fully intending to make you swoon, but knowing your feelings made it easier."

I wondered when Sumner would've told him—the night he found out the truth? The night my dad came into my hotel room? Or had Sumner told him later, after, when I'd confessed my true feelings? "Why would you send your best friend to do your dirty work?"

"He wasn't just my friend," Aaron said, "but my secretary. I worked for Astro Agencies, and he worked under me. I didn't send him as a friend, but as an employee. And if you think about it, how is it any different from someone scoping out companies before investing? Sending a proxy to gauge the situation isn't unheard of."

Looking back at everything, it was almost irritating how well the pieces all fit together, and how many I missed. Sumner coming "highly recommended" from his previous secretary role in California—it never even occurred to me that the company could've been Astro Agencies. I wanted to kick myself in hindsight. "You aren't wrong, I suppose."

"I knew you'd get it." His own confident smile faded a little after a beat, and he hesitated before speaking again. "Sumner...he's a good guy. Better than me."

"I know." I arched an eyebrow. The Keurig behind me kicked to life, groaning as it began brewing my coffee. "You're advocating for him now?"

"He may have screwed up my chance to be a Massey Suites heir, but he *did* call dibs first."

Again with the dibs. This time, though, I frowned for a different reason. "He said you called dibs."

"The Christmas party. The one I said I saw you at. I didn't spot you first; Sumner did." He said the words like he thought they'd shock me. They might've, but I kept it hidden, maintaining my poker face. "I attended with my mother, and he came with me as my secretary. He said you were beautiful. We were introduced to your mother before we had to leave, and she may have mentioned that you were the sole heir to the family fortune, and—well, that piqued my interest."

"You're a crappy friend," I said without hesitation.

"I never said I was a good one."

For a moment, we sat there in his ugly honesty, and I had the strangest urge to laugh. Perhaps it was the sleep deprivation, to find amusement in such a situation. Aaron *was* a bad friend, but couldn't have been the worst if he was here, admitting defeat and talking on his friend's behalf. He had nothing to gain from this. He could've cut his losses and returned to California, leaving a broken mess in his wake, but he tried his hand at picking up a few of the pieces.

Aaron Astor absolutely sucked, but perhaps he had one redeeming quality.

My coffee finished brewing, the scent beautiful in the air, and Aaron's eyes flicked to it. For a moment, I thought he was about to ask for a cup for himself, but he ended up pushing from the table. "You should call him," he said, tapping his knuckles before rising to his full height. "He's at the hotel in Bayview."

"Bayview?"

"Your parents kicked him out of his *complimentary suite*, and my family took our lodging elsewhere until we fly out tomorrow." Aaron flapped his hand in the air. "It was all very dramatic."

I gripped the mug tightly, the heat from the ceramic burning my palms, but I didn't let go. "Yesterday really was a disaster, wasn't it?"

He smiled. "But a fun one."

"Despite everything, you're *smiling*?"

"Life's short. I'll just move onto the next pretty girl who's set to inherit a fortune."

I opened my mouth to say some unkind things, but Aaron held his hands up to keep me from scolding him, heading toward the front door. This time, I was the one trailing after him, still yet to take a sip of my coffee. "It was nice to meet you," he said as he stepped out onto her porch. "More fun than I anticipated."

I didn't say anything in response, but stepped up to the door and peered at him through the screen. A strange feeling stirred in my chest, one that ultimately had me speaking. "I would've married you," I called after him, clutching my cup tighter. Aaron slowed until he halted, but he didn't turn around. "If it'd been you who came out first. If you were the one who bothered to put in the barest bit of effort instead of sending Sumner."

It was true, I knew. Without Sumner, I'd never have

known the feeling of *what if.* At the very least, I never would've been brave enough to pursue it. *Happiness is better*, Sumner had said to me, and it'd never been something I'd thought before. Without him, I never would've known how important it was to choose happiness.

Aaron turned around. He had his hand in the pocket of his chinos, looking like the picture of nonchalance, even now. Nothing fazed him, it seemed. Not even this. "I wouldn't have done it," he replied simply. "I would never have come myself."

You were never worth it enough to come myself. That's what the word said, their hidden meaning too obvious to miss. I looked down at my bare feet as a rueful smile twisted my lips, not watching as he retreated to Ms. Jennings's vehicle. This would be the last time I ever saw him, surely. There'd be no more Aaron Astor hanging over my head, no more worrying about marrying a man I'd never love. That chapter, that fear, was closed and put to rest.

Not a single regret. With that peaceful thought in mind, I shut the door and flipped the lock.

Chapter 30

My phone was dead, and even after I charged it, the screen greeted me with the telltale sign of discontinued cell service. My parents, in less than twenty-four hours, cut it off. They'd followed through on the threat I always knew they'd carry out, and they'd done so swiftly.

I knew I should've felt something at the *no data* signal. It was a symbolic way of realizing that contact with them was fully cut off.

But the truth was that though they were technically the people who gave birth to me, they were never there for me in the way a true parent should've been. They barely paid attention to me growing up, shipped me off to boarding school until the ninth grade. I couldn't think of a single time they'd bought me a birthday cake. They were never parents; we were never a family.

The only reason the phone weighed heavily in my hand now was that I knew life was about to become hard. Very hard. And, in that moment, I was alone.

But not for long.

"I can't believe I still remember your number," I said into the cordless landline, cradling it between my shoulder and my cheek as I attempted to calm my hair into a somewhat "I'm at Nancy's. Come pick me up?"

And just an hour later, there was a sharp knock at the front door. This time, I knew the visitor would be a welcome one. When I hauled it open, I found Destelle standing on the other side, her curls loose and wild. She didn't even miss a beat. "You're crazy," she said emphatically, shoving past me and entering Nancy's home. "Insane. Normally, I'd love that for you—you know I like it when you let your wild side show a little—but you're crazy."

I shut the door behind her. "I do have my moments."

"Listen, am I disappointed in you for ruining all the desserts at the wedding and getting thrown out?" Destelle turned around. "Of course not. But you could've at least saved me a cupcake."

"The icing tasted like chemicals. You wouldn't have been impressed."

"I fly all the way from California, and I didn't get a cupcake."

"I'll buy you one," I said, and then reality sunk back in. "Someday."

Well, that was a mood killer.

Destelle shifted on her feet, looking around Nancy's house. "I haven't been in here in *years*," she murmured, walking up to one of the shelves and looking at the knick-knacks. "That time we came senior year to swim in her pond was probably the only time."

I slipped my hands into the pockets of my dress pants

—because I still had nothing else to change into—and watched her. "Feels like a lifetime ago."

And in a way, it was. We'd both been different people back then, but when I thought back to the type of girl I'd been senior year, it felt like a different life entirely. An alternate timeline, a different reality. When my future still had been everything I dreamed, not yet taken away.

Destelle's thoughts seemed to be moving along the same lines. She reached out and traced her finger across a picture frame of Nancy standing in front of the Alderton-Du Ponte building. "Do you regret what you did last night?" Destelle asked in a soft voice. "Since it made your parents...you know."

"Cut me off?" I finished for her. "No. I don't regret it. In fact, I... I don't know a different time I would've done it."

"I am proud of you. I don't know if I could've done it."

"You *did* do it."

She shook her head. "We already talked about how different it was for me. Me pushing the envelope wouldn't have led to my world completely falling apart; back then, it just felt like it. You pushing the envelope, though... Yeah."

Last night, I hadn't so much as pushed the envelope as torn straight through it. "Yeah."

"Nancy would've been proud of you, too."

Yesterday, I'd had a hard time conjuring Nancy's voice in my head, but now, I could hear her plain as day. "She'd say 'took you long enough.'"

"'I knew you had it in you.'"

"'I guess you are smarter than you look.'"

We both grinned at each other, though the melancholy tone still clung to me like a second skin. We were quiet for a moment, both of us mulling over everything that'd happened in that silence. "What are you going to do, then?"

"Get a job, probably. Know anyone hiring?"

"I meant about Sumner."

I frowned. "How do you know what happened with Sumner?"

"Uh, I think *everyone* knows what happened. Mrs. Astor has a loud voice when she's angry."

So Aaron had been telling the truth about Vivienne ripping my parents a new one. That was more than mildly satisfying.

But...Sumner. That was another thing that felt like a lifetime ago, being in Sumner's arms. It hadn't even been a full day. I thought of all the things I said to him last night, thought of the truth uncovered. I wanted to stick my head in the sand, to add him to the list of things I didn't want to face, not yet. "If someone does something stupid," I began, turning my attention out toward the back door, "does that make them a bad person?"

"Depends on the motive behind something stupid. We're talking about Sumner, right?"

"Not him. Me."

"You?"

My words grew quiet. "I shouldn't have flipped the dessert table. As mad as I was, I shouldn't have done it."

It'd felt good in the moment, and even in the early stages of the aftermath, it'd felt sweet. But now, in the stark light of day, I saw how truly poor of a decision it was.

Destelle walked over to me and laid her hands on my shoulders. "You're not a bad person," she said, gaze serious. In her shoes, she was nearly as tall as me. "You aren't a bad person, because you feel bad about it. Mean people don't feel bad about the crappy stuff they do."

"Like my parents."

"Like your parents," she agreed hesitantly. "And even if you didn't feel bad about it, they deserved it. Maybe that makes *me* a bad person for thinking it, but they did. After the way they've treated you your entire life, they deserved a flipped dessert table and then some."

Destelle reached up and smoothed the palm of her hand down the side of my head, like I was a little kid she was looking after. Even though we'd grown a part, went in our separate directions of life, now that we were back together, the connection of our friendship was still there. While most times, growing up, I'd been the one to comfort her. The tables turned now, and she finally got her chance to comfort me in return.

Comfort. To Nancy, it'd been sarcasm and quips. To Sumner, it was holding my hand. To Destelle, it was petting my head. It looked different for each of them, and I let myself feel it. Instead of pushing away the emotion, instead of hardening my heart to it all, I allowed myself to accept Destelle's touches, and I allowed it to comfort me.

"Do you think you could take me somewhere?" I asked her. "I don't have a car, at the moment."

"As long as I can also take you shopping," Destelle said, scrunching her nose. "Because you look like you've done the walk of shame."

I looked down at my wrinkled pants and rumpled

435

shirt, giving my head a shake. "Fine, but nothing fancy. Something...inexpensive." The words hurt my soul.

And the next words Destelle uttered as she looped her arm through mine stabbed me with the biggest dose of irony. "How about Walmart?"

Chapter 31

$\mathscr{I}$ tapped my fingers along the counter of the Bayview Hotel's front desk, trying to tell myself that even though I felt horribly out of place, I didn't look it. The denim jeans I wore were a looser fit than I was used to—apparently, according to Destelle, tight-fitting jeans were *out*. While my suit pants never usually were that tight, it did feel strange to walk in a pair of wide-legged pants that my legs had so much room in.

Or maybe it was the fact that they were denim jeans to begin with, since I probably hadn't worn a pair since childhood.

The T-shirt I wore had a logo of a band I didn't recognize on it, and Destelle had tied it into a knot at my stomach. "Maybe it's time you discover a new style," she'd said helpfully. "Maybe this could be your new thing!"

It was not. And I had a new note to self: Destelle was no longer allowed to dress me.

But she did buy the clothes, so I shouldn't have been complaining.

"Ma'am," the lady at the front desk said to me, drawing my attention back. It was strange to be regarded the way she looked at me now. There was no discomfort or fear in her gaze like the staff at Massey Suites always wore. There was no goo in her eyes of someone who needed to impress a woman in a fancy suit. No, to her, I was just some random young adult who'd waltzed into the lobby, dressed like a college kid after a night of studying. "If you don't have a room number, I'm afraid I can't place a call for you."

"I know his name. Sumner Pennington. That's not enough for you to look through the system?"

"Do you have a phone number the booking would be under?"

I'd left my phone back at Nancy's since I didn't have service to place any calls. "No."

"A birthdate?"

I blinked. I truly didn't know Sumner's birthday? "No."

The lady gave me an awkward smile. "Then I'm afraid I can't help you. Company policy."

What I should've done, in hindsight, was grab Sumner's number off my phone and use Destelle's to text him. It didn't occur to me until now, with Ms. Gatekeeper over here, and Destelle had already left. *"You've got this,"* she'd said right before I shut the passenger door.

I did not, in fact, have this.

"What about Aaron Astor?" It was lame that I knew his birthday and not Sumner's, but I'd had longer to bounce it around in my head.

She began typing on her computer. "There's no listing under Aaron Astor."

"What about Vivienne Astor? Malcolm Astor?"

The lady's expression was already knowing when she asked, "Do you have a birthdate for them?"

I closed my eyes, fighting for patience.

"Margot?"

I turned to find Vivienne Astor coming in from the revolving doors of the hotel, and she pushed her sunglasses up to the top of her head when she saw me. She, too, wore denim jeans, though hers weren't as loose-fitting as my own. It made me feel slightly better, though. "Hi, Mrs. Astor."

"What—what are you doing here?" Her voice was shocked, though not unkind. "Are you here to see Aaron?"

"Sumner, actually." I tried not to let myself feel awkward, but it was hard to force any sort of confidence into my voice. "I heard he was here."

Vivienne glanced at the lady at the front desk, as if gauging the situation. "Would you like to come up with me? I can show you to his room."

That hadn't been in my plan. We weren't supposed to have this conversation in his hotel room, but outside. We could've walked down to the bay, or gotten coffee— anywhere where there'd be other things to focus on than each other. That was probably my *stick-your-head-in-the-sand* self talking. "That'd...be great."

I walked slightly in Vivienne's shadow as we headed to the elevators, my hands clasped in front of me like I was a kid walking toward detention. With each step, my heart drummed faster and faster in my chest, both at the anticipation of seeing Sumner and being trapped in an elevator with my ex almost mother-in-law.

And, of course, we had to wait for the elevator to

arrive to the ground floor. "I'm sorry for my son's behavior," she said, and her expression was genuinely remorseful. It glimmered in her eyes. "It isn't okay in the slightest."

"Seems like a hassle, doesn't it?" I agreed, rocking back on my heels. "He could've just called me and asked me himself."

"I've always known he's had a confidence issue, but I never thought he'd send someone to feed information about you." She bit her bottom lip. "I thought I raised him better than that."

"Everyone makes their own choices," I said as the elevator dinged. "No matter how they're raised."

My parents raised me to be a good mindless soldier, but it hadn't worked in their favor.

A mother and her young children stepped off the elevator before we stepped on, sealed in a tiny space. It made me feel even more tense. "Last night," she began, looking at me from the corner of her eye. "It definitely will go down in history, won't it?"

I winced. "I'm embarrassed that I did what I did."

"Then that makes two of us—embarrassed of our own actions." Vivienne chuckled a little. "I shouldn't have berated your parents the way I did, not when it was my own son who initiated this mess."

"They deserved it," I answered without missing a beat. "My parents, I mean."

There was another awkward lull in the conversation as we both weighed our words. Vivienne pulled her purse from her side around so she could rifle through it, withdrawing a business card. "I hope you know that, if you ever need anything, I'm here for you. It might not have worked out with Aaron, but... Well. I do feel fond of you, Margot. I want to see you do good things."

Her golden embossed name glittered in the dull elevator light, and I studied it for a moment, her words washing over me.

"And I happen to know a few designers in New York, if you ever decide to pursue fashion. I know they'd love to meet you." Her eyes trailed my attire. "If that's still something you're interested in."

"Please don't let this trainwreck fool you; I definitely am still interested in fashion."

We both smiled at each other, and I was shocked to find how easy it came to my lips now, how genuine it felt. How good.

The elevator stopped at the top floor, and Vivienne told me that Sumner's room number was 608 at the end of the hall. Their room was 620, on the opposite end, and we went our separate directions then. I tucked her business card into my pocket, knowing that I'd keep it close.

I stopped before room 608, staring at the number plaque on the surface. The thought of knocking seemed impossible; my hand was made of lead at my side. My nervousness didn't make so much sense—out of either of us, Sumner, surely, should've been the anxious one. He was the one who had to tell me his story. All I had to do was listen.

And that was why I wanted to go back to the elevator, go back to the lobby, and straight out the revolving doors.

Before I had a chance to run, though, the door ripped inward, revealing Sumner with his phone and wallet in hand. He had been rushing to leave his room, it seemed, because he nearly walked straight into me before he froze, his gaze rising from his phone screen.

We both held perfectly still. I broke the ice first. "Hi."

I didn't know why I was expecting Sumner to look different, but of course he didn't. Of course he wasn't decked out in designer items, with his hair slicked back in the way Aaron's was. He wore the same jeans he'd worn the first time we went out to eat together, with the hole on his knee. His shirt was a deep navy, simple and loose on his frame. He still had the same bright blue eyes I'd looked into the day prior, still wore his hair ungelled. He was still Sumner.

"I—I've been calling you," he stuttered out, reminding me, again, of the first time we met. He'd been just as nervous when I'd approached him then, swiping up the champagne flute from his tray. "All night and morning. I—"

"My parents cut off my phone service." It felt wrong standing before him in an outfit that cost twenty dollars, so much so that I had to actively hold myself back from fidgeting. I looked past him into his hotel room. "I'm ready to hear you out now."

Sumner all but flung himself out of the way. "Yes, please—please come in."

The room wasn't a suite, with his bed in plain sight the second I walked through the door. I tried not to look at it, but there weren't many options for seating. There was the mattress or a velvet chair in the corner.

"Are you okay?" Sumner asked as the door swung shut. He looked at me with that same stormy look in his eye. "By the time I heard about what happened last night, you were already escorted off the property. I figured you went to Nancy's, but I couldn't remember the way there. I used Aaron's car and drove all night, but I—"

"I'm not going anywhere now," I told him, moving to slip my hands into my pants pockets before I remembered I was wearing jeans. "You don't have to talk so fast."

An awkward smile lifted the corners of his mouth, just a tiny bit as he sat down in the velvet chair, turning it to face me fully. "Sorry... sorry."

I thought about Sumner driving around in the dark, searching the hilly roads for Nancy's driveway, a twinge aching in my chest. "You were trying to come to Nancy's when I told you I needed time?"

"I was afraid of you being alone."

It was a good response. It was a *Sumner* response.

I rubbed my palms across the knees of my jeans, trying to think of how to jump into such a serious conversation. the weight of it loomed over us, and if I was being honest with myself, I didn't want to have it. I wanted to push past it, to pretend Aaron Astor never even existed, pretend that Sumner wasn't a part of any scheme Aaron dreamed up.

I was going into this meeting with a mental list, things I needed to check off. I didn't want to get my hopes high, but I couldn't help myself.

"This is the long conversation you said we needed to have," I said as I levelled my stare with his. "I've, coincidentally, cleared my schedule for it today. Start where you think is the best place."

"The beginning?"

"That's always a good spot, yes."

Sumner drew in a steadying breath, knotting his fingers together. I took in his curved posture, his nervous fidgeting, and filed it away. "Aaron sent me to Addison to get to know you," he said. "He doesn't have the best social skills—I'm sure you could tell—and he wanted to know as much about you as he could so he could impress you when he came. I didn't...see the harm in that, at first. It was strange, yeah, but in the world of the rich, people do worse things. So, at first, I didn't think much of it."

That matched with what Aaron had said, more or less. "Aaron sent you because you worked for him?"

"Yes. And because I knew him best. He trusted me."

"So, Aaron was the man you were a secretary for. '*A small startup*' you said."

Sumner winced. "I shouldn't have lied; I just didn't know what else to say—"

"Did you know why he was interested in me in the first place?" I asked, because that was another major factor. "Did you know, going into everything, that he was only interested in my parents' company?"

"Of course not." His response came swiftly, not even skipping a beat. "I swear, I didn't know. At the Christmas gala, he said you were the most beautiful woman he'd seen. He has a habit of falling in love at first sight, so I did know it was on the shallower side, but I *never* thought he didn't mean it at all. If I'd known, I would've refused to come out here."

I listened in silence, trying to remember all the instances between Sumner and me. It made sense he didn't know, given his reaction when he caught what

444

Aaron said to me in the hotel lounge. He'd genuinely been angry. *Say one more word, and I'll throw you out on your ass,* he'd said to Aaron. *How could you say any of that to someone you care about?*

"Honestly," Sumner went on in a quieter tone, "I wasn't mad when he asked me to come out here."

"Because you were the one who fell in love at first sight at the Christmas gala?"

To my surprise, Sumner shook his head. "It wasn't like that. I didn't look at you and think I was in love with you. I thought you were beautiful, sure, standing out on the balcony while it snowed, but I meant it when I said that I knew what it felt like to be alone. Seeing you that night reminded me of myself."

When I first saw you, I couldn't help but think how lonely you looked, he'd said at the diner. Except for him in that moment, he wasn't talking about the fundraiser in Addison as the first time he'd seen me. He'd been talking about the Christmas gala.

"I figured if I was being sent here to learn more about you, I could be someone that made you less alone," he went on, squeezing his fingers. He let out a little breath as he looked at them. "And then...then you smiled at me for the first time—I made you smile for the first time—and it was ridiculous. I knew I needed to do it again...and again. And then suddenly, when I was with you, I wasn't thinking about Aaron or what I'd been sent here to do. I was only thinking about you."

"My smile's that pretty?"

Sumner let out another little breath, a ghost of a laugh. "I can't explain it. Knowing I was one of the few people that could make you smile, make you laugh... Every time, I thought about the same crazy thing—what it would be like to kiss you."

I could remember the times his eyes would drop to my lips as I smiled, the way he'd seemed to revel in it each time. It hadn't only just been one-sided, though. "What else did you lie about?"

A newfound urgency sprung into his pleading blue gaze. "I *swear*." The word was low with his sincerity. "I swear, I meant everything I said to you, Margot. I didn't fake wanting to be your friend, I didn't fake my feelings for you, and I—"

"I know."

They were clearly the last two words he expected me to say. He blinked twice, an echo, taken aback. "Y-You know."

"It wouldn't have made sense for you to fake feelings for me. It wouldn't have helped Aaron, and it wasn't as if you had some vendetta against your best friend. Plus, you're really bad at lying. I knew you weren't faking how you felt." Each of the words, I meant. I might've been angry last night with the shock of it all, but I never doubted him. Not about that. "Reporting everything about me back to him, though... That's where my issue is."

"I didn't tell him the big things," he insisted. "I—I told him about the little things. How you liked suits and fashion, where you went to college, that you liked avocado toast but don't like garlic butter on your mashed potatoes. I didn't tell him the personal things."

I raised an eyebrow. "Aaron knew about my situation with my parents."

"I never breathed a word about your parents or how they treated you. I—I might've said how people at the club treated you like an outcast, but I never said anything more serious. Not about your parents yelling, not about your dad coming into your hotel room—none of it."

That was at least a point—Aaron didn't know about the specifics of the poor relationship. *Besides, I'm from this world too,* he'd said that night in the hotel lounge. *If there's one thing I've learned, it's to read between the lines.* "Aaron knew I didn't want to marry him."

"Because the morning after your dad was drunk, I called him. I thought he'd call the whole thing off." Sumner reached up and pressed his fingers into his eyes, shaking his head. "And maybe I shouldn't have—it would've created more problems for you if Aaron backed out—but I thought... I thought he'd call it off if he knew. I didn't think he'd double down. I guess... it makes sense he would've, doesn't it? Now that I know."

It did make sense. Sumner didn't know it, but calling Aaron and telling him my true feelings most likely had been what Aaron was hoping for. He didn't have to worry about winning over my heart any longer, as he'd said. After finding out I wasn't looking for love, all he had to do was convince my mind.

I knew the lengths people would go to when it came to money. I understood Aaron. He would've manipulated an innocent person in order to inherit her family's company; I would've married someone I'd never met in order to keep my fortune. One was worse than the other, sure, but both stemmed from an unhealthy desire to be at the top.

When I thought about Sumner being Aaron, despite the fact that that would've been a huge breach of trust, there'd been no betrayal there. That thought of Sumner being the elusive Aaron Astor had only brought relief. I would've been willing to take that trick, had it been true. I might've been a bothered he'd lied, but it would've been perfect if he'd been the man I was supposed to marry.

This was a different sort of trick. He wasn't pretending to be someone he wasn't, just hiding the truth of who he was.

"You said that I was showing you it was okay to be your own person," I said, circling back to another point I had on my mental list. "You meant your own person apart from Aaron."

Sumner nodded. "I always listened to him when it came to what to do. For college, for work. Being his secretary only turned me even more into what he wanted me to be. I wasn't happy, though. I never felt like I was living the life *I* wanted to. And if it weren't for you, I probably never would've realized it."

"I meant it when I shouldn't have fallen for you. It *was* a disaster."

"You *have* been liking me selfishly all along," I murmured, remembering what he'd said the other day.

"I have been."

One corner of my lips tipped up ever so slightly. "So we did balance each other out well."

"We do."

The present tense almost seemed hesitant, nervous, as if he was afraid I'd disagree with him. "My parents most likely won't speak to me again," I said slowly, tracing the seam on the side of my jeans. "I was thinking about going back to California with Destelle. I don't have a place to stay here once I get kicked out of Nancy's place, and really, there's no point in staying."

He nodded again, slower this time. Tension still seemed to knit at his shoulders, as if he thought this was my way of teeing up to let him down.

I kept my voice nonchalant. "You live in California, don't you? It's a big state."

He leaned forward. "Where does Destelle live again?"

"Los Angeles."

"What a coincidence," Sumner said in a soft but bright tone. "Me too."

The lie caused a smile to tug my lips up completely before I could fight it—and really, I didn't want to. Sumner's eyes traced the grin on my face, as if savoring the sight, committing it to memory. I wondered if he thought it'd be the last time he'd see it.

I got to my feet and crossed the distance between us. Sumner didn't rise from his chair before I stopped in front of him, forcing him to tip his head back to meet my gaze. It wasn't the first time I stood over him like this, but everything was different now. My life was different, my future. All the choices were before me now, and I could pick any one of them.

Really, though, I didn't need a plethora of choices. I knew my answer. "You said you'd be the breadwinner and put me through fashion school," I reminded him. "That offer still on the table?"

"I told you I'd never change my mind." That was

when he stood up, a few inches taller than me. He reached his hand out and grazed his fingertips along mine, still hesitant to fully grab on. "I meant it when I said I want to find out what that other life is like with you."

The other life. The new life. There'd be no fancy cars, no Gilfman or Malstoni, and no thirty-dollar avocado toast, but it'd be a life of my own. No, not *my* own—*our* own. I wove our fingers together, securing him tight. Securing him to me. "Together."

"Together."

We both moved in at the same time, meeting each other and our new beginning halfway.

My lips met Sumner's and immediately I fell into the moment, the kiss, the warmth. One of my hands gripped the front of his shirt, holding on to keep from floating away or falling to the ground as he kissed me with a firm, bold, beautiful pressure. Warmth speared through me, spreading out through my body until I was nothing short of burning.

Strangely, in that moment, a fierce pressure squeezed my closed eyes, almost as if I could've cried. Sumner didn't erase the fears of the unknown, nor the hardships we'd definitely come across, but knowing I wouldn't have to go through it alone brought a near crippling sort of relief. No, I wouldn't be alone. I'd have my favorite person at my side.

As Sumner deepened the kiss, and his hands wrapped around my body, I was excited for the future. Our future.

The kiss tasted familiar, and I realized it was the promise sealed between us before. *I will treasure you*, it had said, with each gentle touch and each glance of his mouth.

I will treat you well. I knotted my fingers in the hair at the back of Sumner's neck, basking in their softness, and that only I could touch them. *You are mine.*

Sumner's hand curved over my lower back and pressed me closer until there wasn't a millimeter of space that could separate us.

And I am yours.

Chapter 32

*a*fter the wedding and Nancy's funeral, I waited for the other shoe to drop, and on the Wednesday after, a full week since Nancy passed, it finally did.

I sat on the counter in Nancy's kitchen, kicking my legs softly against the cupboard while I watched Sumner rummage through the fridge. He'd gone to the grocery store on Monday, bought a few ingredients, and we'd both been making lunches and dinners there. Or, well, I attempt the first two times—after that, Sumner declared myself cooking-illiterate and banned me from making dinner. "It makes sense," he'd said. "When was the last time you cooked your own meal?"

Outside of preparing a cold-cut sandwich, the answer had been never. I'd always relied on room service or a private chef.

"Are you *sure* you want to try avocado toast?" I asked him now, watching as he pulled out a carton of eggs and a sealed container of leftover salmon we'd had the night prior.

"How hard can it be?" he asked, setting the ingredients on the counter. "Besides, the avocado is getting questionable."

A knock at the door interrupted our perfectly mundane moment, and while it might've been a simple thing, it caused the both of us to still as our heads turned toward the sound.

No one, besides Destelle and Sumner, had showed up at Nancy's besides Sunday when Ms. Jennings brought Aaron over. I'd been waiting for it, though. Waiting for my parents to come and harass me, waiting for whoever got Nancy's house in the will to come and kick me out. Heck, I'd even been waiting for Yvette to storm in with a bill for her daughter's wedding cake. I was surprised *that* hadn't happened yet.

"Do you want me to get it?" Sumner asked me.

I hopped off the counter. "No, I've got it."

Despite my assurance, he still followed behind me as I made my way to the front of the house. It was a little funny, the way we were both tensed over a knock. When I undid the lock and drew open the door, a man I didn't recognize greeted me. He was tall, so much so that the top of his head nearly reached the top of the jamb. Despite how imposing was, some of the weight eased off my shoulders at the sight of him. "May I help you?" I asked him through the screen door.

"My name is Jeffrey Franz," he said with a deep voice, one that didn't quite match his face. He lifted his briefcase a little. "I was Ms. Du Ponte's lawyer."

And just like that, the weight returned. "Oh...hello."

"Are you Margot Massey?"

I could feel Sumner behind me, a silent supporter. "Possibly."

"May I come in?"

I unlatched the screen door before taking a step back. Mr. Franz instinctively ducked his head as he came in, the scent of his expensive cologne filling the air. He proceeded into the house easily, clearly having been here before to navigate his way to the small table Nancy had in her kitchen. "You're a bit difficult to track down," he murmured as he deposited his briefcase onto the surface. "I went by Massey Suites, but everyone I spoke with acted as if they didn't know who Margot Massey was."

That was unsurprising. "Did you tell them you were Nancy's lawyer?"

"I did keep that part to myself."

"You might've gotten more interest had you shared it."

He seemed to understand my meaning. "That's why I didn't share. I did come across a very helpful Ms. Jennings, though, and she pointed me in this direction."

Sumner, a silent shadow until that moment, shifted so he stood beside me. "Why are you looking for Margot?"

The locks on his briefcase clicked as Mr. Franz opened it, shuffling through papers within. "Because she is listed as the executor of Ms. Nancy Du Ponte's will."

I blinked at him. "Excuse me?"

"It's common practice to inform the executor of a will before the passing, of course," Mr. Franz said, and he pulled out a stack of papers now. He peered at them, thumbing through. "It's a lot of work, and it's better if the executor knows what they're going into before things get too busy. Ms. Du Ponte, though, asked to keep it a secret until her passing."

I wasn't sure there'd been another time I'd felt so thoroughly confused. "I—I can't be an executor," I said with a shake of my head. "I don't even know what that all entails."

"I'm here to walk you through it all." When he finally found the stapled stack he wanted, he placed the rest back into his briefcase and laid the stack on the table. "It's not going to be as messy as you might think, given that you're the only beneficiary Ms. Du Ponte named."

Nancy Du Ponte – Last Will and Testament. I didn't read beyond that. "Nancy... Nancy left everything in her name to charity."

"That may have been what she told you, but if you see here—" Mr. Franz reached over, flipped a page in the stapled stack, and pointed at the bolded subline. "On this page, it clearly states otherwise."

I will and bequeath all of my personal and household effects, such as furniture, artworks, clothing, and personal items to Margot Massey.

I leave any real estate property I own, whether residential, commercial, or undeveloped land, to Margot Massey.

I will and bequeath my interests in any businesses, including shares, partnership interests, or other equity interests, to Margot Massey.

My chest had begun rising and falling quickly as I read over everything, and Sumner curved his hand over my shoulder as if to steady me.

"Probate court takes time," Mr. Franz went on. "And it takes time for the funds to be released, but when it does, it will be yours. Given Ms. Du Ponte had no living relatives, it all should move smoothly. It's been signed over to you for a while now, so no one can argue the decision was made in a poor state of mind. Ms. Du Ponte also had a No-Contest clause, which works in our favor."

He continued on with more legal jargon, more explanations of the paperwork in front of me, and it was a good thing Sumner was there, because he absorbed everything that went through one of my ears and out the other. I just reread the lines over and over, gripping the back of the kitchen chair so tightly that my knuckles ached.

This was the other shoe, and it finally dropped. It just wasn't nearly as devastating as I thought it'd be.

"These are what need signatures now," Mr. Franz said, pulling out a different stack of papers. "And if you have a seat, we can go over this together and begin the process. If...ahem, that is, if this is a good time."

"We were actually just about to have some lunch," Sumner said with all the politeness in the world. I could feel his eyes on me, and his hand hadn't moved from its gentle curve over my shoulder. "Is it possible you could come back later? Or...or we could schedule a meeting at your office, perhaps."

Mr. Franz agreed that would work for him, and he pulled a business card from his interior breast pocket and offered it out to me. When I didn't take it, Sumner did. "Ms. Du Ponte did leave a letter, and before I go, I'd like to give it to you."

A letter. It was the next thing he withdrew from his briefcase, and I wished he hadn't. As soon as my eyes locked onto it, a new, sickening feeling weighed down on

456

my stomach. It wasn't a normal letter. Inside the envelope would be the final words Nancy wanted me to hear.

He laid it on top of the will, and I couldn't look away.

Mr. Franz showed himself out, which worked, because I was immobile behind the kitchen chair. I should've sat down. I definitely should've sat down. Sumner reached out and touched the stack of papers Mr. Franz had left me to read in its entirety, gazing at it. "She left you everything."

I was immediately aware of the walls around me. "This house."

Sumner nodded, equally stunned. "The country club."

It dawned on me then, slowly, and then all at once. "The land Massey Suites is on."

We were both silent as we stared at each other, absorbing what it all meant. It was hard to wrap my head around it all—that I went from rich, to broke, to having more assets than I could've imagined. It never occurred to me Nancy had lied about leaving everything to charity—though, in hindsight, that was totally something she'd lie about. Morally gray, she was. It shouldn't have been a surprise...but it was.

"I'll start the avocado toast," Sumner murmured, giving my shoulder a squeeze before leaning in to press a kiss into my forehead. "Why don't you take a look at what Nancy said?"

I wanted to grab his hand, to hold him hostage, but I forced myself to nod. A part of me wanted him to stay beside me as I read it, but the bigger part wanted the privacy in case I bawled like a baby.

I went outside, and though the mid-June heat had become sweltering, it was comforting in that moment. Even the sweat that immediately prickling my skin felt comforting, in a way. I was cold, and the envelope in my hand was cold. The summer sun was like a hug, thawing some of the ice.

Nancy touched this envelope. The contents of the letter...she wrote them. She'd never written me a letter before, I didn't think. She'd written on pre-made birthday cards, maybe passed me a note or two at a fundraiser event, but never a letter. Never anything as serious as the bob in my hands now.

Slowly, I eased the paper from the envelope, the pressure in my chest making me feel like I was going to be sick. *It's just something from Nancy*, I told myself, swallowing hard. *It's not scary.*

But it was. These were her last words she intended for me to read. Her final goodbye.

I unfolded the paper, my hands trembling so badly that I almost couldn't read it. Or maybe it was her scratch of calligraphy. Whatever the case, I had to take several deep breaths before I could focus.

Margot,

Hopefully, you can read my horrible handwriting. I'd have Ally transcribe it for me, but I can just hear her yammering now—best to do it myself.

If you're reading this, Jeffery's come to give you my will. I'm dead, huh! Finally.

Took God long enough to take me home, didn't it? You're probably bawling like a baby while I'm over here, free from drowning in BENGAY every day.

I'm not going to spend this letter yapping on about sentimentalities. You know I never was much for a sappy story. I'm old. My hand's already cramping.

I left you everything. I bet you're shocked, like the thick-headed dullard you are. But on one condition—you go back to fashion school, and you get out from underneath your parents' thumb. I was going to make it on the condition that you don't marry that Aaron boy, but apparently that's only something people do in movies. So go to that fancy fashion school, get your degree, and when you graduate, everything is yours. Until then, I've a fund in place to help carry you along.

Be happy. That's my other requirement. In everything that you do, be happy.

Yes, you're welcome. Stop crying, now. I lived til 90 for you, and have left you everything. Be grateful. I don't want you staying in Addison. You've lived this whole time for your parents. Live for yourself for a change, and leave this world and its champagne problems behind.

God, who writes by hand anymore? I wouldn't be surprised if the cramp is what kills me.

~~I love you~~

It was great seeing you grow up, now go live your own life.

Fondly (I was listening, even if you thought I wasn't),

Nancy Du Ponte

I swiped the back of my hand under my chin, wiping away the tears that had fallen and pooled there. I traced the crossed-out words, because even though she'd written a line through them, they were still legible. *I love you.* Words we never, ever said to each other. They were her final goodbye.

I left you everything. "I never wanted anything," I whispered, rereading her sentences over and over.

And I could hear her response in my head. *And that's exactly why I gave it to you.*

Everyone around Nancy clawed at her for her money, for her estates, for everything she was worth. They were polite to her face, grumbled about her behind her back. They thought they were sneaky, that Nancy wouldn't be the wiser. None of them received a single penny in the end, but Nancy didn't give it to charity the way she said she would.

I had it all now—or at least I would when I graduated from fashion school. Even though Mr. Franz went over it with me, I still couldn't wrap my mind around the amount. The estates, the main shareholdings of Alderton-Du Ponte, the land my parents' hotel sat on.

Of course she'd require me to go to fashion school, the one thing she knew I wanted in the world, and she gave me more than enough to reach for it. *In everything that you do, be happy.*

That'd even been one of the last things she said to me, too. *Choose to be happy. You deserve it.*

I ran my hand across my cheek again, sniffing like a child, before I folded the letter back up.

The back door slid open noisily, announcing Sumner's presence. I turned to face him, not caring if there was still the shine of my shed tears, not caring if my nose was red. There was no stress of making sure I maintained my perfect image anymore, no need to shield my emotions away. I didn't want to hide them from him ever again.

"The toast is done," he said hesitantly, as if also adding *I can give you more time if you need it.*

I tucked Nancy's letter back into the envelope before turning fully away from the pond. "I'm not sure it'll be as good as Pierre's," I told him, starting up the hill. "But we'll find out."

"Hey, I never claimed it would be."

"You offered to make a sacred dish. I assumed it was because you were confident in it."

The closer I came, the more I could see anxiety crease his brow. "I wouldn't say *confident*, but—"

"I'm sure you couldn't have botched it too bad." I stretched my hand out to Sumner as I approached him, and he mimicked me, reaching until his fingers could slide underneath my own. The grip was warm and comforting, just as the sun, just as the letter. Just what I needed. "But we'll find out, hmm?"

Instead of leading me inside, with his grip on my hand, Sumner drew me against his chest. His lips found their way to my forehead immediately, the tender touch enough to make me shiver. "If it's terrible," he murmured against my skin, "I'll let you make me beans on toast."

"You know, it never specified what *kind* of beans. I could use kidney beans."

Sumner's face screwed up. "Never mind, let me remake your toast. I need to improve my chances."

"Too late." I pulled back just enough to peer up into his face. "You already offered."

He started to argue further, but before he could, I surged forward and pressed my lips to his, ceasing his words. His free hand slid its way up my arm to touch the side of my throat, a glancing sort of touch that felt like a whisper itself. I could taste the salt of my leftover tears, and Sumner must've as well, but neither of us cared.

I pulled back and smiled up at him. "Let's not keep my avocado toast waiting."

His eyes traced it, as they always did, as if my smile itself lit something within him. "Let's."

And with that, I tightened my grip on his hand and led him into the house.

Epilogue

The sketch came to life before my eyes, though the process had been slow. Progress *was* being made, and while it took some time, it was beyond satisfying that the image from my mind was able to slowly make its way onto the page.

It wasn't a suit croquis this time, but the silhouette of a dress. It wasn't my first time drawing one, but I still hadn't executed it as I would've liked it to be.

"You ready for a break?"

I looked up from the table to find Sumner coming out of Nancy's back door. He wore a dark pair of cotton pants and a loose shirt, with his golden hair loose over his forehead. He'd finally mastered business casual.

"Just about," I said as he came around the patio table and kissed the top of my head. "Aaron finally hung up, huh?"

"He loves to talk and talk," Sumner said with a little groan, wrapping his arms around me. "I was barely listening."

"I doubt he noticed," I said with a little snort, relaxing in his embrace. The tension in my shoulders from

463

hunching over my paper loosened against Sumner's chest. "He loves listening to himself talk, doesn't he?"

"That he is." Sumner pressed a soft kiss to my temple, lips a quick glance on my skin. His attention dropped to my sketch. "It's looking really good."

I regarded it with scrutinizing eyes, seeing my mistakes stand out as if with red ink. "It's all right."

"Are you actually going to have this one designed this time?"

"Mary-Ana wants me to do this one myself. Apparently, it's vastly uncommon for a designer to have no skills in sewing. Go figure."

I'd missed the deadline to sign up for the fall semester for fashion institutes, but because of Vivienne Astor's generosity, she put me into contact with a few of her friends in New York City, just as she'd promised. Though it wouldn't count toward credits, I'd been able to land an internship position at a small boutique. One that didn't specialize in suits. Unfortunately. But as I built my portfolio, I learned to find sketching dresses fun, in a way. There was a lot of variety in the silhouettes, the patterns, fabrics. Whereas suits require more precision and structure, dresses had ample more opportunities for details and embellishments. It was fun to experiment with it.

The fact that I enjoyed sketching a dress design still made me chuckle.

He gave a soft chuckle that echoed in my ear. "Is that kind of like an architect that can't build?"

I made a pout of an expression. "More like a cater-waiter who can't hold a tray."

"You got me." He kissed my temple again, even though I tried to lean away.

"The clothiers at Gilfman left me spoiled, doing it all for me. I'm excited to try designing something, though." Even though I knew the outcome would be rough, ugly, and probably something I hated with a burning passion, it was an exciting thought that I was *truly* starting my career in fashion design now. I'd sketched all along, but the true designing, the true bringing something to life, was finally set into motion. "I know I'm starting off behind, only learning to sew now, but Mary-Ana promised to help me. And you've seen her designs."

Sumner's hands slipped firmer around me, tucking me closer. "I can't wait until you design me something one day. A Margot Massey original."

"We might start off small. Like a necktie."

"Only if you put it on me."

Sumner extracted his arms from me and came around the table to sit down, blue gaze focused on me. "How did the conversation with Mr. Franz go?"

Sumner and I had come back to Addison for the long weekend—partly because there were papers Mr. Franz needed me to sign, and partly because I missed Nancy's house. I knew, at some point, I'd have to stop calling it that —*Nancy's house*—but I doubted it'd ever stop feeling like her place, even though it technically was in my name. Or officially would be, once the probate case was closed.

The past two and a half months flew by. I couldn't believe it was almost all over.

I sketched a line along the model's hip, but with Sumner's attention on me, I was far too distracted. The dress disappeared from my mind's eye, quickly filled with the awareness of *him*. "He says that he thinks everything will clear probate within the next week or two. Said that things went even smoother than he'd hoped."

"That's a relief." Sumner's eyes dropped to my sketch for a moment. "Have your parents tried reaching out to you again?"

Before, the mere mention of my parents would cause my mood to plummet. Now, it just caused me to sigh in annoyance. "This morning marks the fourth time this week." When they'd learned that probate would be completed soon, they'd started reaching out again. It'd started early in July, when the will became public knowledge once it entered probate. Once they learned that the daughter they'd disowned would soon inherit everything they'd ever wanted. "Apparently, they don't know what the word *wait* means."

"They should learn what the word *no* means," Sumner muttered, his eyes tightening. "You're more generous than I'd be."

I regarded him fondly, mostly because his own annoyance on my behalf was so endearing. "I see it as I can finally be done with it all. I don't want to hang onto it just for the sake of hanging onto it. I'd rather sell it and get them off my back." I set my pencil down and leaned forward over the table. "But that doesn't mean I have to give them a discount."

Sumner grinned. "Of course not."

Really, if my parents couldn't inherit all of Nancy's fortune, they wanted two things: the land Massey Suites sat on as well as the country club itself. Despite the fact that I was permanently banned from the Alderton-Du Ponte Country Club, I would inherit the land and building when the will came out of probate. Since it was a membership-run facility and not a privately owned company, the board of directors still could bar my entry— and they did. I'd gone back and forth with Mr. Franz and Sumner, and I decided that would be another thing I'd let go.

But not to the vultures at the Alderton-Du Ponte, though. No, I'd be donating it to a charity, just like Nancy always threatened she'd do.

The snobby termites that'd moved over the years in had ruined the beautiful place Nancy built; I didn't want to hold on to rotted wood.

Nancy wasn't there, anyway. We held onto her ashes long enough to bring in pond management specialists, and they took the once swampy pond in Nancy's backyard and restored it back to its former glory. The pond Nancy spent her days looking out over, watching deteriorate, was almost a serene oasis now, with the algae cleared and new plants rooted along the edges. The pond specialist even went as far as stocking fish, which could be seen underneath the glittering blue surface.

"We probably won't be back here for a little bit, huh?" I asked with a somewhat sad tone, glancing around the yard. The morning sunlight rose and shimmered beautifully on the pond. "We don't have another long weekend until Thanksgiving."

"We can still come back here and there," Sumner assured. "It's only an hour's flight. We can be here and back in New York in a day."

"Both of us will be tired with work."

Though it'd been a lie before, Sumner truly did work at a small startup now, hired on as a project manager for a small marketing agency. It was a role he enjoyed—and sheepishly admitted he enjoyed it more than being a secretary. *"It wasn't you,"* he'd insisted. *"I just feel like I'm doing something meaningful now."*

"And watching me wasn't meaningful?" I'd teased, to which he gave another small smile.

"No," he'd replied, *"it was* fun."

Sumner tipped his head at me now, his eyes soft. "I'll never be too tired to visit Nancy."

My chest ached, both with warmth at his words and sorrow. It was such a strange combination, but one I'd gotten used to navigating. So much had changed in just a few months. Even though Nancy's absence left an ornery-lady-sized hole in my chest, moving forward hadn't been nearly as impossible as I'd always imagined. I knew it was because I had a hand to hold now.

I'd once told Sumner that I was afraid of a life outside of my golden glitz and glamour, too afraid to lead a life without the comfort I'd always known.

What if it's better? he'd asked. *That other life.*

And it was better. Of course it was. There were hardships and struggles, and the unknown felt a whole lot scarier, but it was better. I no longer felt like a little kid under the directions of her parents, but an adult. One who lived with her boyfriend in New York City, who rode the subway and ate street pizza and walked hand-in-hand with Sumner in Central Park. One who pulled all-nighters and woke up early to go to work.

Navigating this "other life" together with Sumner was far, far more amazing than I could've dreamed, and it felt like my life was truly beginning.

I pushed the metal chair away from the patio table and pushed to my feet, stretching. "What time is it?"

Sumner checked his clunky watch. "A little after ten."

"And our reservation at Pierre's isn't until eleven-thirty, right?"

Sumner watched me approach, his eyes already growing more guarded. "Right."

I laid my hands on his shoulders and looked down at him. His hands rose to rest on my waist, holding me in place. Even through the fabric of my shorts, my skin lit up with the touch. That, accompanied by the wide, tender way he looked up at me, obliterated my self-control.

I leaned down and pressed my lips to his awaiting ones, taking a second to memorize the moment. I always did, even unintentionally. The very first time I'd kissed Sumner, I hadn't been paying attention at all. now, I made sure to mentally file the moment away each time. The scent of him, the sound of his small gasp, the feel as his lips adjusted to mine.

But then I'd melt into the moment, and I'd stop focusing on memorizing and start focusing on *feeling*. Sumner's hand now slipped from my waist around my back, pressing me closer to him. Each pressure of his fingers sent a spark through me, and I combed my fingers through his hair, hoping to elicit the same feeling in him. And it worked, if the sharp breath in through his nose was any indication. Sumner kissed me eagerly, matching each tilt of my head and glance of my lips.

I broke away for a breath. "We could always skip our reservation," I murmured, curling my fingers firmer into the hair at the back of his head. Feathery soft.

"No," he answered at once, equally breathless, but didn't release me from his arms. "I've been told not to keep you from your avocado toast."

"This would be a good excuse." I laid my free hand along his neck, feeling his pulse pound in his throat. "The only good excuse."

"We don't have to skip it." With a firm and smooth tug, Sumner pulled me into his lap. My world was only unsteady for a moment before his arms came around me, and our faces were level now, inches apart. "We have enough time."

A smile inched across my lips. "Do we, now? Enough time for what?"

Sumner's eyes dropped to my mouth, a light illumination his blue gaze, the color as fluid as the pond behind us. Even after so long together, and so many shared smiles, Sumner never seemed to stop his habit of watching my lips lift—nor his habit of smiling in return. "Enough time for me to work on my technique."

"Yours? I thought you said mine needed work."

Sumner pressed a kiss to the middle of my forehead, to my nose, and then to each of my cheeks. "Trust me," Sumner murmured, mouth brushing against mine as he spoke. The words were a whisper, and he barely could get them out. "It definitely doesn't."

I closed the distance between us once more. In moments like this, where there was nothing but the two of us and ample time in the world, it was as if I could physically feel the bond holding us together. Love. Something I once didn't believe in, something I once didn't want, now something I knew I couldn't live without. To love, and to be loved by the same person, was better than any Gilfman or Malstoni.

Falling in love, contrary to what everyone had tried to tell me, wasn't a fairytale. It wasn't nonsense. It wasn't a problem.

It truly was just champagne.

Before You Go!

Reviews are so important for authors, especially for indie authors. If you enjoyed this book, please head over to Amazon and leave a review!

Sarah Sutton

ALSO BY SARAH SUTTON

Love in Fenton County

What Are Friends For?

Out of My League

If the Broom Fits

Can't Catch My Breath

Two Kinds of Us

Christmas As We Know It

Most Likely To

Teaching the Teacher's Pet

Dreaming About the Boy Next Door

Rebelling With the Bad Boy

Fake Dating the Football Player

Made in United States
North Haven, CT
27 September 2024